Darkness Before Dawn

Other books by Ace Collins from Abingdon Press

The Christmas Star
The Cutting Edge (available October 2013)

DARKNESS BEFORE DAWN

Ace Collins

Abingdon Press fiction
a novel approach to faith

Nashville, Tennessee

Darkness Before Dawn

ISBN-13: 978-1-4267-1462-7

Published by Abingdon Press, P.O. Box 801, Nashville, TN 37202
www.abingdonpress.com

Library of Congress Cataloging-in-Publication Data has been
requested.

Printed in the United States of America

1 2 3 4 5 6 7 8 9 10 / 18 17 16 15 14 13

To Jim,
whose life was tragically cut short by a drunk driver

Acknowledgments

My thanks to Kathy Collins, Elizabeth Kelly, and the team at Abingdon Press, including Ramona Richards, Susan Cornell, and Teri Wilhelms.

1

WHEN IT FIRST REACHED THE INNER MOST DEPTHS OF HER DREAMS, MEG Richards thought the distant noise came from the alarm clock rousing her for another day of work at the hospital. As she struggled to rise and shake off her deep slumber, the ringing sound stopped. As it did, she fell back onto the bed. But a second later, like a determined mosquito, it came back for a second strike. This time, awake enough to separate dream from reality, she began to understand her cell phone demanded her attention. She didn't want to leave her dreams to answer it, and, if she had known who was waiting on the other end of the line, she wouldn't have. But she couldn't let phones ring; it wasn't in her nature. When a phone rang, her curiosity always won out over everything, including her need for sleep.

Awkwardly rolling out of bed, her feet finding the cool slats of the wooden floor, she blinked a half dozen times until she could finally focus on her clock. 2:32 a.m.!

Trying to shake the grogginess from her head, she moaned, "What could anyone want at this time of night?" Even as her heavy eyelids closed out the world, she halfway fell forward toward the sound.

"Steve," she mumbled looking over her shoulder to the other side of the bed, "who could be calling at this time of the night or morning or whatever it is?" Then it hit her. There could only be one answer. "Steve, I swear, if this is the hospital calling . . ."

As she glanced over her shoulder, she momentarily froze. The far side of the bed was empty; the covers hadn't even been pulled back. What had happened to her husband? Hilldale's only a couple of hours away. He should have been home long ago. Ah, nothing to worry about, probably just got delayed by something unexpected on his job. Not the first time and wouldn't be the last time that had happened. Besides, with her bizarre schedule, she had no room to complain.

Like a boxer struggling to find his balance in the late rounds of a title fight, Meg unwrapped her lithe, five-foot-two inch frame from the sheet and bedspread and stumbled out of the bedroom. Eight short steps led into the small apartment's living room. Hurrying past the couch, she sprinted to an end table on the far side of the fourteen-by-twelve-foot room.

"I should keep the charger closer to the bed," she muttered as she searched for the lamp's switch. By the time its harsh light flooded the room, the phone had completed its sixth ring. On the seventh, the voice mail would make her short trek a complete waste of time, so she had to hurry. Finally, with a few more of the sleep-induced cobwebs shaken from her mind, Meg cleared her throat, picked up the iPhone, slid it on, and tapped accept.

"Hello?" She spit her one-word greeting with a perturbed and questioning tone. She knew who it had to be. After all, who else would call at this time of the night except the hospital wanting her to come in early again. And this was not a night she wanted to give up her sleep for rounds at Springfield Community. She'd done that far too much the past few months. This week alone she had pulled two double shifts and those had left her dead on her feet. It was time for them to hire a few more nurses, ones that could be depended upon, rather than overworking the staff they already had!

"Mrs. Richards?"

Surprisingly it wasn't her boss, Hospital Administrator John Willis. This was another voice. One she didn't know. Before she had time to answer the man's first simple question, he grew more specific and demanding. "Is this the home of Megan Richards?"

What in the world did this stranger want at this time of the night and how did he get her number? She wavered for a second, questioning if it was wise to share any personal information. She glanced over to her door and made sure it was locked before hesitantly replying. "Yes, this is Megan Richards. Who are you?"

"Mrs. Richards, this is Officer Roland Johnson with the state police. Is your husband's name Steven?"

His query froze her in her tracks. Not only couldn't she answer, she couldn't even breathe, much less move. It was as if a summer fog had invaded the living room and surrounded her in a haze so deep she could barely see. She stole a glance at the wedding photo hanging on the wall just a few feet away. As it came into focus, a chill raced down her spine and then a thousand random thoughts all flashed through her head. Each of those thoughts was crowding another one for space. Her throat grew dry and her knees weak as her brain tried to push out of the fog. Surprisingly, in a few short seconds her mind had driven the fog away and she was once more processing information. And as clarity set in, she sensed the call's meaning. Something had happened! That's why Steven hadn't come home.

She knew the routine. As a nurse, she had seen it play out a hundred times. There had to have been an accident. That's the only reason the police would call. But, no, that couldn't be it. She wouldn't let herself even consider that. It had to be something much more routine. It just had to be!

It suddenly felt as if an unseen hand had found her throat and was squeezing with more force each second. Finding the corner of the couch with her free hand, she slowly crumpled into a sitting position on the arm. Glancing back to the wedding photo, she transported to the moment Steve asked her to marry him. It was in the park, the moon had been full and there were more stars than she'd ever seen. She could now smell the trees and feel the wind. Only the man's distant voice coming from her phone kept her from staying in that "safe" place.

"Mrs. Richards . . . are you still there . . . Mrs. Richards?"

She knew that tone all too well. She'd heard doctors use it when sharing a bleak prognosis and pastors employ it when informing a person their son or daughter had just died. She had heard it so much she had a name for it—"dark music." Now that old familiar, stormy tune had been cued up for her. That man on the phone would soon hit the chord that shattered her world into a million pieces. He'd probably been practicing the words that went with the "dark music" for at least ten minutes. He'd likely said them over and over to make sure they stung as little as possible. What if she hung up the phone and cut the "dark music" off before the song began? After all, if she didn't hear the lyrics, the story they told wouldn't be real. Would it?

Her voice still muted, her eyes glued on the wedding portrait, she studied the good-looking groom. It came to her then, the picture was speaking a phrase he'd once said and it began to bounce off the walls. At first it was just one single voice whispering the five words, but in a matter of seconds it seemed as if a thousand different people were screaming that one line in unison.

'Til death do us part! 'Til death do us part! 'Til death do us part! 'Til death do us part!

She wanted to throw the phone against the wall, cover her ears with her hands, and race back to bed. She didn't want the song to play out because the "dark music" always brought parting. No, much more than separation; the "dark music" always brought death!

"Mrs. Richards." The voice on the phone wouldn't go away. It kept demanding she rejoin the conversation. She knew she had to answer that voice and prayed her premonitions were wrong, but even as her lips began to form words, her heart demanded she remain silent. Finally, it was her lips that won the tug-of-war over her emotions.

"Yes. I'm Meg Richards." The words all but caught in her throat, hanging there like a cough drop that had gone down the wrong way, robbing her of air and stealing whatever hope she had left.

Why did this happen now? Why in the middle of the night? Why when everything had just started to go so right? After another deep breath that did nothing to slow her racing heart or ease her growing fears, she whispered the most painful words that had ever crossed her lips, "Has something happened to Steve?"

"Mrs. Richards," the man's voice was now flat, almost emotionless, as if trying to be empathetic, but lacking the knowledge as to how to accomplish that task. He forced out another "Mrs. Richards," before pausing again. Was he tone deaf or had he not been trained in how to sing the "dark music's" tune. Whatever the reason, he couldn't seem to impart the heartfelt emotion that this number called for. If something had happened to Steve, there needed to be deep emotion in the "dark music," his life demanded that much. But when the voice came back, it was flat and emotionless.

"Mrs. Richards." He was now distant and robotic. No one could do justice to the "dark music" like that. But that didn't matter now. She hadn't got to choose the singer or the song. "I am sorry to have to inform you that there has been an accident. Your husband's car was hit by a vehicle carrying a group of teenagers. I don't know if I should provide you with this information, but from what we have been able to gather, the youngsters had been drinking."

She waited for the cop to continue, but for some reason he stopped—like he had been reading a book and lost his place. As the seconds dragged on, Meg held her breath, hoping for the best but sensing the worst had yet to come. Maybe Steve had just been injured. She could even take him losing a limb or his sight. All she needed was for him to be alive. Yet a minute later those hopes were dashed as the other shoe dropped.

"Mrs. Richards," Johnson continued, "our chaplain is out of town, and I don't really know how to do this, but I guess the best way is to be straight with you. There is no easy way to say . . ."

"Get on with it," a suddenly angry and frustrated Meg barked. "Just tell me what you have to say. He's dead, isn't he? If that is what it is, then say it!"

She could hear the officer breathing, but other than those deep breaths there was nothing but silence. Finally, after at least twenty horrible seconds, a time when she could feel the flames of hell creeping into the room, he continued, his voice no longer flat but now quivering like a violin string, "Mrs. Richards, your husband didn't survive the accident." He paused for another awkward moment, took another deep breath, and continued. "We believe he died instantly. If it's any consolation, he probably suffered no pain."

Meg's eyes darted back to the photo. He'd just celebrated his twenty-eighth birthday. They were just beginning to get to know each other. There were so many things they hadn't done, so many dreams they had only spoken and not lived. Only last week they'd gone house hunting and found one with a perfect little room for a nursery. They'd laughed as they viewed it, wondering if they should repaint it blue or pink. They were going to talk to the bank about a mortgage next week. Monday. But what did it matter now? For Steve, there would be no Monday. Time had stopped and her husband had been lost somewhere between the seconds.

As the reality of the horrible situation pushed beyond her mind and seeped into her heart, she again heard the words bouncing off the walls, "'Til death do us part! 'Til death do us part! 'Til death do us part!"

"Mrs. Richards? Are you all right?"

The voice instantly stopped the mocking chant, and without that chorus employing a wedding vow to rock the room and squeeze the life from her soul, Meg found she could answer the cop's question in such a calm voice that she even surprised herself. "Thank you, officer. I'll be fine."

"If you need anything, we could notify your pastor or . . ."

"No," Meg answered, her tone dry and emotionless, "that won't be necessary, I'll be just fine."

She hit the end call button, deliberately putting the phone down, letting the plastic touch the table gently, almost as if she were handling a fine piece of crystal. As it sat there, under the lamp's stark light, she stared at it contemplating how this night would have been different if she hadn't answered. Why didn't she just let the call go straight to voice mail? Then she could have had a few more hours of security and hope. But those precious elements of her life were now gone, shattered like a broken plate.

Picking up the phone, she punched the button for recent calls. Steve's name jumped out. He'd called her just 304 minutes ago.

"Meg," he'd explained, his voice full of life and exuberance. "Listen, Honey. If I work just a few more hours, I can finish the books here at Wilson's and drive back tonight. That way we can start the weekend, and just as soon as you finish your shift tomorrow, we can celebrate big time."

She had told him to wait in Hilldale, that tomorrow would be soon enough to make that drive, but she hadn't voiced those thoughts with much conviction. She hadn't sincerely tried to sell him on waiting. So this happened because she'd selfishly wanted him to come home just as quickly possible. Why had she allowed emotion to overrule logic?

"Steve, Steve, Steve," she whispered. Yet no one heard her and *he* never would again.

Meg looked down at the blue, lace gown she had put on to surprise him. He loved her in frilly blue things. Although she preferred sleeping in old T-shirts, she'd worn alluring, sexy gowns just for him. Now she didn't need them anymore. There were so many things she no longer needed, too. Oh, why hadn't she made him wait in Hilldale? Why hadn't she insisted he wait? Why didn't she argue? How important could one day be, even if that day was their anniversary? Now instead of one more day, there were no more days. None at all!

The phone rang again and hope suddenly pushed its way back into the small apartment's suddenly cold, stale air. Meg grabbed the cell before the second ring, desperately praying the police were calling back to tell her it had all been a mistake. Maybe Steve had stayed in Hilldale and someone else had been driving his car. Maybe someone else had died. *Please, Lord, let it be anyone else!*

"Hello," Meg whispered as she answered.

"Meg, this is Heather."

Normally, Heather Rodgers's voice would have brought with it good gossip or a great joke. But tonight it would be something else. Tonight, it would be the voice that fully assured Meg there was no awakening from this nightmare and that all hope had evaporated into thin air.

"I don't know what to say," Heather whispered. "I-I-I was working the late shift when the call on the accident came in. It's just so terrible. No one as good as Steve should die—ever— much less so young. I mean . . . I don't know what to do. Your heart must be breaking in a thousand pieces."

Good old Heather, everybody's friend, the nurse who kept them all smiling. How ironic she'd heard it first. If only she could tell a joke and make all of this disappear. Then a thought flashed through Meg's mind, a thought so bizarre that maybe only a medical professional or cop would consider it.

"Heather! Where's his body?"

The voice on the other end of the call didn't hesitate. "It's here right now. They brought it in a few minutes ago."

Why had she said *it*? Steve wasn't an *it*.

"Heather," Meg announced, "I need to see him."

"Meg, I don't think it would be a good idea for you to . . ."

Meg didn't allow her friend to finish. "I'm going to come down! I'll be there in a few minutes. Don't let anyone touch him."

"Meg," Heather was now pleading, "at least wait until they take him to the funeral home. I mean, there's nothing you can do for him now. You'd only be putting yourself through . . ." Heather paused as if trying to find words that would help and not hurt. Finally she blurted out, "I just don't want to see you torturing yourself."

"Heather, I'll be there in a little while. Don't let them do anything to Steve."

Cutting the call off, Meg marched resolutely to the bedroom. There was something to be done and only she could do it!

2

STEPPING INTO THE BEDROOM, MEG TORE THROUGH THE SMALL WALK-in closet she shared with Steve. She considered a half dozen ensembles before picking out a new blue sweater and a pair of jeans. She dressed quickly but carefully, putting on full makeup and fixing her hair almost as if getting ready for a very special date. Before leaving the apartment, she stared into the mirror one last time. Her reflection proved she looked her best. As Steve would have said, "Heads will turn when they see you tonight, Honey." And for reasons she didn't fully understand, she needed them to turn. She needed to look like a woman of strength in control of her world. If not to fool her friends, then to fool herself. And she needed to look like the woman Steve always bragged on.

It was just two miles to the hospital, but the short drive seemed to take forever. Although there was no traffic, Meg missed every light. Ten minutes after leaving her apartment and an hour after receiving the call from Officer Johnson, she finally arrived at the staff lot. Trying to act as though it was just another day at work, Meg got out of her yellow Mustang coupe and turned toward the building she knew so well. As she stared at the white brick building's six floors, a cool, damp breeze hit her face. It was the same kind of breeze that hit her when she had first met Steve, an early fall evening of her freshman year in college. She had blown a tire on a trip back from the library to her dorm and he had stopped to fix it for her. He'd been able to fix everything since then. Except for this. He couldn't fix death. No one could.

Turning her face into the wind, she briskly strolled the forty yards across the parking lot. As she walked through the automatic door into the emergency room, she noticed a young man sitting to her right. Even in the midst of this horrible personal trauma, her training automatically kicked in. In an almost detached fashion, she made her assessment—not too serious, probably just bumped his head in a fall or traffic accident. A few stitches and he'd be told to use ice and take some aspirin. Routine ER stuff. The kind of thing she dealt with everyday of the year.

As she continued her trek across the ER, she heard Dr. Jake Jones, a small, portly man in his forties. "And if you feel any throbbing, just take a couple aspirin. There's nothing broken and except for some pain from those stitches in your forehead, I don't think that . . ." The doctor's words trailed off as Meg rounded a corner and made her way to the emergency room nurses' station.

"Meg," a shocked Judy Lincoln exclaimed. "How are you?"

Meg didn't respond to the fifty-year-old nurse's concerned question. She didn't even acknowledge the older woman's presence. Yet, a voice down the hall did catch her attention.

"Are you sure you want to do this?" Heather asked, her words spilling out like water pouring from a glass. "Listen, Meg, there's no easy way for me to say this, Steve's car must have been totaled and it caught fire. I was in ER when they brought him in and I don't really think you want or need to see him this way. Why don't you just talk to the hospital chaplain

instead? He's right down the hall. I can get him in a flash."
While Heather searched Meg's eyes for some sign of understanding, her pleas fell on deaf ears. Meg had become a force
that pushed her beyond logic or understanding. She needed to
be with Steve.

"Where is he?" Meg's words were delivered in a firm,
demanding, and almost mechanical rhythm.

"But . . ." Heather began.

"Heather, shut it down. I don't need your sympathies or
empathy. I'm a big girl and I'm a trained nurse. And I have a
right to do what I want to do. Now where is he?"

Heather gestured toward a small room across the hall.

Meg nodded. Her need to see Steve was seated in more
than just the love she had for her husband. It was also attached
to a previous family tragedy. Her aunt had lost her husband
in Vietnam. They never found the body. For years, the woman
waited with the illogical hope that he might be a prisoner
someplace and would someday return to her. That looking out
the window, waiting for a call, searching each day's mail had
gone on for decades. Not seeing his body had created such a
deep void, the woman never accepted her husband's death. She
was still looking or at least wishing for his return when she
died forty years later. Meg had long believed that things would
have been different if her aunt had just seen the body. Because
of witnessing that woman's progressive decline into a kind of
silent madness, Meg sensed that only by seeing her Steve now,
at this very moment, not waiting even a few hours much less a
day, could she really accept all of this as something other than
a nightmare.

"I'll go with you," Heather offered. "You don't need to do
this alone."

Meg had never liked being treated like a child, even back
when she had been one, and she didn't want any help now.

"Heather," Meg shot back, "I'm a nurse, have been for a while now, and I've seen it all. I don't need you to hold my hand." Reaching forward, she gently pushed her friend to the side.

"Don't do this," Heather whispered, putting her hand on Meg's shoulder. "You're in shock. You need to take a while and absorb what has happened."

Meg had seen shock put others on autopilot. Shock could twist a person and force them into unwise decisions. Maybe Heather was right. Maybe she was in a bad place now. After all, wouldn't a normal reaction come with a flood tears? Yet she felt very little emotion. Is that how it should be?

Meg looked up and caught her reflection in a window. Yes, that was her face complete with the dark brown eyes, the arched eyebrows, the high cheekbones, and the bee-stung lips. But now she wore an expression that projected a cold, solitary, and hard person. It was a look she didn't recognize. Could that be her?

For a moment she looked back to her friend. She teetered on reaching out and asking for help. Her lips quivered and she felt a bit faint. Then she remembered her aunt. No, shock or not, she had to do this. Pushing Heather's hand from her shoulder, she moved forward. Wise or not, she had to be with Steve. After all, he had made this last trip to be with her. He couldn't rest until his trip was actually completed with her at his side. And that was what this was all about. They both needed to complete the trip.

After taking a deep breath, she walked into the room and flipped on the overhead light. There on a hospital gurney, in a room normally used to save lives, lay a still form covered by a white sheet. The figure under that covering remained rigid. There was no hint of life.

Suddenly, her strength gone, terror gripping her by the throat, she backed up until she felt a cool wall against her shoulders. Her knees rubbery, her stomach churning, and her head spinning, she turned toward the door wanting to run as far as she could from this room. But she couldn't move. Even as she began to hyperventilate, something forced her gaze back to the gurney. She still had to know. She had to see this with her own eyes.

The door pushed slowly open and Heather walked in. "Meg, you don't have to do this and you don't need to do it. But if you're determined to see him, please let me be with you." She opened her arms as if begging to draw Meg in for a hug, but Meg didn't accept the gesture.

"Please leave," the grieving woman asked. "Just wait on the other side of the door. I've got to do this, Heather. Maybe someday you'll understand."

"Meg."

"I still feel his presence," Meg whispered. "I can't accept he's gone. I'll never accept it unless . . ."

"So," Heather softly pleaded, "just let me stay."

"No, please go. I'll be out in a second. I need one more moment alone with Steve."

As her friend sadly pushed the door open and left, Meg closed her eyes and called upon a higher power. "Dear Lord, please wake me up. Please make all of this a bad dream."

As she opened her eyes, she discovered there would be no wake-up call. The body remained on the gurney just as her prayer remained unanswered. There would be no reprieve or escape.

Meg focused once more on the gurney. She'd seen enough dead people under sheets to be able to recognize if the body was a man or woman, a child or an adult. Those experiences now told her something was wrong, very wrong. This couldn't be Steve. The body wasn't big enough. Maybe this had all been a mistake. Clasping her hands together, sweat beading down her forehead, she took the first unsteady steps toward the gurney. As she grew closer, her heart galloped and the room began to spin. For a moment, she felt as she would pass out.

"Oh, Lord," she breathed. "Please stop this. Give me strength."

As if this prayer had been answered, the spinning room slowed down and ground to an unsteady halt. Suddenly, she again had some control.

Once more focused, Meg inched her left hand forward and found the top edge of the sheet. As she touched the linen, her wedding ring sparkled under the harsh light. It was a single gold band, nothing elaborate or fancy, but it represented something and someone she had loved deeply for so long. What did it represent now? Memories?

She suddenly recalled the day he had first slipped it on. As she relived that moment it felt as if Steve was once more with her, holding her hand, grabbing the sheet. With a renewed strength brought on by feeling his presence, she gave a quick, steady pull and was visited by something she hadn't expected. What rested on the gurney took her breath away and made her stomach boil. It was like pictures she had seen of casualties in war zones and it stunned even this trained and experienced nurse.

What was in front of her wasn't so much one body but random, burned parts laid out on a table. They were positioned like broken china awaiting regluing. But this mess could not be put back together. There wasn't enough glue in the whole world. The crash had literally torn this body apart and left it unrecognizable. Unexpectedly, the fact that the man had not just been shredded but burned gave Meg hope.

This can't be my Steve. It's a mistake. Steve could never look like this. It just can't be him! Someone else must have been driving his car.

But that hope was quickly and cruelly dashed when she saw the man's left hand, that same hand that had made him Springfield University's star baseball pitcher and the same hand upon which she had once placed a gold ring. And there on the ring finger of that hand was a simple, plain gold band. It was Steve's ring, the one she'd given him. The one that was engraved inside the band, "'Til death do us part." And death was now not sixty years from now as it should have been.

After one final look, Meg pulled the sheet back up. "As simple as making a bed," a head nurse had once told her about covering a corpse. And it was easy, but still each time she had done this simple act she'd always wondered how many hearts had been shattered by that death? Now she knew that simple act of pulling up a single white sheet over a body wasn't just covering a lifeless body, it was closing and locking a door that would never again be opened.

3

As Meg opened the door to the hallway, Dr. John Seymour, a brash, devastatingly handsome young resident strolled toward her. Yet, even though they were only a few feet away, he evidently failed to see Meg. Perhaps that is why as he approached, his words were directed only to Heather.

"Hey, sweetheart, you really do look fine this morning. No one wears a uniform the way you do." He finished his off-handed compliment with a long wink and a big grin.

Usually Heather had a quick comeback for the doctor's flirting, but maybe because of her concern for her friend she remained mute, only responding with a stern glare. Failing to read her expression, Seymour continued to prod one of the hospital's most desirable single employees, "Why, Heather, who stepped on your tail today?"

"John," she whispered, "there was an accident this morning, and . . ."

Opening the door wider and stepping fully into view, Meg interrupted Heather in mid-explanation. In unison, both nurse and doctor turned toward her.

"We've got to get someone to oil those hinges," the doctor laughed. "The squeaking could wake the dead."

Heather cringed, but Seymour, sensing he had a captive audience, continued. "Well, Nurse Richards, good morning. I didn't expect to see you this early, but it's always a pleasure to be around such beauty even if you're taken. That husband of yours is one lucky man."

"Doctor, Meg is . . ."

Cutting Heather off, Seymour added, "Beautiful. Yes, she is. And I've got some good news for Meg, and I'm not going to keep her in suspense for even a moment longer." His face beaming, he continued, "Nurse, the lab finally got caught up after you left yesterday."

Heather jumped in again, "Whatever the news is, I don't think this is the time!"

A stubborn Seymour just kept right on talking. "Meg, I overheard you saying yesterday your husband would be coming home this weekend for your anniversary and I knew you'd want to surprise him with the good news. Congratulations! Your suspicions were confirmed. Our official tests prove you're pregnant!"

Seemingly realizing that no one else was reacting normally to this bit of wonderful news, a confused look quickly crossed the man's face. "Listen, Meg, I'm sorry if I spoiled the surprise by telling you in front of Heather, but I know how long you've been trying and I just didn't think that you'd want me to hold back. If I was wrong, just remember I've never been known for having any tact."

Meg's eyes met the doctor's momentarily then she lowered her head, turned, and walked toward the ER door. In the background, she heard him ask, "What did I do?"

Meg was out of earshot before Heather could explain.

As she exited, the same accident victim she'd observed when she'd first arrived held the outside door open for her. He was so lucky. He got to go home to be with his family. Or maybe it wasn't luck but fate. Maybe fate had dealt her the wrong hand and him the right one.

Walking resolutely across the parking lot, she again felt the damp breeze hit her face. Like a slap in the face, the cold wind emphasized how quickly things could change. In a split second, good had become bad and pleasure had morphed into pain. Just as quickly, an answered prayer had turned into a meaningless coda in an evening consumed by tragedy. The "wonderful" news she'd been waiting and praying to hear for what had once seemed a long time didn't seem to matter now. How ironic! The only thing she and Steve needed to make their lives complete had only been confirmed after his life had ended.

Sliding into her Mustang, she slammed the driver's side door, tightly clenched the steering wheel, and looked toward the heavens. So this is the way God worked! And if this was the case, then why bother trying to live a good life or even praying? What had it gotten her? She had experienced a few incredible years and then it had become a nightmare of pain and regret.

Looking out through her windshield, she took a deep breath and shouted, "Why? What have I done?"

She had more she wanted to say but she couldn't bring herself to tell God what she thought of Him. Besides, she'd lost her voice and for the first time since the phone had awakened her from such peaceful dreams, tears filled her eyes. She was completely alone and that knowledge spilled out into the night, the car, and her heart. It rolled over her like a powerful ocean wave. A silent voice suddenly screamed unrelentingly that nothing would ever be the same again, that death had come and the parting was real and there was no stopping the "dark music"!

4

For two days, Meg mindlessly walked through the duties that had been suddenly and unmercifully thrust upon her. She graciously greeted scores of visitors as they came into her apartment with arms full of food and mouths spilling out thousands of meaningless words. Some even said they understood just how she felt. She wanted to laugh in their faces. How could they know how she felt? No one could know how she felt. She wasn't even sure herself. She wished they had all just left her alone. After all, alone was now the story of her life and she felt it was time to begin living that story.

She vaguely remembered spending time picking out a suit, a shirt, and a tie to give to the funeral director, but what did it really matter? After all, the slate gray coffin she'd chosen would be closed. It had to remain locked because Steve, like Humpty Dumpty, couldn't be put back together again. He could have been buried in a sheet and no one would have known. So why had they wasted good clothes that someone else could have worn? In fact, picking out clothes that would never be seen reflected the nature of everything about a funeral. The whole experience seemed like a colossal waste of time. There were far better things to do than say good-bye to someone who couldn't hear or reply. Besides, she had said her goodbyes at the hospital. That is where she'd learned the true meaning and felt the full weight of "'Til Death Do Us Part."

So as Meg now waded through all her obligations, she saw no reason for any of this. It was all just social mumbo-jumbo. She seriously thought it should be cancelled; it was accomplishing nothing more than drawing out needless pain. But when she suggested just a graveside memorial, her wishes were quickly shot down. Her mother and Steve's folks insisted on a full-blown funeral. And when Meg balked at attending the church memorial service, her mother raised her voice and scolded her. "How would it look if you weren't there?" Then she'd added, "Steve would want you there." Meg had just nodded and forced a solemn smile. What a joke! Steve didn't want anything anymore, and he wouldn't care if she were there or not. His mind had stopped and with it all his wishes.

With each passing moment, she grew to hate the thought of the funeral even more. She saw no real purpose in it. Was this the way all widows felt? Did they also dread dealing with a ceremony that was really nothing more than hollow words among old friends?

Love had been the anchor in her life and that love had come from Steve. He had radiated it with his touch and his kiss. She felt it in the way he looked at her. It gave her confidence and made her strong enough to handle anything. But now that love was gone. And with each passing moment, it grew more distant. And without that anchor, she was adrift. So why hold a service that pointed out to the world the guiding force in a woman's life had left her?

Beyond the ache in her heart and the sense of incredible loneliness, the worst part of the two endless days had been her meeting with Reverend Cheston Brooks. There was nothing wrong with the man. Brooks, short, middle-aged, and blessed with a gentle spirit and a soft delivery, was the kind of person everyone, including those who didn't ever darken a church door, liked. Yet over the past forty-eight hours she'd come to loath the sight of him. He'd visited with her on two long, drawn-out occasions and each meeting left her feeling more empty and lost. Worse yet, the preacher in his haste to make her feel as though God was with her had actually done just the opposite. Brooks had planted a seed that made the widow wonder if God wasn't really the problem rather than the solution.

The first time he came to see her Brooks read a great number of Scriptures to seemingly reassure her that all of this was in God's plan. Meg actually heard few of his words. What she did hear just made her angry. She wasn't buying any of the "God's plan" bit. Why would God plan such a horrible thing? Why would He break her heart? And then there was the pastor's constant need to stop and pray. Now praying seemed to be a bit like buying a spare tire after your car had been sold. What real good could it do?

On Brooks's second visit, after he had finished mumbling his carefully chosen words, she pressed him on the whys of Steve's death. Brooks admitted he couldn't understand why the accident had happened. And if a man trained to know didn't know, how could Meg begin to understand or possibly put any faith in the God who had killed her husband? And if He is all-powerful and had allowed it to happen, then that was just what He had done. He'd killed her husband. That singular, cruel thought almost caused her to voice her emotions. But before she could tell Brooks that God had to be responsible, he chimed in with more of his evangelical dribble.

"Meg, I don't know what it is in this case, but I really believe that something good can and will come out of this. You need to believe that, too."

She bit her lip and nodded, and then he prayed again.

While Meg didn't accept Brooks's faith in there being a reason for all of this, it had been easier simply to nod her head pretending to agree than to continue to challenge the man. After all, arguing would just needlessly waste more time discussing something she didn't want to discuss. If Brooks wanted to continue to believe in the elementary Christian faith of her childhood, he could, but she had a much different point of view now. When all of this pomp and ceremony ended and Steve was buried, she'd start to live a life based on the present and not the future. She was not going to be hurt again nor live with fairy tales and outdated ideas such as good things happen to those who have faith. It was now all too obvious that had to be a fable. After all, she'd always played by the book. She'd been faithful. She'd tithed. She'd gone on mission trips. She'd prayed for the sick. She'd been the best Christian she could be and look at what had happened! The last thing she needed to hear at this point was "just have faith."

Thankfully, not everyone tossed off the same old, tired, and meaningless lines. There had been one person who hadn't spit out a long litany of clichés. Heather had just been there and she'd been wonderful. She'd done her best to understand what Meg was saying and thinking and hadn't even attempted to talk her out of wearing a blue dress instead of the traditional black to the funeral. After all, Steve had hated seeing her in dark clothing and she couldn't bring herself to wear black even on this day. Heather had understood and even gone to bat for her against her mother. Thanks to her, that one battle had been won.

Somehow, maybe thanks mostly to Heather, the world had moved forward and she and the endless streams of people who had offered their condolences were now seated in the church. There directly in front of her, presiding over it all was Reverend Brooks. And those who had packed the church for the service felt sure he would find the words to bring comfort to Meg. She was just as sure he couldn't. After reading a few Scriptures, Brooks began to speak from the heart and in the process proved Meg right.

"As we consider his death," Brooks began, "we can now fully realize there was no finer young leader in this community than Steven Richards. He meant so much to this church. An active choir member, the leader of our high school Sunday school department, and of course, a tremendous witness to all of our members through his devotion to the wife he now leaves behind."

The preacher's next words were equally glowing as he listed all of Steve's great accomplishments from Eagle Scout to trusted employee. He told several funny tales that captured Steve's sense of humor. He followed those with serious narrative, presenting example after example of his incredible character. But to Meg those words and the stories rang hollow now. They offered no comfort at all. Food had no taste, the wind no chill, the sun no shine, sleep offered no refuge, and words, even those praising the man she loved, meant nothing! She just wanted the words to end. Finally, after thirty long minutes, Brooks seemed to be coming to the real point he wanted the congregation to hear.

"I don't understand why this tragic accident happened, nor, I am sure, does anyone. God does not let us know all the mysteries that are a part of His world, but we can gain true inspiration and insight from Steven's short life and feel true joy knowing that he is now happy with the Master in heaven."

Meg couldn't help it. As soon as Brooks uttered those words she just had to shake her head. Mysteries of His world! Yeah, that was it. Why question the mysteries, just accept them. She'd heard that for two days. She wasn't going to fall into the trap. She would never accept this. This wasn't right and it had nothing to do with God's love. And then, Brooks delivered the clincher.

"You have to trust in the Lord and something good will come out of this."

He just had to toss it out there—that all-encompassing line she had heard from lots of family and friends over the past two days. Her mom was the worst. She kept saying it over and over again. And now, Brooks had fallen into that trap as well. Trust in the Lord and something good will come out of this. Well, if Meg managed to be good, Santa would come visit in nine months, too. Every child in the world knew that and every adult used it to keep those children in line. Something good coming out of this was a joke. She was alone. The love of her life had died. It might have been Steve's mangled body in the gray coffin, but she was in there, too. And when they buried him, they would be burying the part of her that could feel and experience love. She knew that as well as she knew Steve would never again take a breath or say a word. And yet the preacher kept talking as if there could be some kind of opportunity created by Steve's death. What kind of opportunity? What could anyone gain from this? Where was the good?

"For even though the body of Steven Richards has died," Brooks droned on, "we know that Steven accepted Jesus as his savior, and as is promised in the Bible, a believer in our Lord will be safe from death and can be sure that his soul will find everlasting life with Jesus in heaven."

Heaven! Meg couldn't make a cell call to there. There was no iPhone app for that. She couldn't talk to Steve or be held in his arms at his new address. So his being there brought no comfort at all. It didn't stop her pain and didn't fill the void in her life.

Meg's eyes left Brooks and went to those filling the church. Many were nodding, a few were whispering amen, but they all looked sad; some were even visibly hurting. It was as if they had each been kicked in the teeth. The more she looked around the more she realized that pain hung over the service like a violent summer storm. As she took it all in, Meg's aching turned into rage. How could this be called a Christian service when it put so many people through such great anguish? Where was the love in all of this? Better yet, where was the saving grace?

"So, Meg," the pastor's mentioning her name suddenly jarred her out of her raging fog and refocused her eyes on the pulpit. What she heard turned her stomach more than soothed her spirit.

"Even though this time must be very hard for you, try to remember that Steven embraced a mission and a life beyond this one. In fact, he had a mission and a life greater than any we can begin to realize. He had been chosen by God to live and his job is finished, and he is now in a better place than we who are left. Thank you, God, for this man and what his life stood for. Now, let us pray."

Yep, the old mystery angle again. If you don't have an answer for something, then trot it out and hook it to the it-must-have-been-his-time theory. It might work for some, but not for Meg and not today.

Meg tuned out Brooks's prayer. While all other heads in the auditorium were bowed, her eyes remained fixed on the closed coffin. She'd shed no tears since the ones that had fallen in the hospital parking lot and there would be none coming today. Not even the sight of that cold, gray coffin could open her heart. She was too angry to cry and ached to move to a place where she could fully vent.

When this funeral ended, she silently vowed, she'd be walking out of this church for the last time. It couldn't happen soon enough. After the final words were said and they lowered Steve into the ground and covered the casket with dirt, Meg would shake a few hands, accept a few hugs, and even mouth a few prayers, but only for the moment because the mask would soon come off. God had His chance to prove His love and He had not proved worthy of hers.

As Brooks said his final amen and the congregation rose to watch the coffin rolled out of the church, the emotion Meg felt centered not on loss but rage. Before this day ended, she vowed that someone would feel her wrath. All she needed now was a human target.

5

"OH, MEG, I THOUGHT THE REVEREND BROOKS GAVE US SUCH A MEANING-ful message today. Didn't you?"

Meg glanced over at her mother. Barbara Hankins was short, auburn-haired, and a bit chubby. Her fair, round cheeks caused her dark brown eyes to appear larger than they were. She was dressed in a black suit and pumps. She was the stereotypical image of a president of a book review club and she just happened to be filling that role this year.

"I thought Steve's parents handled it very well. It's a shame that they live so far away. I know that they could be such a comfort to you during this time. I mean, all things considered, what a beautiful service! It really did Steve proud. I know he would have liked it. I just wish your sister Terri could have been here. She just couldn't make connections from overseas. She would have loved the service and been touched by it. Do you suppose the church made a video?"

It had been six hours since they'd left the graveside and except for her mother, everyone else had gone home. Standing in the kitchen, looking out the window but not seeing anything, Meg started to acknowledge her mother's comments in the same manner that she had everyone else's, with a simple yes and a line about how glad she had been that all of the family and close friends could make it back to Springfield for the service, but something stopped her.

This was her mother, they were finally alone, and it was time to be honest. After all, isn't that what she'd always preached to her daughter? "Give it to me straight!" She had said time and time again. Well, it was time that Barbara Hankins experienced her daughter's honesty. How could God have dared to take her husband, particularly now? No words or flowers or pretty services would supply the answer, and Meg had grown so tired of pretending that she was grateful for any of those things. It was time her mother heard about what Meg really thought about the service and everything else that had happened over the past two days. This was the moment Meg could toss off the part of the good little wife who would lean on God, make it through this hard time, and let all of her emotions out. Her mother just happened to be in the wrong place at the wrong time. Like a wild stallion freed from a pen, she charged.

"Mom, I don't really care who came and who stayed home. I'm glad Terri didn't waste her time and money trying to get home. I don't give a flip about what Reverend Brooks or anyone else said or did. Steve's dead and no one or nothing is going to change that."

The older woman, obviously stunned at the biting words spewing from her daughter's mouth, rocked back on her heels. Almost joyfully, Meg observed the shock register on her mother's face. This was exactly the reaction that Meg wanted. And before Barbara could find her voice, Meg continued.

"If you want to believe that trash about God's will, you can, but I don't. You just show me what good will come out of this. I defy you to present to me just one thing! You can't and you know it! No one can! You can't give me one good reason that it was best for Steve to die now."

Meg's brown eyes were burning with a cold, calculated fury, her tone now sharp and bitter. She was daring her mother to prove her wrong, verbally slapping the older woman with the faith she had long worn on her sleeve. And watching the confused look on her mother's face gave Meg an emotional lift. After all, this time her mom would not have any satisfactory answers. There would be no Bible verses to trot out or old family stories that would make this all better.

Barbara fidgeted on the couch, Meg's sudden rage evidently shaking her to the bone. Meg could see the confusion written on her mother's face and it brought her a strange sense of satisfaction.

"Now, Honey," she almost whispered, seemingly trying to choose words carefully so Meg would not become more upset. "You're right. Nothing will bring Steve back, but bitterness is not going to get you anywhere. You can't just give up on twenty-five years of faith simply because of one event."

"One event, Mom? Please get serious. Steve was my whole life. I'm not tossing out anything that matters, because I've already lost that. If God is a loving God, how could He have done this to Steve, to his family, or to me? You show me some reason, Mom. You can't, because there isn't any. There is absolutely no good reason for this. Steve didn't die saving a life, didn't die for some noble cause, he didn't die for anything!"

As silence filled the room and her fifty-five-year-old mother toyed with the corner of a magazine, Meg almost felt sorry for her. She almost reached out to hug Barbara. That is what she would have done in the past. She'd always been the perfect daughter. The girl who came home on time, kept her room neat, didn't party, and never caused her parents' any heartache. But she couldn't be that person now. At this moment, with the fresh wounds of grief still raw, she couldn't reach out in love to anyone, not even her mother.

"Meg," Barbara softly began, "I've always found that prayer is a way to understand just what . . ."

Meg cut her off, "Okay, Mom, fine, you go ahead and pray, but I'm not going to. This God, this almighty being that zaps helpless people at random moments, He is not worthy of it. I now kind of think He kills people on whims for His own amusement. I wouldn't associate with a person like that, so why would I speak to a god like that? It'd be like being friends with the school bully. If I have to believe that He works in strange ways, then fine. But if He is all-powerful, he could have saved Steve and He didn't. In my mind that makes Him a murderer. And you know what we do with murderers in this state. We either execute them or put them away for life. Maybe I can't execute God, but I can lock Him up and keep Him out of my life. In fact, I already have! I did it the moment I saw Steve's body in pieces on the gurney. You should have been there, Mom. You should have seen it, too. That would have been a blow to your faith. Might have woken you up like it did me. I wish you'd seen what God did."

"Now, Meg. God wasn't driving the car that hit Steve. He didn't sell the liquor to those teenagers." Barbara continued her rambling discourse, but Meg stopped listening after the word *teenagers*.

Of course, they were the ones really responsible for Steve's death. She'd completely forgotten about them until this moment. The driver of that car is the person who really deserves to feel her wrath.

Meg's heart began to race as she thought of exacting some kind of revenge on Steve's killer. This would focus her pain. Maybe she could even bring the pain she was feeling now to the person responsible for Steve's death. Suddenly wrapped up in devising a prescription to inflict pain, she was only vaguely aware that her mother had stopped talking.

After an awkward moment of complete silence, Meg said, "Mom, I'm sorry. I shouldn't have lashed out at you. What's happened has shifted my perspective."

"That's okay, Honey. I understand."

"Thanks, Mom," Meg said, her tone now much softer. "By the way, who was driving the car that killed Steve?"

"I don't remember, Honey," Barbara said almost absent-mindedly, "I'm not sure the police even released the information. I don't think they could if the driver was a minor."

The realization sent a flood of rage through her body. That wasn't fair. She should know the killer's identity. If fact, she should be the one who judged and sentenced him.

Meg turned back to the window and stared out to the street. If the news reports didn't list the name, then who would know? Spinning around, she grumbled, "There has to be a way to find out who did this."

"Why would you want to know, Darling? What good would it do?"

Her brown eyes locked on her mother. "I'm going to find out, Mom." Smiling for the first time in two days, she added, "And when I do, I'm going to make him wish that he'd never been born."

Meg's cold statement caused her mother to suddenly wrap her arms around her body as if chilled. Meg noted the reaction, but didn't care. An eerie fire burned in her brown eyes as she planned her next move. She had a mission now. She was tossing away the old shell of a warm-hearted, loving Christian. That woman now lived in the past. It was time now to channel her inner Charles Bronson or Clint Eastwood—time to become a driven vigilante. Revenge would be hers and she could already taste it. Suddenly filled with a sense of power and purpose, her life again had meaning. Her misery could be transferred to the killer of her husband, and when that person wore her pain, she knew she would feel so very good.

She glanced at the wedding portrait hanging on the wall and whispered, "Don't worry, Steve, he'll pay for what he did to you. You have my word!"

For the first time in two days, Meg Hankins Richards felt alive!

6

As Meg awoke, she automatically turned to face her husband only to be confronted with the familiar spot where he always lay. The sudden shock of seeing an empty pillow immediately drove home the realization of the solitary nature of her new life, and the void Steve's death had left filled the room like a choking cloud of toxic gas. Turning over and staring at the opposite wall didn't remove the hollow feeling of loneliness; rather it magnified it. Choking back tears, she dragged herself out of bed, grabbed her robe, and wandered toward the apartment's kitchen.

Opening the cabinet, she automatically pulled down two glasses and set them on the counter. Reaching into the freezer, she grabbed the ice tray and dropped six cubes into each of the glasses. After replacing the tray, she opened the refrigerator, took out a two-liter bottle of Coke, and began to fill the glasses. As she waited for the foam to settle, reality hit her.

Suddenly a feeling of rage, the same rage that had kept her awake most of the night, began to envelop her. Taking a still foaming glass in her hand, she spun around and threw it as hard as she could against the far wall. Ice cubes and Coke splattered all over her kitchen as pieces of glass slid in eighty different directions all at the same time.

Turning, Meg stared at the wall, amazed by her own actions but seemingly calmer because of them. Except for the noise made by her fizzing drink, the apartment was immersed in complete silence and that was simply not natural. Steve should have been singing a stupid song or telling a funny story. Sighing, she picked up the other glass and walked to the window.

Trying to push the memory of past mornings from her head, Meg focused on the scene beyond her window, which showed signs of being a typical midwestern March morning. A light snow had fallen during the night and covered the unspoiled ground with a pure and beautiful carpet of white. A strong northerly breeze, evident in the swaying evergreen trees on the corner of the front lawn, coupled with a grayish sky, made it seem even colder than the twenty-eight degrees indicated by Meg's window thermometer. Birds, mostly small sparrows, along with one beautiful male cardinal, played in the white fluff, while a neighbor's cat, partially hidden behind a tree, stalked them.

Meg's brown eyes darted to the far side of the street. Old Mr. Fudge, bundled up as if for a Russian winter, eased out of his front door, across the snow, and awkwardly slid into his trusty 1985 Olds. Meg knew that soon, after the car's motor had sufficiently warmed, Mrs. Fudge would follow her husband's path, and just like they had done for sixty years, the two of them would head for church. Normally she would have been joining them, but not now, not without Steve.

Another old-timer, Herb Lucas, waved at Mr. Fudge from his blue pick-up as he delivered the Sunday morning edition of the *Springfield Herald*. Meg watched, just as she had a hundred times before, as the ever accurate Herb, while never leaving the truck, hit porch after porch with carefully rolled papers.

On most Sunday mornings, she would have timed opening her door at just the moment the paper landed at the base of her stairs. She would have then shouted a hearty greeting to Herb and waved and smiled at Mr. Fudge. But today she didn't want to talk to anyone or have anyone else see the sadness in her eyes, so she simply let the paper land on the concrete and watched Herb drive on.

Taking another sip of her Coke, she stared back at the idyllic scene in front of her. The world still turned just as it always had. Steve's death hadn't stopped anything or anyone. The snow still fell, the papers were still printed, and the birds still sang. It seemed that only her life was different, only hers was empty.

Glancing at the stove clock, she noted that on any other Sunday she would be getting ready for church by now. She knew that the fifth graders in her Sunday school class must be confused and waiting for her. She'd seen some of them at the funeral. They were sweet to come to such a grown-up event, but from now on somebody else would have to explain the mysteries of God and the world to them. She didn't have the answers to their questions any more than she had the answers to her own. While she would miss the kids, she'd already moved church and all that went with it to the past. It was that simple. And why hadn't she made that decision years ago? She could have enjoyed those wasted Sunday mornings with Steve. Think of all the things they could have done. Now she couldn't get them back. That was the problem with life, once it slipped away you couldn't get anything back.

The ringing of her cell phone roused her from her thoughts. Stepping across the now sticky kitchen floor, being careful to avoid the shards of glass, Meg stopped the iPhone's chirping on the third ring.

"Hello." Her greeting revealed absolutely no enthusiasm.

"Meg, it's Mom." Barbara sounded far too caring and for that reason Meg didn't respond with anything more than a deep sigh. Perhaps sensing her daughter was not going to speak, Barbara charged on, "Dear, I do wish you'd let me stay with you last night."

"I was fine, Mom. Besides, there wasn't enough room." Meg hoped her flat tone made it obvious that she didn't want to deal with her mother nor the words of wisdom that would soon spill out of the receiver.

"Well, you should have at least come home with me. It's not good to be alone at a time like this." Barbara waited an appropriate time for a response, and when none came, she continued, "Meg, why don't I pick you up for church and then we can come back over here for some roast."

"No thanks, Mom. I'm just going to stay home today." Her controlled response remained polite, hiding the fact that the mention of attending church had sparked an explosive fire in Meg's heart. And though she likely didn't know it, if she kept pushing, Barbara was walking a line that could transform her daughter's normally calm nature into a violent storm. Meg hoped her mother would read between the lines and drop this spin for togetherness.

"Meg, you just don't need to be by yourself, not yet anyway. I know what you're going through."

Meg was surprised it had taken as long as it had. Now came the time for the older woman to deliver the kicker—the moment when Barbara would try the ultimate attempt at bonding by trotting out the story that Meg knew had to have been on the tip of her tongue for the past three days. Oh why couldn't she just say good-bye and head off to church?

"When your father died," Barbara began, her tone sincere but a bit forced, "all I wanted to do was sit in a chair and look out the window. But, you, your sister, and my friends didn't let me do that. I mean . . ." There was no reason to listen to this old story. She'd heard it many times before. So Meg bluntly cut her mother short.

"Mother, I don't want to hurt your feelings. I know you are trying to make me feel better. But you're not. The fact is that you don't know what I'm going through. Steve was twenty-eight—just twenty-eight. Some drunk killed him! It happened suddenly—without warning! One minute I was a wife, the next a widow. I didn't have any time to think about it or prepare for it. There were no goodbyes."

She could have stopped there and probably should have, but the anger raging in her soul had now taken control. So she spit out another series of thoughts as if they were being delivered by a machine gun. Their impact was almost as cruel as it was deadly.

"Dad had heart trouble for years. When he went into the hospital that last time, he knew he wasn't going to come out. We knew it, too. Dad was sixty-one years old and I miss him. But you can't begin to compare that to what happened to Steve. Dad was within a decade of a normal life span. He had kids, went on fun vacations, and got to spend all of his active years with you. He actually lived life! Steve only got to start living. So don't even try to tell me you know what I'm going through, because you don't."

Barbara evidently had no response to calm her angry, hurt daughter and an awkward silence, made even more awkward by the fact the conversation was taking place on a phone and not in person, filled the next few moments. Finally, obviously struggling to find words, Barbara continued.

"Honey, I know it didn't happen the same way, but . . ."

In a challenging tone now filled with hostility, Meg fired back. "Mom, when Dad died, Terri and I were already out of school. He left you secure. You didn't have to go back to work.

That made it easy for you, at least compared to what I'm going through. Show me one place you had it tougher than me! I dare you, show me one place!"

Her voice now growing louder and more demanding, Meg challenged her mother again, "Show me, Mom!"

Attempting to apply a mother's empathy, Barbara answered with a calm steady voice. "Meg, dear, your father's death was not easy for me, no matter how long I'd had to prepare. We had been together for thirty-six years."

"Mom, be grateful for them, that's an eternity compared to what Steve and I had."

"I know, Meg, but still I had a very difficult time adjusting. Your father and I were a team. We were together all the time."

"Dad didn't leave you pregnant."

The silence that followed had the effect of an immense black hole—all energy immediately drained from both ends of the call and neither woman spoke for almost a minute. Finally, Barbara whispered, "What?"

"You heard me."

"When did you, I mean, how long have you known?"

"I found out right after he died, Mom. How's that for a kick in the pants?"

Meg now sensed her mother had fallen into a complete state of shock. The pregnancy had come from out of left field. Meg knew the older woman hadn't even suspected. Before her mother could sort through her confused thoughts and emotions, Meg bluntly ended their conversation.

"Listen, Mom, if you don't get on the move, you're going to be late for church. Your friends will all be there and they'll want to talk about how horrible this all is. I wouldn't want you to miss that. I want to be alone today anyway. Please respect that. Don't come over and don't call me. Now, good-bye."

Meg didn't even wait for her mother's response. Satisfied she had extracted a full measure of pain, she hit the end call button and tossed the phone onto the couch. Wandering back to the kitchen window, she once again picked up her Coke and looked outside. Mr. Fudge's car was now gone and the only signs of life on the street were the playing birds and the stalking cat. For reasons she didn't comprehend, she found herself drawn to the scene under the elm tree just a few yards from her door. It was escapism at its best, like an Animal Planet documentary created only for her eyes. Best of all, the unfolding drama took her mind off the pain that had so unexpectedly entered her life.

For ten minutes, the cat watched unmoving and unseen, hidden by the tree's large trunk. Little by little, the birds came closer and closer to where he lay. Meg stood perfectly still, amazed by the cat's patience and equally impressed with the hungry stare in his large, green eyes. He had become a living statue, a beautiful work of art. But he didn't stay stone cold for long. With absolutely no warming, in a very carefully planned moment of his choosing, he sprang to life. Landing in the middle of the dozen or more sparrows, his paws reached out, and in a split-second of brutal savagery, broke the neck of the lone, unsuspecting cardinal.

As the red bird dropped lifelessly to the ground, the other birds scattered in a panic, some quickly landing on low limbs then turning back to observe their fallen comrade. Others, pushed by continually exploding fear, flew out of sight. They didn't want to know what would happen next. They didn't have the stomach for it. Yet, Meg couldn't pull her eyes from the victorious feline. The cat quickly surveyed the area before picking up the lifeless bird in his mouth. He violently shook his prize once more and then trotted off, disappearing beneath her window.

These events would have shocked her not so long ago. The brutality of the act might have even brought tears of rage, but now the nature play only served to give her a few minutes of escape from the reality of her own loss. So while it registered in her mind, it came nowhere near touching her heart. Casually turning from the window, she opened the refrigerator and announced to no one, "Well, now that we know what the cat's having, I wonder what I can whip up for breakfast?" After a moment of staring at her choices, she closed the door without making a decision.

Wandering back through the living room, she pulled her oversized, terry cloth robe a bit more tightly around her, stepped out on her second-floor landing, walked down the steps to the apartment complex's first floor porch, and bent over to pick up her paper. A bloody sight stopped her short. Once again standing upright, she studied the form of the newly dead cardinal, lying on the walk less than a foot from the rolled-up paper.

"I guess the cat wasn't hungry," she coldly murmured.

Shrugging her shoulders, Meg once again bent over, grabbed the paper by one end, while using the other end to flick the bird off into the snow-covered grass. Turning, she marched back to her apartment, opened her door, tossed the paper on the floor, walked to her bath, eased out of the robe and nightgown, and turned on the shower. As the water heated up, she attempted to lose herself in soap and steam. But no matter how hard she scrubbed, she couldn't get rid of her anger or pain.

7

WITH THE SHOWER'S HOT WATER POURING DOWN HER FACE, MEG ONCE again went through the *if*s she had considered for the past three days. What if she had told him to wait? What if he hadn't gotten his work done so quickly? What if? What if? What if? Then, as she reached for her shampoo, another question surfaced, the same question that had haunted her the night before. Who? Who was that drunk kid? Who killed Steve?

Putting the shampoo down without ever using it, Meg turned the water off, wrapped herself in a towel, and still soaking wet, ran back to her landline phone. She punched in a familiar number and waited as it rang—once, then twice, and finally three times.

"Come on, Heather, be home."

On the fourth ring, a sleepy voice answered. "Hello?"

"Heather."

The shock of hearing from her friend must have yanked Heather from deep sleep into a complete and fully awake awareness. Somehow, as she framed a question, she also managed to embrace a tone filled with compassion. "Meg, how are you?"

"Heather, do you know the name of the kid that was driving the other car?"

"What kid?" After an awkward pause, she added, "Oh, Steve's wreck. I don't know? Why?"

"You can tell me," Meg was pleading. Her tone was almost frantic. "Surely you've heard. I've got to know."

"I really don't know, Meg," Heather answered sincerely. "If I did, I'd tell you. I just haven't heard anybody say. In all honesty, maybe I didn't want to know."

Meg swore.

In four years of working with her, Heather had never heard Meg utter even the mildest obscenity, so the word likely contained the shock value of a 7.0 earthquake. Maybe that was the reason she didn't offer a response. For whatever reason, before Heather could fully gather her wits and respond, Meg's voice came back on the line.

"Okay, thanks, I'll see you tomorrow at work."

Repeating the process, Meg called over a dozen different friends and the seven she actually reached all gave the same response. No one knew. She looked up at the living room clock. It was 11:17. Still wrapped in a towel, her hair now damp not wet, she got up and walked around the couch toward the kitchen, nearly tripping over the morning paper.

That's it, the paper. Okay, the accident happened on Thursday night, so the story would be in Friday morning's Herald. *I didn't read it, but Mom brought it in when she came over. Where did I put it? The trash, I pitched it.*

Pulling out a large, white, plastic trashcan from the pantry, she dug through empty cans and bottles until she found a newspaper. Yanking the plastic wrapper off, she unrolled it. Reading the masthead, the words "Friday Edition" jumped out. Quickly she scanned the front page, and then page two, and so on and so on. Sitting in the middle of a week's worth of kitchen trash and a now dried Coke spill, surrounded by pieces of broken glass, she desperately searched for some report, only to find nothing.

Come on, Steve was a pretty well-known guy. Where's the story? As her hunt bore no fruit, she grew angry. It just seemed the world was out to keep her from getting the information she needed!

Shoving the pages to one side, she looked around the kitchen. Suddenly her eyes lit up. Almost startling herself with her own voice, she all but yelled, "Of course, it happened too late for Friday's paper; it's got to be in Saturday's."

Standing up, she once again tightened her towel and looked into the trash can, but the paper wasn't there. Wandering back into the living room, she frantically scanned the area hoping that the paper would jump into sight. When it didn't, she screamed, "Where are you?"

Wanting to cry, she fell in a heap on the couch and tried to remember what she'd done with it. There might have been no one to hear her words, but she put voice to her thoughts. "Okay, I got up yesterday morning, got dressed, and drove to Mother's. I had to have walked by the paper, so I must have picked it up and done something with it . . . but what? The car, that's it, I tossed it in the back seat of my car."

She was about to get up when it hit her—the information would likely be online. Firing up her laptop, she did a search for the *Herald's* website. A roadblock once more greeted her. The paper was now subscription only. She didn't have the patience to dig out a credit card and sign up, so she turned her focus back to the paper she'd tossed in the Mustang.

Jumping up from the couch, she opened the apartment's door, charged down the steps, up the front walk, out to the curb, and threw open her yellow Mustang's passenger door. Not once did she notice the cold wind, the snow on her bare feet, or the fact that she was dressed in only an oversized bath towel. Reaching over the front passenger bucket seat, she tossed aside a pile of old clothes and a tennis racket and grabbed the paper. Running back up the walk and the stairs, she raced through her open apartment door and went directly into the kitchen. As soon as she had spread the paper out on the counter top, a front-page headline leaped out at her.

LOCAL CPA DIES IN AUTO CRASH

Her eyes focused on the words that followed.

Steven J. Richards, 28, was pronounced dead on arrival at Springfield Community Hospital due to injuries that occurred when his 2005 Buick Century collided with a 2010 Ford Explorer driven by a local teenager. A blood test indicated that the seventeen-year-old youth was legally intoxicated at the time of the accident.

Accident! What kind of word was that to describe what amounted to cold-blooded murder? Why didn't the writer report it the way it really happened? This was no accident. Wiping away a tear, Meg continued reading.

The teen also received minor injuries. He was treated in Springfield Community Hospital's emergency room and released without being admitted.

Due to the youth's age, police did not release any further information on his identity or the charges, if any, that would be filed against him. District Attorney Webb Jones would only say, "We are studying the case and currently the boy has been turned over to his parents."

Richards, an employee of . . .

Meg stopped reading and once again looked out the window, her eyes involuntarily filling with tears. The paper had been no help. All she wanted to know was who had killed her husband, and no one or nothing could or would tell her.

Charging back into the living room, she pulled a phone book from the end table drawer and scanned its pages for a home number for the district attorney. It wasn't there. Calling information, she learned that the number was unlisted. She once more hit the Internet, but Google gave her the same information as everything else.

Temporarily defeated, she headed back to the bathroom and finished her shower. Pulling on some jeans and a sweater, she applied her makeup, fixed her shoulder-length, light brown hair, and opened a can of tuna fish. She ate directly from the container. Like everything else in her life, the meal left her unsatisfied.

8

For two hours, Meg cleaned up her kitchen, sipped on a Coke, and reread six stories about Steve's death online. Finally, with no new information coming to light and no one whom she could call in order to gain any more knowledge, she accepted she'd have to wait until the next morning to get what she needed. At exactly nine tomorrow she'd get in touch with the district attorney's office and demand he tell her who killed Steve.

Yet tomorrow seemed like forever and the way the minutes crept so slowly by echoed that fact. After leafing through a half dozen magazines and searching in vain for something to watch on television, Meg once again found herself overcome with loneliness. Turning off the TV, she walked back over to her window.

Mr. Fudge had returned from church and swept his walk, and the Smith kids had ruined the beauty of the apartment's smooth, snow-covered yard by building a snowman. Up in the elm tree, a gray and red female cardinal fluttered nervously from branch to branch.

Until Meg spotted the bird, she had forgotten about the events of the morning. Then, when she saw the Fudges' fat yellow cat gracefully balancing on the old couple's porch railing, the episode came back in vivid detail. Pulling on her coat, Meg walked out to her balcony just in time to see the cardinal swoop down and discover the place where Meg had pushed its mate that morning. Bouncing all the way around the now cold, scarlet bird, the female tilted her head one way and then the other, waiting for the fallen mate to rise up and fly home with her. Meg observed the scene for a few minutes then, overwhelmed with a wave of sudden emotion, rushed down the steps and screamed at the poor, confused cardinal.

"He's dead! He's dead!" she yelled. "And you can't do anything to bring him back."

Startled, the cardinal took flight, landing in one of the elm tree's lower branches. Standing directly below the bird's perch, tears now streaming down her face, Meg glared at the frightened bird and sobbed, "Do you want to know who did it? Do you? I'll tell you who, it was Tom, the cat. Yes, that yellow one across the street. He killed your mate without mercy. And he did it just for the thrill of the kill."

As her tears fell in the snow, Meg looked back at the confused bird and cried out, "At least you know who is responsible. I'd give anything for just that much!"

As if taking a cue from the woman's words, the bird flew from the limb and swooped down at the unsuspecting, sleeping cat. Never getting close enough to the animal to allow him to catch her, she swooped again and again. First running for the cover of a bush and then under Mr. Fudge's Oldsmobile, the cat, eyes now opened wide, realized he was marked and any trip out into the open would bring an angry bird swooping down and reigning vengeance from the sky. Reconciled and seemingly unbothered by the hand fate had dealt, Tom closed his eyes and ignored the female cardinal's loud chirping. Within moments, he had resumed his nap, this time safely tucked under the old car.

Meg suddenly saw the cat as the boy who had struck down her husband. She wasn't going to let him rest. Not for a moment. Shaking her head, she whispered a promise.

"Whoever you are, I'll find you, and when I do, I'll make you pay. I'll make you pay!"

Bending over and molding a handful of snow into a ball, she threw it wildly in the general direction of the cat. It hit the fat feline in the rump, sending him back into the open, where the female cardinal resumed swooping down at the perplexed killer. Meg smiled. Tom needed to pay for what he'd done. Everyone should pay and pay deeply for taking a life. As soon as she found out who killed Steve, it would be her turn to swoop unrelentingly down on an unsuspecting enemy.

9

WE DIDN'T EXPECT YOU BACK SO SOON!" EXCLAIMED AN OBVIOUSLY shocked John Willis as a fully uniformed Meg entered Springfield Community Hospital through the emergency room door. The forty-three-year-old hospital administrator peered through his black-rimmed glasses at the woman for a few seconds before adding, "Listen, Nurse Richards, you can take as much time off as you want or need. We'll work around you until you're fully ready to come back."

"I'm fine," Meg, her tone as flat as the plains in Kansas, informed Willis. "And I want to be working."

As Willis looked on, Meg signed in and began going through the checklist of things that all nurses have to do before beginning their shifts. As she and Nurse Jan Greer took inventory of drugs and instruments, word of Meg's arrival quickly moved through the two-hundred-bed hospital. Within minutes, Heather had rushed to her side.

"What are you doing here?" her coworker and best friend asked.

"The count," Meg's replied, not bothering to look up.

"Are you sure you're ready for this?" Heather whispered, "I mean, it has only been . . ."

"Heather, I know how long it's been, and I know that I don't want to be at home staring at his pictures or folding his clothes. If I'm here, at least I'll have something else to think about. Now, I'm checking in and I'm going to my station. Thanks for your concern, but save it for the patients."

"But . . ."

Meg cut Heather off with a wave of her hand coupled with a stern look. "For the last time, I'm fine, and I'll see you later. Oh, and please don't come checking on me every five minutes. I don't need another mother. I have one that's already driving me crazy with her 'sage' advice and deep concern."

Meg had vowed to treat this as just another day. It had to be just like any other Monday. Thus she had taken extra care to insure she looked her best, adding layers of makeup to cover up the dark circles, though she couldn't do much about the redness in her eyes. With her game face on and her emotions under control, she appeared strong and alert. In fact, she was sure she looked normal. But that normalcy was only skin-deep. Beneath the calm exterior was a driven woman, a woman who couldn't wait for her first break in order to call the district attorney and finally discover the name of her husband's murderer. And that was the real reason for her coming to work. Waiting had driven her crazy all through the night. Being at work gave her something to do to pass the time until the district attorney's office opened.

She'd memorized the number the night before. In fact, she had practiced dialing it a few hundred times. Now, her fingers could fly over the keys in a pattern as familiar as stepping from her apartment's front door to her car. At nine, she slipped into a storage room and put her practice into play. As the call went through, she jammed the device to her ear. One ring, two, and the third! Finally, on the fourth ring a matronly sounding woman answered, "District Attorney's office."

After attempting to clear the tightness from her voice, Meg anxiously asked, "May I speak to Mr. Jones?"

"I'm sorry. He's out of town today. May I help you?"

No! He can't be out of town. She didn't wait all night to but put off for another day or more. He has business here in Springfield. And it is very important business, too. This simply wasn't right.

"Excuse me," the voice came back on the line, "is there something *I* can do for you?"

Meg took a deep breath, hoping it would cover her disappointment, and replied, "I hope so. My name is Meg Richards. My husband was killed . . ." Before she could continue, the woman broke in.

"I'm so sorry about your husband, Mrs. Richards," the woman responded, sounding genuinely sincere. "My heart goes out to you."

"Thank you," Meg replied, "but I called to find out the name of the person driving the other car. You see, the papers didn't print that information, and I feel that . . . well, what I'm trying to say is that . . ." Pausing for a second, attempting to relieve the pressure she felt in both her throat and aching heart, Meg searched for the proper words. Not finding them, she took a deep breath and blurted out, "I just want to know who he is!"

The line was so quiet for about ten seconds that Meg thought she'd dropped the call, but then the woman's kind voice came back, "I can understand that, Mrs. Richards. If I were you, I think I would want to know, too. But you see, I can't tell you his name at this time. No matter how much I want to or how unfair it seems, I can't tell you."

"Why not?" Meg demanded. "He killed my husband. I have a right to know who he is. That's fair, isn't it?"

Endless seconds crept by with no response. Finally, the voice came back on the line.

"Mrs. Richards, I can't tell you because of the boy's age. He's a minor, and in order to protect his rights, we are not allowed by law to release any information about him at this time. I'm sure, if this is any comfort to you, that you'll find out his identity in time. But we have to go by specific rules of law and we can't break that process. As unfair as it may seem to you, that is the way it works."

Tears began to fall from her eyes and run down Meg's face. Her frustration and grief surfaced just as they had when she had run into a brick wall of noninformation on Sunday. As she glanced out of the storage room, she noticed Heather walking down the hall. Not wanting her friend to see her out of control, she closed the door and pleaded into the phone, "I have rights, too. Why does the killer get all the protection and I get none?"

"I know it must seem that way now, Mrs. Richards, but if you will be patient—"

Meg snapped, "I'm the one who lost it all, not him. I'm the one who lives by the law, not him. You're supposed to serve me!"

"You're right," the woman answered, "but my hands are tied, and I can't do anything about it. Perhaps you can call back on Thursday. Mr. Jones will be back then, and well, maybe he can tell you something."

"Thursday?" Meg barked. "You expect me to wait until Thursday?"

"Mrs. Richards, my name is Jo Blount. If there's anything I can do for you in the meantime, please give me a call and let me know!"

"Mrs. Blount," Meg shot back, "it's obvious that there's nothing you can do for me. It seems that there is nothing anyone can or will do for me."

10

AN ENRAGED MEG JAMMED THE CELL PHONE BACK INTO HER POCKET, stormed out of the room, and marched down the hall to the break room. Before walking in, she dried her tears and straightened her hair.

"Did I see you on the phone?" Heather asked. "Who were you talking to?"

"It wasn't you, so what difference does it make?" Meg answered much too harshly.

Heather's eyes never left her as Meg dropped seventy-five cents in a machine, hit a button, and watched a Coke fall out. She likely was shocked by the tone in Meg's voice and her sarcastic response. As Meg considered what must have been going through her friend's mind, she almost apologized. Heather didn't deserve to be treated in that fashion. Maybe Meg should explain her frustration, but that would display a weakness she couldn't show, at least not yet. So rather than say anything, she popped the top on the can and took a sip.

"I didn't mean to pry," Heather said as she took a seat beside Meg. "I'm sorry."

"No," Meg replied, "I shouldn't have snapped."

Poor Heather, she was trying so hard to understand and she couldn't.

"Maybe it's good your back," Heather said.

"Why?" Meg asked.

"Because everyone has been asking about you. You're the perfect nurse, not only because you know our business but because you make people feel better by simply being with them. Even today they are asking about you and asking for you."

"Really?"

"Oh, Meg, I'm not saying this will make you feel better, but none of us measure up to you. You have always been the heart of this staff."

"I doubt that," Meg replied. "I'm not sure my heart is even beating anymore."

"Things will get better," Heather assured her.

"Not so sure about that." Meg took a sip of the soft drink before adding, "Heather, you've never been married and you've never lost anyone close to you. So don't judge me now and don't expect me to be like I used to be. I don't think I will ever be that way again. I hope you'll accept that and not try to find a way to change it."

Heather nodded but didn't respond. She probably didn't have the words to answer. Who did?

As both nurses sat silent, not talking or looking at each other, a young, tall doctor wearing a green coat walked in. Looking up, Heather responded first. "Hi, Paul, want a cup of coffee?"

"No thanks, Heather. I didn't come here to flirt or drink this time; I came here to beg! What I really need is for someone to find some records for me. I'm treating a man admitted and released by the swing physician covering the emergency room on Saturday night. You see, because the guy was simply treated and released, no one expected him to need anything else. Well, he came back in this morning and naturally, he can't remember what medicine was prescribed. I've got to know. So I checked with records and found his report hadn't been loaded into the system yet. It seems that everything was down this weekend due to the storms we had last week. We actually went back to using paper on everything. So until they get things fixed and uploaded so I can see it on my iPad, I'm lost."

Heather nodded. "I've got the same issue. I guess we're just spoiled. We think we can make a couple of taps and everything will leap into view. Looking through paper files is a headache."

"I'm not a filing wizard," the doctor explained. "You should see me try to get organized when I do taxes. If it's not on the computer, then I'm lost. And I don't want to mill through the papers that were filled out in the emergency room for the next hour in order to get this guy out of my hair. No one down there seems to have time right now, so could you possibly help?"

Putting her coffee down, Heather got up, but before she could say anything, Meg cut her off. "Heather, you just sit down. You do all the dirty jobs around here and it's time some of us took up some of the slack. You've got another ten minutes left on your break and you've barely started your coffee. You finish it, and Paul, you have some, too. By the time you all are finished, I'll have the records for you."

Pulling a notepad out of a table drawer, Meg looked at the doctor, "Okay. Now, you said Saturday night?"

"Actually," the doctor replied as he took a seat. "He came in about two on Sunday morning. At least, that's what he says. His name is . . ." Before finishing he glanced down at a clipboard he had just set on the table, "Joe Messa."

Writing the name and the time, Meg looked up and smiled. "You and Heather enjoy yourselves and I'll be back as soon as I can."

"Meg," Heather interrupted, "are you sure you don't want me to do that?"

"No, Heather, I need to keep busy. Oh, by the way, if the records are in a big mess and it does take me a little longer than I expect, will you cover for me until I get back?"

"Sure," Heather assured her.

"Don't worry, Paul," Meg explained, "I'll get this information to you just as soon as I can."

Meg stopped just outside the door to study her notes. As she did, she overheard the doctor and nurse speaking inside the room.

"She seems to be doing pretty well."

"I can't tell." Heather's response was sincere and her tone showed real signs of concern. That was just like her. She was everyone's mother hen. "Paul, she seems a little bitter and a bit harsh to me, but I guess that's normal. She's probably just trying too hard to be efficient and not admitting how much she hurts."

The doctor agreed. "I know she's a strong woman, but I'm surprised she came back to work so soon. By the way, I don't mean to change the subject, but you sure do look good today. I couldn't help but note . . ."

That was Paul, always on the make, especially with Heather. Nothing detracted him for very long. Well, at least, Heather and Paul seemed to believe in her strength. That was enough for Meg at this moment. The last thing she wanted was to look weak.

Having something but Steve's death to think about put a special kind energy in her step and she quickly made her way to the emergency room. Thankfully, one of her mother's oldest friends was working in the ER.

Lena Worel was a white-haired, heavyset lady, with pale skin and big blue eyes. Despite the fact that she'd been on a diet for as long as anyone could remember, her whole body shook when she walked. As a child, Meg thought Lena looked a great deal like Mrs. Santa Claus. And her cheery face and laughing voice only added to this perception. In fact, Lena was the reason that Meg had first gotten interested in nursing. She'd loved the woman's uniforms, especially her hats, even though by the time she became a nurse the hats were gone and the uniforms were scrubs. Over time, as they worked together, Lena became more than a friend, she had somehow taken on the role of an aunt.

"Meg, honey, what are you doing here today?" the old woman gently inquired.

"Now Lena, I'm doing what all good nurses do—working! You know as well as I do there's not much that can be gained by sitting at home and looking at the walls."

Hoping her answer would satisfy the woman, Meg began to look around the room for the most recently filled-out forms. One glance convinced her that a hurricane had struck the place. Finding something in this mess would be like finding the proverbial needle in the haystack. Yet it had to be done.

"Lena," Meg asked, "What in the world happened back here?"

"Oh, child," the big woman answered, throwing her arms into the air. "Jean, the unit secretary, got the flu last week and then Katie, her assistant, quit. And except for the really serious cases, nothing has been filed. Worse yet, we still haven't gotten the computer system back up. Even though it's not my job, I organized some of this mess today. I had to because I've had folks ask for a specific file, and I was tired of weeding through all of them to find that one."

Meg began checking through the layers of forms but the longer she looked the more lost she became. Lena finally cleared things up.

"What are you looking for, maybe I can help? Believe it or not, I have created a system."

"I hope you can, Lena," Meg sighed. "I guaranteed I could find the information in a flash that Dr. Mason needed."

"Well, Meg," Lena asked, "what exactly does he need?"

"A patient, who was treated and released this weekend, showed up this morning for follow-up. I came down to find out what the swing doctor had prescribed."

"Okay, Honey, when was this person treated? If you know that, I think we can find the information you need. I spent an hour when I first came creating some order out of this chaos."

"Sunday morning, about two."

Turning to six rows of papers stacked on a table in the back of the small room, Lena pointed to stack number six. "I've already taken a little time to put together at least a system for this organization. These are Sunday's forms," she said, pointing to a small mountain of papers. "You'll find what you need in this pile." The nurse seemed obviously proud of her knowledge and work and her next statement proved it. "When I came in this morning, none of this stuff was organized at all, but now we at least have it by days. What name do you want?"

"Joe Messa."

"Okay, let's see if he's here." As Lena's fingers begin to sift through the stack, a voice came over the hospital's paging system.

"Nurse Lena Worel, you are needed in records," the voice announced.

Glancing up at the speaker, the older nurse wondered out loud, "What do they want now? Oh, well, the last thing I need is to keep Gertrude Johnson waiting. You know how she is." Looking across the room at Meg, she asked, "Can you get along here without me? I know it's in stack six."

Smiling, Meg replied, "Of course, now move along before Gertrude has a cat!"

After Lena cleared the room, Meg began to sort through Sunday's treatment forms. The fourth one from the top, a form filled out on a Jerry Bates, had been misfiled. It should have been filed on the Thursday, March 10 stack. Picking up the short form, she started to restack it in its proper place but a name on the top of the file stopped her cold as a flood of unwanted emotions flooded her mind while they weakened her knees. The name at the top was her husband's.

For a few minutes, she had thankfully been so involved in doing her job she had almost forgotten she had lost him. Now all the horror flooded back and she had to work to restrain the tears. "DOA" had been scribbled across the middle of the form. This was the last thing she needed to see. She knew she should set the report to one side, but instead she slowly picked it up and scanned what had been scribbled there. It was very cut-and-dried indicating that there had been no treatment necessary or taken. And that was pretty much all there was to it. He was simply dead on arrival.

Gingerly easing Steven's form back onto the proper stack, she placed the Bates form on top of it in an effort to eradicate all thoughts of her husband's death. Forcing herself to go back to Sunday's stack, she sorted through until she found Joe Messa's file. Noting his medication, she replaced the paperwork in the stack and turned to leave the room, but as she opened the door, a simple realization froze her in her tracks. She likely was in the room with the information she needed and it was all so easy and so readily available.

Turning, she quickly walked back to the table, her heart racing as she looked down at the stacks of papers. A cold sweat broke out on her forehead and a chill ran down the back of her neck. Using all the courage she possessed, she forced her hands back to the Thursday stack. Taking the pile of forms in her hands, she walked across the room, sat down in a chair behind the desk and began to look at them. She passed over Jerry Bates's form without so much as a glance. She stopped at Steve's for a brief instant, took a painful look at her wedding ring, and then moved on. The third admit, a six-year-old girl named Amy, didn't interest the nurse at all. The fourth, a stroke victim, and the fifth, a heart attack, didn't cause Meg to pause more than a few seconds. She passed by the next three admits just as quickly. But when she got to number ten, a man named Kenneth James, she immediately stopped to carefully study the report.

James had been injured in a car wreck. He'd received stitches above his right eye and then he had been sent home. "It's him," Meg whispered, but then her heart sank. *Come on dummy. Look at the age, this guy's fifty-two.* Putting the report at the back of the stack, she continued her search.

Meg scanned form after form, occasionally glancing down the hall to check if Lena had appeared. Then, just as she was about to give up, James A. Thomas's file appeared. She checked the admit time. It fit. She checked his age. Seventeen, perfect! She then checked the cause of his injuries and discovered they had resulted from an automobile accident. Her heart surged to full race mode. He'd been patched up and released, and further more, he had had blood taken for an alcohol level check. The numbers clearly indicated he had been drunk. The test showed he'd hit 1.4.

Taking out her pen and finding a scratch pad on Lena's desk, she wrote down the name James A. Thomas and followed it with 1034 East Walnut Street. Finally, after gleaning all she could from the paperwork, she scanned the remainder of that night's forms to see if any of those patients also could have fit the profile of Steve's murderer. None did. Restacking the papers on the table, she went to her station, checked in, and paged Paul. Once she'd given the doctor the information he needed, she headed directly back to her post and tried to go about her duties. Yet for the rest of the shift, she could do nothing more than go through the motions. Her mind was a thousand miles away from her job. A name, an address, and a vow of revenge tumbled over and through her thoughts and nothing short of a patient going code red could have changed that focus.

11

Meg couldn't wait to go home. And when the time came, she hurriedly set about the routine that all nurses have to do before checking out. It was time for inventory.

Earlier in her shift, Heather had been swung to another wing to cover for a sick nurse. Meg hadn't seen her since ten.

"Meg!" Startled by Heather's voice, the nurse paused in her counting. Seeing that she had her attention, Heather continued. "How's your day?"

"Fine," Meg sighed. "Just like any other." She went back to her count.

"How about we grab a bite to eat at Pizza Hut tonight?" Heather asked. Countless times over the last four years she and Meg had hit Pizza Hut on nights when Steve was either working late or out of town. "Eating with me might be better than being by yourself tonight."

Waiting a few seconds to conclude her count and sign out, Meg shook her head. "Not tonight, Heather, I've got something to do." Without so much as a wave, she headed down the hall. From the corner of her eye, she saw Heather grab her coat from her locker and reach behind the desk for her purse.

"Are you sure, Meg?" Heather pleaded as she caught her in the parking lot. "I hate to eat alone. I mean ..."

"I know what you mean," Meg replied. Her tone revealed she fully understood exactly why Heather really wanted her to spend some time with her. She was trying to be a good friend and on another night she might need a friend. But not tonight! "Heather, listen, I really do have something to do, and I'm not going home to be alone. Honest!"

When Meg stopped beside her Mustang to dig through her purse for her keys, Heather gave it one more try. "Are you going over to your mom's? I haven't really visited with her in months and I'd love to ..."

Raising her voice so she could be heard above the biting north wind, Meg said, "Heather, if you want to visit with Mom, that would be great." After finding her keys and unlocking her car door, she turned to face her friend. "But you'll have to go by yourself because I don't plan on seeing Mom tonight."

Meg eased into the driver's seat, jammed the key into the ignition, and started the car. Looking back at Heather, she smiled. "Maybe we can do it tomorrow. I really appreciate you being there for me. But right now I have to do something very important. So please forgive me. You have a good evening and try not to worry about me." She closed the door and shoved the shifter into reverse.

Meg, out of habit, pushed her favorite *American Idol* CD into the player. Yet as the music played, she was oblivious to the song or the singer. The only thing on her mind was the address of a teenager who lived on the other side of town. She couldn't believe she had found him. As she pulled off the parking lot, she smiled. This was what she needed. She was sure just seeing where he lived would somehow ease her pain.

Walnut Street was well off the main drag, over five miles from downtown and the hospital, and just a stone's throw from the country club. Meg had been to a few parties at the club during high school, but her family had never had the money to join the social elite on a regular basis. Still, the area was not foreign to her. She had often driven down the broad streets of this neighborhood admiring the houses and beautiful, rolling, tree-covered lots. She and Steve had even dreamed of someday owning one of these large brick homes set on such finely landscaped grounds. But dream homes and notions of wealth now seemed unreal, especially when placed against the reason for her trip today.

She crossed Elm and then Maple, hardly noticing the homes that had once so enthralled her on those streets. Then, when she came to Walnut, she made a sharp right and began to look much more closely at the addresses so proudly displayed on each ornate door. For three blocks, she eased the Mustang by house after house, each seeming larger and more impressive than the former. And then, the one she sought came into view.

It was immediately obvious that the Thomas's house was the most impressive on the block. A two-story red brick, with paned glass windows and a four-car garage, the home itself must have included more than seven thousand square feet. Over the privacy fence surrounding the backyard, she saw a slide and diving board indicating a swimming pool. On the far side of the home was a private tennis court. This wasn't a residence; it was an estate!

Passing the ten-hundred block of Walnut, Meg made a U-turn and parked her Mustang directly across the street from the house. After turning the car's engine off, she examined every facet of what could only be called a mansion.

The roofline reached more than fifty feet at the highest point. There was no wooden or vinyl trim work; the brick went clear to the roof. Many of the windows were rounded at the top. Three reached more than thirty feet up the house. The walks were made of polished stone. A new Mercedes and Lincoln set in the driveway. If they were sitting out in the weather, what was in the garage?

Here were people who obviously had everything money could buy. These were folks that the community always considered important and influential. And these people, this family, were the ones she'd be fighting in order to gain some kind of justice. Suddenly, her simple little plan to extract personal punishment and satisfaction from James Thomas had taken on David and Goliath proportions. And because of these overwhelming odds, hopelessness pushed its way into the car, squeezing her wounded heart like a vice as she lingered and studied an enemy that now seemed unbeatable.

As the car began to lose its heat, Meg pulled her coat a little tighter around her body. Searching through her pockets, she found her gloves. Still, even as it grew later and colder, even after she had looked over the house from top to bottom a dozen times, memorizing even the minutest details, she waited. She didn't understand why, but for some reason, just being at the place where her husband's killer lived gave her some purpose, some identity. And maybe, if he somehow came out of the house, she could put a face to her pain. How she needed that face!

With nothing new to see, time passed slowly, and as the temperature continued to drop, it became more uncomfortable. By 7:30, it had become so cold she could now see her breath. Just about the time Meg was going to give up and head to her apartment, a car drove up to the front curb of 1034 East Walnut. It was a late model sports utility and when it stopped, and the passenger door opened causing the interior light to come on, Meg could clearly see it was filled with teenagers— two boys and two girls.

For a while, the car just sat there, motor running while the kids remained in the vehicle. Then after a few minutes, a boy eased out the rear passenger door. He was tall, about six-foot-two and wore a letter jacket and jeans; his sandy-colored hair was uncovered and blowing in the wind. And in the dim light, Meg spotted a large Band-Aid on his forehead. This had to be him! She strained to get a better look at James Thomas. It only took a few seconds for her to realize this was the kid who had held the ER door for her after she'd viewed Steve's body. How she wished she'd known that then!

As she anxiously took in the scene playing out just across the street, she turned on the keys and eased the window of her car door down in order to catch the kids' conversation. She first heard the driver's voice.

"So, Jim. Your dad say anything about getting you another car?"

"He will," the blond youth answered. "After all, he did the last time I totaled one."

"Yeah, but last time nobody got hurt," the other boy replied.

"Well," Thomas's tone was casual. It was as if the accident was just an insignificant inconvenience that had dropped into his life. As he explained his father's reaction, the boy even smiled. "Dad was pretty steamed about that. He informed me that next time I got drunk, it'd probably be me that cashed it in. Still, I think the fact that I was hurt a little got me off the hook. You know as well as I do, he can spring me from the charges. He's always been able to. Besides, it's not like I haven't had to pay already. You know the coach isn't even going to let me play in the basketball playoffs until I get these stitches out. I've been looking forward to that all year."

Meg was amazed by the boy's tone. His selfishness shocked and enraged her. He obviously felt no sense of remorse. He actually claimed abuse because he wasn't going to get to play in a basketball game.

A girl, now left alone in the back seat, handed Thomas a gym bag. Reaching back into the car to pull it out, the boy gave the young, giggly blonde a long kiss, smiled at the other two kids, and then whirled and ambled up the walk to the front door. Within seconds, he found his way inside and the others had driven off.

Even though she was once again alone, Meg continued to stare at the house. She'd been expecting James Thomas, Jim as his friends called him, to be a punk rocker or a redneck. She had expected green hair, earrings, weird clothes, and a kind of drugged-out look on his face, but James Thomas wasn't like that at all. He was good-looking, clean cut, an athlete, and probably popular with the kids who mattered in the school. The only thing he seemed to have in common with her previous vision was his selfishness. He seemed completely unconcerned about anyone but himself.

Having seen all there was to see, Meg restarted her car and began to drive off. Yet, as she eased her car past the boy's home one last time and turned her head for one final look, a name on a mailbox, now lit by her car's headlights, jumped out and hit her like a hammer—Alfred E. Thomas.

Meg knew that name well. Alfred E. Thomas. *Judge* Alfred E. Thomas. Judge Thomas was a deacon in her church. He and his wife always sat in the same pew every Sunday. He had given countless prayers, served on numerous boards, and had always sent Steve and her a Christmas card. They'd even voted for him in the last election. Yet, for the two years they'd sponsored the high school youth group on Sunday night, she had never seen his son. As a matter of fact, she hadn't even known that the judge had any children. Jim Thomas must have never been to church. What a revelation!

As she drove home Meg felt shaken to the core. The knowledge that she'd be fighting not just a rich kid but a judge's kid—the kid of someone whom she thought she'd known and someone whom she had respected; someone her own church respected—caused Meg to plunge deeper and deeper into a reeling depression. If it had been some poor kid or some punk, someone from the wrong side of town or from a family she hadn't known, then she figured she would've had a chance to see justice done. But now it seemed like there would be little hope of ever seeing Steve's killer made to pay. She had nothing compared to the power this family wielded. And besides, she didn't figure the district attorney would ever want to challenge the Thomas family in court. No wonder the kid didn't seem concerned about the charges.

Once out of the car and safely in her apartment, it was a completely overwhelmed Meg who attempted to put all thoughts of Steve's death out of her mind. She had to try to forget, because just remembering brought on a kind of hopelessness she knew she couldn't handle. Yet even as she opened a can of tuna fish, pulled some chips from the cupboard, and turned on the television, depression shook her like a rag doll. And with every shake, she was reminded of what she had lost and the impossible battle she faced.

When her iPhone chirped, she quickly grabbed it. The last thing she wanted or needed now was to face this alone. She needed to talk to someone, anyone! She checked her caller ID and smiled.

"Heather, I'm glad you called."

"Just wanted to check on you."

"I'm glad you did. I just realized something and I need to share it with someone I trust."

"Do you want me to come over?" Heather asked.

"No, you don't have to do that. But I've got to explain something to you. I need for you to listen because I know I'm not myself. I'm not sure I'll ever be myself again. I've got feelings in me I can't understand."

"Meg, I think that's natural. I just wish there was something you'd let me do."

"Listen friend," Meg began, pausing for a moment, trying to put into words what was written on her heart, "I don't know how to say this, but Steve and I experienced so much love, so much of the joy, that now everything seems to be empty. It is like life is a blank page in a book on which nothing will be written because the story hadn't been and can't be wrapped up. It just seems the rest of my life will be nothing but meaningless blank pages."

"I guess I understand what you mean," Heather replied, "but I'm not sure I can feel it. I never had anyone like Steve in my life. You know me, I'm our generation's oldest and last virgin."

Meg smiled. Heather always used disparaging jokes to make others feel better. She loved that about her.

"Meg, where did you have to go tonight? If you don't mind me asking, what was so important?"

"Maybe it wasn't that important," Meg replied. "I think I was going someplace to get some answers, but instead I just found a big wall that I probably can't climb."

"I don't understand."

"I'm not sure I do," Meg admitted. "Anyway, thanks for calling and checking on me. Maybe tomorrow or the next day I can figure out how to share with you my plans. I don't know what they are yet and even when I figure them out, I'm not sure you'll approve."

"You're not going to leave nursing?" Heather asked.

"No, kid, you're stuck with me there. It has nothing to do with that. See you tomorrow."

"Bye."

Good old Heather! Her call was perfectly timed.

Setting the phone on the coffee table, Heather leaned back on the couch and closed her eyes. Maybe she should have told Heather what she'd seen tonight. But would she be able to handle Meg claiming a personal vendetta as a reason to live? What would Heather think if Meg admitted that the passion of hate had taken root in her heart and was somehow starting to make up for the devastation of lost love? No, Heather was too kind and gentle and she wouldn't have understood those things. To fully grasp it, her friend would have had to hear the words Jim Thomas had said to his friends. Those words had proven that life, the same stuff that she and Heather fought so hard to preserve every day at the hospital, was in reality very cheap.

12

Aᴛᴛᴇʀ ʀᴏᴜꜱɪɴɢ ʜᴇʀꜱᴇʟꜰ ꜰʀᴏᴍ ᴀ ꜰɪᴛꜰᴜʟ ꜱʟᴇᴇᴘ, Mᴇɢ ꜱᴘᴇɴᴛ ꜱᴇᴠᴇʀᴀʟ ʜᴏᴜʀꜱ on the Internet looking for DUI cases similar to the one that had taken Steve from her. Many were settled without a trial and some of those involved sentences that only included community service. Those who received jail time usually were repeat offenders, thus her research was anything but satisfying. The thought of Thomas only getting a few hours picking up trash made her sick to her stomach. Surely, a life had to be worth more than that!

Refining her search, she began to look at sentences coupled to the wealth of those found guilty of the crimes. After researching a few of these, there could be no doubt that money could buy anything, including freedom, for those who could afford the best lawyers. With the Thomas's power and money, what hope did she have? Real justice might have to come outside of the courts. But what could she do to make that a reality? She yanked out a pad to sketch out ideas just as her doorbell rang. Pushing her hair back from her face and tightening the belt on her robe, she ambled across the room and pulled the door open.

"Mom," she all but moaned.

"You haven't picked up on my calls," Barbara said.

"No, I haven't felt like talking."

"It's kind of cold out here," the older woman noted. "May I come in?"

Meg said nothing as she stepped aside. Barbara strolled uncertainly across the room, fiddled with her gloves, finally placing them on the coffee table before yanking off her coat. As Meg watched, her mother patted the couch, something she always did when she wanted her daughters to join her for a conversation. Barbara took her place on the couch. Meg parked herself in the chair that had been Steve's favorite, crossed her legs, and waited for the lecture she was sure would follow. She didn't have to wait long.

"Megan, it's not good for you to be alone—to be here. You need to come and stay with me for a while."

"This is my home and I'm staying here," Meg defiantly argued.

Barbara shook her head. "And I hear you've gone back to work. It's much too soon. You need time to process—"

"Process what, Mom, that Steve is dead? I sleep in an empty bed, have received a hundred condolence cards, and now only set the table for one; I figured it out."

Her dark eyes painfully examined her daughter.

"I'm still me," Meg said. "I'm the same girl you've known for almost three decades. Except it's different now. I didn't scrape my knees. You can't fix what happened this time with a Band-Aid and a kiss. In fact, you can't fix it at all. This is all on my plate and I have to work through it in my own way."

Barbara smiled weakly as she offered a predictable suggestion, "You might talk to Reverend Brooks. He's dealt with this sort of thing many times."

Meg almost laughed. She knew her mother would trot this line out and she was ready for it. "Mom, so Reverend Brooks has had a spouse killed by a drunk driver?"

"No," came the reply, "I didn't mean that."

"Exactly! His wife is still by his side. They sleep in the same bed. They go on vacations together. So he doesn't have a clue as to what I'm going through."

"But he's a trained minister . . ."

"Yeah and that makes him about as prepared to deal with my issue as a trained seal. In the case of the latter, at least, I might get a laugh or two. I know that probably sounds horrid. And maybe I sound that way as well. But Mom, when you are hurting like I am, when you have a person you love die at the age of twenty-eight, well, tact goes out the window. So if you toss something at me, you have to expect me to be bluntly honest when I toss my words back your way. I hope you can deal with that."

"That's just not like you," Barbara argued.

"You're right," Meg agreed. "It's not like the way I used to be. But being sweet and accepting isn't working for me now."

"Well, there's this group of women at church who've lost their husbands. They meet each Thursday night and . . ."

Meg shook her head. "They're all over seventy. Their situations are much different than mine. And they're not facing having an upcoming trial where they'll have to relive the details all over again."

"I don't care what you say," Barbara argued. "You need to go to those meetings!"

Meg rose from the chair and moved back to the door. She opened it and glanced back toward her visitor. "I think it is time for you to go."

"Megan! You better listen to me!"

"Don't use that indignant tone on me. I'm not five years old. The fact is I don't want you around right now. When I need to talk, I'll call. Until that time, give me my space."

"But, Baby," Barbara pleaded as she got up from the couch, "I can't bear the thought of you being alone."

"Get used to it, Mom, that is what I want to be. When I decide to rejoin the social scene, I will let you know. Until then please respect my wishes. And make sure and tell Reverend Brooks I don't want any visits from him here or at the hospital. I don't need any preaching right now!"

The older woman nodded and reached for her coat. It was obvious she was hurt, but she wasn't the only one in the room who was in pain. And no meeting with other widows was going to take care of that pain. What Meg needed was to make someone pay for Steve's death. When that happened, maybe she would be ready to once more show her softer side.

Barbara slowly walked to the door, pausing in front of her daughter, lifting her eyes, and tilting her head. Her lip quivered for a moment before she whispered, "Can I at least hug you?"

Meg opened her arms for the woman who'd raised her. As the two embraced, a tear rolled down Meg's cheek. She patted her mother on the back and then stepped back. Barbara took a final look into her daughter's eyes and rushed through the door.

As her mother walked to her car, a thought rose from Meg's heart and lodged in her brain. She had always known that emptiness brought pain, but until this moment she hadn't understood that it also brought a complete void of positive feelings. There were no longer any memories that soothed her heart. Love, which only last week had been the most powerful force on earth, now seemed like a cancer. So, unlike the women in that group her mother begged her to join, Meg didn't just feel a sense of loss, she had gone numb, focusing not on her own broken heart, but on something else. And it was that something else that called her right now.

Closing and locking the entry, Meg made her way back to the table. Sitting in front of her was a blank legal pad. Picking up a pen, she wrote down the number one and began to sketch out a concept for revenge.

13

THE AFTERNOON AIR WAS COOL, BUT AFTER A LONG, COLD WINTER, THE steady sun, coupled with a southerly breeze, made the forty-degree temperature seem almost balmy. The sunshine, the first Meg had noticed in days, seemed to be a good omen. Perhaps all of her plans and efforts would come to fruition today. Maybe the right things would finally begin to happen.

She stood just a few feet away from a sheer cliff, some two miles out of town on hilly and curving Route 63. This was an area the local kids called Lovers' Leap. A small, two-foot stonewall, built in the 1920s and now crumbling with age, separated the road from the deep valley on the other side. Countless times, drivers coming down old Jenkins's Hill had failed to slow enough to safely make the almost L-shaped turn. The fact could easily be verified by even casual observation as many places on the wall were marked by a large number of different paint scars, the most recent red. Still, because rarely did anyone but locals use the road, most knew just how dangerous the turn was and how tragic going over the cliff would be, so they slowed down. Therefore, this had been the site of only a few significant accidents. The last fatality had been more than twenty years before when a trucker had lost control of a big rig hauling gasoline. That fire had burned for hours.

Checking her watch, Meg wandered over to the edge of the wall. Glancing down at a patch of snow that still stubbornly remained only because it had been safely hidden from the sun's rays by the shadow of the hill, she wondered just how it would feel to go plunging over the wall. What would it be like to hurtle through the air, knowing that within a second, maybe two, your body would crash into a mound of boulders and trees some four hundred feet below? Could a person hope to survive such a fall? From what she'd been told, no one ever had.

Picking up a rock, she stood on top of the wall, her body now just inches from the edge, and pitched the three-pound piece of stone down toward the bottom. She listened as it rebounded from boulder to boulder until it finally reached the end of its fall. Smiling, she glanced toward the road. Even God would forgive her this one time. Everyone would understand, but the best part was that no one would know. Not a single person would suspect sweet little Meg.

The noise of a distant car turned her attention from the cliff and valley and back to the road. Glancing at her watch, she nodded. It was time. Quickly jumping off the wall to the safety of the road's shoulder, she ran to a place she'd picked out weeks before. There, safely hidden by two large oak trees, she could watch every car come down the hill, but the drivers and their passengers wouldn't be able to see her.

Easing her face from behind the tree, she glanced up Jenkins's Hill. There, at the very top, now only a few hundred yards away, Jim Thomas's new Corvette drove into view. She knew it would be him because he was the ultimate creature of habit. His girlfriend, Kristen Jennings, lived just a mile up the road and he brought her home from school between 4:10 p.m. and 4:15 p.m. every day.

The two of them would talk and kiss for two or three minutes before Kristen went inside. Then, rather than take the quick way back to town, he always challenged his driving ability and nerve by going home via Lovers' Leap. Down the hill he would race, accelerating more and more as he reached the curve, and at the last moment, he'd jump down on his brakes, causing the tires to squeal and the vehicle to jerk violently to the point where the rear tires all but lost contact with the asphalt. With a quick turn of the wheel, he would literally slide the car around the outside of the curve, coming just inches from the wall. Today, it would be different.

Earlier, while Thomas sat unknowingly in class, Meg had driven to Springfield High, and after crawling underneath his Corvette, used a hacksaw to puncture his brake lines just enough to make them fail only when he applied a great deal of force. Because she knew that Kristen wouldn't let him drive recklessly when she was in the car, Jenkins's Hill would likely be the first place Thomas would exert any force on the brake pedal. This daily ritual, combined with the fact that he always downshifted to slow the car down, meant he'd barely touch his pedal until he needed his brakes the most. Now, as the red car became a blinding blur, she waited for that moment.

In the car, Thomas was likely unaware of anything other than the thrill of reckless speed. His heart had to be beating faster and faster as he neared the stone wall then, as he had almost every day for a month, he downshifted to third and hit the brake pedal. As Meg watched, a look of pure terror registered on his face as his foot went directly to the floorboard and the brakes failed to take hold. He attempted to adjust his course by yanking the steering wheel to the left, but that move came much too late. Instinctively, he threw his arms up to protect his face as the wall came closer and closer.

Stepping out from behind the tree, Meg now openly observed the speeding car and studied the young man's face, now filled with a mixture of panic and agony; his mouth locked open in a silent scream. Right before the car hit the wall and hurtled over the cliff, Thomas's eyes locked onto Meg. Smiling at him, she raised her hand in a wave and formed a kiss with her lips. She wanted to be the last thing he saw before his car went twirling over and over in a death spin to the rocks below.

Waiting for a few seconds until the sounds of boulders crushing fiberglass and metal ended, Meg walked over to the cliff and studied the sports car burning on the rocks below. She watched, almost in a detached manner, as a badly injured Thomas attempted to climb through the vehicle's shattered roof. Then, just as it appeared he would make it, a huge explosion blew both him and his car to pieces.

"Oh, revenge is sweet!" Meg murmured as she casually turned to walk back to where she had hidden her car. "This is for you, Steve. It was all for you!"

"Did you say something?"

Responding to Heather's upbeat voice, Meg looked up from where she sat.

14

Meg blinked rapidly. How had Heather known where to find her? What was she doing here? As her eyes and mind snapped into reality, she realized she was not at Lovers' Leap but sitting in her usual spot in the hospital cafeteria. Disappointment rushed over her. It wasn't real. It never had been real. It was all a daydream!

Not so much questioning as observing the half-eaten tuna fish sandwich on Meg's plate, Heather quipped, "Got the old dependable, huh?" When Meg only nodded, Heather sat down across from her friend and attempted to draw her into conversation.

"You remember Jamie? The four-year-old girl you met last week."

Meg nodded as she took another bite of the sandwich.

"Well, she's been asking me if you'd come by and see her. Your visits last week meant a lot to her. As a matter of fact, she showed me a picture she drew of you—pretty good likeness. I think the girl's got some artistic talent! It'd sure mean a lot if you could drop in on your break or something."

As Heather's words trailed off, Meg pushed the plate with her still half-eaten sandwich toward the middle of the table.

Looking up but avoiding Heather's big blue eyes, she took a long sip of her Coke before finally mumbling, "Maybe I can drop by this afternoon." Then almost as an afterthought, she added, "But you know my wing has been pretty busy today, so I'm not making any guarantees. So please don't say anything to her."

Heather nodded as Meg got up from her chair, put her tray in its designated return spot, and caught her reflection in a mirror. That brief glimpse proved her shoulder-length brown hair was perfectly combed and fixed. Her makeup, as always, looked as if it had been applied by Max Factor himself. She didn't have to have the mirror to know her figure also still filled her pale blue scrubs—the same uniform that made most women look as if wearing generic flour sacks—as though the outfit had been molded for her shape.

Yet, she'd never thought of herself as beautiful until Steve pointed it out to her in college. After that, it made her feel all bubbly when he'd whisper that she was the belle of the ball or queen of his kingdom. Thus, suddenly looking good became so important to her because of how important it was to him. Still she knew he and everyone else really loved her because of her personality. Even as a child she'd been outgoing, warm and caring. She had been the girl who'd save the lost kitten or find the words to mend a friend's broken heart. And a mirror couldn't catch that part of her; it had to be experienced.

But now the loving nature that had seemingly been born into her was getting hard to find. Even her thoughts and motivations were now disturbing. Why had she gotten so much satisfaction from the daydream of watching Jim Thomas die? And why didn't she want to race down the hall and visit with Jamie? Where was that old Meg now? When she'd lost Steve had that Meg, the one everyone loved, died? If she hadn't had a pulse, Meg would have guessed that was the case, but her heart was still beating. And the image she'd briefly glimpsed in the mirror reflected the person people knew. But she wasn't sure she knew that Meg anymore.

"I have a right to be different," she whispered.

"What did you say?" A tall man in a dark suit asked.

Meg looked up and forced a smile. "Sorry, I was just thinking out loud."

Embarrassed, she moved quickly forward and exited the cafeteria. Yet, like baggage she didn't need or want, she brought her worries with her.

"Hey, girl, slow down." Meg stopped as she heard Heather's voice. When her friend caught up, she lowered her voice and quietly asked, "How are you doing? Really? I find it hard to believe that anyone, even you, could be holding it together this well."

Meg leaned against the hallway wall and sighed. "I really don't know how I'm doing. My focus is fine, so my job's not a problem. But I don't know who I am anymore."

Heather moved closer. "What do you mean? I don't understand."

Meg shook her head. "I don't understand either. Aren't I supposed to be sad? In truth, I'm more angry. I'm so mad I want to punch everyone. That's not the way I was, but I'm thinking the old Meg was a sucker."

"You were never a sucker," her friend assured her. "You just cared about everyone."

"And that's just it—I don't think I care about anyone anymore." She paused and looked into Heather's deep eyes. "I don't know if there is room for the old Meg and this new Meg in my heart or head. One of them is going to have to move on. And I find myself rooting for the angry one."

"You'll work through it," Heather assured her.

"Could you work through knowing your husband had been murdered?" With those final cold words, Meg turned and strolled resolutely up the hall. Within seconds the wondering as to who she was had been forgotten. The all-consuming image in her head was that of seeing Jim Thomas going over the cliff.

"Your lunch break's not over for another fifteen minutes," noted Jan as Meg arrived at the station.

Her trance now broken, Meg offered, "Why don't you go early and catch a little extra time?"

Evidently not wanting to look a gift horse in the mouth, Jan quickly shot out from behind the desk, saying only, "I didn't know Christmas came on Thursdays in March."

Initially, Meg didn't take note of what the other nurse had said. The words had no meaning and made no impact. Then one of those words rang out and began to bounce around all the corners of her mind. Thursday! Why did that day seem so significant? What did she have to do today? What was it about Thursday?

Sitting in a chair behind the counter, she tried to refocus on her work, but Thursday wouldn't leave her alone. Why couldn't she think? Why couldn't she remember what made this day important? Her mind had been numb since watching Jim Thomas outside his house on Monday night. The desire for revenge, coupled with a feeling of overall helplessness, had made her even more depressed. Still, seeing him, knowing who his parents were, hearing him talk, and finding nothing of redeeming value in what he said had given her something on which to focus her thoughts. And those thoughts had crowded out everything that wasn't written on charts or appeared on iPad screens. And there was nothing on either that suggested Thursday was important for any reason at all. It was just another long day.

With the frustration of not being able to remember what she felt was so important, Meg realized how much each day seemed like the one before it. Even though this was only her fourth day back at work, the routine, filled with the same questions, the same requests, the same duties, began to run together. In the near past—a time that seemed years ago, a time before Steve had been killed—she had enjoyed her job. Each day had seemed fresh and alive with new faces and new challenges. And when the day ended, she knew that each evening with Steve would also be filled with new discoveries and newfound passions. Now, each day seemed to last forty-eight hours and each night, an eternity. As she glanced at her watch for the fifteenth time in half an hour, she wished she could turn back the clock. But that wasn't possible. Death had changed everything.

In this new life, the daydreams had become the reality and life was nothing more than a place to stumble through. She felt no real emotional attachment to her job, her mother, or her friends, and talking with them, answering their questions, even taking care of the patients was accomplished through little more than memorized mechanical reactions. Even things like cooking, cleaning, and putting on makeup were just time killers. They seemed to serve no purpose. Life had no purpose.

Yet, when she allowed herself to dream, her feelings and senses were brought back and the world again had color. From the time she had found out about Steve's murder—she refused to call it an accident—until the day after the funeral, she had dreamed about him. In those dreams, he brought her surprises, said funny things, and made love to her. He was alive. But now, since the moment she saw Jim Thomas, her dreams were filled with passionate plans for revenge. For now, Meg's world was one where reality and fantasy had somehow changed places, and this was the way she wanted it until life offered her some kind of personal satisfaction. That satisfaction could only be fully realized when her sworn enemy was brought to justice.

A ringing phone prompted her to look up from the chart she'd been staring at but not really seeing and move across the small cubicle to the counter separating her from the wing's hallway. "Wing Three," Meg answered tersely.

"Yes, I'm looking for Nurse Richards," a man explained.

Pausing for a moment in an attempt to remember where she had heard this voice, she replied, "I'm Meg Richards."

"Mrs. Richards, this is Webb Jones, your district attorney. My secretary said you called while I was out of town."

Suddenly, Meg was alive again. Here was the reason she had mentally marked Thursday as important. This was the day that the district attorney was to return. This was her bridge to hope! Now she had someone who could give her some answers. How had she forgotten about Thursday?

15

Tall, handsome in an Ivy League sort of way, Webb Jones was the cookie-cutter image of a Hollywood district attorney, with his green, wide-set eyes, wavy, dark hair, and strong, firm jaw. Yet what was most impressive about the man was his deep voice. And he used it effectively on the street and in the courtroom.

Jones had worked his way up from nothing. His father had been a clerk in a hardware store. His mother cleaned other people's houses. He was the only one of his four siblings who went to college. Pushed by a desire to escape a world in which he was always the poorest kid, he'd not been satisfied just to earn a college degree. He yearned for much more. He wanted to be the guy who lived on the right side of the tracks, drove the big car, and wore the expensive suits. He wanted to be important. And he felt the best way to earn this status was through law. His degree from the Indiana University Maurer School of Law brought him a sense of satisfaction. From there, he clerked for a federal judge and then became a part of the state attorney's office. While working in the capitol, he focused on a twenty-year plan. The first step was realized when he was elected district attorney. The second was when he married a daughter of a wealthy and influential stockbroker. Now six years after leaving to become the area's top prosecutor, he was primed for the next move—the governor's office. But that meant he was going to have to avoid the pitfalls that trapped many aspiring politicians. This case could be one of those traps, so he had to be very careful.

"Mrs. Richards. How I wish I had been in the office when you called. I'm so sorry I was out of town on business."

"Mr. Jones"—her voice was now filled with an excited tremor and she wasted no time making her point—"I want to know what you're going to do about my husband's death."

Jones was prepared for her question. The widow's response was not atypical in cases like this. The victim's family always wanted swift and hard justice. Even as he'd placed the call, Jones felt sure the conversation would quickly turn in this direction.

"Pardon me for not saying so earlier," Jones began, choosing each word with special care to hit the right note, "but I was very deeply saddened to find out about Mr. Richards's accident."

"It was no accident," Meg cut in.

The woman was combative. There was no mistaking that. She seemed primed and ready for a fight, and she would be in for one. This would be no easy case, not with the Thomas family and their money and power on the other side. And that was the problem. This case was one of those pitfalls that could kill a career. Thus, Jones would really rather avoid it all together. The best way to defuse this bomb was to get the family to cover medical and funeral costs, pay a few thousand in a settlement, and maybe have the kid do a bit of community service. But this woman's tone indicated she would likely not be satisfied with that answer. Still, he had to try.

"Mrs. Richards, bringing a case like this to trial can be very, very painful. You can't begin to imagine what you will have to go through. It could take months and that means you'd be forced to relive your husband's death over and over again. The toll it would take on you could be enormous and the end result would not bring your husband back. When dealing with a case like this, where a widow is left alone, it might serve your interests best to cut a deal."

"A deal?" Meg asked. "I don't understand."

Jones took a deep breath as he shifted into a tactic he often used when faced with a situation like this. It was time to gently present himself in the role of a big brother. "Mrs. Richards, what I'm going to suggest is for your own good. I can probably get the driver to plea guilty to a charge that would require him to do some community service, pay a fine, and serve a long probation. And then, in a separate agreement, his family would pay you a large settlement."

Her response was immediate. "I don't care about money. That won't bring Steve back. I want the kid to know the kind of pain he has caused me. I want the satisfaction of watching him convicted and sent to jail. He has to serve time. He killed my husband!"

It was so much easier when money could buy influence. And a lot of the time it could. But the tone in this woman's voice assured him she couldn't be bought off. Her pain was too deep, her resolve too strong. So that made things much more complicated. With the elections coming up in the fall, this case needed to disappear, but it appeared she wasn't going to let it. How much money would it take to change her mind? Did she have a price?

"Mr. Jones, are you still there?"

What to say now? He was far too pragmatic and logical to get emotionally involved in his cases and he'd never been very good when it came to sympathizing with or understanding grief. Still, at least for the moment, he had to give the appearance of caring. Find a safe, noncommittal reply and then, after he got the woman off the phone, come up with a game plan that would not include his going up against the Thomas family.

"Mrs. Richards," he began, "as I started to say, I had the good fortune to meet your husband on several occasions and I can't begin to explain how deeply saddened I was by his senseless death. It was tragic, simply tragic, and it shouldn't have happened."

Surely this was what the woman wanted to hear. Those words would assure her Webb Jones was a man who wanted justice. After all, he had just indicated how wonderful Steve had been.

"So, what do we do now?" Meg inquired.

"Well," Jones quickly answered, maybe now that he was on the familiar turf of law he could spell out in language the woman would grasp why this case didn't need to go to trial. "We are dealing with a juvenile and the initial thing that will have to be done, if we try him, is have him certified as an adult. If there is no problem in Justice of the Peace Court, I'll present the case to a grand jury. If that jury decides to indict him, then we'll try the case."

"Mr. Jones, what do you mean *if* the jury decides to indict?" There was a certain desperation now obvious in the woman's tone that grew stronger as she continued. "He was drunk, he killed my husband, and he is guilty."

"I agree with you," Jones answered defensively, "but sometimes justices of the peace and grand juries have strange ways of looking at things. Still, don't worry about that." Jones paused before coming back with what he considered a small fib. "I want justice, Mrs. Richards, and I'll do my best to get justice."

Jones had figured that his strongly phrased promise would bring the woman the satisfaction she needed and allow him to end the phone call on a high note. Yet Meg's next demanding question quickly convinced him of one painful fact. This woman would not be intimidated by his voice, knowledge, or promises. He hated working with people like that!

"Does this mean," Meg demanded, "that you'll go after my husband's killer with all the power you can muster, even though his father is who he is? I mean the Thomas's are important people in this town."

He was stunned. The woman knew much more than he figured. That information hadn't been in the paper. Where did the leak come from? Leaning back in his leather desk chair, Jones attempted to recover from the bomb that had just been dropped. With this new card in play, he only had one recourse—he had to buy some time.

"Mrs. Richards, would you hold on just a second? My other line is ringing." Before the woman could reply, the district attorney pushed the hold button, got up from his desk, and stormed into the outer office, stopping only when he stood over his administrative assistant's desk.

"Who told her that Judge Thomas's son was driving that car?"

"Told who?" Jo Blount quickly asked.

"Meg Richards, you know, the other driver's widow."

"Well, don't accuse me. I didn't."

The woman's tone assured Jones he had not been betrayed, at least not by her. She had been with him for ten years, first in state office and now here. She knew better than to release the name of a minor or give anyone any information that might make his job more difficult. But who did it then? Groping for answers, he scratched his head, turned back to his office, and then, just before reentering his office, looked over his shoulder and asked Blount one more question.

"The news media didn't get a hold of it, did they? If they did, I'll go after them—"

The woman didn't let him finish. "No, the press did not get it," she paused before adding sarcastically, "Not even your favorite, Robyn Chapman, from Channel 10."

"Well, I wouldn't put that woman above it," Jones barked. "You know what she did to us on that Morris affair. Anyway, we've got a leak somewhere and I want it found!"

Marching back to his office and slamming the ten-foot high oak door, Jones took a deep breath and punched the hold button. "I'm sorry, Mrs. Richards, an important call came in on the other line. I hope that you will forgive me."

"No problem," Meg answered. "Now what about my question?"

"No matter who the person is on the other side of the court-room," he firmly assured her, "I'll do my dead-level best. The law doesn't play favorites around here." After pausing a second to sense if the woman seemed to be accepting his promise, he asked, "Mrs. Richards, the other party in this case is a minor. How did you find out his identity?"

"Not from your office," she replied.

"Did someone in the media tell you?"

"No," she shot back. "No one told me. I just found out."

Concluding she wasn't going to volunteer how she uncovered the information, Jones wound up his call with a promise to keep Meg informed. He added as an afterthought, "Justice will be served." Before the woman could press him anymore he finished with a quick, "I'll be in touch and good-bye."

After putting the handset back in the cradle, Jones brought his fist down hard on his desk. *Who told her? Who gave the woman confidential information.* A knock pulled him out of thought.

"Come in," he barked.

"What was that all about?" Blount asked as she entered.

"We've got a problem," he admitted as he turned toward the window overlooking Springfield's town square. "The Richards woman is a deeply wounded animal, and the Thomas family will expect me to fix this for them just like I and all the locals have always done in the past. This might be one that really blows up in our faces and I can't let that happen."

16

As his administrative assistant looked on, a worried Webb Jones got up from his desk and crossed to his third-floor window. With his hands shoved deeply into his pockets, he studied the courthouse square. Except for the storm that had just entered his world, everything looked normal. But this storm was dangerous and the damage it could do might wreck his political aspirations. It was time to trust his instincts.

"Jo," he said, his eyes still studying the scene below, "this case is a time bomb."

"No doubt," she replied. "But since I've worked for you, you've always figured a way to avoid being in the wrong place at the wrong time. There has to be a way to handle this and not be hurt."

She was right about his timing. He'd always been one step ahead of the game. Anticipating a voter shift, he'd changed parties at just the right time. He'd been careful to groom the right friends and dump them at just the right moment, too. He'd married well and his wife was a member of all the right clubs. His record in the successful prosecution of violent offenders was perfect, largely because he never went to court unless he had a pat case. And through a series of deals and favors, he'd earned the support of the powerful Judge Alfred E.

Thomas. And now all of that might fall apart simply because of the death of a man in a car wreck had placed Jones between a rock and a hard place. How could he go after the Thomas kid and hang onto the most influential force in state politics?

Turning back toward his assistant, Jones shrugged, "I'm cooked. If I don't win, my next opponent will hit me with two punches. The first is that I blew an open-and-shut case. The second is that I tossed in the towel because the Thomas family was involved. And both charges will stick in the voters' minds. My political career will begin and end with this office. Then I become just another small-town lawyer."

Blount nodded.

Pushing his hands even deeper into his suit pants pockets, Jones leaned against a case filled with dusty law books. Shaking his head, he looked up toward the ceiling. Worry deepened every crease in his face. His house of cards didn't look very secure right now.

"Jo," he sighed, "if I win, Judge Thomas will ruin me."

"Has he called you?" she asked.

"No, he knows he doesn't have to. I've fixed things for his family for years. If only this had been just a DUI, I could easily sweep this under the rug, too. But a man died this time. The papers reported it. Mothers Against Drunk Drivers will no doubt parade in here for the trial. I can't snap my fingers and make this go away."

Blount grimly smiled. "The case won't go away, but you can."

Confused, Jones looked across the room. "What?"

"Your knee. The doctor told you that you needed to have it operated on."

Jones shrugged. "It's just an elective procedure."

"That doesn't matter," she assured him. "Get the surgery and rehab scheduled during the time the Thomas case goes to trial. To be fair to the state, you'll have to withdraw from the case."

The district attorney smiled. "Yeah, I see where you're going with this. If I don't handle any of the case, then I can't get blamed either way."

"You can talk out of both sides of your mouth," Blount added. "You can tell Thomas you were in his court if the case goes against his son and you can show the voters you aren't soft on crime. If the kid gets off, you can pretend outrage."

"That's not bad," Jones laughed.

"So," Blunt added, "we just give it to Cheryl."

Jones's eyes went to the ceiling. What a wonderful suggestion! His assistant was too young and too green to win a case like this. Thomas's legal team would tear her up. And if she somehow did happen to get lucky and win a conviction, Jones would be completely out of the picture, so he couldn't get blamed for it. If Thomas had to pay the price, let it be the woman who gives the kid the bill. She will become the sacrificial lamb.

Jones looked back at Blount. "As soon as the trial is scheduled—and let's face it, the grand jury will push this to trial—get me an appointment for surgery that week. Once we have that on my calendar, get Cheryl in here. We'll let her take charge of this one from the get-go. She can't battle the Thomas clan. And when she loses, she'll be seen as the woman who let the Widow Richards down. Then, I can use my assistant to show voters just how disgusted I am with the sentence and her inept work on the case."

Blount wryly noted, "That would keep you out of hot water and maintain your image as being tough on crime."

He smiled and walked back to the window. The train hadn't bounced off the track after all. He could just avoid this bump in the road and let it ruin someone else's career—someone who wasn't nearly as important as he was.

17

For Meg, a small promise was better than none at all. And with just the knowledge that Jones had made his way back to his office and now planned to prosecute, she felt better than she had in days. She even mustered a small smile for little Jamie, thanking her for the pretty picture she had drawn, and accepted an invitation to go to Pizza Hut with Heather.

Over supper, the nurses discussed television shows, movies, and work. Steve was the one subject they both ignored. Then, after they had paid their bill and were putting on their coats, Meg asked Heather if she would mind going for a drive.

As they rode through town in the Mustang, Meg rattled on about the times she and Steve had enjoyed while dating. As the minutes passed, Meg's conversation became more and more current, even talking about how she and Steve had just paid off their school loans and had been saving to make a down payment on a house. Then, just as it appeared Meg had begun to confront the demons that had been causing her to feel so bitter toward life, the car stopped in front of huge brick home. Meg smiled as she considered the bomb she was about to drop.

"You know who lives there?" she asked, pointing through Heather's window.

Heather just shook her head.

"That's Judge Thomas's house," Meg explained.

Meg let Heather take in the magnificence of the structure—a splendor that even the darkness couldn't hide. Then she slipped the car back into drive and eased it down the street. The two didn't speak again until Meg dropped her friend off at her car. After they had said their good-byes, and just as Heather opened her own car's door, Meg pushed the Mustang's passenger window button. After the window opened, Heather leaned down and was greeted with a strange smile.

"Heather, that house, the big one?" Not waiting for a response, Meg continued. "That's where Steve's murderer lives his little, happy life. When I get done with him, he and his family, all those who called that big house home, will never see another happy day as long as they live."

Before Heather could reply, Meg raised the window and the Mustang rolled out of the parking lot and disappeared into the night.

18

THE RUDE BEEPING ECHOED THROUGH THE ROOM AT THE SAME TIME IT DID every weekday morning—5:15 a.m. Groping in the darkness, Meg reached over and hit the snooze. The room at once took on a tomblike silence as she fell back into a deep sleep. Five minutes later, the loud buzzing woke her again. This time she managed to hit the off switch as she tossed the covers back and rolled out of bed. Not bothering to turn on the lamp, she sleepily stumbled to the bathroom. Temporarily hiding her eyes with her left arm, she flipped on the light switch, and after waiting a few seconds for her vision to clear, stared at the image reflected there.

"If only Heather could see me. She wouldn't think I looked so perfect."

Pushing her hair back in some semblance of order, she plugged in her electric curlers, automatically pivoted 180 degrees, and turned on the shower. The routine had become so familiar over the years she could do it without thinking. But today something different and unexpected had been added.

With no warning, a strange, dizzy feeling came over her. The whole room began rolling and she felt as though she were on a ship fighting against storm waves. Balancing by holding onto the sink, she managed to keep from falling, but that didn't stop her head from spinning for another thirty seconds. The dizziness left almost as soon as it came. Refocusing, Meg straightened herself and tugged her favorite T-shirt over her head. Just as she dropped it on the floor, a queasy roiling hit her like a hammer. She'd never gotten this sick so quickly. She'd always hated being sick. She'd always fought giving into any kind of illness. Yet this time she had no choice. Her stomach had a mind of its own. Dropping to her knees, she found the commode and quickly lost what little food she had in her stomach.

Pulling herself off her knees, she turned on the sink's tap and rinsed her face with cool water. Drying her cheeks with a towel, she glanced back at the reflection of her now ashen, white face and muttered, "No more pizza after work. Heather will have to find someone else to pig out with."

Feeling slightly better, she stepped into the shower and spent the next few minutes reviving herself. By the time she had dressed, fixed her hair, and put on her makeup, she was not just feeling well, she was ravenous. With energy brought on by desire, she prepared a huge breakfast of pancakes, bacon, eggs, and hash browns and quickly devoured every bite. Not satisfied, she munched passionately through a half bag of potato chips. She would have eaten the remainder, but it was already well past time for her to be on her way to work.

As no one in their right mind was ready to be a part of the real world this early in the morning, the short trip was uneventful. It was just another drive through lonely, dark streets on a route that never changed. Except for Mr. Kim working in the donut shop and a lone police car, there were no signs of life. The hospital parking lot was all but empty as she pulled in and shut off the Mustang. And the solitude was the best gift Meg could imagine. If Steve could never again be with her, then she saw no real reason to be with anyone. But as soon as she hit the employee door, that peaceful isolation would be transformed into organized chaos.

"Hi, Meg." Heather's voice sounded as chipper as ever. "How are things today?"

Meg shrugged as she hung her coat on the rack. "They'd be a lot better if we hadn't had pizza last night. Boy, I was sick this morning."

"Wish I looked like that when I was sick," Heather replied.

"You always look fine," Meg returned.

"Hi, nurses!"

Heather and Meg stopped their drug counts as Dr. Mason walked into the room.

"Hi, Paul," Heather said. "I thought you had the day off."

"I did, but Dr. Parks has a touch of the flu, so . . ."

"I think Meg might be coming down with it, too," Heather shot back.

Meg almost grinned. She could see right through her friend and coworker. Heather might have been attempting to make casual conversation and sound like she had no interest in the male in their midst, but she would give her right arm to go out with him. It was so obvious it was almost sad.

"How many did you get, Heather?"

Glancing over to see what the other nurse had been inventorying, Meg answered, "Twenty-two."

"So did I. Let's sign in."

After the two nurses initialed their reports, Heather hovered around the desk attempting to make small talk with the doctor. Meg saw no reason to watch the sad scene play out and headed down the hall to the nurses' station. Life would be so much easier if love were not a part of it.

19

Cheryl Bednarz looked more like a Zumba instructor than a prosecutor, a look she worked hard to maintain. She knew that her age—twenty-seven—and her size—diminutive—had to be overcome by strength. So she made an effort to make up for those with boldness. As a child, she'd been both fearless and impulsive but now possessed drive and intelligence to temper her courage. Though not yet a seasoned attorney, she possessed a confident nature that belied her lack of experience. She knew the law backwards and forwards, yet she could never seem to impress her boss. Thanks to the trivial assignments she was handed, it had become more evident with each passing day that Jones had no faith in her at all. Two years of a practice filled with small victories still left her on the edge looking for one bit of praise and it had never come. Now, he'd dropped this into her lap. She was in change of a firefight with the most powerful man in the community and maybe the state. It was the biggest case that had come into this office in years, so why did Jones make this move? Had he suddenly decided she was up to the task? No, she knew she hadn't earned this case; it had to be avoidance. Jones had decided to punt the ball and now she had to not just catch that punt but find a way to make it to the end zone.

"Webb turned this case over to you?" Lauren Bass marveled while standing in front of the assistant district attorney's desk.

Cheryl nodded as she glanced back at her assistant. Just two years younger than Bednarz, she too was green. While bright and well educated, the tall, attractive, African-American woman had a lot more miles to travel to get to the top on the learning curve. Thus, she seemed as unprepared to deal with this matter as the assistant district attorney. Yet in spite of her lack of seasoning, Cheryl had complete faith in Lauren. She also had as much faith in her own abilities.

"Kind of shocking," Cheryl noted as she sat down at her desk in her small, windowless office. "He told me he had surgery planned for the week of the trial."

"What kind?" Bass asked, taking a seat in an antique wooden chair beside the desk.

"Knee surgery."

"Couldn't he have put that off?"

"Of course," Cheryl replied, "but the fact he didn't isn't a matter of his physical health. This is all about his political health. I've been set up. Jones wouldn't touch this one with a ten-foot pole. If he loses, he gets beat in the election because his opponent will paint him as a political stooge giving in to the power of the Thomas family. If he wins, Thomas will see to it that his political career is over and there goes Webb's dreams of being governor. He bailed on this because he knew he'd be ruined either way."

Bass shook her head. "Where does that put you?"

Cheryl smiled. "As old Webb says at least three times every day, between the old rock and the hard place. If I win the case, I'm cooked, but Jones is fine. Thomas can't touch him because he's going to be out of the office due to surgery. If I lose, Jones fires me because I'm soft and can't win the easy cases. So no matter which way you look at it, I'm going to lose and you'll be working with someone other than me."

"You don't seem to be too upset about it," Bass noted. "In fact, I seem to hear a bit of glee in your Texas drawl."

"Lauren, Jones is sure I can't take on Thomas and win. He's sure I'll fall on my face or maybe something else. He's confident that I don't have the experience to make the charges stick. But he doesn't know one thing."

"What's that?"

Bednarz stood up, moved to the side of her desk, and grinned. As she rubbed her hands together, she said, "I've been preparing for this for a decade. I know more about this kind of case than Jones ever will. And I don't give a rip if Thomas tries to ruin me after I put his kid away. I will just move back home and work there. For Jones, Springfield is a launching pad, but for me it is a jumping-off point."

"Hope you have a parachute," Bass jabbed. "Thomas is powerful and it might be a long fall."

"Don't need one when you know how to land the plane," Cheryl shot back. "You will soon understand why Webb's nightmare is my dream! Now, let's start going through these files. We've got work to do and a lot of ground to cover in a short amount of time."

20

Heather turned her eyes toward the doctor, smiled, and asked, "How do you like your new BMW?"

When he didn't respond, she repeated her question. This time he noticed.

"I'm sorry, Heather, what did you say?"

"It's not really important," she shrugged. "Something on your mind?"

"Yeah," Paul's voice indicated a level of concern that he rarely showed. Tilting his head in the direction from which Meg had just walked, he queried, "You know her pretty well. How's she doing today?"

Names were not necessary; Heather knew exactly whom Paul was talking about. "She seems to be doing all right. I mean, we went out for pizza last night and she sounded okay. Hey, she even spoke about some of the fun times that she and Steve had."

Making eye contact with the doctor, she asked, "You knew him, didn't you?"

Shaking his head, Paul responded, "Not really. Saw him once or twice, but I never really knew him."

"A lot of people thought he was a hunk," Heather said. "You know the type, good-looking boy who always appeared full of himself." She paused, wondering how to fully explain a man she'd so admired. Shaking her head, she continued, "He wasn't that way at all. Yes, he was athletic and had a fun personality, but he was bright and kind of a saint, too. I know that sounds weird, but he was just that nice. In fact, he seemed just about perfect. I don't think I'll ever meet anyone who could come close to measuring up to him. Boy, and how Meg loved him."

Heather moved away from the desk to a far wall and leaned up against it. She folded her arms across her chest as Paul watched her every move. Sensing he wanted her to say more, she took a deep breath and continued. "Last night she talked about that, how much she loved him, how great he was, and I actually began to think she had found a way to work through it. I mean, I knew it would take a while, but for the first time since the accident, she seemed to be looking at the good things."

"Well, Heather, then it sounds like she'll bounce back pretty well." Paul's inflection caused his statement to come across more as a question rather than an observation.

"I don't know." Heather sighed moving from the wall and back to the man's side. Only when she drew next to him and stared deeply into his eyes did she say what was really on her heart. The words came out in a whisper.

"After we finished eating, she did something that worried me all night. She took me by the home of the person driving the other car. She told me that she'd promised herself there would never be any good times in that home again. She said it with such conviction it caused chills to run up my back." As she finished her story, Heather's blue eyes searched his face with an expression that demanded a response.

"I wouldn't worry too much," he answered. "We would all probably feel the same way." He waited a second as if to compose his thoughts before continuing. "You know, we watch people die almost every day—old people, young people, from disease, accidents, even suicide. When it happens, we shake our heads, even pat the hands of a family member, and then we walk away. We all get so caught up with illness and fighting it that when we lose a battle, when someone dies, we con ourselves into believing that at least the pain is over. Heather, in cases like Meg's, the pain is just beginning."

There were no more words to say. Paul turned back to a patient report he had been studying. Heather, her heart now aching, pretended to recheck the inventory she and Meg had finished earlier. Suddenly, a muffled voice broke the silence.

"Nurse, this is Minnie Evans in 109, could I have some ice?"

Responding to the intercom, Heather leaned over and checked the computer file to see if the patient could have ice, before punching a button and saying, "Be right there."

"Hey, Heather, before you go—" Paul interjected, stopping her with not only his voice but with a light touch.

"Yes, doctor."

"Since you mentioned my car, I'd love to run it through the paces for you say—Saturday. You know that's tomorrow night. Now, I've checked and you don't have to work."

Trying hard not to sound too excited, Heather replied, "If the ride includes dinner, I might be convinced."

"How 'bout a show, too?"

"Okay, I'll bite," she answered, laughing. "Why not?"

"I'll get hold of you this afternoon and we'll decide a time." He shot her a huge smile as he walked off.

Turning so that Paul wouldn't see the flush on her cheeks or the ever-brightening smile on her face, Heather headed off to get a bucket of ice. Assured now, that for her, this would be a good weekend.

21

For the remainder of the day, Heather's eternally happy voice seemed to bring a glow to every room on the wing. Meanwhile, Meg was anything but a positive force. As the day dragged on, she become even more burdened by thoughts of how slow the wheels of justice were going to turn, wondering if they would ever turn at all. At the moment it seemed the odds were against her finding satisfaction through the legal system. The Thomas family simply had too much power in this town and she got the idea Webb Jones didn't want to challenge that power. After all, didn't he suggest she let the family buy her off? Therefore, she was probably going to have to find a way to extract her own brand of justice. Yet, how could she act? What could she do? What power did she have to call on?

Last night, after an evening with Heather, she felt empowered. But as the night went on and she confronted the task she faced, her sense of power faded. When she woke up sick to her stomach, she lost all her confidence. Sitting in front of her commode, she had felt weak, alone, and frightened. And that sense of helplessness had now worked its way into everything she had done on this day. Yet as much as she didn't like dealing with patients or even the other staff members, it was better than being home. She absolutely dreaded going through a second weekend without Steve. As long as this day had been, she knew the next forty-eight hours would seem like an eternity. And as the minutes slowly moved that reality closer, she sank deeper and deeper into despair. Yes, walking the halls, cleaning bedpans, and listening to complaining patients were better than being in her lonely apartment.

As Meg and Heather were checking out, two more nurses, Jan Greer and Molli Cassle were waiting to check in. Like all veterans, they knew that Friday and Saturday nights often presented problems and people who would test both their knowledge and their patience. It just seemed the weekend brought out the worst in people and that kept the emergency room hopping.

"I'd give anything not to work this weekend," Jan stated to everyone and no one.

"Who wouldn't?" Molli tossed back. "Did you see there's a full moon?"

Heather couldn't help but gloat a little. "Well, while you two are slaving away, bandaging heads and tossing out pills, I'll be sitting by a fire, being held in the arms of the ever suave and handsome Paul Mason."

Heather was sure her statement would bring out some type of jealous remark from the two nurses. She was partially right.

"He's one heck of a good lookin' man," sighed Jan.

Meanwhile Molli seemed caught between silence and a full-blown confession. When she spoke, she opted for something in between. "I've been out with him a few times." Jan and Heather both turned toward her. Still seemingly unsure of just how to put what she wanted to say, she continued. "And in person, the good doctor is a whole lot like he is in surgery."

Jan started to grin, but poor innocent Heather, a confused look on her face, just walked right through the door Molli had opened.

"How's that?" she inquired.

"Oh, Heather," Molli laughed, "Paul is such a fast operator. I hope you know how to handle yourself, because if you don't, he certainly will."

Heather blushed a bright shade of red, Jan and Molli turned toward the wall so their giggles would go largely unnoticed, and Meg, now finished with her count, remained oblivious to everything. Well, almost everything! While she waited for Heather to complete her part of the count, Meg walked over to where Jan and Molli were sharing an inside joke. Not waiting for them to finish, she said, "Listen, I'll work somebody's shift this weekend, if one of you would rather go out or something. "

"Saturday evening?" Molli quickly inquired, not wanting to take a chance that Jan might jump before her.

"Sure," Meg answered.

"You wouldn't want to work Sunday night, too, would you?" Jan asked.

"Anything to keep me busy and away from home," Meg responded. Turning back toward Heather, she asked, "Are you done yet?"

"Yeah, just got it." Heather answered. "I'm out of here." The words had no more cleared her mouth when she grabbed her coat and hit the door.

Turning back to the other two, Meg nodded. "I'll get it cleared with the head nurse's office. If there are any problems, I'll tell you." A small smile couldn't mask her solemn expression as she disappeared around the corner.

22

WEEKEND WORK COULD BE A REAL PAIN, ESPECIALLY THE LATE SHIFT. YET, for Meg, just having something to do seemed like a blessing. Still this blessing had a price. Sunday night she was dog-tired and actually grateful she had the late shift on Monday. Too weary to mourn her loss or even plan revenge on Steve's killer, she dropped off to sleep almost as soon as she hit the bed. She remained dead to the world until a familiar noise invaded her dreams. At first, she thought it was her alarm, but when she clumsily hit the snooze button the noise only momentarily stopped. Then it came back again louder than ever. Slowly sitting up and rubbing her eyes, she finally recognized the ringing of her telephone. Dropping back down on her bed, too tired and too disoriented to be curious, she decided to wait it out and go back to sleep. "They'll call back," she mumbled to her pillow. Sure enough, a few minutes later, they did.

"Okay. Okay. I'm coming," she yelled, as she untangled herself from her sheet and staggered into the living room. She glanced at the clock. It was 10:30 a.m. After clearing her throat, she picked up the receiver and answered, "Hello."

"Mrs. Richards?"

"Yes, this is Meg Richards."

"I'm Cheryl Bednarz with the district attorney's office. Mr. Jones would like to talk to you for a moment. Do you have the time?"

Finding the arm of the couch, Meg dropped onto it, pushed her hair out of her face, and, her voice trembling, answered, "Sure."

"It'll be just a moment," and then the sounds of some nondescript elevator-type music filled the receiver. For almost three minutes, Meg listened impatiently to a string version of "Honky Tonk Man," followed by part of an equally unsettling rendition of "Stand by Your Man."

"Who in their right mind picked those tunes?" Meg groaned.

"Mrs. Richards?" Webb Jones's voice broke into the song. "Did you say something?"

"Not really." Meg's heart raced as she attempted to cover her embarrassment. "Has something happened on the case?"

"Yes, that's what I'm calling about." After pausing for a short moment, the district attorney continued. "The Thomas kid has been certified as an adult in the justice of peace court. That happened yesterday afternoon. Normally things don't work this fast, but as the grand jury met this morning, I went ahead and presented them with the information we had already put together. After all, it seemed pretty open-and-shut to me. They must have thought so, too, because they asked for an indictment. By the end of the day, I'll issue a warrant for the boy's arrest."

Meg's heart almost leaped from her chest. She had hoped Jones would act fast and that Jim Thomas would be arrested and put behind bars, but because of his family's power she'd begun to doubt that would really happen. Now, maybe justice would allow her to extract her revenge in the proper way. Taking a deep breath in an attempt to calm her excitement, she asked, "Does this mean that he's going to be in jail?"

"Not really," Jones answered. "He will be arrested, bail will be set, and I'm sure that his family will post bail. He'll be out until the trial or until we settle this with a plea bargain."

Disappointment showing in her voice, she shot back, "No bargain. He has to be convicted. When is the trial going to be?"

"We'll meet with his attorneys and Judge Truett later in the week, and a date will be set then. I'm betting the Thomas family's legal team will want to take care of this thing in a hurry in order to get it out of the news and buried. So I figure a month, maybe six weeks. Until that time, we'll just wait. Believe me, the waiting will be worse for Thomas than for us." As Jones completed his sentence, his intercom buzzer sounded. "Mrs. Richards, I'm going to put you on hold for just a second. I'll be right back."

As he pushed the hold button, the sounds of "Cold, Cold Heart" came over the receiver, this time a small ensemble of flutes was miserably trying to twang. Why do people think music is such a wonderful way to pass time while on hold? Silence would be so much better. Trying to ignore the Hank Williams tune, she looked out the window. The sun had just broken through the clouds and a brightness she hadn't seen in weeks filled the snowy streets. In a strange sort of way, a way she couldn't describe, Meg felt really good. It wasn't getting-a-new-car good or winning-the-lottery-good, but it was still a hopeful kind of good that, as she waited on Jones, grew into a euphoric state that led to a strange sort of peace.

"Mrs. Richards," the voice that had come back on the line belonged to the woman who had first placed the call. "Mr. Jones extends his apology but an emergency just called him out of the office. I'll be happy to answer any other questions you might have. As assistant district attorney, I'm very familiar with the case."

Meg had assumed that Cheryl Bednarz was a secretary, not a lawyer, and this new information stunned her a little. The woman sounded so young. After coming to grips with her misunderstanding, Meg turned her mind back to the reason for the call. There was something she needed to know. Unable to find what seemed like the perfect words to pose the question, she bluntly and awkwardly inquired what had been on her mind and heart since the first time she'd driven by the Thomas's palatial home. "Can we get him?" After the words tumbled out, she felt like she had just delivered a stock line from a 1940s crime movie. Why hadn't she put it another way?

"If you mean the Thomas boy," Bednarz's voice was reassuringly calm, "I haven't talked to Mr. Jones to get his opinion, but in my mind I think we can. The evidence seems to be very substantial. Of course, there are no guarantees, Mrs. Richards. I want you to know that if Mr. Thomas decides to plead not guilty, the actual proceedings might be pretty hard on you. A lot of times a defense attorney will put the victim on trial. It can get pretty rough."

"I've already lost my husband." Meg's tone filled with resolve as she continued, "I can do anything it takes to get his killer."

"Mrs. Richards, did Mr. Jones give you the charges on which we'll be trying the defendant?" The assistant district attorney's tone indicated she seemed to believe Meg already had the facts.

"No, I just thought it would be . . ."

Ms. Bednarz broke in before Meg could finish. "It's vehicular homicide, reckless driving, and DUI. That means driving under the influence of alcohol or drugs. In this case alcohol."

This couldn't be. It was not right at all. Leaning back in the couch she glanced back over at a photo of Steve. He'd been killed just as surely as if he'd been shot with a gun. His life had literally been snuffed out. Shaking her head, she took a deep breath and asked, "Not murder?"

"We can't do it that way in this state," the woman explained. "Not on a DUI."

Pausing to consider this new turn, Meg suddenly felt deflated. The euphoric feeling was gone. This was not nearly enough.

"If he's found guilty, how much will he get?" Meg demanded.

"Well," the assistant district attorney explained, "there are a number of variables. But if the sentencing were to go to the harsh side, considering Thomas's age, we could expect maybe ten years, with most, if not all, to be served while he was on probation."

"That's all?" Meg's voice had fallen to a disbelieving whisper.

"Under the circumstances, I'm afraid that is it. Juries and judges are not known in this state for dealing out long prison terms for those who have combined alcohol and a car to make a lethal weapon. It has been a very frustrating situation for me, but I'll do my best to make this case different."

"Ms. Bednarz . . ."

"Please call me Cheryl."

"Cheryl," Meg continued, "Steve meant everything to me. He hadn't lived much of his life. He was a good man . . . a wonderful man. You can't begin to imagine how much he didn't get to do. We had so many things planned. He never even got to hold his children." She stopped as tears stung her eyes.

For a few minutes, an awkward silence fell upon the conversation before Cheryl's compassionate voice filled the receiver. "I know that he was cheated out of a lot and so were you. But in some ways maybe it's better that you don't have any children. It can be very hard explaining to a child a tragedy that even you and I can't even fully understand."

"I don't think you know what I mean," Meg, tears now running down and falling from her face, whispered. "You see, I'm pregnant."

The assistant district attorney must have been at a complete loss. She must have been searching the air around her for something comforting to say. Evidently, nothing came to her mind because her answer contained just two words, "I see."

"I don't think you do," Meg coldly snapped. "He never even knew he was going to be a father."

"Mrs. Richards, Meg, if I may. Maybe we just need to let you think for a while on what we've talked about today. Later, we can get together for lunch, or dinner if that's better for you. I'm pretty flexible this week. I can answer all your questions and tell you what to expect from the trial."

Rubbing her tears with her left hand, Meg composed her voice. "Sure, that sounds fine. Supper on Thursday?"

"Seven o'clock all right?"

"That would be okay with me."

"We'll go casual, just someplace where we can get to know each other. I'll pick you up. My email is Bednarz@springfield.gov. Just email me where you want to eat."

Meg reached for a pad on the table and jotted down the address.

"Thanks," she said as she tossed the pen down.

"Good-bye."

Setting her phone down, Meg considered the fact that Thomas would likely pay very little for what he had done. As she let that reality take root in her mind, an overwhelming wave of nausea come over her. Jumping up, she ran for the bathroom.

A few minutes later, after the sickness passed, she washed her face and fixed herself a big breakfast. In spite of the daily bouts with morning sickness, her appetite for food had grown almost as large as her appetite for justice. As she ate enough for two large men, she considered what she'd been told.

She wasn't satisfied with the charges or the possible penalty that Jim Thomas faced, but she was at least glad that there had been movement. If he spent some time in jail, it would be a start. As she finished her third piece of toast, she resolved to first get what she could out of the courts then take the rest her own way.

After a shower, a trip to the grocery store, some clothes shopping, and a late lunch, Meg headed off to work. And today, she had something special to share with Heather.

23

Meg," Jan Greer's voice was unmistakable. "You're looking better today. More color. You finally licking that bug?"

"Maybe," Meg replied as she took off her coat and prepared to check in. She wondered how much longer she could hide the fact she was pregnant or maybe Jan knew and was just being diplomatic. After all, it wasn't that big a hospital, probably even the janitor had heard by now.

"Glad you're on the mend," Jan stated as she began the routine of checking out. "A lot of folks went home today and there were only a couple of admits. No cranks on the wing, either. You'll probably find this the easiest shift you've had in a long time."

"Good, I want an easy one. I'd like to sit back and watch the time go by for a while," Meg replied while she picked up the clipboard and waited for Heather to arrive and verify the other nurse's drug count. Finally, after five minutes of looking at the door and waiting on Jan to finish, Heather walked in.

"Hey, gang. You waitin' on me?" Anyone who heard Heather's happy voice would have known something good must have just happened. She was on top of the world. Jan piped up first.

"What's the story?"

"Oh, nothing much," Heather replied, a huge smile belying her off-handed explanation. Pulling off her coat, checking her hair in her compact, and then storing her purse behind the counter, she finally offered, "Well, if you must know. Paul just asked me to go skiing with him this weekend."

"Hot mama," Jan exclaimed as she left. Looking back over her shoulder she added, "You'll be the talk of the hospital for the next week. Way to go, Honey."

An enormous grin covering her face, Heather turned toward her work. "Meg, you look really nice tonight. Are you feeling better?"

"I tell you what," Meg replied, sarcasm filling her tone. "I must have really looked bad before. You're the second person to say that to me tonight. But to answer the question for hopefully the last time, yes. Except for a brief spell this morning, I've felt good all day."

Finishing their check-in count, the two prepared for the light routine promised them. As they looked over charts and readied medication, Meg told Heather of her conversation with the district attorney's office. When she finished filling in the details, her friend offered an observation. "It sounds like they're really going to try to get him."

"I think they'll do their best," Meg agreed. "But it's not enough. Steve's life is worth more than a bit of jail time and probation. You know, I hope that when I talk with the assistant district attorney on Thursday, I can convince her of that too. Maybe they can bring stiffer charges or something. I've been studying some cases online today and there are people who serve as much as twenty years or more for things like this. We need to go for the max!"

"I don't know anything about law," Heather answered. "But I think you're right. I agree that probation isn't enough. But if that's all you can get, then it's better than nothing."

Turning so that her eyes met Heather's, Meg, her tone suddenly bitter, shot back, "Just barely better than nothing. But don't worry, Heather. I'll let the law get its piece of Jim Thomas, and then I'll take mine! One way or the other he will pay dearly."

A muffled voice, a patient calling in over the room-to-nurse's station intercom, ended the conversation at that awkward point. "Excuse me, but could I have some ice?"

Checking the name on the Kardex that corresponded to the caller's room number, Heather made sure it had been approved, and then answered, "Sure, Nancy. I'll get it in a moment." At that instant, another page came over the main intercom system. "Heather Rodgers, you have a call on line three."

"Meg, would you?" Heather looked at the ice bucket.

"I'll take care of the ice," Meg agreed. "You get your call. Ice *is* all right for her, isn't it?"

Nodding her head as she picked up the phone, Heather punched line three and added, "She's in room 211."

Meg, now halfway down the hall, ice bucket in her hand, waved, "Got it." She could hear Heather's voice in the background but she didn't note what her friend was saying. She was far too busy daydreaming about a car careening out of control over a stone wall.

24

Hi, I HOPE IT WASN'T TOO MUCH BOTHER?"

The cheery voice that issued that equally cheery greeting in room 211 came from a small, attractive, impish woman, who looked to be in her late twenties or early thirties. She was sitting up in her bed, an open book in her lap. An iPod Touch in a speaker box on a table next to the window played music by a female vocalist. Meg knew she'd heard the singer before but at the moment she just couldn't place the name.

"I'm Nancy." A smile came with the introduction. "I don't think I've met you, have I?"

"No." Meg's reply, while not unfriendly, lacked the soothing warmth it would have displayed a few weeks ago. "Where do you want the ice?"

"On the table will be fine. Let me see, your name tag says Meg, so unless you're working incognito, I assume that's who you are."

Nodding while not acknowledging the patient's attempt at humor, Meg answered, "It is actually Megan, but no one has ever called me that, except my mother when she's trying to make a point—which she does all too often." After placing the ice on the table next to a water pitcher, she asked, "Would you like some ice water?"

"That'd be nice," Nancy replied. "Is the music too loud? I'll turn it down if it is. I love Sandi Patti so much that there are times when I get carried away with the volume."

Of course! That's the singer's name. She and Steve caught her last summer at a concert with the youth group from church. She was a gospel singer and a good one with almost unlimited range. The kids had been impressed. Meg had even been moved enough to buy one of her CDs. Where had she put it? Oh yeah, it had been in Steve's car. That sobering thought plunged Meg into a semitrance. There was another thing among hundreds now missing from her life. Something else she wouldn't get back along with goodnight kisses, evenings out sitting across from each other at Dino's, visiting antique shops, or arguing about baby names. Just like the CD, all of that was gone.

Shaking herself back into the moment, she spun toward the patient only to realize she was being studied. Nancy's eyes were following every move she made. And that gaze made her feel a bit uncomfortable. This woman seemed to be reading her, and at this point, Meg didn't want her life to be an open book.

Meg ambled toward the window and still the patient's eyes followed. Trying to focus on anything but the small woman in the bed, she tidied up a table, restacking a few magazines then turned her attention to straightening a jacket that had been casually tossed across a chair. From behind her, Nancy cleared her voice and repeated her question.

"The music? Is it too loud?"

Meg turned. "No, the music's fine. Oh, I forgot to give you your water." She hurried to the table and retrieved the glass then moved quickly to the woman's side. As the patient took the water, the nurse studied her carefully for the first time.

With her perfectly applied makeup, immaculate nails, and stylish hair, Nancy really looked more like a visitor than a patient. Her attitude and the strength in her voice certainly didn't indicate much illness either. So what was the problem? Meg made quick survey in an attempt to ascertain the nature of the patient's illness. Nothing jumped out even to her trained eye. Outwardly, Nancy appeared very healthy. When she smiled, she glowed and her skin color looked good. There were no tubes or IVs, and there was no sign of any recent injuries. She wasn't hooked up to any monitors either. As no obvious symptoms came into view, Meg scolded herself for not taking a look at the Kardex. That would have given her the answers she now wanted. Of course she could look at the patient's chart; it was right in front of her, but as all she did was come in here to deliver ice that seemed unnecessary and rude.

"Are you new to this wing?" Nancy asked after she set the glass on the night table.

"It has been a while since I have worked over here," Meg explained. "But I'm going to be here for the rest of the week." She wanted to ask Nancy, "Why do you care, anyway?" but she bit her tongue.

"Where do you normally work?" This woman seemed more than a little too nosy. But she also could be lonely, and in the past Meg had sought those patients out and tried to bring some comfort to their world. This was just a lonely person desperate to make conversation. Nancy was likely trying to hold Meg here so she wouldn't be alone.

"Recently on the pediatric wing," Meg informed her questioner, a bit of the old Meg bubbling to the top. Pulling up a chair and taking a seat, she asked, "How are you doing?"

"Feeling fine today. Thanks." Nancy's enthusiasm for conversation was obvious. There was warmth in her eyes and her smile came effortlessly. Her manner was not that dissimilar from what Meg's had been up until two weeks before.

"Wish all my patient's felt great," Meg replied.

"Pediatrics must be a bright place to work," Nancy chimed in. "All those happy little faces. I'm a teacher, or at least I used to be one. And I miss the kids. You know, all their strange questions and unique observations. There's nothing like a child to remind you how wonderful life is."

Meg marveled at the woman's delivery. She could fire off a long string of words faster than most people could utter a single sentence. And after just a tiny breath she continued. "I would have loved to have children, but . . ." for the first time, a slight note of sadness crept into the woman's tone. Turning her eyes away from Meg and toward the window, Nancy took a breath and continued, "But it just didn't work out. Some things don't. And there are always reasons."

As Meg studied Nancy, the patient once again turned her gaze back to the nurse, and noting the wedding ring on Meg's left hand inquired, "Do you and your husband have any children? Maybe you have some pictures?"

A chill ran down Meg's back. She'd never expected anyone to ask that question. Looking away from Nancy, she got up, moved across the room, picked up a stack of old newspapers, and placed them in the trash can. Without glancing back toward her patient, she turned to the far wall and asked, "Would you like the shades raised?"

"No, they're fine," came the quick response. "I'm sorry if I said something wrong. I didn't mean to. I guess I ask too many questions."

Spinning toward the patient, Meg's eyes met Nancy's. Biting her lip, fighting back tears, she almost walked past the woman and out of the room, but something kept her there. It was like her feet were glued to the floor. For thirty seconds, the room filled with an awkward silence then, not really understanding why, Meg lashed out.

"I don't know why every patient thinks a nurse's private life is her business. It's not. I'm tired of having people prying into my life. And I'm tired of people asking me personal questions. I got your ice and unless you need something else there are a lot of other patients on this wing who are obviously a lot sicker than you are. So just let me do my job without the third degree. I'm here to be your nurse, not your friend. If you want to talk to someone, pick up the phone and use it. But bother someone else. Okay?"

As she finished, Meg rushed out of the room, not giving Nancy an opportunity to respond.

"Did you get the ice?" Heather asked when Meg returned to the station.

"Yeah."

"Nancy is something else isn't she?" Heather continued.

"Yeah," came the almost sarcastic reply.

"It's absolutely amazing to me"—Heather paused for a moment as she looked in the mirror and checked her hair—"that anyone who is dying of cancer can be that up—you know—that happy. But she always is. And no matter how down I am, she makes me feel better."

As Heather continued to rattle on about the woman, Meg turned her face toward the wall as a wave of embarrassment and guilt washed over her. How could she have been so rude to a patient, any patient, but especially one who was dying? Why didn't she check her file? All Nancy did was ask a question. A few weeks ago that question would have been welcomed, too.

For the rest of the evening, a war raged inside Meg. Every time she walked by room 211, she wanted to stop, go in, apologize, and explain. But another force, a more powerful, bitter one, kept her from carrying through on what she knew would have been the right thing to do. When her shift ended, she still hadn't gone back to room 211.

"Night," Heather said, yawning as the two walked out into the cold night air. Then, as almost an afterthought, she said, "Oh, yeah. I don't know why, but you know Nancy in 211?"

Meg looked back, not speaking. She awkwardly stood, the wind blowing her hair and biting at her cheeks, as if waiting for a shoe to drop. And one did!

"She told me to tell you she was sorry. She didn't tell me for what, just said she needed to apologize. You know why?"

Nodding, Meg walked away leaving Heather to wonder about the reasons behind the apology. A few moments later Meg eased herself into the Mustang, started the car, snapped the seat belt, and drove off.

25

Cheryl Bednarz was vastly different from what Meg had expected. This third-generation Texan, who had moved to the Midwest to attend law school and stayed to ply her trade in public service, was bubbly and energetic and had all appearances of being a determined winner! Maybe having a young woman working on the case was a good thing. Perhaps Webb Jones needed a partner like this to take on the powerful Thomas family.

Though petite, Cheryl possessed an athletic build and strength that made her seem much larger. She also possessed the brightest blue eyes Meg had ever seen. The assistant district attorney's thick black hair swirled around her head in a style that seemed more appropriate to a beauty queen than an attorney, and her skin still hung onto a tan that should have faded months before. Beneath her long, black coat, she was dressed in a gray wool suit that fit as if it had been tailored especially for her and a silk blouse that exactly matched her eyes. Her square jaw presented a determined look, her smile came easily, her teeth were perfect, her handshake firm, her nails long, and her voice still resonated with a twang that gave away her roots.

During the meal both women ate salads while occasionally throwing out small talk. Finally, when the waiter brought coffee for Ms. Bednarz and a Coke refill for Meg, the attorney began to advise Meg about the upcoming trial. Her words were direct, honest, to the point, and disturbing.

"Usually, the defense will attempt to do one of two things in situations like this. One of the tactics would be to attempt to find some way to prove that one of the two vehicles involved might have been faulty. If this fails, they'll often resort to a tactic that represents the dirtier side of my profession." Pausing to take a short sip of coffee, Cheryl continued. "It's too bad that you don't like coffee, this stuff is great! Now, where was I? Oh, yes!"

That sparkling life leaping from Cheryl's eyes almost mesmerized Meg. The woman had the enthusiasm of a new puppy, but it also appeared, that unlike a puppy, the attorney's energy was organized and directed.

"Jasper Tidwell is representing the Thomas kid," Cheryl continued. "Jasper has a great record for putting the victim on trial. One way or another he will attempt to convince the judge and the jury that your husband was at fault and that his client is not only innocent but is a full-blown saint. I've seen him do it before. He actually got one jury to buy that a prostitute with a ten-year string of convictions worked the streets only to support her family, not her cocaine habit. He paraded a host of witnesses through the courtroom that practically canonized the woman. You would have thought that we were trying Mother Teresa. I'm betting he'll do the same thing here."

"But, Cheryl," Meg interjected, "Steve was so perfect, you know the all-American guy. How can a lawyer possibly do anything that would imply that he was at fault and that little, rich, spoiled heathen who killed him is anything but guilty?"

"I don't know, and I won't know until we get to court what he will do. But he *will* try something like that. He always does. But I'll be ready."

"You're trying the case?" Meg's voice showed her surprise, almost shock. She immediately liked her, but Cheryl was just the assistant district attorney and she looked so young! Surely it would be Webb Jones who would be in charge when the trial got under way.

"Yes, Mr. Jones gave it to me," Cheryl explained confidently. "I hope you don't have a problem with that."

"But, I mean . . ." Meg found that words were failing her.

"You thought," Cheryl began, "that Webb would do it himself. Well, off the record, he's scared of the judge's family. He's afraid that he might lose this one, or more important, lose a political connection. So, I got it. More than that, I wanted it! I'm glad that Webb's acting like a coward." Letting her words sink in for a minute, Cheryl continued. "In all honesty, in certain ways I'm better than he is. Yes, he has the soap actor's looks, perfect hair, and that deep voice, but he's not as smart as folks think. It is his administrative assistant who often thinks for him. Besides, I know how you feel. He can't and he never will. He just doesn't grasp how important this case is. You see, my daddy was killed by a drunk driver, and that son of a dog, as my grandmother used to say, didn't serve a day. So, for a lot of reasons, I want this kid in the worst way."

Those last words, said with a piercing anger, quickly convinced Meg she had the right woman in her corner. The two were united by a common goal of revenge. Now, as she looked across the table, it was like a bright light had been turned on. United by a loved one's deaths gave them a very special bond. Not one built on friendship or common ground, but one constructed on a need to see vengeance carried all the way through. With that thought, a warm surge filled Meg's heart.

After finishing the last of her coffee, Cheryl set her cup down and, while staring intently into it, spoke. "Meg, do you know how many people are killed by drunks each and every year?"

Watching as the attorney picked up a package of crackers from the center of the table with her left hand and then placed it deep in the palm of her right hand, Meg just shook her head.

"Last year," Cheryl began," alcohol mixed with driving killed over 12,000 men, women, and children."

Meg watched as Cheryl's fist closed, crushing the crackers into tiny little crumbs. Dropping the now-wasted package into her empty salad bowl, she continued. "You'd think that we'd do something wouldn't you? I mean, can you imagine what the government and the FAA would do if 12,000 people were killed in plane crashes each year? The whole air industry would be shut down. But you see, plane crashes are spectacular events that kill a hundred or more at a time. The news media flocks to the scene with cameras and reporters, and so we see these images of dolls without little girls and luggage without anyone to claim played out on every station on our sets. And we are horrified. We are so shaken we demand better inspections for planes and pilots.

"But when your husband or my father died, ABC didn't set up a remote from the crash site. Nor did CNN interview the victim's relatives or those that were responsible. As a matter of fact, no one did much of a story at all. Even the local paper pretty much buried it. No one demanded legislation, they only offered consolations. And except for a few organizations like MADD, everyone turned the page."

Cheryl let her gaze drift up to the ceiling and then, in a much quieter tone, revealed some of her own pain. "My father was just a simple farmer. Mom died when I was born and for seventeen years Dad took care of me. I never knew why, but he always called me Bunny; he never used my real name.

"One day a worthless, good-for-nothing, filthy rich businessman had spent too much time at a bar celebrating a big strike in the oil field, crossed the center line, and hit my daddy head-on. As luck would have it, I had just gotten out of school and was on the road a couple minutes behind him. When I got there, he was still alive."

Cheryl paused for a moment, using her napkin to wipe a few stray tears from her eyes, then picked up where she had left off.

"His truck was so bent up they couldn't even get him out, but he was still alive. I walked up to him. As I leaned over, he took my hand and said 'I'll love you forever, Bunny.' Then he died. Forever didn't last too long. And the drunk didn't even get bruised." Cheryl pointed toward another section of the restaurant.

"Look over there." Meg turned and glanced at a small bar were five or six businessmen and two women appeared to have few cares and lots of time. As she took in the scene, Cheryl continued in a bitter tone. "Those folks right there are past this state's limit for intoxication, I'd bet on it. But if they get in a car and get caught driving home, odds are four-to-one they won't ever pay a fine or spend any time in jail. Meg, I want to change that!"

While Meg continued to gaze at the people gathered around the bar, Cheryl made a promise. "So, for me, this case is about more than your husband. It is about my father, too. And I'll admit it is more than about justice. It is about revenge. I hope that doesn't bother you."

Meg turned her eyes back to the other woman. Nodding her head, she smiled. "No, I like it."

Cheryl smiled. "This drive and bitterness, this focus on getting those responsible for stupid and unlawful behavior, well,
it probably cost me my marriage. My husband just hadn't been
able to understand the hate that filled me. He couldn't adjust
to coming in second place to law school and then the district
attorney's office. Losing Greg hurt. But that doesn't matter
now, because I finally have the case for which I have waited for
years, and I know a woman who shares my need for revenge.
I'm just sorry it had to be your husband. But just remember, I
do understand."

"I know that now," Meg assured her.

Yes, this was the perfect woman for the job. She had the
passion and she was fearless. Maybe together they could turn
the Thomas family upside-down and bring a lifetime of pain
into their home. And they could celebrate together after they'd
won!

"Meg," Cheryl's voice brought her attention back from
thoughts of revenge to the moment. "You mentioned on the
phone the other day that you were expecting a baby."

Meg nodded.

"Have you thought about what you're going to do?"

At first, the question made little sense to Meg. What was
there to do? You carry it for nine months and then take care of
it for twenty years. She had never really considered any other
option. What else could she do? What other choice did she
have?

After waiting an appropriate amount of time for an answer,
Cheryl continued. "I guess what I'm really trying to say is that
a lot of people in your shoes consider having an abortion. And
since you're obviously not very far along, I thought that maybe
you were thinking along these lines."

Abortion—a word that Meg, the nurse, was certainly familiar

with. But Meg, the woman, had never spent much time thinking about such a thing. But why not? This might well be the
best piece of advice she'd had been given in her life. She didn't
have to have this baby. She didn't have to look at a child and be
reminded of Steve and all she'd lost.

26

As she drove home, Meg wondered again why she hadn't thought of this before. Had her mind been in that much of a fog? Or perhaps something remained from the old Meg causing her to still cling to a morality system that died when Steve did? Whatever the reason she had not considered her real choices in the past couple of weeks, but she would consider them now. After all, as a woman she did have choices.

As soon she returned to her apartment, Meg leafed through several of her own medical books and then hit the Internet. Over the next two hours as she dug up everything she could on abortions, she was lost in study. While she uncovered no new information, everything she had learned in nursing school still held true. Just seeing the words, reading a description of the procedure, and realizing that thousands of women—respected women—turned to this option every day, reassured her this was a path she could use. A few minutes later, when she lost her supper to morning sickness now visiting her at night for the first time, she was much closer to making her final choice.

Putting a damp washcloth over her head, she lay back on the couch and tried to focus. This decision required logic. Emotions needed to be left on the doorstep; they couldn't enter in. And logic told her that without Steve this baby would be nothing more than a haunting reminder of the past. She didn't want to have to look at the baby's face and see Steve's eyes. When that happened she'd feel a flood of painful memories that would rock her to the depths of her heart. It would be far easier to pretend that the past didn't exist and that the future was to be spent alone than to have a piece of her husband reminding her of how he looked on that gurney the night he died. By getting rid of the baby, she could more easily accomplish this. This was the direction she needed to go. And if folks didn't understand, so be it.

As the world stopped turning and she regained her equilibrium, she pulled herself off the couch, turned off the living room light, and headed toward bed. As she changed into her pajamas and brushed her teeth, she knew that for the first time in the weeks since Steve died, she would sleep well. With Cheryl's firm resolve, she was sure her case was in good hands, even better hands than those of Webb Jones. And with an option to rid herself of this now unwanted pregnancy, she realized she'd soon be feeling strong again. She was back on track, maybe not the same track she had spent her life traveling on, but a track that could get her things she needed and take her away from the things she had to forget.

The phone's ring stopped her just before she turned out the light beside her bed. Walking back to the living room, she wondered who would be calling her on her landline. A glance at the receiver told her it was a hospital exchange. But this wasn't one she was familiar with. She almost let it go, but, as she was in a good mood and seemed to have the world by the tail, she decided to gamble this would be someone she wanted to talk to. She picked up on the third ring.

"Hello." For the first time in weeks, Meg's voice had an almost upbeat ring to it.

"Hi, this is Nancy."

"Who?" Meg inquired flipping through a mental catalogue of the people she knew at Springfield Community.

"Nancy Leslie," the woman explained, "the nosy patient in room 211."

Of course, the woman she'd been so rude and insensitive toward earlier in the day. Why would she be calling her at home? A little embarrassed, Meg blushed and awkwardly mumbled, "Hi."

"I suppose," Nancy continued, "that you're surprised to hear from me, but I felt I owed you something. After all, I was pretty thoughtless. Nurse Rodgers told me what you'd been through, and well, I really put my foot in it, didn't I? I hope that you can forgive me."

"Don't worry about it," Meg assured her. "I just had a bad day."

"You know, folks like me . . ." Nancy's voice halted for a few seconds, and then in a rather unsure manner she picked up her thoughts. "I guess what I mean is that I often take it for granted that no one has any problems but me. Joe—he's my husband—was in this evening, and I told him about what I'd done and the tough situation that you were in. After we talked I realized I'm much luckier that you."

"What way is that?" Meg's asked. "I mean you're . . ." She stopped herself before going any further.

"You can say it," Nancy began. "I've gotten use to hearing it. I'm dying. But sometimes I think that my dying is tougher on Joe than me. I mean, I don't want to die, but at least I'm a lot closer to finding out why it had to happen than Joe is. Do you know what I mean?"

As she considered Nancy's words the old Meg resurfaced to such a degree she almost said a prayer. While the prayer never came out, a bit of compassion did bubble to the top."

"Nancy, I think I follow you," Meg softly replied, "but what you're going through is—well—it's horrible. You're too young and according to Heather, you are too special to die." She almost choked on the last word and after it had come out she regretted even saying it.

"The world's not perfect," Nancy replied, "but I've been blessed more than some who live a hundred years."

"Isn't there something someone can do? They've got incredible programs at MD Anderson Cancer Center in Houston. Maybe someone down there has a new treatment that could help you."

"I've been there," Nancy assured her. "And a lot of other places, too. I think I'm a decade too soon."

Meg heard the words but refused to accept what Nancy was saying. It was just too painful. Rather than respond directly to the question, she threw out a trite statement that carried little weight and one she'd heard a half dozen times in the days after Steve died. "It has got to be tough on you."

"Yeah, maybe it was for a while. I mean, I want to live as much as the next person, but after a lot of soul searching, I finally decided that it was better me than someone I love."

"What?" Meg asked.

Nancy didn't hesitate with her reply. "God's given me a ticket to a better place and I'd be a fool to question His timing. So I just say why not me? From what Heather told me about your husband, I think he'd rather it have been him than you."

The woman was probably correct. Steve always put her first. But this wasn't about a choice; it was about a murder. Steve didn't get cancer, he'd been murdered. If that was God's will, then didn't that make God an accessory to that murder?

"Nancy," Meg asked, as an image of Jim Thomas once more entered her head, "don't you feel like God cheated you?" Meg's voice hid none of her own bitterness. She was angry about what had happened to Steve. And she was suddenly angry about what was happening to Nancy. In fact, in a strange sort of way, she was beginning to identify with Nancy. They'd both been treated unfairly, and therefore, they both had every right to ask that the world cater to them. Yet, why didn't this woman demand that? Meg figured if she pressed all the right buttons, Nancy would reveal these emotions and if Nancy would just admit her anger it would be easier for Meg to quit feeling sorry for her. And Meg didn't really want to feel sorry for anyone other than herself. But right now she couldn't help but feel sorry for Nancy.

"No," the woman answered, "cancer isn't something that God created." Her voice was firm and resolute as she continued. "You see, the earth He created was perfect. It was people who messed it up. I really believe that God feels just as cheated as I do. But He hasn't forgotten me; He really wants to comfort me. It took me a while to figure that out."

"I just can't buy it." Meg's answer revealed her pain. "In fact, I think anyone who says that God cares about us is pretty stupid. I don't even know if there really is a God. But I do believe the devil is the kid who was driving that car that killed Steve."

"I think I understand," came the calm response. "I was pretty angry when the cancer came back the third time. I thought I had it licked after the first two battles. It just didn't seem fair. Then I got to thinking about my family and friends. I sure wouldn't want them to have to deal with this. So I decided I'd gladly take it if that meant they wouldn't get cancer. That probably doesn't make any sense to you right now."

"No," Meg replied, "I'd rather anyone else in the world, even one of my friends, would be going through this rather than me. I would do anything and sacrifice anyone to get Steve back."

Nancy answered rapidly. "But given time . . ."

"No, you don't understand." Meg's tone was much like that of a mother talking down to a child. "In my case, I would rather have died than lose Steve. It would have been easier. Especially the way I lost him." Without realizing it, Meg had suddenly been drawn into revealing her true feelings—feelings she hadn't even voiced until this moment and feelings she didn't want to voice. Now that the door was open, there didn't seem to be a way to close it. Why had she gotten caught up in this conversation? Why had she answered the phone? It was just too painful. Never had the truth hurt so much.

With Meg struggling not to cry, Nancy offered another observation. "Joe and I always wanted kids, but my first surgery prevented that. If we had had a child, then Joe wouldn't be so all alone when I die. I probably shouldn't, but I have to admit that I know that you're pregnant. I also know that your child is something you can live for. Your child will be the product of the love you had for your husband and he had for you."

"I don't want the child," Meg shot back. "I'm sorry to say that, after finding out that you couldn't have any of your own, but the only thing I really want is to make sure that Steve's killer is punished. One way or the other, I will do that."

"Meg, Heather told me that you and your husband had always been very dedicated Christians. I know you worked with kids in church. Surely the mere fact that Steve had accepted Christ and is in heaven . . ."

Meg didn't have any patience for this. She didn't want to hear one more thing about God. She snapped back. "There isn't a God, at least not in my world. The con job that I got my whole life was that if I were good then I'd be blessed. Well, you see what that kind of thinking got me. My life is in my hands. The things I want, I'll get. The things that I don't want, I'll get rid of."

Before Meg could conclude, Nancy cut back in, "Does that mean your baby?" Her voice was almost a whisper.

"Yes," the answer was firm.

"Have you talked to anyone about this?" Nancy's tone was now somewhat frantic. "I mean, maybe you could speak with your preacher or a family counselor or someone. You really need to be sure that this is the right decision. You can't just do it and then change your mind."

"I don't need to talk to anyone else," Meg retorted. "It's my decision, mine alone. I don't need anyone else to tell me how I feel. I know how I feel!"

For several long seconds the line was deathly quiet. Finally, Nancy spoke.

"I know that I'm once again being nosy. I know that I have no right to even ask this, but I have to. What would your husband think of your decision?"

Why did she have to call at all? Why did Nancy have to ask that question? This question was one that Meg hadn't considered. And she didn't want to consider it now because she knew what Steve would want. He would want her to keep the baby. He'd so wanted to have a little girl to spoil. And then later, he wanted a boy to take fishing and to ballgames. He'd always thought that kids were special and he loved their innocent views of life. He'd gone to the park just to watch them play. He'd even spent hours teaching the neighbors' kids how to throw a baseball and shoot a basketball. He had forced her to go to toy stores when they went shopping and pointed out which toys their kids were going to have. Yes, she had to admit, she had once felt the same way, but now she couldn't let herself feel anything. The past was the past. Everything had changed. She had to stand up for herself. She had to be strong. If she wasn't, she might change her mind.

"Well, he would . . ." Suddenly, the assurance, so evident in Meg's voice just minutes before, was gone. Though she wanted to lie, she couldn't. Finally she just said, "Steve would have understood."

She knew her answer hadn't convinced Nancy, but she hoped the other woman wouldn't pursue this angle any further.

"It sounds like your husband was a very special person." Nancy's statement was phrased more like a question.

"He was the most special person on earth." Meg's response brought back a flood of memories as to just why Steve had been so incredible. She remembered the cards he had sent, the clothes he had surprised her with, the picnics in the middle of the living room, and the way he had held her in the middle of the night. Those memories brought back an overwhelming need to see him again, to hold him in her arms. Still, she knew that those times were gone forever. Glancing down at her wedding ring—the one that she kept meaning to take off but never did—she attempted to put together some kind of sentence that would explain to this woman just how wonderful Steve had been. "There just aren't any words," she finally offered, her voice now much softer. "He was thoughtful, loving, and so much more. When he was here, I was so alive. Now"—her voice caught on the words—"now, I'm just not complete."

"Yes." Nancy's voice showed real sympathy. "I know you're not. Steve's life was very precious, wasn't it?"

Without even thinking, Meg responded, "Yes."

"You don't have to answer this," Nancy began. "But don't you think that his baby's life might be just as precious to someone, someday? Maybe even you? That child can't take your husband's place, no one can. But doesn't the fact that it has a part of your husband in his or her genes make it special enough that you would fight for it? Maybe even die for it?

"Listen," Nancy continued, "I have no business bothering you again. And believe me when I say that I didn't mean to get into all of this. So I probably owe you another apology for overstepping my bounds again, and you're right, whatever you do is your decision; still, I want you to know that I'll be praying for you." She paused for a moment before concluding, "If you get a chance come by and see me tomorrow. I promise, no lectures."

"If I have time," Meg murmured.

"Good-bye, Meg."

"Bye." A click and a dial tone followed.

The call had no more than concluded when tears began to stream down Meg's face. She didn't want anybody praying for her. She just wanted to do things her way and be left alone. Suddenly a feeling centered deep within her stomach signaled the baby was haunting her again. That feeling brought the true reality of the situation into sharp focus. She was living in a nightmare and the best way to end it was to at least rid herself of the cause of her sickness.

27

So, you can do it next Monday?" There was a firm resolve in Meg's tone. "Good, I'll come in around ten o'clock. Thanks."

Meg slipped the phone back into her pocket and turned around. She was shocked to see Heather behind her. When had she come in and what had she overheard?

"Who was that, Meg?" Heather asked.

Why did everyone in the world want to know her business? Her mother, Nancy, and Heather all seemed ready to gang up on her. Well, that wasn't right. They were concerned and that was understandable, but they couldn't live her life for her and they had no right to either.

Lowering her chin and shooting a hostile glance across the room was all it took for Heather to avert her gaze and mumble, "Can you cover the station? I think I'll go down and check in on Mrs. Burlson."

Meg nodded. Heather was only twenty steps down the hall when a patient's voice over the intercom claimed Meg's attention.

"I need some help, please."

Meg immediately recognized Nancy's voice. Great. Just when she got rid of one of the tormentors, another showed up. She'd somehow managed to avoid Nancy for five days and she didn't want or need to have to deal with her now, but it appeared Lady Luck had run out. Stalling for over a minute, hoping all the while that Heather would return, Meg finally leaned over the microphone, pushed button number 211 and said, "I'll be right there."

Forty steps to the next lecture—oh, how she dreaded it. Why couldn't she just get rid of the baby and put the guilt trips behind her. She paused at the door, took a deep breath in order to shore up her resolve, and marched in. She was once again greeted by gospel music. While the music hadn't changed, the woman playing it had changed a great deal since the one other time Meg had seen her.

Although she had done a thorough job of making herself up, Nancy looked nearly a decade older than she had just a week ago. Her eyes, the same ones that had so brightly sparkled, now were dull and watery. Even though she smiled when Meg walked in, the smile was weak. It was as if it took all her strength just to lift the corners of her mouth for a few seconds.

"I'm sorry to have to bother you," Nancy said sincerely.

"That's why I'm here," a suddenly concerned Meg answered.

"I thought that I could get by without any pain meds, but the last couple of days," she paused and took a labored breath, "I mean, it has been getting to me." She stopped talking, probably not because she was finished saying what was on her mind, but likely due to the fact she was too tired to go on.

"I'll get you something," Meg gently whispered. "Don't worry now, I won't be long."

Leaving the room, Meg hurriedly walked back to her station, pulled the Kardex, found Nancy's name, and noted the kind of medication that had been prescribed. Getting the pill, she checked the time on the card, and started to leave the desk.

The desk phone caught her just as she rounded the station's counter. She retraced her steps and answered.

"Nurse Richards, here."

"Meg," the operator replied, "I have an outside line call for you on four."

"Okay." Putting the pill into a paper cup and placing both on the counter, Meg punched line four.

"Hello."

"Meg, this is Cheryl Bednarz in the district attorney's office. We have a trial date. You got something to write with?"

Reaching into her pocket for her pen, Meg grabbed a notepad from the other side of the counter. "Go ahead."

"Five weeks from today," Cheryl sounded like a horse tugging at the reins. "We will be ready for that day, too. Circle April 26. It'd be good for our case if you show up for all the sessions."

"I'll definitely arrange to be there," Meg assured the assistant district attorney.

"I've got a few more things that I want to share with you about the case," Cheryl continued. "In spite of our losses and our pain, I really did have a wonderful time getting to know you the other night. Have you got an evening free so that we could have supper again?"

"Yeah, just a minute," Meg answered. "Let me check the schedule." She pulled out her iPhone, called up the calendar, and looked at her week. "How about Sunday?"

"Okay with me. I'll pick you up around six."

"I'll be ready," Meg answered while loading the trial date onto her phone's calendar.

As she hung up a special rush covered her. She suddenly felt very sure that in a little more than five weeks she would have some personal satisfaction. Then maybe she could get on with her life.

"Who are the meds for?" Heather asked, pointing to the small paper cup in Meg's hand.

"Nancy in 211."

"You want me to take it back to her?"

Meg almost handed the cup to Heather, but then, changing her mind, shook her head and walked down the hall. This was a job she really needed to complete.

"I'm sorry it took so long," she announced apologetically as she entered the room. "I had a call."

Nancy reached out, took the pill cup from Meg's hand and placed it in front of her on the bed table. Simply by routine, Meg got a glass, filled it with water from the pitcher on the nightstand, and handed it to the woman.

"Would you take it?" Nancy asked.

"Take what?" came Meg's puzzled reply.

"The pill."

"Sure, I guess," a now confused Meg shrugged. "Why not?"

"I've never taken them in the past." Nancy explained. "I wanted to feel every bit of life I had left. I didn't want to miss any of it, not even if it hurt. I'm just afraid that if I start this, then I'll not really ever experience . . . well, you know, clear thoughts and feelings. I'm probably not making any sense, am I?"

As she watched Nancy stare intently at the pill, Meg could see not only pain but also fear written on the woman's face. A week ago, she hadn't looked sick even to a nurse's trained eye, but now anyone could guess that there was something terribly wrong. She had no color. Her skin appeared drawn. But more than anything else, there was a look in her eyes—a frightened, tortured look.

"Could you change the song for me?"

Nancy's voice brought Meg to immediate action. As she shuffled through the play list menu she asked, "What do you want?"

"Why not Barbara Mandrell's 'He Set My Life to Music'? I used to listen to that on a cassette tape back when I was a teenager. Things have sure changed a lot since that time. Back then, it was a big deal to hang out at a music store where they had CDs, tapes, and even albums. Those places are all gone now." She paused, took a deep breath, and sadly added, "Yeah, a lot of things have changed."

Meg scanned the album list on the menu and finally discovered the number Nancy had requested. After selecting it, she pushed play, and then as the music began, she pulled up a chair and took a seat beside the bed.

"It's nice," Meg said referring to first song. When Nancy didn't respond, she continued. "My husband liked Barbara Mandrell, but I've never heard this one."

Raising her head on the pillow in such a way that their eyes met, Nancy smiled and said, "She won a Grammy for this album. The songs, especially the words, meant a lot to me when I was a teen. It was kind of like my journey of faith, I guess. This was about a year after a friend of mine took me to church for the very first time. You see my family never went. Did yours?"

"Every Sunday," Meg assured her, "and often a couple of more times a week. It was my second home."

"I missed that part of my youth," Nancy sadly replied.

"There were some good times," Meg admitted. "I especially enjoyed our youth group. There was a mission trip to a slum. . . . I'm sorry, no reason to talk about it now. In fact, there is no reason to look back."

Meg didn't want to look back to anything that reminded her of the good feelings of the life she'd once led or the faith she'd once embraced. When she did, the old Meg gained control. That Meg forgave easily and loved even more easily. That Meg wasn't welcome, at least not yet.

"Your friend, Heather," Nancy said. "She was right. You really are nice. You aren't cold at all. I wish I could have known you before."

Meg didn't react because she didn't really know how to respond. She just let the remark drift away, much like a leaf falls from a tree to the ground. After a few minutes of listening quietly to the music, she glanced back at Nancy. "You'd better take that pill so I can get back to work."

"No, I've changed my mind," Nancy announced, her eyes now showing signs of a sparkle. "I don't think I need it yet. I was scared for a few minutes. You know, I kind of doubted my faith. I felt really alone. When that happens, well . . . you just feel the pain. I guess I was just trying to handle it all by myself. Now I know that I'm not alone. You made me realize that. Just having a friend beside me helped ease my pain and restored my thankfulness for having another day. And I don't want to sleep through it, I want to experience it!"

Meg got up from the chair, reached over, and picked up the pill. As she held it in her hands, her eyes flashing from the patient to the pill, she asked, "Are you sure?"

"Yeah."

"Well, if you change your mind, just give us a call."

"Meg," Nancy gently breathed, as the nurse left the room. Catching the door, Meg responded, "Yes?"

"Thanks."

Meg just nodded her head.

"How is she?" Heather inquired when Meg got back to the station.

"Not good. I've seen that look before. She doesn't have much time. But she decided she didn't need the pill after all."

Meg put the pill back and changed her notation on the chart.

"I wouldn't let myself go through that kind of pain." Heather's words were blunt and matter-of-fact. Still, there was a note of admiration in them. "I'd demand my pill every time I got a chance."

"She wants to experience life, even if it's painful," Meg explained. The comparison between Nancy's situation and her own suddenly hit Meg full force. She didn't want to feel anything, but Nancy did. Pain was a part of life and women with cancer knew that. So why did Meg want to run from it? Why did she want to erase all memories of Steve and everything else she had lost from her mind?

"Am I selling out?" Meg whispered.

"Did you say something?" Heather asked.

"Not really," Meg replied, "just thinking out loud."

Speaking her thoughts was dangerous. She had to watch that. She couldn't afford to even look into her heart right now, much less expose it to anyone else. She couldn't show weakness

"I haven't looked at the case in detail. What kind of cancer does she have?"

Heather looked up from a file and asked, "What?"

"Nancy," Meg inquired. "What kind of cancer does she have and why aren't they treating it?"

"Beyond treatment. Started out as breast cancer. As I understand, she beat it a couple of times, but now it is pretty much everywhere."

Meg nodded. "But why is she here? Why not in hospice?"

"Something about the insurance. They cover us but not hospice care. And, as her husband has to keep working to keep the insurance, she can't stay at home. She has no other family. She's kind of alone. Really sad!"

Meg nodded. It was more than sad—a lot more—it was tragic. Yet that is the way life is. Tragedy was everywhere and you just had to deal with it. Like she was. And while Nancy didn't have anyone to lash out at, anyone to punish for what happened to her, Meg did. And when she was given the chance to extract a measure of personal justice, surely she would feel good again.

28

WHEN SHE LEFT THE HOSPITAL, IT WAS MID-AFTERNOON. THE WARM SUN
had melted what little snow that was left. April seemed to be
coming in like a lamb. Winter was giving up. Its cold winds
had now been chased away by the promise of new life. There
were even hints of green in the grass and a few buds on the
trees. If Steve had been here, it would have been a perfect day.

As she drove home, she passed Corely's flower shop. Steve
had often stopped there just to buy her a single yellow rose.
She had no idea how many yellow roses he had brought her
over the years, and all of them for no reason at all, that is,
except to tell her he loved her. It had just been one of the
many little ways he had always showed his devotion. Quickly
making a sharp right on Franklin Street, she drove around the
block and parked in front of the shop. Unbuckling her seat
belt, she opened the car door of her Mustang and strolled into
the quaint, little store.

The fresh scent of carnations greeted her as she strolled
through the door, and after she closed the door, a hundred
different arrangements filled her eyes with all the beauty of a
spring day in the country. Smiling, she noticed a small African
violet, heartily growing in a vase decorated with a Norman

Rockwell painting of two lovers sitting on a park bench. The plant brought back memories of her grandmother. For the first time in years, she thought about the rows of violets sitting in the old woman's spare bedroom. She had died before Meg had even started school, and at this moment, she couldn't even remember what her grandma looked like, but the violets in that bedroom seemed as clear as if she were standing in front of them now.

As her gaze wandered from the plant to the vase, she couldn't help but remember the many times she and Steve sat on a bench just outside the university library enjoying the sun, watching other students stroll across campus, and speaking of dreams of a wonderful future. Just like Rockwell's painting, those times had been simple, well defined, and idyllic. The memories of those days caused an unexpected warm feeling to surge through Meg's heart.

"May I help you?" a middle-aged woman's voice startled Meg back to reality.

Turning, Meg nodded and answered, "Yes. I need to buy a single yellow rose."

"That shouldn't be any problem," the woman replied. "Would you like it in a vase or in some type of arrangement?"

"No, I don't need an arrangement," Meg answered, shaking her head. "And I don't need a vase. I just want a rose."

"It will be just a moment." The clerk exited the showroom through a curtain, leaving Meg once again alone. Turning back to the African violet, she checked the price. $9.95. Too much to pay for something she would kill in a matter of weeks, but the plant was beautiful.

"We've got a special on roses today," the clerk announced as soon as she reappeared. Presenting the white box to Meg, she added, "This one will only cost you $2.75 plus tax. Let me see, the total is $2.93."

Meg dug through her purse, found three one-dollar bills, paid the clerk, picked up the rose, exited the store, and walked back to her car. Laying the rose box on the passenger seat, she backed out of her spot and headed the Mustang in the direction of the city cemetery.

"Well, Steve," she whispered. "It has been a while, but I think it's time I start returning a few gifts to you. This should look nice on your grave. And it is such a beautiful day."

Suddenly her train of thought was interrupted as a car pulled out of a parking lot directly into her path. Jerking her wheel to one side, she slammed on the brakes and managed to miss the other vehicle by inches.

What in the world? Meg thought as she straightened her wheel and passed the now stalled sports car. A stern look on her face, she stared at the other driver. Sheepishly, he returned her stare then shrugged his shoulders and lifted his hands as if to say, "Sorry, I didn't see you." When his right hand became visible just above the dashboard of his car, Meg noticed the man was holding an open can of beer.

A sudden rage burned through Meg. Shaking her fist, she hit the gas and rushed from the scene. First Steve and now her! Forgetting all about the rose and the cemetery, she turned her car around and headed home. By the time she got there she felt very alone, very abused, and had little patience for people of any age, description, or size. She just wanted the world to leave her alone.

After parking her car in its place, she reached over, picked up the box containing the yellow rose, and then, walking by an empty trashcan, pitched the box in with scores of other things that now meant nothing. This act seemed to calm her nerves and as she quickly mounted the steps to her apartment, her temper slowly began to burn out. Digging the keys from her purse, she managed to unlock the apartment door just in time to answer the phone.

"What is it?" she demanded as she picked up her landline on the second ring.

"Hello, is this the Richards's?" a man's voice asked.

"Yes."

"This is Comet Cleaners. We've had some clothes down here and if you don't get them soon we'll have to sell them or give them to the Goodwill or something. They've been here a very long time."

"I've still got my coat on," Meg assured him. "I'll run down right now."

Comet was only five blocks away and the drive took about two minutes. As she drove, she mentally inventoried her closest. She was sure she'd picked up her good coat. Hadn't she worn it last month? Or was that the month before? And almost everything else she owned didn't need to be dry cleaned. Maybe it was the blue, wool suit. She remembered dropping it off in February and perhaps she hadn't picked it up. Pulling up to the shop, she parked her car, got out, and hurried in.

"I'm Meg Richards," she announced to a heavy, balding man behind the counter as she entered the store. "Someone here just called me about some clothes that I had forgotten to pick up."

"Yeah, that was me who called. Let me get 'em." He turned and ambled back to a clothes rack and began to search. As he did, Meg picked up a brochure from a stack on the counter and, for lack of a better way to kill the time, began to study the different services that Comet now offered. Who knew that a cleaners would have a Facebook page? And what did a small town cleaner have to tweet about? As she mulled over those questions, she was vaguely aware of the door opening behind her. Out of the corner of her eye, she noticed a young high school girl come from the back of the shop in order to wait on the new customer.

"Jimbo," the girl said in a dreamy, lighter-than-air voice. "Love your new wheels. When you gonna take me for a ride?" The way the girl emphasized that last part of the sentence made Meg wonder just what the word "ride" meant.

"Some day, baby," came the young man's response.

That voice! Meg knew that voice! Looking into a counter mirror, her eyes flashed past her own reflection and to the image of the high school student. Even though she'd only seen him twice in person, she immediately recognized the other reflection as that of Jim Thomas. This was the closest she'd ever been to the kid who killed her husband since that night she'd left the ER after seeing her husband's mangled and burned body.

"You here for something special?" the girl asked.

"My old man's cleaning. Hope you know where it is because I'm in a hurry. So get moving!"

Taking the order in stride, the girl quickly disappeared through the door to the back of the shop.

Left alone in the room with Jim Thomas, Meg's knees grew immediately weak, her stomach began to churn, and boiling blood rushed through her veins. In the quiet room, she was fully aware of the loud pounding coming from her chest. Surely, he must hear it, too. But he said nothing, apparently unaware of her wildly beating heart, much less her presence. Too scared to look at him, she turned her eyes back to the brochure, pretending to study it.

With a whoosh, the door to the back once again opened and the bald man reappeared, this time carrying a blue, pinstriped suit covered by a clear plastic bag embossed with Comet's logo.

"Here we go," he said. "One suit. That'll be $3.75."

As Meg once again looked up, Thomas's eyes met hers in the mirror. He obviously didn't know who she was. Still, he did stare at her—an intent, unembarrassed stare. It only took her a few seconds to realize he was actually sizing her up! Feeling uncomfortable under his gaze, Meg glanced back down, fumbled with the latch on her purse, and finally pulled out a ten-dollar bill. Handing it to the clerk, she grabbed the suit off the counter.

"Just a second and I'll have your change," the man said. Ambling slowly to the cash register, he greeted the boy in the letter jacket. "Tell you what, Jim. That basket you made the other night to win the game against Centerville, I never saw anything like it."

"Well, somebody had to do it, Mr. Weaver," the boy answered cockily.

"Yeah, but nobody could but you!"

A nervous Meg watched the man lethargically open the cash register and deposit the money. Then, before he could get her change, the phone rang.

"Comet Cleaners?" The owner announced. The shop's owner waited for a moment before explaining, "That's a big order. It might take a couple of days to clean eighty band uniforms."

As the bald man and the potential customer quibbled on time and price, Thomas continued to leer at Meg, and for lack of anything better to do, she continued to study the brochure she had picked up a few minutes before. Finally, when the call ended, the bald man slowly counted out the money and walked back to where Meg anxiously stood.

"Six and a quarter," he explained, handing her the change. "And we appreciate it."

"Just a minute, Jim," the man stated, turning to his other customer. "I'll see what's taking Candy so long." The man disappeared into the back room, leaving Meg alone with the boy.

Picking up the suit, Meg tried to move quickly past Thomas and out the door. But in haste to exit, the now panicky Meg, tripped over a cardboard display and fell against the boy's arm. Pushing herself off, she dropped her cleaning on the floor. As she picked it up, the boy laughed, "What's the rush, sweetheart?" Noting the scrubs and her hospital ID he added, "You in a hurry to give somebody mouth-to-mouth?"

Straightening herself, Meg ignored the kid's smart remarks, took a deep breath, and walked toward the exit. Grabbing the handle, she started to open it but stopped when she saw his reflection in the glass. He was staring at her legs, a grin spread from ear to ear, so he obviously liked what he saw. Now she felt like little more than a piece of meat.

Turning back to face his grinning face she asked, "You don't know who I am, do you?"

"No, but I'd sure like to!" came the boy's cool retort. "That is, if you're game? I've always thought older woman were hot, and they like me, too."

A rage deeper than the one she had experienced the night she had spied on him from her car bubbled up in her gut. If she had had a gun, Meg knew that she would have shot him. He was even worse than she imagined. He was coarse, crude, and disgusting. What was most disturbing was that no one else seemed to notice these traits, or if they did, they overlooked them. Certainly, the hero-worshiping clerk or the gum-chewing bimbo who waited on him didn't see Jim Thomas for what he really was. But Meg did.

Her eyes glaring, her jaw set, she stood up to her full five feet two inches and with a voice so strong that it even surprised her, she replied. "My name is Meg Richards. My husband, Steve, was the man you killed in that car wreck a few weeks ago. Are you sure you want to know me?"

The boy's cocky smile quickly evaporated. Seconds later the color drained from his face and his jaw had grown slack. Meg allowed the introduction to hover in the air for only seconds before adding, "You take a good look at me. You remember what I look like. Because I'm going to get on a witness stand in a courtroom in a little more than a month and I'm going to put you away. But that's not all."

Meg formed her free hand into a fist and added, "When they let you out of jail I'm going to be at the gate waiting. Because when the state's satisfied that it got its due, I'm going to begin to exact mine. I'm going to be your shadow. You're going to see me on every corner and in your every dream. I'm going to haunt you for as long as you live. And then when you die, I'm going to meet you in hell!"

Meg almost couldn't believe what she had just said. More than that, she couldn't believe how good it felt to say it. She lingered a moment, a vicious smile now etched on her face, a frightening wrath burning in her eyes, watching as the boy seemed to melt in front of her. His lips now pale and just barely open, visibly trembled, and his hands alternately reached in and out of his letter jacket's pockets. He was almost too shocked to breathe and probably too stiff to walk.

Satisfied she had made her point, Meg turned, flung the door open, and hopped into her car. Just before she pulled off, she stared back at the shop and caught Thomas in her line of sight one more time. As her eyes met his, he looked down. She had won round one. Round two would be fought in a court-room and she now figured that she could win that one, too.

29

As Jim Thomas's eyes followed the Mustang down the street, Candy reappeared at the counter with Judge Thomas's clothes. Her lighter-than-air voice announced, "It's $45.32."

The youth didn't turn around, much less acknowledge the girl's pronouncement. Frozen in place, his mind was whirling. So *that* was the widow! Who knew she looked like a fashion model? Until a few moments ago, he'd figured her as just another washed-out relic for another age. And who knew she had that kind of fire? She went after him with more energy than any defender he'd ever met on the court or the gridiron.

"What's wrong, Jim?" Candy questioned as she came up beside him and glanced in the direction he was looking.

Turning away from the window, Thomas swallowed hard. "What do you mean?"

"You look like you just saw a ghost."

"No, not a ghost," he murmured, almost under his breath. Then, once again looking back in the direction in which Meg had driven off, he shook his head. "But maybe I just met the devil."

"What?" She all but laughed.

Turning, Jim grabbed the girl's shoulders and looked her straight in the face. "You know that woman that was in here?"

"I don't know her," she answered. "I guess I might have seen her before, but I don't know her name." Candy grinned, "Jim, she's too old for you."

"It's not that," he said dropping his hands and walking back to the counter, "not that at all." Pushing his fists into his letter jacket, he tilted his head to the side. What were the odds of his walking in when she'd had been here? And why had he stupidly said anything?

"You look really weird," Candy noted as she strolled to the other side of the counter. "Was that woman kind of sketchy or something?"

His eyes once more caught hers. "You know the guy that died in the accident?"

"You mean that night after the party by the lake?"

"What other night would I mean?" he barked.

"Hey, I'm not stupid," she said, her eyes drifting down to the countertop, "just wanted to make sure we were on the same page. Sure, I remember the night. How could I forget it? Watching that other guy burn was not something I can erase, if you know what I mean? You were so out of it you don't remember anything about that night. At least that's what you've claimed. Is that true?"

He nodded. "Yeah, it's true. That night's a blank for me. Anyway, that guy we hit, well, that was his wife."

"Hey," she shot back, "you were driving, so I had nothing to do with hitting him." After fully justifying her innocence, she folded her arms across her chest and whispered, "Wow, bet she's hurting."

"More than hurting," he explained, "she's creepy! She wants a piece of me."

Candy looked back to her friend, "You're not scared of her are you? After all, your dad can fix anything."

Jim nodded as he turned back toward the window. His dad could probably keep him out of jail. He'd already bought him a new car. But there was still something about that woman that spooked him. He'd never felt fury like that. Her words had scorched him like a flamethrower. He reached back, grabbed the cleaning, and strolled toward the door. The girl's voice attempted to stop him just as he reached the exit.

"What about the bill?"

Without looking back, Jim answered, "Put it on my dad's account."

Stepping out into the street, he glanced both ways. There were no yellow Mustangs and there was no woman with fire in her eyes. Still, he didn't feel safe. Rushing to his car, he jumped in and drove straight home.

30

MEG HAD AVOIDED HER MOTHER SINCE THE FACE-TO-FACE JUST DAYS AFTER the funeral. Yes, she had talked with her on the phone, but the simple explanation of her wanting to be alone had surprisingly kept Barbara from her door. So she was shocked when that Thursday evening knock on the door came from her mother's hand.

"What are you doing here?" Meg asked in a harsh tone, as she watched her mother push by her.

Unbuttoning her coat and tossing it on the chair, Barbara had a strange look in her eye as she studied her daughter.

"What's this all about, Mom? I thought you understood I wanted to be alone. Thought we agreed that I'd come to your place when I was ready to move on."

"Heather told me," Barbara answered, opening her arms as if she wanted a hug.

Crossing her arms, Meg asked accusingly, "Told you what?"

"About the baby." Her mouth was now framed with a huge smile.

Why didn't Heather keep her mouth closed? Why did she have to blab that information to, of all people, her mother? This was news that should have never seen the light of day.

"This has to be one of the greatest blessings in the world," Barbara continued. "Imagine the comfort it must be to know a part of Steve will still be with you. God is good!"

Shaking her head, Meg answered, "I wouldn't call it a blessing and let's not even go to that part of about God."

"What do you mean? Every child in a blessing."

"Sit down, Mom. I've got something to tell you."

Meg moved past her mother and took a seat in Steve's recliner. Barbara found a spot on the couch. For a few seconds, Meg stared at her mother trying to figure out how to give her the news about the choice she'd made. Try as she could she simply couldn't find the words.

"Mom, I don't want this child."

"I can understand that, but in time, when you have come to deal with what happened, you will treasure this gift. I mean, there is nothing like a child. You and your sister have meant so much to my life. Even more with your father gone."

As Meg watched her mother, sitting there with her hands in her lap, a compassionate look on her face, and obvious hope in her heart, she wanted to run. Yet she couldn't. Monday was just three days away and the woman had to know what was going to happen.

"Mom, I'm terminating this pregnancy."

"What?"

"I'm having an abortion."

"You can't."

"Actually, I can and I will."

"But," Barbara struggled for words, "it isn't right. This goes against everything I've taught you. And what about Steve's parents? They deserve a grandchild from their only son."

"It is not about Steve's parents," Meg gently cut in. "It is about me. It is about what I want and what I can live with. And

I can't live with carrying a baby much less dealing with Steve's child. It would be too painful."

"I-I-I just can't believe that any daughter of mine would consider something like this."

Meg knew exactly what the "this" was and she was ready with a response that would put her mother in her place. Though not embracing the rage she had hurled at Thomas, her tone still displayed a calm but derisive fury, "Oh, I'll bet you that Terri wouldn't think twice before doing it. She's probably had one or two."

Meg grinned as she watched her mother wilt under the spot-on observation.

"All right," Barbara looked down at her lap as she spoke, "you may be right. But the daughter I was talking about was you. You'll regret this decision, Meg. Oh, I just know you will."

"Listen, Mom." Meg's voice showed little patience. "If you're going to start this, then leave now. You're not welcome here or in my life. You support me or you get out."

"I just can't let you do this," Barbara answered mournfully.

"You can't stop me."

"You're right," Barbara admitted. "I can't stop you the way I did when you were sixteen and you wanted to go on that overnight trip with those kids from school. You were fit to be tied that I was such a prude to not let you go that time. But when those kids got arrested and Julie turned up pregnant just a few weeks later, well, you—you—you had to admit that I was right. And I'm just as sure about this."

"Mother," Meg snapped. "Maybe you were right then. But even if you had let me go, I wouldn't have gotten into any trouble." Then, seizing on something her mother had just mentioned, she continued. "You know, Mom. I'll bet you that if Julie had had an abortion rather than having that kid, she'd be alive today."

Julie Evans's life was indeed tragic. She'd been so young, so misguided. At one time, she had been an honor student with a future. Then next, a dropout, working in a cheap diner, caring for a child she hadn't wanted and didn't need. Meg had visited her a few times and had never seen a person so unhappy. Then one night, Julie had been walking to the ratty old apartment she and the baby had called home, and someone, no one knew who, had raped and killed her. She had only been seventeen. Now Julie's tragic ending was the trump card Meg needed to put her mother in her place.

"Meg," Barbara quietly argued. "Julie's situation was very much different from yours. She didn't have anyone who really cared about her. You do. I'll help you. You know that. It can bring us closer together. It will be good for both us and our relationship."

Meg had the upper hand and she realized it. Quickly grabbing her chance, once and for all, to shut her mother up, she cruelly lashed out. "If it hadn't been for people like you—folks from our church—Julie would have had an abortion. She wanted one, but the guilt you and your friends laid at her feet got to her. There's no telling where she would be today if you all had allowed her to do what she wanted."

She took a deep breath then spat out, "Mom, Julie didn't want that kid, she wanted a chance to be a kid. And look, her kid is being raised in the filth of her alcoholic parents' home. What chance has that kid got?"

"We couldn't have predicted that," Barbara quietly said. "We had no idea her baby would end up back with her parents. That was and continues to be sad. But I'm praying for them."

"Well, Mom, you can pray all you want to, but let me assure you, Julie and have I something in common. I don't want this kid either. I want to feel good again. Today I've thrown up six times. I'm sick of that and I'm sick of being pregnant. I don't need a child to remind me for the rest of my life of something I loved and lost. There is nothing, not even this baby, that will bring Steve back. And I'm going in on Monday and having an abortion and that is it. There's nothing that you or anyone else in this world can do."

"Meg," Barbara pleaded. "If you abort this baby, then you're just as bad as that kid you hate so much for killing Steve. As a matter of fact, every newborn baby that you see for the rest of your life will haunt you just like seeing people drink and drive will haunt you. Think about it!"

"Shut up, Mom," Meg stood up as she yelled. "Why can't you just leave me alone?"

"I'm going to pray that you change your mind. I'm going to pray that God wakes you up!"

"Stop it, Mom. Praying is not going to get you any nearer to me. It fact it will drive us further apart. Now, pick up your coat and get out of here. Don't send anyone to see me either. I don't want to hear from the preacher or anyone else. And I don't want you to call me until after this is over. And don't call Steve's parents. They're never to know about this! You understand? If you tell them, it means you and I will never have a chance at being close again!"

Grabbing her unwelcome visitor's coat, Meg tossed it to her mother. Barbara stood and slipped on the gray wool jacket, looking all the while as if she wanted to say something else, but held back. Instead, she swallowed hard and slowly and sadly walked to the door. Just before she opened it, she looked back at her daughter.

"I love you."

"I know you do, Mom. But don't say anything else. The subject is closed. Nothing you can do will change my mind. I'm not doing this to spite you. I love you, too."

Barbara nodded, opened the entry, and walked out. Meg followed her to the threshold, pushed the door shut, and locked it. Moving back across the room, she once again sat in Steve's favorite chair. She'd won. She knew she had. What she'd said made more sense than what her mother had countered with. And yet, the victory seemed so hollow because, like Nancy had, her mother said a few things that rocked her.

Meg was extinguishing a life, but at least this life didn't have a family or loved ones yet. It didn't have a past and now it wouldn't have a future. And even though Meg felt a little bit ashamed that she wasn't willing to give birth, she was sure that she couldn't face the pain of having to deal with someone who would remind her of Steve. Even at this moment, just glancing at his picture caused her to hurt in more ways than she could believe possible. No, she had to keep her mind on the goal. A baby and old memories combined with the words of a woman dying of cancer and her mother couldn't get in the way. Not now and not ever!

31

ON FRIDAY MORNING, THE FIRST THING MEG DID WHEN SHE ARRIVED FOR
her shift at the hospital was to share every facet of the Comet
Cleaners encounter with Heather. She described in great detail
the way the boy had tossed off his crude remarks and how she
shocked the teen by turning and putting him in his place. As
the story ended, Heather gave her a big hug and told her how
proud she was of her.

Just before she had concluded her rounds that day, Meg
even stopped by Nancy's room to tell her about the unexpected
meeting. Nancy sympathized with Meg, especially concerning
the boy's cocky attitude and unnecessary flirting, but unlike
Heather, she hadn't laughed when Meg informed her how
she'd blown him away. In fact, the only thing Nancy said was,
"That child needs help." Meg assured the patient that Thomas
would soon be getting all he deserved.

After relishing in her small victory all day Friday, Meg spent
Saturday being lazy. She never got out of her nightgown and
didn't call or text anyone. Instead, she just flipped on Turner
Classic Movies and watched every classic film the channel
aired. Fortunately, most were comedies, and none dealt with

the death of a spouse. So, for one day only, the bad memories stay buried.

Sunday, Meg got up, read the paper, and did a thorough cleaning of the apartment. She even reorganized her drawers in the kitchen and bedroom. After taking a late afternoon nap, she looked out the window and noted that the signs of the winter's passing had been premature. As Meg slept, the skies once again had turned gray and a strong, cold wind whipped out of the north. Still, despite the fact she'd always hated cold weather, Meg felt strong and strangely satisfied. That strength and satisfaction had been born during her chance meeting with Jim Thomas in the cleaners. Now she felt like she could do anything. That unexpected meeting had been exhilarating. It was as if she'd been reborn! In the span of five minutes, she went from a frightened kitten to a ferocious tiger.

And tomorrow was the day when she would no longer be carrying the nightmare in her body. The child that would have been so welcome another time seemed more an unwelcome invader now. Not carrying it would lift a huge weight from her shoulders.

As she finished dressing, Meg glanced at the stove clock. Cheryl would arrive at any moment, so she didn't have any spare time to paint her fingernails. Strolling back into the living room, she picked up the coat she'd earlier laid out on the couch and checked her hair one more time. Glancing out the window, she saw the assistant district attorney's gray sedan pull up to the curb. Hitting the light switch, she left her apartment and skipped out into the cold air.

Dinner went smoothly. Cheryl had a small steak. Meg, her appetite still controlled by her all-day, come-and-go morning sickness, had a salad and several packages of crackers. Thankfully this kind of diet would be ending soon. Neither of them spoke of the case until after their meal. It was Meg who opened the conversation by rehashing the story of running into Jim Thomas at the cleaners.

"Well," Cheryl noted when Meg delivered her finale, "he sounds like an even bigger jerk than I had him figured to be."

"I wish you could have seen him squirm," Meg grinned.

"Believe me." Cheryl's voice was now filled with enthusiasm. "If he gets on the stand, I'll see him squirm and I will keep him on the edge of his seat for a long time."

After delivering those words, Cheryl became less an attorney than a partner in a plan of revenge. She listened to Meg's fantasies of seeing Jim Thomas going flying over cliffs or wrapping his car around trees. She smiled and nodded her head when Meg spoke of getting the maximum sentence possible. In both scenarios she mirrored the widow's emotions and daydreams. She agreed how important it was to exact some kind of personal justice. The only thing she voiced reservations about was Meg going outside the law.

"Fantasy is one thing," Cheryl explained, "and I've had a lot of them concerning the guy who killed my father. But if you really do anything like that, then the weight of the law comes down on *you*. If you go to jail because you claimed your revenge in an unlawful fashion, then the guy gets both Steve and you and he wins again. You understand me?"

Meg nodded. "I won't go far enough outside the law to be brought to trial. I'm smarter than that."

"I hope so," Cheryl said. "You know, since we last spoke I've been doing a lot of thinking about this case. In fact, it is all I've thought about. I really believe you're the reason that we'll win."

Meg didn't verbally respond to the assistant district attorney's insight, acknowledging it only with a nod and smile. She hoped the look in her brown eyes coupled with that smile would prove she wanted to hear more. Taking the cue, Cheryl continued.

"Up until this generation, there was not as much publicity about drunks killing or maiming people on the highway. Today, thanks in large part to Mothers Against Drunk Driving and the Internet, there is a lot more information out there. Hence, laws are becoming more strictly enforced. So, I feel that just because of this change in public perception, we have a good chance at getting a conviction. Still, considering who Thomas's father is, as well as his own Superboy standing in the community and particularly in his high school, I believe it will be a tough battle. I was worried that a conviction would only lead to a reduced sentence. But then, you offered us a way to paint this young man as more than a kid out for a good time who used poor judgment. If fact, you have given us much, much more. You are the trump card. You are a prosecutor's dream!"

"I am?" Meg answered, reacting to the information by pointing the index fingers of both hands to her chest.

Cheryl paused for a moment, took a sip of coffee then continued. "What I have to say sounds terrible. If it was printed in the newspaper it would read like every bad lawyer story you have ever heard. It links me with many in our profession who have a horrible reputation. It makes me look like a person who will use anything in order to win a case. Yet, the fact is, you're pregnant. And that child you are carrying may well be the key to putting Thomas away rather than seeing him walk out of the courtroom with probation."

For at least a minute, nothing was said. It was as if Cheryl was waiting for some confirmation Meg understood the real advantage they had. But she didn't respond. She couldn't. This strategy had been so unexpected it had left her totally stunned.

"Meg, what I'm saying is that a judge and a jury will no doubt feel a lot more sympathy for you as you sit there in maternity clothes and wait for them to make a decision about the person who killed your child's father. It sounds low and cruel, and maybe it is, but I think that it will win the case for us."

Meg nodded. There was no other explanation necessary. It was all very clear. Maybe there was a God and He was just as mean as she thought He was. While her mother's and Nancy's prayers had been answered, Meg had been punched in the gut and all the wind had been pushed from her lungs. In the process, all her plans had been turned upside-down again. As she sat there not fully believing what was happening, Cheryl continued.

"I know that I could have told you all of this on the phone, but that would've seemed a little cold to me. After all, Meg, I'm using you and your unborn child in a way that almost seems dirty. But in all honesty, I don't mind getting a little grime on my hands if it will help me put away a piece of scum. Do you understand?"

Meg nodded. She understood all too well.

"Meg, I was so relieved when we talked last time. Simply by your reaction when I brought it up, I discovered that you weren't considering an abortion. Can you imagine what would happen if you'd done that and it had gotten out? In this town, and in reality, this state, abortion is still murder in many people's eyes. When Tidwell got through trotting that information out, the jury would've probably thought of you in a lower light than Thomas. Consequently, an abortion probably would've finished us, and yet, if I had been in your shoes, that's exactly what I would have done. In this case, I'm so glad you didn't react like I would have."

Meg had never considered how it would affect the case if she opted for having her pregnancy terminated. When she had resolved that it would be best for her, she hadn't considered the repercussions. What if it did get out? Those kinds of things always did. How would it affect not only this trial but the rest of her life? Why did this have to be so complicated?

The rest of the conversation took place in a dense fog. She was there, Cheryl was explaining steps in the case, but Meg wasn't hearing any of it. Her ability to process information had terminated with the news she couldn't have an abortion. To have what she really wanted, she was going to have to hang onto something she didn't want. It just wasn't fair. She didn't want to raise a child by herself. She certainly didn't want a little image of Steve staring back at her for the rest of her life.

Later that night, long after Cheryl had dropped her off and long after Meg had turned off the lights and gone to bed, a war raging deep inside her soul kept Meg from sleeping. This war was tearing her apart. It was a war she knew she would fight all night long and she couldn't win.

If she got an abortion, she'd be the one on trial. She couldn't deal with that. If she were the reason Thomas got off, then she would never forgive herself. Giving up on sleep, she struggled out of bed and wandered into the kitchen. After pouring herself a Coke, she looked out the window. The sky was filled with stars. There were no cars on the streets and certainly no people out at this time of night. The world was quiet—so quiet that Meg could almost hear her heartbeat. A sudden churning in her stomach reminded her that another heart was beating inside her, too.

Looking up, she shook her head and whispered. "You got me again, didn't You, God? One way or the other, things have to be Your way. You wouldn't let me get rid of the kid, even though I could have done it with no guilt feelings at all. No, You made it where I have to keep the child because it is the key to my getting the justice that I have to have.

"Well, tell me this, God," Meg whispered. "Where were You on that night when Steve was driving home? You could have turned the tables then. Thomas could have been killed. Now You are making it not only impossible for me to have what I want, You're not doing anything to keep Nancy from dying. And what about poor Julie? She was nothing more that a frightened little child who made one mistake. I mean, she'd worked her way up from nothing and she had positioned herself at a place where she could have gone to college and escaped the rotten life she had at home. If it hadn't been for the wonderful Christians at our church, she would've had an abortion. Great present, wasn't it? They had her keep her baby and lose her life. And where were You when she was walking home that night when some guy raped her and then left her to die in a cold, dark alley? And where is the guy now? He's probably running around doing the same thing to someone else.

"Well, God, if You wanted me to have this child, then You're going to have things Your way. But remember, I'm not doing it for You, or Mom, or Nancy, or anyone else. I'm doing it to get Jim Thomas. So, if You're expecting any wonderful signs of a loving mother to jump out, just forget it."

Meg walked slowly back to her bed. The clock on her nightstand told her that midnight had become three and that in three hours of debating with God and herself her mind was still a jumble of confused thoughts and unwanted options. The fact that her appointment for the procedure was just hours away only added to the pressure. Why the devil couldn't she have scheduled it for later in the week? Better yet, why hadn't she already done it? Finally, just before dawn, she resolved to cancel her appointment for the abortion. How ironic that this child, conceived in love, was now having its birth guaranteed by her own boiling hate.

32

As she'd already arranged to have the day off, Meg made the call she didn't want to make, canceled her procedure, and spent all of Monday in her nightclothes watching TV. What she viewed was unimportant; the programs were nothing more than just something to keep her busy. At six, her mother called. When she found out Meg hadn't gone through with the abortion, she was thrilled. After she listened to Barbara go on for over five minutes about how right the decision had been and how time would show Meg this was so, the phone call finally concluded. In a very real sense, the conversation left Meg completely humbled and humiliated. She was sure her mother thought she'd changed her mind for the wrong reasons.

The second call, also unwanted, was from Nancy Leslie. As she now recognized the number, Meg considered letting it go through to voice mail, but, in a fit of compassion due to the caller's terminal condition, she picked up.

"How are you feeling?" Nancy asked after greetings had been exchanged.

"A little sick," Meg responded truthfully.

"I guess that's to be expected," Nancy said. "I'm sure that within a few days you'll feel wonderful again."

"I doubt it," Meg replied wearily. "I didn't have the abortion."

"Really, you changed your mind?"

"Not for the reasons you would have expected," Meg admitted. "The district attorney's office believes it would be better for the case if I were pregnant. It seems that my being in a motherly state might well sway the jury to give Thomas a harsher sentence."

"I'm glad for the decision," Nancy answered, her voice a bit breathy. "And I hope and pray that it'll work out the way that you want it to."

"Well," Meg said, "we'll find out in a month or so. Won't we?"

Nancy didn't reply to Meg's observation but simply issued a warm good-bye.

Only after the phone had gone dead did Meg realize that for Nancy a month might be longer than a lifetime. She might not be around to find out what was going to happen. Just more proof that life wasn't fair.

33

THE NEXT FOUR WEEKS PASSED EVER SO SLOWLY FOR MEG. THE GOOD news, much of it lost on her, was that there was new life everywhere. Winter had finally ended and fresh buds signaled the beginning of spring. Yet, she hardly noticed. She'd been too busy working at the hospital, experiencing morning sickness, and finding uniforms that would fit her ever-changing shape. The only date that meant anything was the one when the trial started.

She was hovering at her station, going over charts, when the call came in.

"Nurse Richards," the voice asked after she'd answered.

"This is Meg Richards."

"John Willis here. I need to see you in my office. Can you get away now?"

"Sure, Heather can cover the wing."

"Good, come straight to my office. There are things we need to discuss."

Meg set the phone back in the cradle. *Wonder what this was about.* She hadn't missed a single day of work. She'd done her job. So what did he want?

"What's up?" Heather asked. "You have a distant look in your eye. Is it about the case?"

"No, Willis wants to see me. I'll be back in a few minutes."

Meg walked through three long wings and then took an elevator to the first floor to get to the hospital administrator's office. His secretary was out, so she strolled right up to his door and knocked. A muffled voice on the other side told her to enter.

Willis was sitting at his large desk staring at a computer monitor through his thick glasses as she entered. Looking up, he hit a save command and turned his attention to his visitor.

"Have a seat," he ordered, more than said.

Feeling like a student being sent to the principal's office, Meg eased down into the chair. Willis wasted no time with formalities.

"Nurse Richards I realize that your husband's death was an incredible blow to you. So over the past month or more I have been willing to cut you some slack."

"Sir," Meg cut in, "I have not checked in late once. And I haven't missed a day due to illness. I've even put in a bunch of overtime hours. You can look at the records."

Willis waved his hand and sternly continued, "Your hours are not the issue; it is your demeanor. I have a stack of complaints here about your attitude. In many cases, your bedside manner had been horrible. As you've done your duties, which you've done well, you have barely acknowledged patients and shown little regard for the feelings of staff members. You've been sour at best and completely lacking in compassion at worst."

"Mr. Willis," Meg said, but was once again cut off by the wave of his hand.

"I could dismiss you. You at least have earned being reassigned. But because of what has happened in your life, I'm going to give you another chance. I expect to see a dramatic change in attitude, and if I don't, then you need to be updating your résumé. Do you understand?"

She took a deep breath but didn't retreat, "What have I done wrong?"

He shook his head. "We have a reputation at Springfield for offering a loving hand and a compassionate voice with our care. That goes back decades. You might just act like a machine at another hospital, but not here. There is no doubt you know your job and rarely make professional mistakes, but your attitude is much different than it was before you husband died. We can't have that. Look at your job description. Attitude is covered in great deal there. Do you understand?"

Biting her lip, Meg nodded.

"Nurse Richards, I've always had the utmost respect for you. Until your husband's death, you were the model nurse. I'd never seen anyone bond with patients the way you did. They loved you because you cared so deeply about them. You were empathetic, kind, and compassionate. You defined your profession as well as anyone I'd ever met. What I want to see is that person back in this hospital. Can you do that for me?"

Meg responded with a tone that belied the hostility boiling inside, "I will try."

"Thank you. You may go back to your station."

Meg clenched her jaw as she walked out of the office and down the hallway. What did he know about compassion? Had he shown any to her? He was demanding and aloof. No one liked him. So why should she listen? After all, nurses were in short supply, she could get another job, one where a boss would work with her and not demonize her. No she couldn't do that, either. She had vacation time coming that she was going to need for the court battle. She had to hold on to this job until after the case was over. That meant falling into the form Willis wanted—no demanded—she adhere to. With this in mind, she forced a smile at two visitors as she joined Heather at the station.

"What was that all about?" The other nurse asked.

"Compassion," Meg replied.

"What?" Heather asked.

"It's time for me to show compassion. Well, I won all kinds of awards acting in high school, so looks like I will have to trot out my old stage skills again. I might not feel like Florence Nightingale, but I guess I'm going to have to act like her."

"I don't get it," Heather answered. "They should cut you some slack.

Meg noted a call light on. Not missing a chance to show off her fake smile, she announced, "I'll get that and the patient will love me."

34

WHAT'RE YOU DOING?"

Jim Thomas glanced up from stuffing his bat and glove into his equipment bag and watched the cute blonde walk up to his car. Once again fate was on his side and the script for this day couldn't have been any better if he'd written it himself. The temperature was in the seventies, there wasn't a cloud in the sky, and one of the most beautiful girls in school was so close he could smell her perfume. Best of all, Candy had a huge crush on him. It had always been that way and probably always would be that way. She'd been following him since elementary school. Back then she'd been a scrawny moppet, but now she was an explosive bombshell. What a transformation!

Yet, other than her being the shortest of his harem, Candy was really no different than a dozen others. She'd do what he wanted, when he wanted it, and ask for nothing in return. Why was that? He was good-looking, but no better than a half dozen other boys. Yes, he was a star athlete and that carried weight. It seems girls loved guys who scored touchdowns, dunked basketballs, and hit home runs, but there were other guys who did that as well. And they didn't have the luck with the girls he did. So he figured the major reason Candy and all the others flew to him like a moths to a flame had to be his money and connections. He could take them to the nicest places, buy them anything they wanted, and get them in to see people they never dreamed they'd meet. No one else at school could offer those things. Best of all, once they tasted what only he could give them, it became a drug and they constantly had to have more.

"Did you see my home run?" Thomas casually inquired as the blonde threw her arms around him. The hug lasted long enough that a couple of the other players started howling at them from the other side of the parking lot. Yet those catcalls didn't dissuade Candy from planting a kiss on his cheek.

As she broke away, her eyes met his. Those eyes told him all he needed to know. She'd do anything he wanted. Sadly that easy-to-read invitation meant nothing on this night.

After zipping his bag, he looked back to the young woman admiring him as if he were made of gold and diamonds. She had it bad. Leaning down, he drew her close to him. But rather than kiss her, he asked, "I'll ask you again, did you see the homer?" After popping the question, he pulled back, leaving her standing with eyes closed and waiting for a kiss that never happened.

"That's mean," she whined.

He shrugged, "About my question?"

"Yeah, I got here just as it was sailing out of the park. I couldn't get here sooner because we had a big day at the cleaners. It seemed everyone was bringing stuff in."

"You didn't miss much," he assured her. "I did get three more hits and pitched a great game, but that long ball was the key to our win. It's what folks will be talking about tonight and reading about in the paper tomorrow. You know being a hero isn't easy."

Tossing his bag in the passenger seat of his new Corvette, Thomas waved at a couple of team members who were already driving away. They pointed at Candy and gave him a thumbs-up.

"You guys have fun!" He called out as they roared by in the Ford pick-up. "And don't do anything I wouldn't do."

"That leaves things wide open," the girl noted.

"Yep," he laughed. "Just want them to have a good time when they're celebrating the victory. After all, we're on top in our district." Folding his arms across his chest, he looked back toward the field. With that long ball, he'd proven once more that he was king of Springfield High, and how he liked being king.

"What's on your mind?" Candy asked, leaning into his body in what was likely an attempt to have him turn his attention back to her.

"Just thinking about how unfair life is," he said as he draped his arm over her shoulder.

She looked up at him, "Unfair? You think your life is unfair? You with the new car and you with the home run! How could life be unfair?"

"Maybe you just don't see the whole picture," he explained. "My life pretty much sucks right now. Everybody gets to go do what they want to do tonight but me. Ray and Cliff are headed out to the lake to party. A bunch of the others are going out for pizza, but I've got to go home."

The blonde shook her head, "You're going home? You never do that. How can the guys have a lake party without you? You always supply the booze. What's up?"

"Got that trial in two weeks," he explained. "Dad's being a real jerk about it. His attorney gave him a list of questions and answers that I have to memorize. So I study them every night just like I would if I was prepping for a history test. Except this is worse. Dad puts me in a chair and drills me as if I'm in court. I can't wait for this mess to get over."

His words had barely cleared his lips when Candy said, "She was in today."

"Who's she?" he asked.

"You know, the woman whose husband died in that accident." She paused and looked back toward the field. "I wish I could get that scene out of my head. I can still see him trapped in that burning car."

Thomas shot an angry look her way. "I don't need to hear you or anyone else telling me about that accident. I get that every night at home. I'm constantly having to relive every detail. I don't care how she feels, I'm the one with the real problem. The law is going after me."

"She probably lives with it every night too," Candy noted while pulling away from Thomas. She walked two steps toward the field before turning back. Rubbing her arms as if she'd suddenly felt a chilling wind, she added, "You should have seen her. She was cold and hard. Her words had a bite to them. She scares me. Does she scare you?"

Slamming the passenger door, Thomas stomped around the car to the driver's door. After throwing it open he slid in. For a few seconds Candy watched him through the windshield before saying, "I figured your dad could fix it. I thought you wouldn't have to go to trial."

He didn't answer. Starting his red Corvette, he jammed it into drive and pulled out of the parking lot leaving Candy standing alone and confused. He was sure his father could fix it as well. That's what the judge did; he fixed things. But for some reason the old man couldn't make this go away, and until it ended, it looked as if the king of Springfield High would remain a prisoner in his own castle. Life just wasn't fair.

35

I'M GLAD YOU COULD MEET ME ON SUCH SHORT NOTICE."

Meg nodded as she took a seat on a bench beside Cheryl. It was cloudy and rain was predicted for later in the night. So, except for two old men playing checkers on a table a hundred yards away, the city park was empty. That's probably why Cheryl chose this place for their meeting.

"I take it you have something new on the case?" Meg asked.

The assistant district attorney shook her head. Leaning close, she whispered, "They're worried."

"You mean the Thomas family?"

Her blue eyes sparkled as Cheryl answered, "The whole defense team. They've even put out feelers to see if we can work out an agreement to avoid going to trial."

"What do you mean not go to trial?"

"Unofficially, they've approached us with an offer. Jim Thomas will accept a guilty plea in exchange for attending alcohol abuse classes, five years probation, a stiff fine, and community service."

"No jail time?" Meg asked, her tone clearly showing her disapproval.

"No," Cheryl admitted, "he'd never spend a day in jail. But there is something else. This deal also means you could find a lot of money in your bank account. They're offering a quarter of a million to make the case go away. I think you could probably double that."

Meg's hands formed two fists, her blood boiled, and her heart raced. They thought she could be bought! Toss a little money her way and they thought she'd just go away and leave them alone! Who did they think they were?

A light mist was starting to fall, driving the checker players to their car. Yet as one minute became two and two became three, Meg said nothing. As the silence dragged on, the assistant district attorney leaned back into the bench and shoved her hands into her pockets.

"Meg," Cheryl finally chimed in, "you've got a kid coming in the near future and that is lot of money. Let's face it, you could use it. Steve's life insurance barely paid for his funeral."

Meg clinched her jaw and shook her head.

"You have to carefully consider it," Cheryl said. "This means security. And there is no guarantee that we will win. Even if he is found guilty, Thomas might even get less punishment than what is in this deal we've been offered."

Pushing off the bench, Meg stood facing the north wind. The mist was now thicker and within seconds her face was moist and cold. They were trying to buy her off! The mere fact Judge Thomas thought she would cave for cash was a cutting insult. Steve's life and death could never be erased with money.

Whirling around, she stared at Cheryl, "I suppose you think this is a good deal."

The assistant district attorney shrugged. Standing, she walked over to Meg, pulled her hands from her coat pockets and placed them on the hurting woman's shoulders. "It is a good deal. I'd be lying if I said it wasn't."

Meg hadn't felt this alone since the night Steve had been killed. Even the one woman once driven in an effort to get justice had now seemingly deserted her.

"What can I do?" Meg coldly asked.

"You can do what you want to do."

"I can't spend the rest of my life knowing I can be bought."

Cheryl nodded. "So you want to reject the deal and move on with the case?"

"I do." Meg's reply was resolute. "But what about you?"

"I never settle," she smiled.

Stepping forward, Cheryl took Meg into her arms. In an instant, the two had been transformed from allies to friends.

"You're giving up a lot," the assistant district attorney said as she broke the embrace. "There is nothing guaranteed if we do it our way. And there won't be any money for you even if we win."

"I can't be bought!"

Cheryl smiled, walked over to the bench, and retrieved her briefcase. Looking back to Meg, she said, "Webb Jones bet me you'd take the deal. I love it when I'm right and he's wrong."

36

IT ALL STARTS ONE WEEK FROM TODAY," MEG EXPLAINED.

"And you're ready?" Nancy asked, her tone breathy and hoarse.

"Well," Meg explained, "I've been prepped. I have an idea of what the defense will try to do and the questions they will ask. So I guess I'm as ready as I can be."

"I'm ready, too," Nancy grimly said.

Meg didn't know how to reply to the small woman's pronouncement. She was also scared to ask what it meant. What she did know was that her habit of not leaving after work until she had visited with Nancy had become very meaningful and she didn't want it to end. The tiny woman had a strength that awed Meg. Others would have given up by now. Their funerals would have been weeks ago, but not this lady. She was a fighter. She was determined to cling to every second she could. But, even though Meg didn't want to think about it, there was an expiration date looming.

"The pain must be getting bad," Meg whispered.

"I can handle it," came the quiet reply. "Besides, if I was on the meds, I probably wouldn't be awake when you came by each day. I look forward to that time. And, as I know you don't work everyday of the week, I appreciate that you come to see Nosy Nancy on your days off, too. It's kind of like having a sister."

Leaning closer to the bed, Meg patted the small woman's hand. "I think you're the reason I've learned to care about my patients again, so I still have my job thanks to you. I guess you're the person who keeps the old Meg alive."

"You don't need to lose that part of you," Nancy warned. "After all, that's who Steve fell in love with."

Though she hadn't meant it, Nancy's words cut to the bone. She was right! Steve wouldn't have fallen for the person Meg had become. In fact, he wouldn't have recognized the person who now carried such rage in her heart.

"Did I say something wrong?"

Meg smiled, "No, Nancy you said something very right. When I met you I was mad at everyone and everything in my life. You've caused me to refocus. I'm not angry with the patients anymore. I'm not mad at my mother. I'm not ready to pal around with her yet and I need my space, but I no longer feel a desire to push her completely out of my life."

"But you're still carrying a lot of rage," Nancy pointed out.

"Only for those who deserve it," Meg admitted. "I focus now on the Thomas family, especially the judge and his son."

"What about God?"

Meg cocked her eyebrows. This woman really had a way of pushing buttons. "God is not on my good side. If confession is good for the soul, then I'll confess I don't like Him much, either."

"Even a little hate can chew you up," Nancy warned. "It's like cancer; it starts small and grows. If you don't cut all the anger out of your life, it will kill everything that is good in you."

Meg leaned closer to her most special patient. "You go places others dare not tread."

"Tact is not very important when your days are numbered." Nancy paused, smiled, and added, "But friendship is. Thanks for being my friend."

"If Steve had met you first," Meg whispered, "I don't think I'd have ever caught his eye."

37

Thanks to Willis's warnings and Nancy's influence, Meg was once more acting like the perfect nurse at Springfield Community; yet in almost every other situation, she was aloof and distant. Many who had once cared deeply for her, those who had once thought that after she had time to work through her pain she would return to her values and her beliefs, now tried to avoid her. Meg didn't care that she was being avoided. In fact, she liked the separation. It made it that much easier for her to embrace her private little pity party.

When she wasn't at work, Meg didn't have to act like she was happy. She could be as miserable as she wanted. And she usually was. She had quickly gotten used to being by herself, but that didn't mean she liked it. Even she had to admit her life was depressing. There would be no happiness or satisfaction until Jim Thomas got what he deserved. That goal kept her going. Seeing the teen declared guilty was her first thought each morning. To emphasize the coming of that special day, every night she crossed out the day on the kitchen calendar. Thus she was able to clearly see just how much time she had left before putting the boy in his place. The big X over today's date meant April 26 was now just two days away. That was reason to celebrate.

As an act of cleansing, she had given some of Steve's things to Goodwill and almost all the rest she had shipped back to his folks. She'd removed all the photos and other items that reminded her of him from the apartment and put them a locked trunk in the closet. She had also gotten good at purging thoughts of her husband. She'd replaced Steve's memories with plans as to how she could best exact retribution for his death. It was when she was making those plans she felt most alive.

Meg was looking over notes in preparation for the beginning of the trial when her iPhone rang. It was Heather.

"Didn't get to visit with you today."

"Things were kind of crazy."

"You're right on that," Heather replied. "I'm exhausted. I barely had time to get off my feet today. Guess you went by to see Nancy after work."

"Yeah," Meg admitted. "I feel sorry for her. Her husband can't get there 'til after seven each night and there is no one else. It has to be tough waiting to die like that."

"I'm surprised you've bonded with her," Heather noted. "I mean, you put a lot of distance between you and the other Christians in your life."

"She's different," Meg explained. "She doesn't judge. Nancy sees the whole story and therefore looks beyond my actions of the moment. She seems to have the faith to believe that given time, I'll work my way back to having a solid outlook on life. You know, she even gives me books to read. I've got a whole shelf full of them."

"What kind of books?" Heather asked.

"The kind I'd throw away if Mom gave them to me. They're devotional books. I'm guessing they must mean a lot to her. So I keep them."

"Have you read them?"

"Heather, you know better than that. But I won't get rid of them. I kind of like having a piece of her heart in my house."

"She's gotten to you. Hasn't she, Meg?"

"I wouldn't say that. But you know there are some patients that each of us bond with. Like you and that burn victim on the south wing. You spend a lot of time with her."

"I guess," Heather admitted, "but it seems like Nancy has become more your friend than a patient."

"She hasn't replaced you," Meg assured her.

Yet in a way she had. When Meg was angry, Nancy would sit through every story, never once giving an impatient look or harsh word. When she wasn't feeling well or she was concerned that maybe Jim Thomas might get off, she informed Nancy. She even told Nancy the story of her high school friend, Julie Evans. She had almost laughed when Nancy pointed out that Julie's killer was probably having a tough time living with the pain of what he had done. She not only disagreed, she reminded the dying woman of the remorse that Jim Thomas hadn't been feeling. On that occasion, Nancy only smiled in a way that said she didn't want to argue. But the two of them did argue—mostly over God. But it was a lot different than arguing with her mother. Nancy never pushed God down Meg's throat.

"Heather."

"I was wondering if you were still there."

"You don't have to worry about Nancy replacing you. I just feel for her. I can't imagine facing death like she is."

"So you put up with her for that reason?" Heather asked.

"I think that is it," Meg admitted. But it was a lot more than that. There was something about the way Nancy saw life that puzzled Meg, and she'd always been a sucker for puzzles. Even as a kid, she wouldn't stop until she figured them out.

"Heather," Meg asked, "my land line is ringing. Can I call you back?"

"Sure."

Ending the call on her iPhone, Meg walked over and checked her caller ID. She knew the number well. Picking up the receiver she said, "Hey Nancy, Heather and I were just talking about you."

"I'm sorry, I'll let you get back to her."

"No," Meg assured her, "I can call her back. Do you need something?"

Nancy's voice sounded stronger than it had earlier in the day. "I just wanted to tell you that God loves you. And He loves everyone and we should, too."

"You've told me that," Meg said. "But can I ask you a very personal question? One that is tough and unforgiving."

"Of course."

"Nancy, if God loves you, then why is He killing you?"

"God's not killing me," Nancy explained, her tone seemingly tinged with anger. "Cancer's killing me. God gave us control over this earth because we demanded it. Check it out in the story of Adam and Eve. When we got power over the earth, we also screwed it up. People just aren't good at giving in to anything, and that includes God. But He is a loving father and He doesn't zap people in car wrecks or with cancer. It is the evil we invited into this earth that does that. You need to understand that."

"Okay," Meg quietly replied. "While I don't understand it, I'll think about it."

"Good," Nancy answered, all signs of anger now gone, "I think I need to sleep now. Will I see you tomorrow?"

"I'll do my best. Good night."

"Night."

As Meg set the phone back in the cradle she considered this strange new friendship. She and Nancy were so different. Maybe opposites did attract. Nancy's life was all about love and each day the little love that still existed in Meg was being buried deeper and deeper by her need for revenge. Maybe Nancy was right, perhaps this lust for vengeance was a cancer. Maybe it was eating at her, just like the disease that was working its way through Nancy. In Nancy's case, it was destroying her body; in Meg's case it might be destroying her heart. And yet, while Nancy fought her cancer with everything in her, Meg treated hers like a welcome guest.

38

It was early Sunday morning and Meg was preparing for another day at the hospital. Since the day Willis had called her on the carpet, she had grown to hate her job; but now, with the trial just forty-eight hours away, she had a good reason to be happy. Even work—a routine day of sick people and bedpans—was not going to mess up her feeling of anticipation.

When she arrived at Springfield Community, Heather greeted her with a sleepy, "Hello."

As the two of them checked in, Meg couldn't help but notice just how tired her coworker looked. "Did you and Paul play doctor last night?" she finally asked.

Choosing not to answer the question directly, Heather asked one of her own, "Paul and I have been going out quite a bit over the last few weeks and he's starting to put a lot of pressure on me to give up the prize. Do you think I should?"

"The prize?" Meg asked raising her eyebrows.

"You know what I mean," Heather shot back.

"Why ask me?"

"Because I want to know if hanging onto it is worth it," Heather responded. "I thought that you could tell me. After all, you were a virgin when you got married."

"Listen, Heather. What you do with your body is your business."

"Meg, I don't think you understand." Heather was more than a little concerned about what she should do. "I'm not tired from partying. My date ended early. Paul began to put pressure on me to go all the way, and when I wouldn't, he got mad and left. I spent the night wondering if I had messed up."

Meg jabbed, "You're such a prude. I know I used to be one too, but that was back in high school. We're not kids anymore."

"Two years ago you told me not to sleep with John," Heather said. "And I didn't. You said it would be wrong. Well, it took me two long years to find someone who cares about me and someone that I care about, and if I continue to say no, then I might lose another guy. Is it worth that?"

When she asked Meg for advice, Heather probably didn't stop to think about how much her friend had changed over the past few months. If she had, she might have turned to someone else; but she didn't, and with sweating palms, she waited for Meg's words.

For Meg, raised in the church and brought up with a strict moral code, there had never been any question as to her virginity. She had never had any reason to doubt her choice. After all, she'd won the one love of her life without giving anything up. Still, as she looked into her friend's distressed eyes she knew that being twenty-one and being twenty-six like Heather were two different things. If she'd had to wait that long and if she had been lonely, would she have made the same decision as she had so many years ago?

Heather hadn't had the greatest of upbringings and she hadn't even gone to church until Meg and Steve had taken her. Even now, she didn't go very often, but she still made her decisions based on what women like Meg did. So, Heather likely wanted her to give her a reason to stay a virgin.

"Heather," Meg casually said. "If I were in your shoes, I'd probably go for it. After all, there are no guarantees as to how long any of us have and sometimes you have to take your happiness wherever you can find it. Do what will make both of you happy!"

Knowing that a patient in 217 was due for a new IV, Meg got the needed bottle and began her day. As she did, a now relieved Heather picked up the phone.

"Paul, I'm sorry about last night." her voice drifted off as Meg walked down the hall, but Meg still knew what Heather must have had in mind and how this conversation was going to end.

39

THE NEXT TWO DAYS, DAYS THAT MEG HAD ONCE BELIEVED WOULD LAST forever, flew by. There had been a huge patient load and her duties had kept her busy from sign-in until sign-out. She'd been so covered up she hadn't even had an opportunity to ask Heather about what she did. Yet flowers delivered to Heather at the nurses' station on Monday afternoon served to assure Meg her friend had followed her suggestion. And there had been that unique glow on the young nurse's face for the whole day that seemed to confirm her suspicions. Still, not a word was said about what had happened. Probably none needed to be said. It was now just water under the bridge. Heather had finally grown up.

After Meg checked out on Monday, she stopped by Nancy's room. Knocking but receiving no answer, she eased the door open enough to look in. She heard one of the same songs she had heard at least a dozen times before, and Nancy, looking a little paler, was napping. Rather than disturb her, she shut the door and left. Later than night, when the phone rang, she was not at all surprised to hear Nancy's voice.

"I wanted to call before the trial."

"Thanks," Meg answered. Holding the phone with her shoulder, she continued ironing a new maternity dress that she was going to wear the next day.

"I hope you find what it is you're looking for Meg." Nancy's tone was strangely serious.

"How are you feeling, Nancy?"

"A little tired, that's all," Nancy answered. Then, after pausing for a moment, she continued. "You know, the pain hasn't been too bad recently. But the treatments make me exhausted. I guess taking them may be a waste of time and effort. After all, the result's going to be the same. All I'm doing is trying to give myself a few more days."

Meg had almost forgotten that Nancy was dying. She'd simply put that fact in the back of her mind. Nancy's personality—her life—had almost caused Meg to believe the young woman might really beat the odds. But in reality, there weren't any odds given on this race. All bets were off. Nancy was going to lose. She was living on borrowed days as she had already beaten the doctor's timetable by over two months.

"Nancy," Meg's voice was soft. "You love life a great deal."

The statement was a good one, one that must have caused Nancy to stop and think a minute before answering. What she said was more than just the simple yes Meg had expected.

"Oh, Meg. I don't know that I love life that much, but what I love is what life brings me. The longer I live the more wonderful people I get to meet and the more people I get to love. Beating the odds gave me a chance to get to know you. It may sound kind of funny, but you've made me feel very fortunate. You have made me think about things that I'd never thought about before. Your doubts have even brought me closer to God."

Putting the iron down and sitting on her bed, Meg quipped, "I've brought you closer to God?"

"Yes," Nancy returned. "You see, I've never had anyone I loved taken from me. I was raised in a children's home and then foster care. So in a way, maybe I was feeling a little sorry for myself until I realized that those who are left behind have it the worst. My husband will know the real pain—the kind of pain a pill can't cure. I realized that from watching you."

Nancy took a deep breath. "And that boy, the one who is going on trial tomorrow, he's going to know pain, too. Maybe you won't think it's enough, but if your attorney does her job, he will still know pain. I wish I could give you the peace that I feel to go along with the drive that's pushing you on to get the justice you are sure you need. I think if you had that peace, the kind that only the knowledge of knowing God gives you, you could do something far more special to commemorate the way Steve died than just put his killer away."

"Nancy, I'm not sure you really want to go there."

"Meg, I'm sorry, there I am again getting into areas I don't need to get into. Forgive me, won't you? Sometimes I sound just like a know-it-all old woman. I guess in a way I am old."

Strangely this time Meg felt no anger over what Nancy had insinuated. It didn't change the way she felt about the trial or Jim Thomas, but it did give her another viewpoint that sounded a little more constructive than "this is all in God's plan."

"Nancy," Meg answered, "no apologies needed. You at least attempt to give me reasons rather than pat answers. Folks like my mother claim to have all the answers, but they don't seem to have anything concrete to back them up. You make me think and I appreciate that."

Nancy weakly laughed and then added another bit of unsolicited advice, "I really think the only map we need to live by can be found in Matthew 25:35-40. In fact, that's what has driven me to be your friend."

"Those are the verses on touching the least of these?" Meg asked.

"Yeah. They are."

"But you are the one that's sick," Meg argued. "I should be touching you."

"And you have. But while I'm sick, you are the one who has been broken. I was put here to reach out to you."

Nancy let her words linger for a moment and then came back on the line. "There's one more thing, Meg."

"What's that?"

"My folks died when I was two," Nancy explained. "I never really knew them."

"I'm sorry," Meg said.

"So am I," the woman replied. "But how can you miss what you don't remember? Anyway, you need to know what happened to them."

"Go ahead."

"They were killed by a drunk driver." Nancy let the words soak in before adding, "I was in the back seat and was uninjured. So, you have given me something else that is very special. I now feel their loss for the very first time, because I see how Steve's loss has hit you. I suddenly believe my dying would be easier if I'd had parents to hold my hand. I can only hope they will be on the other side to greet me."

Meg was dumbfounded. She didn't know what to say. Alcohol-related accidents took thousands of lives a year, but up until this moment she'd only measured that cost in her own terms. Yes, Cheryl's story had further fueled her need for revenge, but it had not touched her heart. Nancy had now put what happened into a whole new light. There were millions of people living right now that shared Meg's pain. They probably also shared her need for justice.

"Good-bye, Meg." Nancy said.

The phone went dead before Meg had a chance to reply.

40

Even though several people, including her mother, had offered to accompany her, Meg wanted to make this trip on her own. With road construction along several streets, a water crew dealing with a massive leak on Elm Street, a four-car police chase along Pine, and a half dozen erratic drivers pulling out in front of her all along her route, she now wished she had ridden with someone else as the drive to the courthouse had been nerve-wracking. She felt lucky just to get there in one piece. On the top of those hair-raising and heart-stopping experiences, the gloomy skies offered another ominous sign. It just didn't look like a good day. As Meg parked the Mustang and stepped out into the damp air, she felt as through there was a huge weight on her shoulders. Even after taking a deep breath, that weight was still there. It continued to ride her back as she strolled quickly and fearfully across the courthouse grounds and to the front stairs.

Standing on those limestone steps she looked back toward her car. Suddenly the deal she's been offered looked good. She'd probably have upwards of a half million dollars if she'd taken it. On top of that, she wouldn't have to be facing a trial whose outcome she couldn't predict. As she considered the price she was paying her eyes literally found the writing on the wall. She'd been in this building hundreds of times in her life but had never noticed the cornerstone until this moment. There it was plain as day and it was speaking directly to her. Under the date of construction, "1897," there were four words, "Justice will be served." She stopped and studied that pledge for a few moments. Would it ring true this week or would this be a time when the system failed to bring justice? Right now, she felt anything but confident.

As the pledge burned into her head, she glanced up at and studied the imposing four-story structure. Built of white limestone it was impressive but also foreboding. Why not? People paid taxes here, they tried criminals here and they filed complaints here. For all those reasons and a hundred more the courthouse just seemed to be a place you didn't want to visit. But, nevertheless, this was a place she had to be. She owed it to Steve.

After climbing the outside steps, Meg pushed open the ten-foot doors and made her way into the hall. There were steps to the right leading to the second floor. Made of granite, they were worn from more than a century of men and women climbing them to see if justice would be served. And though she now wanted to turn and race out the door, to not make this final climb, Meg solemnly put her feet where so many others before her had trod. Reaching the top, she noted a friend marching down the hall toward her.

"This is the day." Cheryl grimly announced. "Are you ready?"

A knot blocking her throat, Meg could only nod.

She had also gotten up an hour early on this special morning just to make sure that her hair, as well as her makeup, painted the picture Cheryl needed. She chose a royal blue maternity dress, dark hose, and pumps. She picked this dress because it made her look much further along than she actually was.

Cheryl stepped back and studied Meg. "You look perfect. It's just what we need."

"Thanks." At least one thing was going right. The assistant district attorney had requested Meg look like a demure mother-to-be—a woman that a jury would take pity on—and she had evidently succeeded.

"Your look will earn the jurors' sympathy," Cheryl assured her. "That is the first step in getting the maximum sentence."

"Thanks. I went through four or five dresses before I felt right about this one."

"It's just what we need," Cheryl added.

As she seated herself in a chair directly behind Cheryl's place at the prosecutor's table, she didn't know how to deal with her contradictory emotions. She was experiencing butterflies, and while she had expected that, she also had a conflicting deep-rooted confidence the case was so cut-and-dry that they had to win. These two polar opposites were fighting a war for her mind. And right now neither was winning. In an effort to dismiss these emotions, she spent the final few minutes before things began taking stock of those who had gathered in this historic chamber. She didn't know most, but there was one who really stood out.

Jasper Tidwell was heavy, white-headed, and probably mid-sixties. Meg had expected the attorney to be slick, refined, and polished, but Tidwell was rumpled and wrinkled. He wore a baggy gray suit that must have been at least twenty years old, unpolished and scuffed brown shoes, and a wide, ugly, dark green tie decorated with yellow dots held in place by a large, brass tie clip, all pulled together, or maybe torn apart, by a light blue shirt. A month overdue for a haircut, his glasses seemed permanently attached at the bottom of his rather large nose. He really appeared to be more a feeble but kindly old man who spent his spare time feeding pigeons at the park than a member of the state bar. In fact, due to his attire and unkempt look, Tidwell seemed to be the lovable, gullible, grandfatherly type. Could this be the famed lawyer she had been told to fear? At first glance, he did not seem like the sly, evil man Cheryl had painted him to be.

As Meg continued to study Tidwell, he leaned over the railing and started a conversation with two well-dressed gentlemen who looked to be businessmen. All three men were smiling as they spoke. By the time Tidwell spied Meg, he'd finished his conversation and pulled a pocket watch from his coat. After checking the time, he nodded and shot her a pleasant smile.

"Meg," Cheryl whispered.

Turning her gaze back to the assistant district attorney, Meg raised her eyebrows to indicate an affirmative response.

"Don't let his looks mislead you," Cheryl's eyes were directed toward the defense table. "He's a shark and a smart one, too. If he smells blood, he'll go for it. There are hundreds of guilty folks walking free, thanks to Tidwell."

Meg nodded, not quite able to reconcile Cheryl's words with what she was seeing. Still, the warning did serve to put her on guard.

Standing up, Tidwell turned toward the back wall. Throwing his arms out and forcing a huge smile, he robustly welcomed Jim Thomas into the courtroom.

"James, my boy, and how are we today?"

Thomas, dressed in a conservative dark blue suit, white oxford cloth shirt, and silk tie, managed to force a smile of his own as he replied in a polite voice. "Fine, sir."

Now showing his true colors, the grandstanding Tidwell made a big show of walking halfway down the center aisle of the room to embrace the boy. Then, in a voice just loud enough so the crowd could overhear but not loud enough to appear as if he had wanted them to overhear, he asked. "Is your father, Judge Thomas, coming?"

"He'll be along in a second," the younger Thomas assured the attorney.

"Oh, good." A whimsical smile now filled the Tidwell's face. "There's no doubt, my son, of all the men I have practiced before, your father, Judge Alfred E. Thomas, is the finest. Our community is blessed to have him. Fine man, a very fine man!" Glancing around the almost-full room as if to make sure that all those present had heard, the attorney then slapped his client on the back and the two of them walked toward the front of the courtroom. As they passed the row where Meg sat, Tidwell announced just loud enough for Cheryl and Meg to overhear, "Don't worry, James, we'll have this little misunderstanding cleared up in no time."

Cheryl shook her head. She had likely seen this kind of stuff out of Jasper Tidwell on many occasions. She'd even warned Meg that the old man always played the crowd to try to unhinge the prosecution's emotions. Yet while those from the district attorney's office had long since learned to handle it, Meg's blood was boiling. How dare this man refer to Steve's death as a little misunderstanding! She glared at the bench where Thomas and Tidwell were sitting, and just as she did, the attorney turned around and smiled at her. He continued to stare and grin until she finally turned the other way.

"Meg," Cheryl's tone was very assertive. "Ignore him. He wants you to get mad. That's his plan. Don't let him get to you. Stay cool." Cheryl reached over the railing and patted Meg's hand in an attempt to calm her down. It didn't work. There were now two people in the courtroom the young widow hated.

A tall, thin man Meg hadn't noticed suddenly stood up and cried out, "All rise, this session of the Third District Court is now in session, the honorable Judge Scott M. Truett presiding."

Judge Truett, a short balding man in his mid-forties, walked through a door in the front of the room, up three steps, took his seat, and signaled for all to do likewise. Afraid to move her gaze back to Tidwell, Meg stayed focus on the man in charge of these proceedings.

The judge appeared to be a no-nonsense person, someone whose face Meg would not be able to read. She sensed he might not buy the stunts the defense team was sure to try. But would that make a difference? Would anything make a difference? Had she made a mistake in not taking the money and running? She would know soon enough.

After the charges had been read, the judge recognized Jasper Tidwell's motion to approach the bench.

"Your Honor, it is indeed a pleasure for me to practice in front of such a scholar of the . . . "

"Jasper, you gave me this speech just a few weeks ago, so cut the flowers, and get right to the dirt. What do you want?"

Tidwell smiled, momentarily bowed his head, and continued. "All we request, Your Honor, is to do away with a jury trial and try this case directly before you. We know you to be a wise and fair man, sir."

Judge Truett glanced down at the list of charges, read them over again, and didn't look up. "Mr. Tidwell, you and your client want to try this case in front of me, thus waving a jury by this man's peers. Is that right?" There was irony in his tone.

"That is correct." Tidwell replied with a slight grin.

Looking past the attorney, Judge Truett spoke directly to the defendant. "Young man, do you understand that I will be the sole judge of your guilt or innocence?"

Jim Thomas simply shook his head.

Truett then turned his attention to the other side of the room. "Ms. Bednarz, will you agree to this request?"

"May I have a short conference, Your Honor?"

"You may."

Cheryl turned and leaned over the railing toward Meg. As the women's heads came close, the attorney whispered, "I think this will work in our favor. It will be easier to sway one person rather than twelve."

"So this is all right?" Meg asked.

"Do you trust me?" Cheryl asked.

Meg nodded.

The assistant district attorney turned back to the bench and announced, "The prosecution has no objections Your Honor."

"Very well," the judge said. "That will save us some time. If you are a part of the jury pool and are here waiting to be questioned, you may leave." After two dozen men and women of all shapes and sizes had made their way from the courtroom, the judge looked at Thomas. "Will the defendant rise?"

Thomas stood up beside his lawyer. As soon as he did, Truett asked, "Mr. Thomas, how do you plead?"

Jasper Tidwell answered, "My client pleads not guilty, Your Honor."

"All right, then," Truett flatly replied. "Let's get on with the opening arguments. Ms. Bednarz, as you will be representing the prosecution, are you ready to proceed?"

"Yes, Your Honor."

Cheryl, pushing her chair out from behind the table, stood up and began her opening remarks. "Your Honor. We the people will prove that James Thomas, even though under age, did illegally possess, consume, and become intoxicated on alcohol. And then, while in this state, caused an automobile accident that resulted in the death of Steven Richards. Thus, making Mr. Thomas guilty of the crime of vehicular homicide as well as each of the lesser crimes that are listed in the indictment handed down by the grand jury."

As she finished her initial remarks, she looked directly at James Thomas. The boy's eyes coldly stared back at her. After a span of at least thirty seconds, Cheryl broke off her gaze and continued her opening remarks.

"Your Honor, this case is special, not just because a man has been killed, but because this death was such a waste, a terrible tragedy. The man who died was a model citizen, an important member of our community, active in both civic and church work, and an expectant father. Hence, James Thomas's reckless nature, as well as his consumption of alcohol, has cost not only a community, but a wife, a mother, and an unborn child."

As Cheryl set down, the judge pointed his gavel toward the defense table. "Mr. Tidwell, you may give your opening remarks now. If possible—and after many years of watching you first hand, I doubt it will be possible—make them brief."

"Thank you, Judge," the old attorney replied as he stood. Turning toward the audience, he made a big show of removing his glasses, taking a handkerchief from his pocket, carefully cleaning both lenses, and then returning the glasses to their place on the tip of his sizeable nose. During his entire performance, one that lasted nearly a minute, he didn't speak a word and he never took his eyes off of Meg. She'd never felt so uncomfortable.

"Your Honor," Tidwell began, turning toward the judge's platform, "no one in this courtroom will argue that the loss of Mr. Richards's life was a tragic one. Surely, all of us feel for his widow and unborn child, my client as much as anyone. Judge Truett, I can't tell you how deeply this young man's death has affected Mr. Thomas. Still, there is nothing that he can do that will bring Mr. Richards back to life. Furthermore, we will prove that James Thomas was not the reason that Mr. Richards died."

As Tidwell allowed his words to sink in, he glanced back toward Meg. He studied her intently for a few seconds and continued to push his withering gaze in her direction as he picked up his remarks.

"The charges that have been presented by the prosecution are simply inaccurate and a wild attempt to pin the blame for an accident on someone who was just as much a victim of this tragedy as Mr. Richards. As a matter of fact, even though my only duty here is to prove that my client is not guilty of those crimes and to see that justice does prevail, I will also show through my witnesses, the real party who was at fault, as well as show the extent that some within the local district attorney's office will go to in an attempt to embarrass one of this community's finest families."

Turning his gaze from Meg to Cheryl, Tidwell paused for a moment, and then, in a strong, powerful voice roared, "That is all, Your Honor."

Meg was in shock, anger consuming her like a fire would a pile of dead brush. She glanced back toward Cheryl hoping her ally was mirroring the same emotion. Yet the assistant district attorney hadn't even raised an eyebrow.

Judge Truett, a pencil in hand, wasting no time, said, "Your first witness, Ms. Bednarz."

"The state calls Silas Ragsdale," Cheryl responded.

After the witness was sworn in and took the stand, Cheryl began her examination.

"Mr. Ragsdale, how do you earn your living?"

"I'm a state trooper," the tall, rugged, uniformed man answered.

"In that capacity were you called to an accident on Route 44, on Friday, March 4?"

"Yes, I was."

"Officer Ragsdale, in your own words, can you tell us what you found that morning."

"Officer Bill Johnson was with me and when we arrived at the scene we observed that two cars had been involved in a head-on collision. The first car I came to was on fire with a man trapped inside. I grabbed an extinguisher, as did Officer Johnson, and we put the flames out enough to check on the status of the man, an individual whom I later learned was Steven Richards. He was dead. On checking the fate of the persons in the other car, I discovered all but one of the five passengers to be unhurt. That one, James Thomas, had a cut on his head. Paramedics who had arrived just as we did informed me that the boy—Thomas"—Ragsdale pointed toward the defendant—"would need to be transported to the hospital. As I had already noted a large number of beer cans and empty bottles of Buffalo Scotch in the car in which the kids were riding and upon finding out that Thomas had been driving that vehicle, I asked the paramedics to order a blood test on the individual when he was treated at Springfield Community Hospital."

"Officer Ragsdale," Cheryl broke in, "according to your report, who was at fault?"

"In our report, we concluded that the car driven by James Thomas caused the accident. If you like, we have some slides that will explain why we came to that conclusion."

The courtroom had already been prepared for this visual aid and within two minutes the lights had been turned down and the computer began flashing color images up on the screen.

"As you can see in this photograph, the skid marks on the highway indicate that the Thomas car crossed the center lane and ran head-on into the Richards vehicle. From the damage shown in the next slide, as well as the length of the skid marks, we have concluded the Thomas vehicle was traveling at a very high rate of speed. In excess of eighty miles an hour."

Meg's eyes focused on what had been left of Steve's car. She had not gone to the wrecking yard to see it nor had she given much thought as to what kind of shape it must have been in. Still, as image after image demonstrated the extent of the damage, she quickly understood why he had been so brutally injured. The last slide, one of the inside of the vehicle, showed large amounts of fresh blood dripping from where the door had been torn from the car, forming a pool on the street. Even though she was a nurse and was used to gory injuries, Meg had to turn her head to keep from throwing up.

For the first time since the night of the wreck, the trauma began to take its toll. This impact was so great her head began to swim, causing Meg to close her eyes and take a deep breath. Try as she could to focus her energies and attention back on the stand, the picture of the car still invaded her mind, forcing her to consider time and time again her great loss. Tears welled up in her eyes as she thought about what Steve must have felt and been thinking during his last moments. The image of various parts of his own car piercing his body cut through to her heart. It was some minutes before she was able to regain enough control to glance back at the stand. When she did look up, the Thomas car was being shown. It, too, had been wrecked beyond recognition, and yet, except for one small cut on Jim Thomas's head, the kids had walked away unhurt. How?

The lights came back up as Cheryl turned her attention from the screen toward Thomas and Tidwell and announced, "I'm finished with this witness."

After the assistant district attorney took her place behind the table, Tidwell slowly rose and approached the trooper.

"Officer Ragsdale, you stated that your investigation proved that the Thomas vehicle was at fault. You said that the skid marks from that vehicle were on the wrong side of the road. Tell me, in your expert opinion, could it have been possible for those skids marks to have been on the wrong side of the road because James Thomas had been forced to cross to that side of the road in order to avoid Steven Richards's vehicle that had been traveling on the wrong side of the road?"

"I guess it could have been possible, but . . ." The trooper's answer was cut off by Tidwell's response.

"Not only was it possible, but that is the way it happened." Turning away from the stand and facing Meg, Tidwell struck again. "Officer Ragsdale, can you be 100 percent certain that Steven Richards's vehicle was not the one traveling at too high a rate of speed? I mean, the skid marks end where the two vehicles plowed into each other, so how can you tell which was going the fastest? That is with 100-percent certainty."

"Well," the officer answered, "our tests showed that . . ."

"Officer," Tidwell jumped in, "and the independent tests that I had done by a former lead investigator for the FBI show just the opposite. Can you say, and I want you to listen to this very carefully, to 100-percent certainty, that you are right and the tests that noted expert Jason Rolling conducted were wrong?"

"I can be pretty sure . . ."

"Officer Ragsdale," Tidwell whirled and stared directly into the trooper's eyes. "Pretty sure is not enough. Did you get any alcohol blood test on Steven Richards?"

"No, we didn't. We didn't feel . . ."

"Thank you. Your Honor, the defense is through with this witness."

And so it went, for every witness and every bit of solid testimony that Cheryl brought to light, Jasper Tidwell found a small hole. Could those small holes Tidwell uncovered influence an experienced Judge Truett enough to toss out the district attorney's case? In Meg's eyes, Cheryl was presenting ironclad proof that Thomas was guilty and Tidwell was bluffing, but what about the judge? How did he see it?

It was late in the afternoon when Cheryl called Meg to the stand.

"Do you swear to tell the truth, the whole truth, and nothing but the truth, so help you God?"

"I do."

"State your name."

"Megan Elyse Hankins Richards."

Cheryl smiled at Meg before beginning her questions. It was a reassuring smile meant only to calm her jitters. It didn't work. Meg felt both Jasper Tidwell's and Jim Thomas's cold stares, and these overruled the assistant district attorney's warm smile.

"Mrs. Richards . . . Meg," Cheryl began. "No one would have known your husband any better than you. Hence, we have you here to back up the other things that his close friends and coworkers have already said about him. Did your husband drink?"

"No, he didn't."

"Of course, I can and will enter his driving record into the court, but to the best of your memory had he ever had a ticket or an accident?"

"No," Meg answered, her nerves now calming.

"Mrs. Richards, we all know how tough these proceeding have been on you today." Using a Tidwell tactic, Cheryl turned toward the crowd. "And a woman in your condition doesn't need to answer needless questions. So thank you for your time."

As Cheryl took her seat the attention of the courtroom turned toward Jasper Tidwell. Glancing down at some notes on his table, he slowly pulled his large form from the chair and ambled across the room until he stood before Meg.

"Mrs. Richards," he stated in a gentle voice. "Just like the assistant district attorney, I don't want to keep you up here too long. I'm a considerate man, but there are a couple of questions that I must ask.

"You stated that your husband did not drink, it that correct?"

Meg nodded.

Tidwell continued. "Let it be shown that Mrs. Richards answered in the affirmative."

Pausing for a moment, he walked back across the courtroom, looked at some printed pages, and after picking them up, strolled back to Meg. "I have several sworn statements from college friends of Steve Richards that say they knew him as a drinker."

Glancing at Cheryl, Meg swallowed hard. "Steve did drink in college. He quit when he started going with me."

"Oh," Tidwell raised his eyebrows and glanced back toward the crowd, "so you are saying that he didn't drink around you?"

"I didn't say that," Meg retorted, a bit of frustration and anger now evident in her tone.

"But, Mrs. Richards, when your husband was gone on business, you weren't there, so you can't be sure that he didn't drink. After all, we have no blood alcohol report to verify that he didn't. The state didn't think one was necessary. I'm not blaming you for this, but in this case the state failed to do its job. So we don't know how much Mr. Richards had to drink that night."

Now visibly shaking, Meg watched the attorney once again cross the room. Glancing at some more notes, he looked back up, and from the defense table asked, "Your husband called you on the Thursday before his death and stated that he was almost finished with a big job. Is that right?"

"Yes," Meg whispered.

"Excuse me, Mrs. Richards, what did you say?" Tidwell asked.

In a stronger voice, Meg answered, "Yes."

"Well, if he had just finished a big job, maybe he celebrated a bit before he came home . . ."

"Steve wouldn't have done that," Meg argued.

"So you say, Mrs. Richards." Tidwell's tone was now sarcastic. "But you told the court that he didn't drink either. Now, we have discovered through other testimony that he had been working long—twelve, fourteen, even sixteen-hour—days, in order to get home to you before your anniversary on that Friday. Mrs. Richards, Your Honor, all of you who are here in this courtroom, I propose that it is just as likely that this tired man fell asleep. I mean if he had worked as hard as his coworkers said and then maybe had a drink or two to celebrate. Or maybe even three or four . . ."

Meg, her eyes now filled with tears of anger, lashed out, "You didn't know him. How can you say those things?"

"Your Honor, I object!" Cheryl's words shot out like a cannon blast. "There is no excuse for this woman to be badgered like this. It only serves the purpose to satisfy the defense attorney's huge ego."

"Your Honor," Tidwell yelled. "I will not stand here and take these insults from an attorney who is just learning her trade. Put her in her place!"

After banging his gavel, Truett pointed it at the defense attorney. "Jasper, cut the theater or I'll hold you in contempt. And don't think I won't do it. But in fairness to the case, I must also overrule Ms. Bednarz's objection. This testimony does tie in with the case and I must allow it. I do agree, however, that a more gentle tone is in order from Mr. Tidwell."

Cheryl sat down. It was obvious she was not happy. Tidwell only smiled as he again approached the witness box.

"Mrs. Richards," Tidwell began again in a softer tone. "How well did you really know your husband?"

The attorney looked directly at Meg, his eyes not leaving hers for at least fifteen seconds. Meg stared back but said nothing. In her blushing face, she showed a contempt that anyone in the courtroom could read; her brown eyes flashed fire through her tears.

Satisfied, the defense attorney smiled. "Your Honor, I'm finished with this witness. Thank you, Mrs. Richards."

Meg was trembling with rage as she slowly stood. How dare he imply what he implied! What kind of a person would assassinate the character of a truly good man? How could he live with himself? Composing herself the best she could, Meg, her head down, quickly made her way through the gate and to her seat. Only after she sat down did the judge look at his watch and address the entire room.

"Ladies, gentlemen, as the hour is late, I recommend that we adjourn this proceeding until tomorrow morning at nine."

With the pounding of the judge's gavel, everyone arose, the session ended, and those watching got up to go home. But Meg remained seated.

"Meg, you okay?" Cheryl leaned over the railing and whispered.

She shook her head. Taking a deep breath, she looked toward the defense table and hissed, "Tidwell's a snake. He's as bad as Jim Thomas."

"Don't worry about Jasper," Cheryl assured her. "I'll take care of him. And in all honesty, I think we did pretty well."

"Cheryl," Meg inquired, "can you tell me now why no jury?"

"If Tidwell had lit into you like that in front of a jury," she explained, "they probably would've tried to lynch his client right then and there. A judge usually doesn't let that sort of thing affect him like a jury does. Hence, Tidwell got to use you, and abuse you, a little more than he would with a jury. Besides, Judge Truett and Judge Thomas have got to know each other pretty well and Tidwell figures that Truett might take that into account when deciding the case. So, the old man has got to paint his boy to be the saint and your husband to be something less. But he can't step over the line and make himself look like the devil. He's getting close to that right now. I think he blew it with you!"

"So I didn't mess up?" Meg asked, her mournful eyes meeting those of the assistant district attorney.

"Meg," Cheryl advised, "you were fine. Now you can't do anything more here. Go home and get some rest. Come in here tomorrow looking even more pregnant. Tomorrow very well may be a wrap."

With that bit of advice, the two women walked side by side out of the courtroom. As they emerged into the wide, old hallway, Cheryl turned right and headed for her office to go over her notes. Meg made a left, marched down the steps, and drove straight home to take a shower and try to pull herself back together.

41

Nightmares so haunted her that as the hours wore on Meg grew too fearful even to attempt sleep. Every time she closed her eyes, she was back on the witness stand and Tidwell was badgering her again and again. As he ripped into her, he also tore Steve apart, taking the man she'd loved and transforming him into a monster. Worse yet, in spite of Cheryl's warnings, Tidwell had found a spot in her head. In her dreams, the frumpy attorney pointed to the back of the courtroom where Steve was standing, cut and burned, looking like something out of a horror movie and holding a half-empty bottle of Buffalo Scotch in his right hand.

And then there was Jim Thomas. Every time she awoke from her fitful dreams he was there standing over the bed and smiling. It was almost like he was a ghost. And when she tried to reach out to hit him, the room was filled with wicked laughter and he disappeared—just evaporated into thin air.

Why was she so scared? Why had sleep become a prison? She knew why. It was because no matter what Cheryl said; Meg had blown it. She'd allowed Tidwell to get under her skin, prick her heart, and light a fire in her brain. And everything she'd said had helped the evil man paint Steve in such a dark light. If the judge let Thomas off, it would be her fault. She'd let Steve down and in the process she'd cooked her own chances of revenge. If she'd taken the deal, this would have never happened. What she thought she had been doing for Steve was destroying the only thing he had left—his character.

After a long night with little sleep, she yanked herself from bed, showered, and once more carefully got ready for her day in court. Too sick to eat a real breakfast, she was munching on a couple of saltines when her phone rang. She glanced at the caller ID before picking up.

"Hi, Mom."

"How are you doing?" Barbara asked, her voice just as sweet, caring, and condescending as it was when she taught the preschoolers at Sunday school.

"Okay, I guess. I think I messed up on the witness stand yesterday. I'm not so sure we aren't going to lose the case."

The line was silent for a few seconds before Barbara continued. "You want me to come down and sit with you. I'd be happy to. I'd have been there yesterday, if you'd asked."

"No," Meg quickly assured her. "I don't want to be there with anyone I know. I need to do this by myself. But thanks for asking."

Maybe it has been the discouraging day in court or perhaps the nightmares, but for the first time in weeks Meg actually felt a bit of warmth for her mother. She didn't want her hovering around yet or once again becoming too involved in her life, but hearing her voice did offer a strange bit of comfort.

"If you need me, please call," Barbara said.

"I will. Now I must get moving so I can be there when things start. I hope today is better than yesterday."

"Megan, it will be."

"Thanks, Mom, bye."

Grabbing her purse, Meg made her way out the door and to the car. It was cool with a slight but bitter breeze. The sky was covered with clouds. Before this day was over it would likely rain. How she hoped the ominous weather was not a sign of what would happen in the courtroom.

42

M s. Bednarz," Judge Truett's voice was strong as the trial's second day began, "you may call your next witness."

"The prosecution rests, Your Honor."

Glancing up, the judge gave a nod toward Cheryl's table and then turned to Jasper Tidwell. "Mr. Tidwell, do you have any witnesses?"

"We do, Your Honor."

"Then let's get on with it."

"The defense calls Sam Chambers to the stand."

Meg recognized Chambers as one of the two men she'd seen talking to Tidwell before yesterday's session had begun. Appearing to be in his mid-thirties, he sported a clean-shaven face and thinning, light brown hair and looked very sharp in a dark blue suit and white shirt. If Tidwell wanted to begin the day with someone who appeared successful, he had chosen well.

"Mr. Chambers, just what is it that you do for a living?" Tidwell was looking at the prosecution's table when he asked the question.

"I own Wilson Construction," the witness stated matter-of-factly.

"Did you know Steven Richards?"

"Yes, he and one of his partners audited our books the week of the accident."

Jasper Tidwell sought a degree of clarification. "The accident that we have been discussing in this court proceeding is the one to which you are referring?"

"Yes, sir."

"How was Mr. Richards's work?"

Exasperated, Cheryl voiced a complaint. "Your Honor, I hardly see how this has any bearing on this case."

"Your Honor," Jasper Tidwell interceded, his voice roaring. "I can clearly show where I'm going, that is, if you will just be patient enough to allow me to continue along this line for a few more moments."

Judge Truett, weighing both requests, looked the defense attorney directly in the eye and said, "I will allow you a few more attempts to justify this line of questioning. But, Jasper, this had better not be one of your famous fishing expeditions. I don't want this court's time and money wasted. Now, answer the question, Mr. Chambers."

"His work was superb. The best."

Meg was hardly surprised by the response. What she couldn't believe was that Tidwell was opening a door that made Steve look like such a model citizen. Maybe this day wasn't going to be so bad after all!

"And were you surprised when he finished that work late on Thursday night?"

"No," the businessman answered. "I mean, he pushed himself hard. I don't know when he rested. He and his partner were great. I was so impressed with how fast they worked that I sent them a case of beer as a reward."

Meg's eyes darted to Cheryl and then back to the stand. So that was it. It was a set-up to make Steve look like the drunk driver.

"And when was this?" Tidwell asked now turning to look directly at Meg.

"Right after they finished on Thursday," Chambers replied. "They deserved it. I had it sent right over to their room. Made sure it had already been chilled. I had no idea that either of them would be driving that night or I would have made different plans."

"Thank you, Mr. Chambers," then pausing for just a moment, the attorney turned to Cheryl and smiled. "Your witness."

The assistant district attorney nodded but didn't return the smile. Not bothering to glace at her notes, she pushed her chair back and quickly walked over to the witness.

"Mr. Chambers, I only have one question. Did you see or do you have any knowledge of Mr. Richards consuming any of that case of beer?"

"Well, ma'am, he didn't return it," Chambers' reply brought a small giggle from two or three members of the audience.

"Do I have to repeat my question?" Cheryl sternly asked, ignoring the witness's initial response.

His smile erased, Chambers quickly answered, "No, I didn't see him drink any of the beer I sent over."

"Did anyone else see him drink?"

"Not that I know of," Chamber quickly answered.

"Do you even know if any of the beer was consumed at all?"

"No, ma'am. I don't."

"Thank you, Mr. Chambers. Your Honor, I am finished with this witness."

If Tidwell was surprised by Cheryl's savvy counterpunch, he didn't show it. Instead, he seamlessly moved on to his next witness.

"Your Honor, I call Drake Reason to the stand."

After the witness was sworn in, Tidwell went to work.

"Mr. Reason what is your occupation?"

"I am an engineer for the Consumer Protection Agency."

"What have your tests shown about the make and model of car Mr. Richards was driving on the night of the accident?"

"Some tests have indicated that this particular year and model had steering linkage problems that caused a loss of control."

Tidwell smiled and continued, "So there could have been a malfunction that caused Mr. Richards to lose control of the car."

"It is possible," Reason explained. "It has happened before. There was a wreck in Boston last year where a failed linkage was determined to be a factor in the accident."

"I see," Tidwell said and nodded toward the opposing table. "Your witness."

After Cheryl glanced through some notes, she looked back toward the witness stand. She didn't bother getting up as she posed her question.

"How many wrecks?"

"Excuse me?" Reason replied.

"How many accidents have been attributed to the steering linkage issue?"

The expert licked his lips and moved his eyes toward the defense attorney. As he did, Cheryl pounced.

"Mr. Tidwell might well know the answer," Cheryl said, as she got up from her chair and crossed to a point where the witness's view of the other attorney was blocked, "but Mr. Tidwell is no more an expert in this matter that I am. So, as you are the expert, why don't you answer the question? How many accidents?"

"Two," Reason whispered.

"A bit louder," Cheryl demanded.

"Two."

"And those two accidents attributed to steering linkage were the only two reported in the six-year run of that make and model of car?"

"Yes," Reason answered.

"And there was no recall ever requested by the government?"

"No, there was not."

"I'm finished, Your Honor. And, if so needed, I can provide photographic proof and expert testimony that the steering linkage on Mr. Richards's car was still in perfect condition after the wreck. As a matter of fact, I can even bring the vehicle to this court to prove that point, if necessary." Cheryl shot a glare back to the defense table before calmly saying in her deep Texas drawl, "The ball is back in Mr. Tidwell's court."

Undaunted, Tidwell played his next card by trotting up a host of witnesses, who testified to the nature and character of James Thomas. These talking heads ranged from fellow students, to coaches, neighbors, scoutmasters, teachers, and businessmen. Each of them painted a picture of Thomas as a perfect model for American youth. The testimony made it sound as if the boy was up for sainthood. Still, Cheryl was able to knock holes in these stories, too.

Upon cross-examination, a number of the students admitted that the underage Thomas had been known to drink, even occasionally get drunk. The linchpin moment came when Cheryl cross-examined Matt Craig.

"Mr. Craig, you claim to be James Thomas's best friend, is that correct?"

"Yes," the six-foot, solidly built young man answered. As he waited for the next question, his dark brown eyes sought out Tidwell. The attorney smiled.

"Mr. Craig," Cheryl continued, "you were not with Mr. Thomas on the night of the accident. Is that correct?"

"No, I was home that night."

"I believe you were grounded. Is that correct?"

All the color abruptly drained from Craig's face, his confused expression clearly spelling out his shock. As he struggled to find words, Cheryl continued.

"I can bring witnesses, including your mother and girlfriend, who will not only confirm that you were grounded but will give the reason as to why."

"Your Honor," Tidwell barked from his table, "the fact that he was grounded that night has no bearing on this case."

Truett looked down at the assistant district attorney, "Can you justify this line of questioning?"

"Yes sir, and as this is Mr. Tidwell's witness and he opened up the door, I plan on walking through it and revealing the skeletons in the closet."

"Then go ahead," Truett suggested.

"Mr. Craig, why were you grounded by your parents?"

The boy sheepishly answered, "I got caught drinking."

"Was it at a party?"

"Yes, ma'am."

"At whose house?"

Craig took a deep breath. "Jim Thomas."

"And did Jim Thomas supply the alcohol that night?"

"Yes, ma'am." The kid scratched he head before adding, "well, actually his father did. The judge always got the booze for us. He didn't want his son getting picked up buying with a fake ID."

Cheryl smiled as she glanced back to Tidwell and then deeper into the courtroom to Judge Thomas. "I think that is all I need from this witness."

Truett dismissed Craig. When the teen had exited the courtroom, he glanced over to the prosecution's table.

"Miss Bednarz, if an investigation has not yet begun, I suggest your office get with the police chief and validate Mr. Craig's testimony. If he has lied about who supplied the alcohol for these parties, then I will charge him with perjury. If what he says is true, then the adult who supplied that alcohol needs to be charged and dealt with." Glancing at his watch, the judge looked up and said, "This is the end of the morning session. We will begin again at 1:30."

As Meg got up, she felt a lot better than she had when she'd walked into the courtroom. Cheryl had anticipated every move Tidwell was going to make and was ready to counter. Her preparation had likely come as a shock to the defense, but what would the crafty old attorney do next?

43

OVER LUNCH AT A NEARBY SUBWAY, MEG ASKED CHERYL THE QUESTION that was likely on the minds of everyone who witnessed the morning's proceedings. "How did you know what Tidwell was going to do? Every time he made some kind of move, you pulled out a trump card?"

"It was nothing really," she modestly explained. "Everyone knew he'd trot out folks who'd attempt to make Thomas look like the all-American, innocent kid. So I spent the last month looking at every possible person that Tidwell would likely use and did research on them. The Craig kid likely hadn't told Tidwell about his checkered past. So I went to his girlfriend and mother to discover why the guy who was usually Thomas's shadow was not there that night. The mother slipped up and said she was so glad she grounded him. The rest of the information came easily after that."

"But the consumer affairs guy," Meg noted. "How did you have the information you needed at your fingertips?"

"Oldest trick in the book," Cheryl explained. "When you can't blame the man, blame the vehicle. I did full research on the make and model to see what Tidwell would find. The car was simply well-made and had few problems. But I'm sure

Tidwell thought I was too green to already have those facts in hand. He was expecting me to be surprised by that move. I loved watching him wilt when I had more facts on the matter than he probably did."

Meg nibbled on her sandwich before posing the question that she really was afraid to ask. "Are we winning?"

Cheryl shrugged. "I can't read Judge Truett and I doubt if anyone can. I do know he is a pretty good friend of the Thomas family. But he also has the reputation of not letting anything stand in the way of the truth."

"So you think he'll make a judgment just on the evidence?" Meg asked.

"Yeah. Let's review what has happened in the first day and a half. Tidwell has attempted to cast doubt upon Steve's character and I just don't think he's done it. He also attempted to paint Thomas as an angel and I think we beat that one, too. Then, in a move I had expected, Craig volunteered that it was Judge Thomas who supplied the booze for the kid's parties. So I think Jasper has to be worried, and if I am right, the only thing he can do to shore up his case is to call Thomas to the stand. I sure hope that's what he does."

"So you want to take on Thomas?" Meg asked.

"If I were Tidwell," Cheryl shot back, "I'd be scared of having me go after him. He has seen how well I've been prepared. But Tidwell is in a hole and he really has no choice because the blood evidence doesn't lie. His client was drunk. So he has to put him there and let the chips fall where they may. That may shore up his guilt, but not putting Thomas up there will certainly seal his doom."

Meg nodded, a rush of warmth filling her heart. Maybe they could beat the Thomas money after all.

Cheryl's eyes drifted to a far window. As the light caught in those baby blues, she smiled grimly. "Meg, I want him to feel my wrath. I want to treat him like I wish I could have treated my father's killer. I want the chance to deliver the final blow for the prosecution by personally knocking the cover off the man who was responsible for killing your husband. I want Jim Thomas to pay the price for every person who has ever used a car and a bottle as a weapon. I can't begin to explain how badly I want that!"

Cheryl turned her attention back to the woman across the table. "How did you sleep last night?"

Shaking her head, Meg answered, "Not well. I was so mad I just tossed and turned."

"Well," Cheryl smiled, "tonight you'll sleep, and if I'm right, sleep very well. I think we'll have a verdict by the end of the afternoon." Looking at her watch, she continued, "Okay, time to get back."

Meg took a last sip of her Coke. Would this be the day when she could put this huge weight of retribution off her shoulders and onto the person who should be carrying the load? Would she be able to visit Steve's grave tonight and tell him that she had won?

44

ONCE THE AFTERNOON SESSION OPENED UP, JASPER TIDWELL DID JUST what Cheryl had predicted. Still, it was easy for anyone to see the defense attorney didn't look very pleased when he called Jim Thomas to the stand. Maybe sensing the verdict was no sure thing, the young man looked nervous and afraid as the questioning began.

"Mr. Thomas," Tidwell's voice was kind and gentle, almost grandfatherly as he began, "on the night in question, in your own words, tell me, and this court, exactly what happened?"

"Well, sir," the boy began, "a few of my friends and I had been out having a little party. Nothing big, just laughing and stuff around a bon fire out at the lake. The fire was dying down and it was getting cold so we decided to go to Susie's, excuse me, Miss Milam's house. On the way, I looked up and saw this car barreling around a curve, his lights on bright, in my lane.

"I guess I just reacted, I don't know, but I swerved into the other lane and he followed me, probably trying to avoid me and correct his own mistake. I put on my brakes, but I couldn't miss him."

"I see," Tidwell stated, nodding his head as if in approval of the story. "Now this is very important. Think carefully before

240

you answer my next question. Had you been drinking that night?"

"No, sir," the boy quickly replied. "The others had, but I didn't because I was driving. I didn't feel that would be responsible, sir."

Meg could hardly believe the piety the boy was attempting to show. She looked around and noted that very few other folks seemed to be buying it either. But what about Judge Truett? She couldn't read his face. He remained as stoic as he had been throughout the entire trial.

"But, James," the attorney said, "at the hospital the blood test indicated that you had some alcohol, an amount over the state's legal limit, in your blood. If you didn't drink, how can you explain that?" Tidwell turned after asking the question, strolled over to an area just in front of the prosecution's table, faced the audience, and waited for a response.

Clearing his throat, Thomas began his explanation. "Well, when the wreck happened, I hit my head. As a matter of fact, you can see the scar," he pointed to a long mark on his forehead. "Anyway, I was knocked out cold and in an attempt to bring me around, one of the kids poured some scotch down my throat. When I came to, my girlfriend poured some more in my wound to help stop any chance of infection."

"So," Tidwell, now turning back toward his witness, concluded, "you actually had nothing to drink before the accident. And the car driven by Steven Richards, the one that the prosecution claims you struck, blinded you with its bright lights and actually hit you. Is that correct?"

"Yes, sir."

During the entire line of questioning, Thomas delivered his answers like a pro. Not once did he ever sound or appear anything but completely sincere.

"Ms. Bednarz," Judge Truett asked, "do you have any questions?"

"I believe I have some pretty good ones," she replied from her seat.

A few seconds later, Cheryl got up from her chair and moved like a cat toward the witness. She glared at him for about thirty seconds and then in a low, steady voice inquired, "Mr. Thomas, do you actually expect us to believe that your blood count went to 1.4 because of one shot of whiskey administered to bring you around after you hit your head?"

"That's the way it happened," the boy resolutely answered. He then continued, "Of course, I'm no chemist, so I couldn't tell you the levels or anything."

"No," Cheryl smiled, "you're not a chemist, and you are not a very good liar either."

"Your Honor!" Jasper Tidwell's voice roared throughout the courtroom.

The assistant district attorney was ready. With no hesitation she marched to her table and picked up two stacks of paper. She dropped one stack on the defense table and handed the other to the judge. As the two men looked through the documents, she explained what they would find.

"In each of these reports you will find sworn testimony from every teenager who was at the bon fire the night of the accident. They were deposed in front of a court reporter and witnesses. Each one stated very clearly that James Thomas, the defendant, was drinking both beer and scotch that night. In fact, he actually taught them a drinking game."

Cheryl glanced back toward Tidwell. He'd pushed both his hands into his hair. She studied the old man for a moment before turning back to the judge. "We can produce these eleven high school students and put them on the stand if you and Mr. Tidwell would like."

"It's your call, Jasper," Truett announced.

"Your Honor," the defense attorney stammered, "I had no idea. I'm just as surprised as you are in this matter." He glanced back to the depositions and shrugged. "I see no reason why we would need anyone to verify what they have already sworn to."

Cheryl smiled. "May I continue my questioning of Mr. Thomas?"

"You may," Truett assured her.

"I believe you told us that Steven Richards's car lights were on high beam and thus blinded you as you rounded the curve. Is that correct?"

"Yes, ma'am."

Cheryl walked quickly back to the prosecution's table and picked up a piece of paper. She studied it for a moment before moving back to the bench and handing the document to the judge.

"Your Honor and Mr. Tidwell, Mr. Richards had an appointment with Gene's Auto Service, located on Abbott Road in Springfield for the Monday after the tragic wreck that claimed his life. You will note this on the service agreement I have presented to the court." She paused a moment, looked back at Tidwell and smiled. "The week before he was killed, Mr. Richards had received a warning ticket because one of his bright lights was not working. He informed the head mechanic at Gene's of this and that was the reason for the service appointment. Thus, he was not driving with high beams that night and the low beams would not have caused any distractions for other drivers including Mr. Thomas."

Tidwell flew toward the bench where Truett handed him the document. The lawyer studied it for just a moment before moving slowly back to his seat.

"No more questions, Your Honor," Cheryl snapped as soon as her adversary sat down.

"Any follow-up questions, Jasper?" the judge asked.

Tidwell shook his head.

"Mr. Thomas," Judge Truett flatly stated, "the court is finished with you. You may step down." Turning toward the defense table, the judge asked, "Mr. Tidwell, do you have more witnesses?"

"No, the defense is finished."

"Ms. Bednarz, is the prosecution completed?"

"Yes, Your Honor."

"Okay," Judge Truett said, "if there are no objections, I will initiate a fifteen-minute recess then I will come back and hear closing arguments. Court will reconvene at 2:20 p.m."

Meg couldn't believe Cheryl hadn't drilled Thomas more. He had lied! Why hadn't she gone for the throat? Why hadn't she really lit a fire under him? She had him in her sights. Hadn't she thrown in the towel too soon? Even with all the testimony working in their favor, maybe this wasn't a sure thing after all.

45

Using the recess to get a drink of water, Meg was shocked to run into her mother walking down the hallway. Why was she here? After all, Meg had asked her to stay home.

"Mom, I thought we agreed you weren't coming?"

"I know," Barbara answered, "but I couldn't stay away either. Will you please let me sit with you? Please let me be your mother again?"

In truth, that wasn't too much to ask. Meg hadn't anticipated that being alone was going to be this disquieting. Meg needed someone there—especially if things didn't work out.

After Meg nodded in approval, Barbara asked, "What's going on?"

As they walked side by side down the hall, Meg caught her mother up on the events of today. The session was just beginning when the two of them reentered the courtroom and seated themselves behind Cheryl.

Judge Truett looked out at the scene before him, adjusted his robe and glanced over to the prosecutor. After catching the assistant district attorney's eye, he asked, "Are you ready Ms. Bednarz?"

"Yes, Your Honor."

Cheryl stood at the table and, after taking two steps toward the bench, began, "I don't think there is any doubt that we have proven, despite all of the smoke screens that Mr. Tidwell has thrown up, that James Thomas is guilty on all charges. If the court does not rule so, not only will we in the county be guilty of freeing a man who took another man's life but we will be making a larger statement to any man or woman in this county, this state, and even this country who drinks and drives in the future. That message is 'go ahead, you can get away with it.'" She paused, took a deep breath and added, "Even if you kill someone.

"At some point the American system has to protect us against those who maim and murder through the use of alcohol. If James Thomas," Cheryl pointed toward the youth with both her hand and eyes, "is cleared, then how many more of our youth, and even the adults in this community, will think nothing of drinking and then driving?"

As she allowed the words to soak in she moved toward the center of the room. She stood there a moment before picking up her arguments. "It is time, no, it is way past time for us to get this kind of abuse off the streets and away from those who can be hurt. The actions of James Thomas have left a pregnant woman alone and will leave a child to wonder what his or her father was like. While the defendant lives, the innocent party, as well as those who needed and depended on him, must pay a huge price. Meg Richards and her unborn child have already been sentenced to a life without a husband and a father. This happens over 12,000 times a year in this country. In these cases, no court decides who dies, but rather that decision is in the hands of an alcohol-fueled executioner. Now the time has come to find one of those executioners guilty."

The assistant district attorney turned toward the Thomas family and continued, "In this case, as in almost every other case involving underage drinking, it was an adult who supplied the alcohol. The fact that the adult in this matter might have been a member of the bench shows how little regard most in America view the problem of underage drinking.

"In conclusion," she said, once more facing the judge, "Your Honor, we have proven our case. There can be no doubt. Now is the time and the only verdict that the evidence can possibly call for is guilty. Thank you."

"Thank you, Ms. Bednarz," the judge said from his bench. After she had taken her seat, he turned to the defense. "Are you ready, Mr. Tidwell?"

Jasper Tidwell rose from his chair and stood behind his table. He exhibited little of the confidence he'd displayed earlier. Far from employing his normal dramatic flair, he glanced up at the bench and quietly said, "Sir, I do not believe that the prosecution has proven its case beyond a shadow of a doubt. I believe that the law enforcement agencies not only bungled their investigation but that there was a rush to judgment against my client simply because of his youth. The police failed to check the blood alcohol level of Steven Richards. That in itself shows a rush to judge. I also would like to point out that in my view nothing presented by the prosecution has conclusively proven who was at fault. Further, the thin evidence the state presented has been successfully challenged by testimony and reports supplied by the defense."

He looked back at his notes before picking up again. "Still, there has been a significant loss here. A woman has lost her husband in an unfortunate accident. This accident might just as easily have been caused by his impaired judgment, but we will never know. Still, at the urging of my client, his family has shown their incredible compassion by endowing a scholarship in the name of Steven Richards at our own university. That is how forgiving the Thomas family is."

Tidwell pulled his handkerchief out to wipe his brow and added, "If there is even the faintest doubt as to who was at fault, then there can't be a guilty verdict and this is nothing more than a tragic accident. Your Honor, James Thomas is guilty of nothing but attempting to avoid that accident. His very conduct through his entire life has been much like any other youth in our community. His fiber is that of a young man who will become the best we have to offer. You cannot find him guilty with the proof of innocence so heavily in his favor. Once more, and I can't emphasize this enough, the evidence against him is flimsy at best. If anyone is guilty, it is the hungry prosecution that so needlessly wasted your time and the county's money.

"So, toss this case out the door, and then I suggest that you take a long look at the manner and the reasons the grand jury and district attorney's office use in deciding who is persecuted," smiling, Tidwell paused a moment, "I mean prosecuted in the county. Thank you."

With that, the grand old man wiped his brow in dramatic fashion and sat down.

The judge shook his head, "Jasper that is the shortest summation I've ever heard you present." Looking back to the rest of the court, Truett continued, "Ladies and gentlemen, this court is now adjourned until such time as I have studied the testimony and feel ready to render a verdict. I suggest that you stay close so that an officer of this court can advise you when I have reached a decision. I can guarantee this case will be decided by no later than early this evening." With no further words, he got up and departed for his chambers.

46

Two hours is barely any time in the span of a life or even a week. But when waiting for a verdict, two hours is an eternity.

During the time that had already passed, Meg had thrown up twice, downed three Cokes, paced the hall outside the courtroom, and spent countless minutes replaying in her mind both the trial and the events of the last two months. During these long minutes, every person who came out of the courtroom raised her hopes, but each time when that person had proven not to be a court officer, she had seen her hopes dashed.

Now as she sat at the conference table in the district attorney's office, Meg felt as if the world had stopped moving. Speaking to no one in particular, she asked, "How long is it going to take?

"As long as it takes," was the only reply Cheryl could muster.

"Don't worry, Darling," Barbara said in her best Sunday school teacher, comfort tone. "It'll all work out for the best."

Meg glared at her mother. She was supposed to be here to support Meg and that meant leaving her pious attitude at home! That eternal faith of hers! Why couldn't she just pitch the positive sentiment and get mad once in a while? Didn't she ever get frustrated? Didn't she ever realize that things don't always work out for the best? Was there ever a point that she felt was worth fighting, really fighting for, or did she always accept everything as God's will?

As the two hours became three, Meg was questioning more and more if justice would really be served. The testimony Tidwell had presented seemed so transparent to her, but maybe the judge had not seen through it. After all, he hadn't seen firsthand just what kind of person Jim Thomas was. He hadn't been publicly humiliated by Thomas like she had at the cleaners. He hadn't observed the way the teen really viewed the world and life. So maybe the judge could be fooled by what Tidwell had done!

And what about Steve? Did Judge Truett really believe the horrible, unreal picture that Tidwell attempted to paint? If he did, would he blame Steve for what happened? This was a nightmare, one that apparently wasn't going to end. As the time dragged on, she rued more and more not taking the money.

Meg glanced over to Cheryl. "Is his taking this much time to reach a verdict working against us?"

"I don't know," she admitted. "In most cases like this, we are waiting on a jury. A judge is different. Each works at his own pace. Old Jasper is hanging this whole case on the fact the police did not test Steve's blood. That might convince one person on a twelve-person jury, but I just can't see that working with a judge deciding this case. But you never know, after all, sometimes it rains even in West Texas."

The assistant district attorney had no more than finished her analogy when there was a knock at the door. A few seconds later a young man stepped into the room and announced, "Ms. Bednarz, the judge will call the court to order and render his judgment in five minutes. I suggest you come back into the courtroom now."

"Finally," Meg breathed. But what almost kept her in her seat was the question of whether this was going to be good news. Was this the ruling she wanted to hear?

As Meg, her mother, and Cheryl took their places, Tidwell and the Thomas family filed into the room from a side door. Over the course of the next three minutes, the spectators and press filled the remainder of the seats. When the judge entered the room, the milling throng grew silent.

Meg's heart jumped into her throat as the stoic bailiff stood and announced, "This court, the Honorable Judge Scott Truett presiding, is once again in session."

As the judge sat down, he looked over the packed courtroom as if taking inventory of those he knew and those that were strangers to him. Finally, after what seemed like a lifetime, he began to speak. His voice was strong and his tone deadly serious.

"Ladies and gentlemen. The case that I have studied over the past few hours is not one to take lightly. There are lessons to be learned from what transpired in both the courtroom this week and on the highway not that long ago. I hope that those lessons will not be overlooked by the press or by those members of the public who have viewed these proceedings.

"I would like to ask that when the judgment is read, those present refrain from any outbursts of any kind. And I will enforce that request if it becomes necessary."

Picking his glasses up from his bench, the judge looked at the defense table. "Will the defendant please rise?"

Slipping his glasses on, the judge began. "Mr. James Thomas, it is the judgment of this court after hearing the case presented against you that you are . . ."

Meg crossed her fingers as the judge paused, her vision focused on Thomas. As his fate hung in the air, he swallowed hard. He must have never expected it to get this far. He must have thought his father could have had the case tossed out. Now the next words could ruin his entire life. At this, the most important moment of his life, he looked incredibly pale, sweat lined his brow, and his hands tensed and relaxed at regular intervals.

Meg's eyes darted from Thomas to the other side of the room. Cheryl Bednarz projected an air of cool professionalism. Yet she had to be churning on the inside. After all, she had never wanted to win so badly.

The judge, reading from a piece of paper he held in his right hand, continued, "The court finds the defendant guilty of one count of operating a motor vehicle while under the influence of alcohol."

Tidwell had already failed once. Meg sighed deeply as she waited for the judge to go on.

"The court finds the defendant guilty of one count of endangerment and reckless driving."

Meg clenched her fist as she waited for the judge to rule on the big one.

"And the court finds the defendant, James Thomas, guilty of one count of vehicular homicide."

Thomas's jaw grew slack. He would have collapsed into his chair except for the support of Jasper Tidwell's arm. Thomas's father and mother looked completely stunned as they sat in the row directly behind their son. It was a slam dunk for Cheryl, yet her face remained blank as a sheet of unused copy paper. Somehow, she was holding her emotions in check.

"This court," Judge Truett continued, "will meet for the sentencing phase of this trial tomorrow at ten o'clock. The defendant will remain free on bail until that time." Glancing around the room once more, the judge struck his gavel and quickly disappeared into his chambers.

Turning, Cheryl finally flashed a smile as she reached across the railing to embrace Meg. "We did it, kid; we did it, kid; we did it, kid. You should sleep well tonight!"

A rush of different emotions hit Meg like a blast of winter wind. She didn't know quite how to react. She was more numb than happy and she suddenly felt very tired. The one thing she didn't feel was real joy or satisfaction. Even though she couldn't explain it, this victory seemed hollow. She now fully realized that winning in court was not going to bring Steve back.

As Meg turned to leave the courtroom, another familiar face greeted her.

"Mrs. Richards, this is Robyn Chapman, Channel 10 News. We are live. Do you have any comment on this verdict?"

"A-a-a," Meg stuttered. Then, forgetting about sounding prepared or intellectual, she simply stated what she felt. "He was guilty of killing my husband. He deserved worse, far worse, but we'll take what we can get. It won't bring Steve back, but maybe it will be the start of putting Thomas in hell."

"Thank you, Mrs. Richards." The reporter probably hadn't expected those last words or that kind of reaction. Still, she was a pro and didn't let what she hadn't expected throw her. Glancing around the hall, Chapman found Cheryl and immediately signaled the cameraman to follow her. Heading off the assistant district attorney, she inquired, "Ms. Bednarz, what will you go after in the punishment phase?"

"The max!" Cheryl shouted over her shoulder as she walked off. "We'll ask for as much as we can get." Grabbing Meg by the hand, she dragged her down the hall and away from the media. "Well, Meg, why don't we go get something to eat? I'll buy."

"No, Cheryl, I'll buy," Meg answered. "You deserve to be treated for the job you did. After all, you got him for me."

Cheryl nodded in agreement. "Not just for you. I got Jim Thomas to win a decadelong war. I can finally close the door on the greatest loss of my life, too!

47

Dinner was much more than just a meal. It was a victory celebration. Those who joined them, Barbara Hankins and Kent
Reynolds, the current man in Cheryl's life, and three more
employees from the courthouse, were all pleased the case had
gone in the state's favor. But none of these people knew or felt
the real triumph that Cheryl and Meg jointly embraced.

For Cheryl, it was an almost decadelong dream come true.
She had beaten all the arguments of the best defense attorney
in the state and won an alcohol verdict outright and in full
measure. She felt as if her father was with her—smiling, laughing, and reliving each moment of the case. While she knew she
would continue to press for convictions in cases like this for as
long as she practiced, she had already exorcised a demon that
had been driving her for years. With this case, a certain phase
of her life had ended and she was ready to go on to the next
knowing a certain kind of peace and with a need to expand her
life beyond her present work. And, as it was likely the Thomas
family would put pressure on Webb Jones to can her, her days
in Springfield were surely numbered.

Meg was experiencing a different kind of pleasure. For her,
winning meant being able to put aside her fantasies of gain-

ing a measure of revenge. The guilty Jim Thomas, with his pale face and slackened jaw, was the picture she wanted to see. While she felt no sadness or remorse for what she was sure the courts would do to him, his image no longer controlled her every thought and action. With that demon exercised she could actually enjoy these moments with friends. And for the first time in months she could laugh.

Still, even this great joy, realized by rehashing each detail of the case, was not as sweet as Meg thought it would be. In victory, she was still a woman who was defined almost entirely not by what she had but by what had been lost. And the hate that had ruled her daily life for so long likely couldn't be sustained much longer. But she also couldn't imagine a time when warmth and love would come back into her heart either.

After the party broke up, she left the restaurant and slipped into her car. When she placed the key into the ignition, she noticed again the wedding ring she still wore on her left hand. In the dim light of a street lamp, she studied it, touched it, and then, for the first time in over five years, slipped it off.

The reason for the celebration was also the reason she was so alone. That solitary thought hit her like nothing ever before had. It was like a lead weight had just fallen onto her stomach. And all through her body the repercussions could still be felt, especially when she thought about the child she was carrying—a fatherless child!

It wasn't supposed to be this way. It was supposed to feel good, satisfying, not cold and unemotional. So, in victory, the senselessness of what had happened was now a bigger factor in her life than the actual ruling. Even though Jim Thomas had been named officially responsible, this didn't change the fact that Meg was still the one suffering the greatest loss. So while she had what she wanted, she didn't have what she needed.

Meg hadn't cried in a long time. She'd reigned in most of those emotions just after viewing Steve's body. For weeks, rage and anger had controlled her to the point where she wouldn't or couldn't feel anything else. Now, with the guilty verdict, she discovered that the hate and rage couldn't totally sustain her anymore. Meg, now maybe for the first time, felt the real pangs of a person living without love.

So as she drove out of the parking lot she didn't turn left toward home but rather right toward the hospital. She couldn't face an empty apartment. She had to have someone to talk to—someone to tell just how much she missed and needed Steve. She needed to be with a friend who could explain why she wasn't as happy and why she felt more alone than she ever had. There was only one person she knew who might be able to do that.

The mournful pain that had appeared as she left the victory party didn't subside as she got closer and closer to the hospital. If anything, it grew worse. The tears were now coming in torrents and she was having problems seeing clearly enough to even find the turn into the parking lot. Swinging into the first empty parking spot, she let the car idle for a moment. She didn't want anyone to see her this way. And because of that pride, she couldn't allow anyone to know how lost she was. Thus, she almost backed out of her space, getting as far as putting the shifter into reverse. Yet, when she couldn't think of anywhere else to go, she pushed the transmission into park, reached up, and switched the key to the off position. Then, finding a handkerchief, she began to cry again. And for the next half hour, she cried months' worth of tears.

When she finally was able to gain some control of her emotions, she flipped on the interior light of the car and repositioned her rearview mirror to take stock of herself. Grabbing a tissue, she wiped the makeup runs from her face and dabbed a bit more in its place. Still, even after the makeup had been vigilantly applied and the hair combed, she looked far from perfect. Her eyes were bloodshot and her face noticeably swollen. Turning off the light, knowing that she had done her best, she got out of the car and walked the fifty feet to the employee entrance.

The night air, the moonlight, and the stars, all so romantic in nature, only served to make Meg feel that much more alone. And it was this sense of loneliness that pushed her across the parking lot. A light breeze blew her hair around her face and her maternity dress to hug her now slightly rounding midriff. Pausing just before she entered the building, she took a deep breath, forced a smile, and then, satisfied she was fully composed, shoved the door open.

"Meg!" There was genuine excitement in Jan's voice. "Congratulations! Heather called a few minutes ago and told us that you won."

"Thanks," Meg answered, wondering all the while if Jan noticed the shaking in her voice. "We won. Of course, they still have to sentence him. It'll be tomorrow before we know just how much we won."

"Listen," Jan's voice was now a decibel softer and more sympathetic, "I'm sorry if I lost my patience with you during this whole thing. I understand why you've been on edge. If I've been short with you or anything, well . . ."

Waving her hand, Meg forced a smile. "You haven't said or done anything you shouldn't have done or said. Besides, I've been pretty weird." Glancing around, she continued, "Where's Molli? I thought she had the shift tonight."

"She did," Jan replied, "but she got Karry to switch off with her. It seems that Paul called . . ."

"Paul Mason?" Meg was a little confused.

"Yeah."

"I thought that he was going out with Heather?"

"I guess he thought he would like to go out with Molli again, too," Jan answered. "It's not like he and Heather were engaged. Anyway, he asked her out and she accepted."

"I wonder if Heather knows," Meg asked.

"I don't know." Jan shrugged. "But that's the good doctor, one conquest right after another. Heather had to be aware of his reputation. No one is going to tie him down any time soon. Thankfully, Molli is just out for a good time. Don't you think that's what Heather wanted?"

A stunned Meg shook her head. What about the advice she'd given Heather? This was going to hurt her. Why had she said what she said?

"Anyway," Jan's voice brought Meg back into the moment, "I'm sure she didn't take him seriously." Jan waited a second, as if searching for her train of thought, before asking, "What kind of sentence are they going to give the kid?"

"I don't really know," Meg answered. "But Cheryl Bednarz believes the way the judge sounded when he delivered the verdict, he would go for the maximum or at least close to it." Pausing a moment, Meg concluded, "He'd better!"

Changing the subject, Jan inquired, "What are you doing here, anyway?"

"Oh, I just stopped by to see a patient—Meg then glanced at the clock—"and I'd better do it before it gets any later."

Visiting hours ended at nine o'clock, so they had been officially over for forty-five minutes when Meg began walking down the long hallway. Still, she was a nurse, even if she was off duty, and the rules at this small hospital were generally lax for regular folks, much less hospital personnel. She knew that no one would mind her stopping by to see a sick friend. In fact, it might earn her some brownie points with Administrator Willis.

She knew Nancy would want to know the outcome of the case and Meg figured she should be the one to tell her. As a matter of fact, she'd expected Nancy had been calling her house all evening just to find out what had happened. And for some reason, now that Meg was so lonely and filled with so many different emotions, Nancy just seemed to be the one person she could turn to who could make some sense out of her life—not just what had just happened but also what the future held. So as much as she didn't want to admit it, she wasn't really here to give Nancy the news, she was here to have Nancy help her understand what this news really meant to Meg and her future. After taking a moment to touch her hair, she knocked softly on the door to room 211.

When no one responded, Meg knocked a little more loudly. When Nancy still didn't call out, she turned to walk away. Disappointed, Meg figured she could catch Nancy before the morning session. She had only walked a few steps from the door when something stopped her. Deep down she knew that no matter how tired Nancy was, no matter how sick she was feeling, even if she were asleep, she'd want to be awakened if someone needed her. So, retracing her steps, Meg slowly pushed the door open.

The room was dark. Gently closing the door behind her, Meg felt her way across the floor until she touched the edge of the bed.

"Nancy," she whispered.

There was no response.

"Nancy." This time the whisper was a bit louder. "Hey, sleeping beauty, it's Meg. C'mon, wake up. I've got some great news. At least, I think it is."

Still there was no response. Reaching out to where she knew Nancy's shoulder should be, Meg found only an empty bed. In shock, she reached up and yanked the string on the reading lamp. The room was empty. No patient, no books, no iPod, and no flowers.

They must have moved her. She has gotten worse and they probably put her in ICU. Walking out the door and back to the nurse's station, Meg noted Marsha Kolinek now seated behind the counter.

"Hi, Marsha." Meg's voice was friendlier than it had been in months.

Looking up, the nurse responded. "Hey, I understand congratulations are in order. I hope that he gets what he really deserves."

Nodding, Meg asked, "Nancy, the patient in 211, she's not there any more. Where are you all hiding her?"

A genuinely puzzled look came across Marsha's face. "Gosh, you're right. She's not in 211. I hadn't thought about it. I don't know what happened to her. She wasn't there when I came on. Let me check."

Meg glanced down the hall and saw Jan. "Never mind. I'm sure that Jan knows."

"Jan, I need some information."

"You're asking the right person," Jan shot back. "Who runs this place?"

"You do," Meg laughed.

"And you'd better not forget it!" the nurse said. "Now, who needs an executive decision?"

Smiling, Meg went on, "Well, we just thought you might know where a patient has been moved to."

"It's so good to see you smile," Jan answered sincerely. "Now, what patient?"

"The terminal cancer patient in room 211," Meg explained.

Jan glanced down at her feet for a moment and without looking back up asked, "Why do you want her?"

"She's kind of become a friend," Meg replied. "I wanted to tell her what happened at court today."

Jan stared deeply into Meg's brown eyes. Then, in a quiet voice, she announced, "Nancy's not here."

"I know that," Meg replied. "But where is she?"

Jan shook her head, "She's gone. She died Monday night."

"No," Meg moaned. "Not yet. Not this soon."

Before anyone could say anything, Meg rushed back into room 211. It had been cleaned and was ready for another patient. It was as if Nancy had never been there. Her eyes searched for something of the woman she'd come to know and maybe even love. There was nothing to say she was ever here— not even in the wastebasket.

Tears once again flooded her eyes as she sat down in the chair beside the bed. Just hours after she had experienced what she had thought was such a wonderful victory, she had to face another tragic loss. Standing up, she clenched her jaw, shook her fist, and whispered, "Why?"

Opening the door, she turned the light off, and swallowing hard, straightened herself and strolled back down to the station. As she walked around the corner, she choked out, "Well, I broke the cardinal rule. I got too wrapped up in a case."

Marsha just nodded. Getting up from her seat, Jan went to the head nurse's desk, opened a side door, and pulled out a small, carefully wrapped package. Looking up, she took a deep breath before she spoke. "On Monday night, late, Nancy called the desk and asked if I would come down and pick something up. A few minutes later, when I got there, she handed me this. She said it contained something for someone very special." Jan paused until Meg's eyes met her own. "That special person was you. She explained it was a road map. That's all. I don't know what that means."

Setting the package on the nurse's station counter, Jan continued, "I took it and put it in the desk over here. A few minutes later when I went down to check on her, she was dead. It was kind of weird. Her iPod was playing some kind of gospel song and the girl who was singing sounded so happy and here Nancy was dead."

Meg walked the four feet to where Jan stood, gently reached out, and took the package from the counter. Not bothering to look at it, she stuck it in her purse.

Meg choked out, "Was the song entitled, 'He Set My Life To Music'?"

"Yeah," Jan replied, "I think so."

"She played that a lot," Meg softly explained. "I guess that's better than going out with the 'dark music'?"

"What's that?" Marsha asked.

"Nothing," Meg quietly replied. "It's just a tune I have known far too well."

"I wonder what she gave you," Marsha asked. When no one replied, she glanced up at Meg and inquired, "Do you know?"

Meg shook her head, turned, and sadly strolled down the hall and out the door. The breeze had gotten a little colder and a little stronger in the few minutes that had passed since she had gone inside. Clouds had begun to gather and it looked like the storm that had been brewing since morning now might hit within a few hours. But all of this went unnoticed, overpowered by a sense of loss too deep to fathom. Meg was alone, really alone. There was no one left on earth who really knew her heart.

As she drove, numbness joined fatigue, and by the time she got home, they had double teamed her to the point she could barely climb the steps to her apartment. When she got inside, she simply fell into bed, fully dressed. She didn't even bother to take off her shoes or turn out the lights. Within seconds, she was deep in sleep. Not the kind of sleep that brought rest and relief, just the kind that promised escape.

A few hours later, she awoke enough to set her alarm and turn out the lights. But her eyes closed again before she remembered Steve or Nancy or even the courtroom victory.

48

Meg awoke well before the alarm sounded. The first thing she noticed was her bedroom appeared as if it had been hit by a tornado. Her purse was pitched on one corner of the bed and her clothes were scattered around the room. There was simply no system, no organization. Walking to the bathroom, she drew a sink full of cold water, splashed it over her face, and then, slipping on an old terry cloth robe, stumbled to the kitchen. Once there, she tossed a couple of pieces of bread into the toaster, and while she waited for them to brown, poured herself a glass of Coke.

An hour later, at nine o'clock, she'd already eaten, showered, fixed her hair and makeup, and dressed. It was too early to leave for the courthouse, so she picked up the morning paper, found a soft spot on the couch, and in an effort to stay warm against the morning chill, pulled her legs against her body. She glanced over the front page. A bold headline on the bottom right side jumped out at her.

Thomas Convicted of Vehicular Homicide

That headline was followed by four words in even smaller letters—*Judge to Announce Sentence Today.*

Meg quickly read the report of the trial, and then, taking her scissors from an end table, clipped the entire story out of the paper and slipped it into her purse. Checking her watch, she grabbed a sweater, rushed out the door, and down the steps to her car. After the short drive, she found a parking place and walked about a block to the courthouse.

"Some kind of storm last night, wasn't it?" Cheryl noted as the two women met in the hallway outside the courtroom.

"Rain?" Meg exclaimed. "I didn't notice. I guess I slept right through it."

"Well, you must have slept real well then because it almost washed the town away. Reminded me of some of the thunder boomers we have back home." All of Cheryl's Texas accent came out when she said the word *home*.

"Do you ever go back there?" Meg inquired.

"Back where?"

"Texas . . . you know, home?"

"Oh," Cheryl glanced past Meg out a window at the courthouse lawn. "No. Dad's dead and I don't have anyone left there. No real reason to go back. Though I do still miss the country and the way people talk. Still, I guess that this is home now. That is until Judge Thomas puts the pressure on my boss. Webb is sure to cave, he wants to be governor someday, so my tenure is about up at the courthouse. And Thomas will make sure I don't work anywhere in this state. So I may just have to go back to Texas to find a job. Or at least go somewhere where the judge has no connections."

"I'm sorry," Meg said. "Kind of my fault."

"I played the game by my rules," Cheryl assured her, "the right ones, and besides, you gave me something I've been wanting and needing for a long time. I'll gladly take my lumps and like it. Not only did I win, but I proved to myself I'm good at this."

Glancing at her watch, Meg asked the now-beaming attorney, "Do you still feel like the judge might give Thomas the maximum?"

"I hope so. But in cases like this, you never know. Judges are simply unpredictable. We'll find out in a few minutes." Smiling, Cheryl made a big waving motion with her right hand and added, "You ready to go in?"

As Meg took her seat directly behind Cheryl, the assistant district attorney leaned back and asked, "What if he doesn't?"

"Doesn't what?" Meg replied.

"What if the judge doesn't give Thomas a stiff sentence? What are you going to do then?"

Without thinking, Meg answered, "I'll put him through another kind of hell."

Cheryl had to know how Meg felt. After all, she had admitted to making a vow of revenge once and it was a vow that didn't rest until yesterday. Now, so long after the fact, what the courts hadn't done to her father's killer had likely taken the edge off the attorney's emotions through the verdict she won in a courtroom yesterday. She could probably move on. Meg was craving that same kind of feeling. That is really what she'd wanted to talk about with Nancy. Nancy was supposed to give her a roadmap back to acceptance, maybe even happiness, and most of all peace. But that talk with Nancy would never happen and Meg trusted no one else. So, could she put the world right and bring the old Meg back?

Meg crossed one leg over the other and glanced to the other side of the room. Jim Thomas appeared exceptionally ragged. The cockiness that had been so much a part of his personality was now gone. It had been replaced with a look of genuine fear. He appeared scared to death that the next door that closed behind him might have locks and bars on it. Meg considered the kid's position. This might well be the first time in his life he was at the mercy of someone that his father could not buy. She smiled. Thomas was where she wanted him to be—an animal, caught in a trap, just waiting to see if he would be turned loose or slaughtered. The not knowing must have eaten at him for the whole night.

Satisfied Thomas was a defeated soul, she scanned the rest of courtroom. The boy's family looked as if they were going to a funeral, and old Jasper Tidwell was no longer glancing her way today. He was too busy studying his notes.

Checking her watch, she smiled. Each minute now brought her closer to finding out if her nightmares were finally over or if they were just beginning. If he got a stiff sentence, then her fight was done. It would be time to get back to living. If he didn't, she didn't really know what she would do. It was a quandary that had been eating at her fiber for weeks. Was this the way it was for every person left behind after having a loved one killed by an alcohol-fueled driver? Did the pain and sense of loss ever go away? Would those emotions revisit her every time she saw someone throw a beer can out of a car or see an alcoholic beverage ad on TV? Could her heart be completely healed when she heard the judge toss out a harsh sentence?

"All rise!"

The bailiff's voice brought the proceedings to a beginning and dragged Meg back to the present. She listened intently as Judge Truett presented his opening remarks and then asked Cheryl to deliver her arguments concerning sentencing.

The young woman stood up slowly, took a few moments to sum up the case by not only speaking of the loss of Steve's life but the loss for the community, church, and his family. Then she pushed into words that were incredibly personal.

"Your Honor, the cornerstone of this building promises justice. Today this justice must be the kind that sends a statement to every driver in this area. That statement must be that drunks can no longer travel the streets of Springfield maiming and killing without paying a considerable price for their actions."

After glancing over at Thomas and Tidwell, she continued, "In the past, this type of crime was treated much more casually. That lax attitude led to countless deaths, including, not just Steve Richards but my own father. Consider that the maximum judgment you can give today in this case, when compared to the death sentence given by the defendant to the victim, is still very lax. Steven Richards cannot be brought back from his grave. His child will never know his loving touch. He died with more than two-thirds of his life in front of him. So, it is my argument that anything less than the maximum would have the same effect as voiding the verdict of the court.

"Your Honor, in your hand is a key toward helping begin a change in the way all of society looks at drinking and driving. In your hand is a key for changing the perceptions that parents and kids have about partying with booze. In your hand is a chance for a safer life for all of us.

"Yes, I am asking for you to make Jim Thomas an example. I am asking that we deprive him of some of the best years of his life. Yes, I know that this may sound harsh and it will not bring Steve Richards back to his family, but it might stop a thousand more families from losing their Steve Richards.

"Your Honor, it is in your hands. Will you serve justice or will you ignore the first step in a solution to a problem that kills more than 12,000 people a year?

"Thank you."

Meg's eyes, which had filled with tears, fell down to where her hands were folded across her lap. Cheryl's words had cut through her like a knife. Steve wasn't coming back. And the baby she was now carrying would never know him. Surely, the judge would understand that and act accordingly.

As Meg composed herself, Jasper Tidwell pushed his chair back and began his well-rehearsed speech. In dramatic fashion, his words dripping like a gentle rain off a roof, he made his case.

"This boy—and that is what he is, Your Honor, just a boy of such a tender age—has learned his lesson. He accepts the mistake he made and fully realizes the cost to Megan Richards. Yet this mistake, when contrasted to the boy's fine reputation as a student and leader, is an anomaly. James is normally the kid who is the leader and who does the right thing. In fact, ever since the accident he has not missed a single Sunday at church and has even spent his Saturday mornings working as a volunteer at the local Boy's Club."

Though numb, Meg was not so insulated that she didn't take great offense at what Tidwell was doing. She'd met Thomas face-to-face, she'd seen what kind of person he was. His attitude was not anything like the picture the attorney was painting. And he wasn't a boy. He was almost eighteen years old! Men his age were fighting and being killed in wars!

"Your Honor," Tidwell continued the theme that was so eating at Meg, "my client is but a lad, a boy, a youth who has his entire life in front of him. You have already judged him to be guilty and the shame of this will follow him for all the days of his life. But if you sentence him to prison, it will interrupt and probably halt his education. His future will be altered irrevocably and whatever service he could be to humanity will be lost. He does not deserve to be placed in an environment filled with cold-blooded killers and professional crooks. No child does.

"A maximum sentence, really, any jail term, will mean that this accident hasn't just cost this community the life of Steven Richards but of James Thomas, too. Mr. Thomas can build on the experience he has been through and, if you allow him to learn from it, those lessons can be applied in the productive life he will lead from this day forth."

Tidwell took a deep breath, ran his fingers through his tangle of white hair, and glanced back toward Meg. As their eyes met, she suddenly felt like she had the advantage. The attorney's arrogance and combative style were nowhere in sight. Suddenly he wasn't challenging Steve or professing the innocence of James Thomas. Simply put, he was admitting that a mistake had been made and was begging for mercy. He was no longer the seasoned attorney; he now sounded more like a father pleading for a son.

Turning his face back to the bench, Tidwell continued, "No jail term will bring the victim back, but a jail term will make a victim out of my client. He doesn't need a cold, hard cell; he needs the challenges of the world and the understanding of people who love and care for him.

"Please, Your Honor, don't waste a boy's life because of this one tragic mistake in judgment. I thank you and this court."

Truett allowed the attorney to move back to his seat before speaking. "Ladies and gentlemen, we will now dismiss for lunch and will meet again at two o'clock this afternoon when I will then pronounce sentence. I thank you for your time and ask that you return promptly at two."

The last thing Meg needed or wanted was time for her mind to drum up more nightmares, yet that was what was on her plate. She would now have one hundred and eighty more minutes to dwell on what had happened and what would be done about it.

49

THE NEXT THREE HOURS WERE LONG AND LONELY. MEG DECLINED LUNCH with Cheryl, opting instead to walk through the shops located in the downtown business district. Beyond the tense wait for the judge's decision, she was still numb from Nancy's death. And though she'd only known the woman for a short time, she missed her. How she needed to feel Nancy's compassion and tap into her enthusiasm for life. And now there was no way to do that. Nancy would never tell her anything again.

In an antique mall, Meg searched through old, long-playing, vinyl albums and found the Barbara Mandrell record that had the song playing when Nancy died. Though she didn't own a record player, she bought the album. Just being able to carry it with her made her feel less alone.

After her purchase at the antique mall, she walked through another half dozen shops and bought nothing. When she ran out of places to window shop, she grabbed a sandwich at a hamburger stand and ate on a park bench. As she finished her lunch, it suddenly dawned on her that she hadn't gotten sick that morning. Was that passed now? Wouldn't it be great to get all the bad stuff behind her on the same day?

After lunch, she ambled slowly back toward the courthouse, passing the last forty-five minutes before the sentencing sitting on a bench watching old men play dominos. At five before two, she climbed the well-worn stairs leading to the second floor, strolled down the hall and into the courtroom, and took her regular seat. Her attention should have been riveted on the judge as he entered the room. Strangely though, it was miles away. All she could think about was an empty hospital room numbered 211, an equally empty apartment, and a grave occupied by a man she once dearly loved.

"Ladies and gentlemen," Judge Truett began. "I can't tell you how many different ways I have tried to look at the case. I have a host of mixed emotions concerning what is right and what is the proper thing to do. And I have fought a war with myself on this matter.

"As a member of a body of officers given the duty of judging the law, I am very troubled with the problems we have concerning the loss of innocent lives by the careless use of alcohol. As Ms. Bednarz so correctly pointed out, more than 12,000 deaths last year alone were caused by people using this drug while driving."

The officer of the court glanced down at his notes before continuing. This pause allowed Meg time to study Cheryl. She was calm and appeared confident. What a trooper she was! Truett's words pulled Meg's attention from her friend and attorney back to the bench.

"I am personally appalled at the way our high school children and college students blatantly and unthinkingly consume liquor as a means of making a social statement. I am equally upset and disturbed that the parents of these children seem to treat this great problem as a mere facet of growing up, a stage that their children will work through. At some point, someone must step in and show the problem in the proper light. Maybe I should be that person."

Yes, this was what she needed to hear! Meg glanced over at Tidwell and Thomas. Both were pale. The youth actually looked as though he might pass out. This was going well! She couldn't have scripted it any better.

"I must agree," Truett continued, "that our laws do not adequately cover the crime of killing by mixing booze and cars. Surely, if the defendant had gotten liquored up, taken a gun, and shot Steven Richards, all of us in this courtroom would think that ten years in prison was far too short a term for such a vile and outrageous act."

Turning toward Meg, he solemnly said, "I feel for the victim's pregnant widow. Her life and the hardships that she must surely endure due to this careless action, few, if any of us, can imagine. If I were her I would be bitter and unforgiving."

Directing his gaze at the defendant, the judge pressed on with his statement. "Still, being a father, I question if prison is the place for a young man. While I must admit that he is clearly in the wrong and his past actions have taught him little about what is right and wrong, I question whether prison will serve to direct him toward a more mature view of the importance of leading a responsible life. In fact, I am more than a bit disappointed I have no power at this time to sentence those who supplied the alcohol—his parents—more specifically his father. I have laid the groundwork for Judge Thomas to appear before the State Bar and explain his actions."

Cheryl glanced back at Meg and shrugged.

"So be it assured that I have considered all of these things and considered them long and hard before I decided the proper punishment phase of this case."

Stopping, Truett nodded toward the defense table, "Will the defendant rise?"

The youth and his attorney slowly pushed their chairs back and stood. Tidwell rested his hands on the table and actually crossed two fingers. Thomas, his eyes cast downward, rocked from side to side.

"James Thomas, it was the finding of this court that you are guilty on all three of the charges that the state had brought against you. On the first judgment of driving under the influence, I will order the state to void your driver's license and further instruct the state not to issue you a driving permit of any kind until at least your twenty-first birthday.

"On the second count of reckless driving, I am sentencing you to two years' probation and a five-hundred dollar fine.

"Finally, on the most serious count of vehicular homicide, I sentence you to five years . . ."

Thomas looked from the floor to the judge, his face displaying shock and panic. Meg, while disappointed he hadn't gotten the full ten, was still pleased. Her pleasure clearly showing in her eyes. Cheryl, her fist clenched, grimly smiled.

After allowing his words to sink in, Truett continued, "Those five years will be a probationary sentence. During this time, the defendant must see an alcohol counselor at least once every two weeks for a minimum of one year and he cannot break any of the stipulations of the first two assessments. He will also be required to do ten hours of weekly community service, service that the local state social services office will assign, for at least a two-year period. And, he will be assessed and must pay a $10,000 fine. If you, Mr. Thomas, violate any of these stipulations, you will serve the full five years in a state prison. Mr. Thomas, report to the social services office Monday afternoon to receive your assignment.

"Thank you, ladies and gentlemen, this court in adjourned."

Pounding his gavel, the judge quickly departed into his chambers.

Meg bolted up right. She was in shock. Grabbing Cheryl by the shoulder, she demanded. "What kind of justice is this?"

The attorney just shook her head.

"What can we do about it?" Meg demanded.

"Not a thing." Cheryl quietly explained. "It is over now."

Shifting her focus to the other side of the courtroom, Meg noted Jasper Tidwell vigorously shaking hands with anyone who came near him. Judge Thomas and his wife, obviously relieved, were quietly talking to another couple standing beside them. Meanwhile, Jim Thomas was sitting rock-solid still in his chair, his eyes focused on the surface of the table before him.

Meg, observing that no one was close enough to stop her, walked purposely through the swinging gate separating her from the front of the courtroom and marched to a position directly across the table from the teen. He looked up when he felt her presence, and for several long seconds neither of them spoke. Finally, he broke the silence.

"I'm really sorry," was all he could manage.

"You don't know what sorry is," Meg hissed. "I told you once that I'd meet you in hell. I'll go one better than that now. I'll personally deliver you to that destination."

She pointed a finger toward his face as she continued, "Every time you look over your shoulder, I'll be there. If the phone rings, check your caller ID. Odds are, it will be me. When you go out riding with your friends, glance out the back window because I'll be following you.

"I guarantee that prison would have been easier on you than I will be. My vow to my husband and to myself is to make you miserable until the day that you die. I'm your judge and jury now, and don't expect any mercy from me."

"Meg," Cheryl's whispered as she grabbed her arm. "He's not worth it. I'll walk you out."

"You mark my words," Meg spat. "The rest of your miserable life is in my hands!"

Then, turning, she and Cheryl dodged reporters and left the room.

50

A RAPID AND HOT RAGE FILLED MEG. IN HER HEART, SHE KNEW THAT JIM Thomas had gotten off scot-free. He had killed her husband and wouldn't spend a day in prison. None of Cheryl's words served to calm her down at the courtroom or later, while she sat alone at home dreaming up ways to even the score. A call from her mother only served to anger Meg more.

"Listen, Honey," Barbara began, "today man's justice might have seemed light, but God will deal with the boy."

"Sure, Mom, the same God who let that jerk kill Steve is going to deal with him now. I don't think so. But I can and I will." Meg's words were sharp, vindictive. It was clear she planned to follow through on her promise.

Meg now had no use for sleep. She stayed up, formulating and writing down plans of retribution in a journal. The scenarios she spun were gory and cruel. No longer did she dream of cutting brake lines or mowing him down with bullets, her new plans were much simpler, much less lethal, and were things she could actually accomplish. She wanted to haunt him until she'd driven him over the edge. At the very least, she wanted him to make a mistake and violate his parole. At most, she wanted to drive him so far and so hard that he would actually think about killing himself rather than live in the same world as Meg.

She knew that to accomplish her goal she would have to devote herself to this task like she had never devoted herself to anything in her life. Every waking hour would have to be spent in developing new plans, getting information, doing surveillance, and planning execution. And she was willing to give up everything else in her life in order to make this project a success.

Steve was dead and Nancy was not here to temper her mind-set. There was no one who now could hold a mirror up to her and demand she see what she'd become. Internet searches and message boards kept her up most of the night. They also gave her ideas. And she could begin putting those ideas into action almost immediately.

Having taken a week of vacation for the trial, she didn't have to go back to work until the following Monday. So, on Friday morning, after a few hours of sleep, she began to gather ammunition. Taking a picture of Steve from her desk and obtaining a photo of his car from the insurance company —the photo showing the bloodstained interior—she scanned them into her computer, worked with Photoshop, and printed off one hundred copies of her artwork. She then went to the high school, got past security using her nurse's ID, purchased an extra yearbook, cut a headshot of Jim Thomas from the book, and took that photo back home. She scanned the image then began designing the page. She placed "WANTED" in big, bold type at the top. On the bottom she added text that read, "This man is guilty of murder. He is probably armed and dangerous and if apprehended see that he is delivered straight to hell." She then sized and pasted his picture in the middle. She printed out 250 copies of the new poster.

Picking up both stacks of printed work, she got into her car, and drove by Jim Thomas's home. Seeing an old man mowing the grass in front of the house, she stopped, and through some casual conversation, discovered which of the many windows led to the teenager's room.

From there, she went back to the high school. Once inside, she cornered a young lady who was walking down the hall between classes and discovered which one of the hall lockers belonged to Thomas. Taking tape from her purse, she taped the two posters she'd made on the locker and left the building.

Fifteen minutes later, while Meg was waiting just outside the building, the final bell rang, and in a few seconds the kids hit the doors and headed toward the parking lot. One by one she scanned their faces, looking for his, wanting to see the shocked expression that she knew her surprise would bring.

Suddenly, walking beside Kristen Jennings, there he was. Unnoticed, she fell in a safe distance behind the two of them in an attempt to overhear what was being said.

"It was just some kid's idea of a sick joke," the girl said. "One of your friends is playing with you."

"I don't know," Thomas answered, "that woman said she would haunt me and maybe she's going to. This might be just the start."

"Well," Kristen said, "if she gets on your case, then have your father do something about it. He's a judge. He's got the power."

"No way," Thomas said, shaking his head to reemphasize the point. "He's mad about this. He told me I got off light and now, because of the trial, he may lose his job. I'm not going to let him know about this. He'd probably help her. Maybe he's the one that's doing it."

"Oh, you don't believe that," Kristen replied.

"No," the boy admitted, "but he is mad and in big trouble. I wouldn't put anything past him."

Meg stepped out from behind the two of them and moved behind a van. When they were well up the walk, she hurried back inside the school, waved at the security officer who'd let her pass earlier, stopped and chatted with him about the spring weather, and then moved down the hall. When no one was looking she folded up two more pictures and slipped them into Thomas's locker through the vents.

As she walked back outside, the pair was driving off in Kristen's blue Dodge Stratus. She made a mental note of the car before hurrying back to her own apartment. As soon as she got home, she used the Internet to search for anything that might have the boy's cell number. She was shocked when she found it listed on one of the local sports club websites under "contact information." Writing it down, she made a trip to five phone stores and purchased several different prepaid cell phones. She registered each in a different name.

Heading back to her apartment, she put the second phase of her plan into operation. Calling Thomas's cell, she waited for him to answer.

"Hello," the young man's voice sounded distant and a little unsteady.

Meg said nothing.

"Hello," Thomas said again. "Who is this?"

Again, Meg said nothing. When he finally hung up, Meg smiled. She waited five minutes and then picked up the next phone.

Again, he answered, and once more she said nothing.

Waiting ten minutes, Meg called again. This time the line was busy. Alternating phones Meg continued to call the number for the rest of the afternoon and each time the result was the same. She knew that for at least one night she had taken Jim Thomas's phone away from him. But that was just the start.

After dinner, she grabbed the phone book, and once again scanned the numbers until she came to the name Jennings. Stopping when she discovered a number that matched Kristen's address, she noted it and called.

"Hello," an older female voice answered.

"Hello, Mrs. Jennings?"

"Yes."

Meg, using a Texas accent she picked up from being around Cheryl, continued, "I hope that I haven't disturbed you. My name is Jenny McCall, and I just moved here from Atlanta. Anyway, your daughter, Kristen, is in a couple of my classes and she has been such a big help. I was wondering if I could talk to her a moment about an assignment."

"I'm afraid she's out right now," Mrs. Jennings answered. "Maybe she could call you tomorrow."

"Oh, no," Meg replied. "I've got to get this research book back to her by then. Goodness. Well, maybe I could catch her somewhere. Do you know where she might have gone?"

"Let me think a second. Of course, she and her boyfriend were going to see that new movie down at the Multiplex tonight. Something about vampires."

"Thank you, Mrs. Jennings. Maybe I can catch her there."

Meg grabbed the paper and opened to the theater listings. Checking her watch, she grabbed a couple of flyers and headed out the door. When she arrived at the theater, she searched the parking lot, found Kristen's car, and slipped two more flyers under the driver's side wiper. Then, taking white shoe polish out of her purse, she wrote the word *killer* in bold letters over the passenger's side of the windshield. Returning to her car, she waited for the show to let out.

A few minutes later, she saw the two teens walking arm and arm out the door. Both seemed perfectly at ease until the moment Thomas saw the shoe polish. Running to the Dodge, he grabbed the two flyers from under the wiper, took a quick look at them, and threw them down.

"Come on," he exclaimed. "We've got to get this off before someone sees it. Get in and get the washer working."

"It doesn't work, Jim . . . no fluid," the girl explained.

"Well, have you got a towel or something?" There was now panic in Thomas's voice. "We can't leave here until this comes off."

"I have some tissues," Kristen said, digging through her purse.

Meg eased the car window up, turned on the ignition key, and pulled out to the main street. Then she pulled over into a parallel parking spot and waited.

When the blue Dodge came out of the parking lot, she followed it. Kristen and Thomas rumbled down the drag for about a mile before stopping at a teenager hangout called Ron's. There the two got out of the car, went in, and sat at a booth in the back. A few moments later, Meg followed them as far as inside the front door.

"Hey, Betty," a raspy female voice cried to another waitress, "could you get that back booth?"

The woman then looked at Meg. "Table, Sweetie?"

"Just looking for someone," Meg replied.

Meg observed a large woman in her forties, take a huge bite on a Twinkie and then go to the back to fill up a couple of glasses with water and ice. Noting the menus positioned on the corner of the counter, she picked up the top two, stuffed a wanted poster in each one, and put them back on the stack. Then Meg carefully strolled across the floor, taking a place in the booth that backed up to the one where Kristen and Thomas were sitting.

"Hi, kids," Betty's cheery voice boomed out as she placed the water and menus in front of the teens. "Ya'll take your time, I'll be back in a moment."

Meg observed in a mirror as Thomas took a long drink from the glass, opened his menu, and gasped. "How did she know we were here?"

Kristen whispered, "How did *who* know that we were coming here?"

"Look in your menu," he ordered. "No," reaching across and taking it from her, "let me."

The young man literally tore the menu open and was greeted by a smiling picture of Steve Richards. Kristen reached across the table and grabbed the other menu containing the photo of the car. Both of the teens shook their heads and closed the folders.

Satisfied, Meg quickly got up from her booth and exited by a side door. Stopping back by the old Dodge, she placed two more flyers under the wipers, jumped into her car, and sped off. Her first day of retribution had gone well.

51

THE NEXT DAY BEGAN WITH TWO MORE CALLS TO THOMAS'S NUMBER. Neither was answered. Satisfied she had him spooked, Meg typed a short letter on her Macbook Pro and hit print. She grinned as she read it.

"Dear Jim, looking forward to having you join me at the cemetery. Steve."

Placing the note in an envelope and printing Thomas's address on it, she walked to the nearest box and dropped it into the mail. Returning home, she opened the *Herald*. Checking the sports page, she noted that Springfield High had a home baseball game that day, and a story on the game indicated Thomas would be playing first base rather than pitching. She made plans to get there early and sit right behind the dugout.

With the temperature in the seventies, it was a beautiful day for baseball. But as the teams warmed up, Meg was hoping the sky would quickly turn gloomy for Springfield's star player. She waved and smiled as he looked her way. Maybe it was feeling her eyes on him that caused him to strike out every time he got to the plate. His fielding wasn't much as it was his error on an easy ground ball that cost the team the game. When he got on the bus to make the trip from the field to the high school, he discovered a wanted poster taped to the door. Looking out the window, he noted Meg sitting alone in the stands staring at him.

That night as he got in from his date with Kristen, Meg was waiting. She had already taped a wanted poster to the outside of his bedroom window facing inside the room. She didn't have to wait long to wonder if he saw it. Within thirty minutes of getting home, he appeared in his sleep pants and a T-shirt, raced around the corner of the yard and tore the poster off the window.

A few minutes later, when a happy Meg returned home, she found Heather sitting on her steps. She couldn't fathom why the nurse would be waiting on her.

"What are you doing here?" Meg inquired. "It's past midnight. Shouldn't you be home or on a date or something?"

An obviously distraught Heather looked up and mournfully wailed, "I need to talk to someone."

"Well, come on in." After Heather had entered and the door had been closed, Meg asked, "Want a Coke?"

Heather simply nodded.

As Meg fixed the two drinks, she bluntly asked, "What's the problem?"

"It's Paul," Heather answered, her gaze never leaving the floor. "He hasn't called me or gone out with me since last Monday."

"Well," Meg offered, "he's a doctor and he's busy."

"Yeah, going out with other women," Heather quickly shot back. Taking the Coke from Meg, Heather continued her woeful tale. "He hasn't even called me since the other night"—tears filled Heather's eyes and her bottom lip trembled as she moaned—"when I, well, when we . . ." She paused again. "When I slept with him."

"Well," Meg said with a sigh, "I guess he got what he wanted and now has moved on. I wouldn't worry too much, you'll get over it."

Looking up, Heather replied angrily, "Meg, you told me to do it! And that's all you've got to say?"

"What are you talking about?" Meg argued. "I didn't tell you anything of the sort."

"No, that's not true." There was now a building rage evident in Heather's voice. "You told me it was time to give it up. Life was short and all that rot."

"No," Meg quickly denied the accusations. "I told you that it was your choice. And if you came over here to blame me for your going to bed with someone, forget it. Losing your virginity isn't as traumatic as losing a husband and being raped by the court system. I don't have any patience for people who can't handle their own problems. Especially when they're as small and insignificant as this one. In case you hadn't noticed, you're a big girl now. You made your bed and what's bothering you is that you slept in it, too."

Meg took another long sip from her Coke. She couldn't believe that Heather was so upset over this. After all, she didn't have cancer; she wasn't dying! "So Paul dumped you. If you're going to be mad at someone, try him. Bother him in the middle of the night, not me. I have enough problems of my own! I don't have time for trivial stuff like this."

Jumping up from her seat, Heather shouted, "I thought you were my friend. I stuck by you when everyone else cringed when they saw you on the street. I was wrong about you. You don't care about anything or anyone other than yourself." Picking up her purse, she stormed across the room, turned the knob on the door, and jerked it open. Pausing, she spun around and glared at Meg. "Of course, you couldn't care about me. You can't feel or express love to anyone anymore. You're so tied up in hate you've lost whatever it was that made you a human being."

Heather's eyes dropped to the posters resting on the coffee table. "What's that all about?"

"Part of my plan to make Jim Thomas pay," Heather shot back. "There's much more to it. He's going to feel every bit of pain that I felt and more."

Heather shook her head. "I don't know what you've become, but it's not human. The Meg I knew wasn't capable of anything like this. The kid's going to pay! What he did will haunt him forever. Everyone is saying his dad's going to lose his job, too. You don't have to do this. You've already won."

"Steve's dead," Meg spat. "Thomas is alive! The score is no where near equal."

"Meg, look in the mirror. Take a look yourself. You're ugly! Hate is stealing your soul faster than cancer took Nancy's life. What do you think she would think about you now? Maybe it's good she's dead. She believed in you. And what about Steve? What would he say?"

"Don't you dare talk about Steve," Meg screamed.

"I feel sorry for that baby you're carrying. You should have gotten an abortion. The child would've been luckier. Evidently, Steve was the only thing that brought out the good in you. I thought when the trial was over you'd be back. But the old Meg is lost and she might as well be buried with Steve and Nancy. You've become a monster!"

After a deep breath, she turned and slammed the door behind her.

Meg stared down at one of the posters. Her friend was right. She was no longer the person she once was. Yet being that person wouldn't serve her purposes now. If she were the old Meg, she'd be too soft. If she let her heart care about others, then she might stop this campaign. She couldn't do that because then Steve's killer would never know the taste of real justice.

52

Still cognizant of her meeting with the hospital administrator and having to have the job to pay her bills, Meg's nursing was fine. She didn't allow her attitude to spill over at the hospital. Still she was not the warm professional that she had been in the past. Now her nursing had a stiff mechanical feel. She was polite, but distant. She was not warm, but not cold. Patients were not drawn to her, but they were not repelled either. She had become a walking, talking machine not much different than those used in rooms to monitor conditions.

However, there was an undercurrent at the hospital that Willis would have found disturbing, if he'd taken the time to discover it. The other nurses avoided anything more than professional communication with Meg. They resorted to this because she either ignored them or tossed out sarcastic jibes as a response to any of their observations. So rather than take the abuse, they just quit talking to her except concerning professional issues. No one even sat by her during meals.

Ironically, Meg found the other nurses' silent treatment refreshing. She loved being left alone. This allowed her the opportunity to lock herself in her own world and her own thoughts, thus giving her time to work on what she really felt was important in her life—the haunting of Jim Thomas.

She had done a good job of this. Over the course of three months since the trial, she had made his life a complete wreck. Through constant Google searches, she'd found new ways to pop up and haunt him. She used Facebook and texts to her advantage. She'd grown so good at it that Thomas rarely checked either. He'd quit going to his favorite hangouts because she seemed to always be there. He also looked as if he'd lost over ten pounds and there were dark circles under his now almost lifeless eyes. He had developed nervous twitches, had quit the baseball team, and couldn't even go outside without constantly looking over his shoulder. Even when she was hidden and he couldn't see her, Meg noted that Thomas jumped every time he saw a pregnant woman or a Mustang. Through one of Steve's old friends, a school administrator, she'd discovered the youth's grades had fallen to the point where he had barely graduated. But these obvious outward signs were only the beginning.

Now, rather than toss Meg's posters away, she discovered through high school gossip circles that he kept them in a stack on his desk. He no longer answered his phone. When anyone called, he'd just sit and count the rings. He didn't go to movies or watch television. He'd become so withdrawn and sullen, his friends had quit calling him and Kristen had broken up with him.

With Thomas all but a prisoner in his own home, Meg was winning the war. After his graduation, the only times he went out were for his community service work and alcohol counseling sessions. Yet, besides Meg, no one really noticed. His friends, enjoying all the fun summer offered, had moved on and his parents were too wrapped up trying to save their reputations to think much about their only son. In fact, they blamed him for all their problems.

So, in a way, because it was becoming so easy to win, the haunting was now becoming boring. There had been far more satisfaction in watching Jim sweat, in seeing him tear up flyers and wonder where she was going to be next. He still had some fire then. But she had killed his cocky attitude, his flash, ruined his daily life, and driven him completely inside himself. With the challenge gone, the results weren't nearly as dramatic or satisfying.

Ever since the trial, it had been Meg's after-work routine to drive by the Thomas's home. Even though she hadn't seen the young man outside in over three weeks, she still continued to make the trip, occasionally planting a flyer or poster, sometimes even parking across the street and sitting and watching. But now, he was never outside to smile at or wave to. On a misty July 15, she almost decided to go directly home, to give up her surveillance. She was tired and the weather looked like it would get worse. But, whether from habit or a devotion to her goal, she once again turned left instead of right and made the trip to Walnut Street. As her wipers swept the mist from her window and the lighting flashed and thunder rolled, promising much heavier weather very soon, she was surprised to see Jim Thomas sitting on the curb in front of his home.

As she got closer, she noticed he was looking directly at her car, his eyes fixed on the driver's side. His unblinking stare unnerved her a bit and for the first time in weeks, she felt as if she wasn't controlling the situation. Her instincts demanded that she speed off or turn around, but with chills racing down her spine, she eased off the accelerator and slowed down. Still, she wouldn't have stopped if he hadn't stood up and waved at her.

Pulling over to the curb, she turned off the car and stared intently at the boy. He looked ragged and worn. He was barefoot, dressed in old jeans and a T-shirt. His hair was damp from the mist and his expression was drawn. As he exhibited no signs of hostility, she opened her door, pulled her obviously pregnant body out of the car, and slowly walked around the front of her car to the curb. And for the first time since that one occasion in the courtroom, she confronted Jim Thomas, one-on-one, face-to-face.

"Hi," the boy meekly greeted her.

"You want something?" Meg inquired coldly.

Studying her for a moment, Thomas responded, "Only to tell you that I wish it had been me and not him. I wish that I had never been born. I'm sorry for what happened."

"That makes two of us," Meg spat back. "But it doesn't do any good for either of us to make that wish, does it?"

Looking away, Thomas sighed. "I give up." Glancing down he whispered, "You win."

She shook her head. "I lost my husband. I can't win."

Raising his face to where he looked directly into her eyes, he moaned, "I'm eaten up with guilt. It is not just you; it's my own lies. I lied on the stand, even lied to myself. I'd rather go to prison than face you. No matter how bad it is, it can't be as bad as this. You said you'd meet me in hell, well welcome to it. I'm there and you are, too!"

"You're not there yet," she tossed back. "You've got a long way to go."

"Listen, lady, I was drinking Buffalo Scotch on that night." His words trailed off as if he couldn't bring himself to finish the thought.

"You mean the night you killed my husband?" she spat.

He nodded. "And now I'm drinking it again just so I can go to sleep at night. And you know what is the worst thing in my life?"

"Me?" Meg offered.

"No, it's just that my parents, my friends, none of them know what is happening to me. They don't pay enough attention to even notice what I'm doing. My friends think I was lucky to get off and my folks think I'm the family loser who messed up their perfect world.

"Listen, Mrs. Richards. I don't really blame you for doing what you've been doing. I mean, at first, I was really put out, but then I got to thinking about your being pregnant and all and what you went through on the stand, and I get it."

He glanced back at his home and almost under his breath muttered, "But please understand this, when I got in the car that night, all I wanted to do was have some fun. Not kill somebody. I mean, I still can't believe that I did it."

He studied her face. The only thing there was Meg's hatred.

"You know this morning"—the boy's blue eyes now looked right into hers—"I rode my bike over and spent some time at his grave. I wanted to apologize, but I found out I couldn't. Not to him anyway. It was too late."

Thomas stopped for a moment, as if searching for words then continued, "There is no way I can make it all up to you. I know that. And I'm feeling like you do—I wish that they'd put me in jail or something. You know," he looked past her to the house across the street, "my friends still go out drinking and driving. They didn't learn anything. When I tried to get through to 'em, they just laughed and said they can handle it and wouldn't get caught."

He paused and threw his hands in the air. "I'm not making any sense, but what you've done, well, it's working. I'm paying, I'm feeling it, and, well, you know . . ."

As she began to speak, Meg's voice was hard and her words flew quickly from a mouth dripping with hate. "It has only been three months since I began my little exercise in justice. And you know, I've lost a lot of sleep, missed a lot of TV, screwed up every relationship that I've ever had, but it has been worth it. Just four or five months ago you were so cocky and proud. You even hit on me. Then at the trial you came down a little. But now, you look as though you can barely walk. Well, for some folks that would be enough, but not me."

The youth looked back at the woman and pleaded, "What do you want, lady? I'll do whatever it is you want."

"Justice," Meg replied. "I want an eye for an eye and a tooth for a tooth. I want you to crawl and beg and I want to watch it happen. I want you to rot in hell. And I don't even know if that will satisfy me. I do know it's not enough for what you did to my husband."

"Listen, Mrs. Richards," Thomas pleaded. "You've already ruined my life . . ."

Her sharp laugh cut him off.

"Your life? No, I've only ruined three months—ninety short days. That's just the beginning of a life. There's a lot more to it than just that. You're young, and I've got a lot more time to make you pay!"

Convinced that there was nothing more to say, she reached into the passenger seat of her car and pulled out a box. Handing it to him, she smiled and said, "Thought you might want some more posters."

Walking back around the front of her car, she got in, waved, and shouted, "See you soon." She took one last look at her victim, switched on the starter, and hit the gas. In her rearview mirror, she watched as he turned and slowly walked to his front door.

Meg had never felt more alive. Her heart was pumping a wild rushing torrent of blood through her body. Her baby, kicking up a storm in the confines of her womb, seemed to be enjoying this moment just as much as she was. When she got to the apartment, despite being almost six months along, she almost flew up the steps to her front door. Just as she unlocked it, the phone rang.

"Hello." Meg said, her voice almost gleeful.

"Hi, this is Heather," an unemotional voice began. "I tried to come up with someone else, but no one else could do it. Would you work the graveyard in the emergency room for me tonight? I've got a terrible headache, and I just can't shake it. I may be coming down with the bug that everybody else has. I think making it through the shift would just be too much."

"Sure," Meg answered without a moment's hesitation.

Heather had probably expected Meg to turn her down. She hadn't worked an extra shift or switched out for a couple of months. So, Heather sounded shocked when Meg not only responded in the affirmative but didn't complain about the late call.

"You will? I appreciate it, Meg. I owe you one for this."

Meg's singing voice replied, "No, you don't. Just get well soon."

"Meg, you know with this virus going around you may not have much help tonight."

"That's no problem," Meg replied. "Not much usually happens on a Wednesday night anyway."

"Thanks, Meg," Heather said again. "If you get into a bind, call me, and if I feel better, I'll come up."

"Don't worry about it, just go to bed. Now, bye, Heather."

Meg hung up the phone and then, picking up a notebook, spent the next hour recording the events of her confrontation with Jim Thomas. She had written down every experience since the trial and by looking back through her log, she was able to see clearly just how much she had broken the spirit of the young man. After she reviewed the whole journal, a deep feeling of satisfaction filled her heart.

"Oh, Steve," she whispered, "we almost have him."

Checking her watch, she decided a nap was in order. Turning off her phone, she set her alarm and fell into a deep, satisfying sleep.

The alarm woke her at nine o'clock, giving her plenty of time to fix herself a light supper, take a long, warm bath, and then get ready. Before she stepped out the door, she looked at herself in a full-length mirror, something she hadn't taken the time to do in quiet a while. Her breasts felt swollen and seemed almost unbelievably huge, and her stomach, that once thin, flat tummy that had made all the other nurses at the hospital so jealous, was now round and large. Patting it, she smiled. "Well, we're stuck with each other, kid. And in a way, I'm glad now. I can use you to help me really put Jim Thomas through the wringer. He hasn't seen anything yet!"

Hitting the light switch, taking one last swig of a Coke, she literally ran out the apartment's door, down the steps, and jumped into her car. Thinking of the broken look that she'd seen on Thomas's face when she had left him that afternoon, she couldn't help but smile as she drove to work.

53

Hope you brought a book or something," Marsha announced as Meg strolled into the emergency room. "It's been like a morgue tonight. There's absolutely nothing happening."

"Slow, huh?" Meg asked, surprised the other nurse was even talking to her.

"Slow's not the word," Marsha answered. "There's no one here and you don't have to look at a single report. Count the drugs and you're in. At the rate things are going, you'll have the same count when you check out."

Taking her light jacket off, Meg picked up the report and began the process of checking in. It was a duty she knew as well as anything in the world.

As Marsha signed, she asked. "Did Heather tell you that you'd probably be alone tonight?"

"Yeah," Meg replied. Then, right before Marsha walked through the door, she asked, "Who's the doctor on duty?"

Sticking her head back through the door, the departing nurse hollered, "McCullen." Then the whoosh of the door signaled her exit.

As Meg settled in for the evening, she immediately sensed what Marsha had been talking about. The hospital was so quiet and the activity level so light that the only sounds were made by an occasional nurse walking past ER on her way for a break. If the whole night continued like this, Heather could have stayed home and no one would have missed her. This promised to be the easiest gig she'd ever experienced. The phone didn't ring, no one stopped to visit, and absolutely nothing stirred. It was almost eerie.

Rummaging through one of the counter drawers, she came up with a fairly current issue of *Glamour* and slowly studied the magazine's contents. Two Cokes and four complete passes through the periodical's pages managed to kill only two of her shift's eight hours. Six more to go! If they're like the first two, she was going to have every page in the magazine memorized.

Finding a new information brochure on the latest heart surgery techniques, she attempted to drum up some interest in its contents. Yet, after she looked up to check the clock for the third time, she found she had no idea what she'd just read or how far she had gotten. Pitching the brochure back on the desk, she leaned over the counter and eyed the blank hallway. Nothing was stirring.

Now completely immersed into boredom, she thought back to her confrontation with Thomas. He'd been on the curb waiting for her? Why? Oh well, didn't matter, by now he was probably fast asleep. Then remembering his haggard state, she grinned, no, he was probably lying awake and wondering if she'd call. Patting her stomach, she whispered, "We got him spooked, baby, you and I have him spooked."

Reliving the emotions of the confrontation could only bring so much satisfaction. Soon thinking about Thomas grew old. Getting up, she stretched and strolled through the ER looking for something else to occupy her time.

Someone had tossed a newspaper in the trash. Recently she hadn't given herself much of an opportunity to read the paper.

She had devoted so much time to haunting Thomas that she'd usually picked up the editions, and then, without even opening them, thrown them away. Maybe the printed news would offer some escape from the dullness of her shift and also bring her up to date on many of the current local happenings. Retrieving it, Meg checked the date, found it to only be a day old, went back to her seat, and began to read.

Scanning the front page, she noted a headshot of Cheryl Bednarz. Quickly reading the story, she discovered the assistant district attorney had resigned her position and was moving back home to Texas to open up a private practice in her hometown. Cheryl had predicted as much. Probably forced out because she won the case. If it hadn't been the middle of the night, Meg would have called the woman and wished her well. But as she hadn't talked to her since the trial, that bond had been broken anyway. They'd used each other and moved on. That was the way life was.

Flipping through the first and second sections of the paper, she finally found "Dear Abby." She was halfway through reading it when she heard a car driving up to the emergency entrance. Maybe it was finally time to go to work. Setting the paper aside, she looked up to see who would come in.

"Nurse?" The woman who asked the question looked to be in her late twenties. She was fairly plain and thin and had obviously been asleep before coming to the hospital.

"Yes," Meg answered, stepping out from behind the counter.

"My husband, Ed." Glancing behind the woman, Meg saw a heavy, balding man whom the nurse judged to also be in his late twenties, enter the doors, a bloody towel, covering his right hand. "You see, he couldn't sleep and he got up to fix something to eat and cut his hand on a Spam can." Looking back at the hulking figure standing behind her, the woman angrily barked, "He just can't do anything on his own without making a big mess out of it."

Meg smiled and stifled the urge to say, "Evidently not even get married."

"Well, don't just stand there, stupid," the woman growled at the man. "Show the nurse your hand, Ed."

Meg took a look at the man's cut, picked up the phone, and paged Dr. McCullen.

Turning back to the couple, she said, "Okay, Ed, why don't we go into room 2, it's right across the hall and we'll get this wound cleaned up. Then the doctor will look at it and probably give you a few stitches."

"Nurse," the woman asked, tapping Meg on the shoulder. "What should I do?"

Reaching behind her, Meg grabbed a clipboard with the proper forms already attached and handed them to the woman. "There's a pen on the counter. Why don't you fill these out?"

Meg had just gotten finished cleaning the man's cut, when she heard more noise outside.

"Things are picking up," she said to no one in particular.

"What?" It was the first time Ed had said anything.

"Ed," Meg smiled, "you do have a voice!"

Leaving the man by himself, Meg briskly walked out into the receiving room to find out what was going on. As she stood by Ed's wife, who was still struggling with the paperwork, things looked normal, but there was a terrible commotion outside the emergency room doors. Excusing herself, Meg walked outside to see what the problem was. She had no more than gotten through the doors when she heard a female voice screaming hysterically. "He's dead! He's dead!"

54

WHAT IN THE WORLD?" MEG EXCLAIMED, AS SHE HURRIED DOWN THE ramp to the parking area.

"Help me, please. Somebody help me."

Meg could now see it was a teenage girl who was doing all the screaming. She was standing by the rear door of her car, it was open, and she was jumping up and down, crying hysterically as she peered into the backseat. Seeing Meg, she ran up to the nurse and pleaded, "You have got to save him. Please, you've got to do something! Hurry. I think he's dead!"

The girl tried to pull the nurse back toward the car. Reaching out and grabbing the young woman by the shoulders, Meg demanded, "What's wrong?"

Still, crying and screaming, the girl sobbed, pointing to where the boy lay. "It's my friend. I don't think he is breathing . . . he's in the car. I think he's dead."

Rushing down the ambulance ramp, Meg reached into the darkened car. Finding an arm, she grabbed the wrist and searched for a pulse. Nothing. Reaching further into the vehicle, she found the boy's neck and checked again. Nothing. Turning back to the girl, she hollered, "How long has he been like this and what happened?"

"I found him in his garage," she frantically replied. Then, she began crying so hard she couldn't talk.

Jumping up from the car, Meg grabbed the girl, shook her hard, and shouted, "I can't help him unless you tell me what happened. Now!"

Taking a deep breath, the girl rattled out. "He'd turned the car on in his garage and the door was down. I found him that way. I brought him here as fast as I could."

"How long since you know he was breathing?" Meg demanded.

"It couldn't have been over ten minutes." Then she must have remembered something else. "No, he coughed once when we pulled into the parking lot."

If the young man had coughed as they entered the parking lot, he had a chance. Pointing toward the ER, Meg ordered, "Find a doctor and get him out here with a gurney! Go now!"

Running back to the car, she pulled the young man out of the backseat and onto the ground. "Okay, kid," she exclaimed as she fell to her knees, "don't give up on me." Pushing his body into the proper position, she put her hand behind his neck, and then, just as she was about to begin CPR, she froze. For a few seconds, she looked into the boy's face, staring at the anguish written in his now twisted features. Jim Thomas! Reaching into her pocket, she took out a small flashlight. Lifting his right eyelid, she checked for a reaction. A big part of her was hoping she would get none.

When the pupils responded to the light, she knew the kid still had a chance. Yet his only chance at life was if she reacted quickly. It was up to her.

She heard the emergency room doors open behind her. Glancing over her shoulder, she saw the teenage girl.

"Is he going to be all right?" she sobbed.

Looking up at the girl, Meg shook her head and said, "I think he's gone. I think you got to him too late." Turning back toward the boy, she almost choked on her own lie, but it was a lie that no one would ever catch her in. She was safe. The girl was too ignorant to realize that Meg was allowing precious seconds tick by and doing nothing.

She looked back into Thomas's face. This was a moment she thought she would have once given anything for. Victory was hers. But once the "dark music" started to play, as she watched the life slowly ooze from the young man's body, she felt dirty. Only a monster would let this happen and that is what she'd become. She was a monster. Fighting with herself, she looked away from the boy and tried to think of Steve.

He was in a cold grave and that was where this boy deserved to be, too. By letting him die she would be faithful to Steve. Her plan had worked. Luck had been on her side, and thanks to Heather's illness, she was here at just the right moment to make sure it all played out. This was the way things were meant to be. So, she wasn't a monster, only an instrument of fairness. This is the way it should be—an eye for an eye, a tooth for a tooth. Almost choking on her own thoughts, she whispered, "And a life for a life."

Looking back up at the girl, Meg shouted, "You can't do anything out here for him. Go back inside. When you see the doctor, send him out."

For a second, the frightened girl stood anchored in place, anguish etched on her face. Then she turned and walked slowly back up the ramp. This was probably the first time she'd ever heard the "dark music."

Meg turned to once again face the young man she'd driven to suicide. Somehow, seeing the life drain slowly out of his body didn't give her the satisfaction she had expected. She felt no thrill, no triumph. A small part of her, buried somewhere deep in the hidden recesses of her mind, actually wanted to help him—to save his life. Still, even though his life clock was running out, she did nothing.

Noting a crumpled piece of paper in Thomas's hand, she bent over and pulled it out. It was one of her wanted posters. Even in the palely lit parking lot, she could see that he had written something on it. Lifting the page closer to her face, she read the hurriedly scrawled words.

I blew my shot at life. I had everything and I tossed it away. Worse, I killed a man I never knew and then turned his wife into an ugly creature filled with hate. I don't deserve to live. The world is better off with me dead.

Crumpling the note in her fist, Meg slowly rose from her knees and began to walk up the ramp. When she passed the front fender of the car, she stopped.

What had she done? God had given her exactly what she'd asked for, and now she wondered if she really wanted it. Was this the way it had to play out?

Maybe I'm not too late. Maybe I can do something. God, please help me do something. I can't let this happen. I can't be a murderer. I just can't! I've got to stop the "dark music." It has played way too much in my life.

Stuffing the note into her pocket, she turned and rushed back to car. Falling to the ground, she cleared his air passage and began the process of mouth-to-mouth resuscitation. As she worked her one-woman CPR, she prayed her first prayer in months. With her lips to his, she kept working, praying, and hoping for a miracle.

"Breathe, come on, breathe," she demanded.

Panic now began to come over her, and only her professional training kept her from breaking down into a pitiful mass of jumbled nerves and sobs. From out of nowhere, a light rain began to fall, the drops combining with sweat on Meg's forehead and the tears now running down her cheeks blended together and ran down over the boy's face. Still, even as the rain grew harder and the lightning began to flash and the thunder roared, she worked on.

"Now, breathe. Come on, Jim, breathe! You can do it. You have your whole life in front on you. Breathe for me, come on, breathe!"

As the rain began to strike her back with more fury, this time in big, cold drops, she glanced back toward the ER doors. There was no one, not a doctor or another nurse or even an orderly. It was up to her. As the lightning flashed again, she clearly saw Thomas's face. It was just like seeing the cold mask of death.

"No!" she whispered as she went back to work on reviving him. "Come on, don't do this to me. Don't you go away! Not now, not here. Don't leave me with this kind of guilt trip. Breathe!"

She felt her baby kick her hard as she continued to administer CPR.

It is the right thing to do, Baby. I'll explain why at another time. Then turning her face into the rain, she screamed, "C'mon, God, I know I was wrong. I'm sorry. Don't do this to me. I can't handle this. I thought I could, but I can't!"

She put her mouth to the young man's and silently pleaded, "C'mon, breathe!"

Inside her brain, Meg was aware of a clock ticking. It was a life clock, the kind that couldn't be wound or turned back. With every tick, it brought Jim Thomas closer to the point of no return. For all she knew, he'd already passed that point. He might have passed it as she read the note or even when she walked away. She had no way of knowing and the ticking in her brain kept getting louder.

"Oh, God, Please!"

And still, the boy just lay there. She would breathe in, but he wouldn't help her. She would push on his heart, demanding that it beat, and she would get no response. As the rain grew harder, Meg took one last deep breath and placed her mouth on his one final time.

Suddenly, she felt a weak cough come from the boy's throat. "That's it!" she whispered lowering her lips to his once again. "Now, keep it up," she urged as she took another deep breath.

Suddenly, she heard the doors behind her open and the sounds of heavy footsteps splashing through the rain to her side. "Sorry it took me so long. Had a heart attack in ICU. What's the story here?"

Looking up at the doctor, Meg hurriedly explained, "Carbon monoxide. I've got him breathing shallowly now. We've got to get him inside. I think we can save him!"

As they lifted the boy onto a gurney, the heavens cut loose with a torrential downfall. Soaking wet by the time they got inside, they wheeled Thomas directly into room 3 and went to work.

"Get an IV in him, nurse. I'll get the oxygen going."

Meg went to work, all the while haunted by the thought that she had done this. She had been the one who might have killed this boy.

55

AN HOUR LATER, AN ORDERLY AND A NURSE WHEELED THOMAS TO INTENsive care. As Meg rested on an empty stool, Dr. McCullen went directly into the other room to treat the still-waiting Ed's injured hand. Wiping her brow with a cloth, Meg took a deep breath and walked out of the room into the lobby where she sat down beside the teenager who had brought Thomas to the hospital.

"Is he going to die?" the girl asked again.

A tired smile coming to her lips, Meg looked at the frightened kid with warm, loving eyes, and said, "I don't think so. He's not out of the woods yet, but he should make it. At least, I believe he will."

"You saved his life," the small, sandy-haired teen said in amazement.

Meg just glanced away and shook her head. Turning back to the girl, she asked, "Want some gum? I have some in my purse."

The girl nodded.

Getting up, Meg went behind the counter, opened a drawer, and pulled out her handbag.

"What's your name?"

"Katie ... Katie Davis," the girl answered.

"Well, Katie," Meg explained, "you saved his life by getting him here in time. You are a good friend."

The girl just shook her head. "Not really, I only went by because he had something I needed. He never sleeps much, so I figured he'd be up. Nobody really likes him anymore. He's gotten so weird. But I couldn't let him die. Oh no, what time is it? I need to call home and tell my folks where I am, and my cell is still in the car."

"Use this phone." Meg offered the one on the desk. As the girl called, Meg picked up her purse to look for the gum. Opening it, she reached in and pulled out a small, wrapped package. As soon as she saw it, tears filled her eyes.

"Is there anything wrong?" Katie asked.

"No," Meg responded. "I just picked up the wrong purse when I left home. I haven't carried this one since . . ." It had been the day of the verdict. After trying unsuccessfully to push a tear back into her eye with her finger, she continued, "Well, anyway for a long time." Searching in the purse, she pulled out a piece of gum and handed it to the girl.

"Nurse." Dr. McCullen's voice caused her to look across the room. "You've done some great work. I'll cover here. Why don't you take a break?"

Nodding, Meg picked up the wrapped package, slipped it back in her purse, and walked out behind the counter and down the hall to the break room. After getting a soda, she sat down and once again retrieved the package from her bag. Staring at it for a few moments, she placed it in her lap.

What was in it? What had Nancy thought was so important that she wrapped it and left it for her on the day she died?

Pulling away the string and tissue paper, Meg finally saw the gift she'd forgotten she'd had.

"A Bible," she whispered as the paper slipped off. The name "Nancy" was written in gold on the bottom right side of the cover. As Meg lifted the book from her lap, a piece of paper fell to the floor. Bending over, she picked it up and saw it was a note meant for only her.

Meg, I know that you will find the satisfaction that you so badly want to find. But, trust me, you will not find it in the place where you now believe it to be. I once thought that true happiness and peace would only be found when they developed a cure for cancer. Now, I know that answer would have only been a temporary one. I've found that the answer does not come from the outside, but from within. So, what you need has already been placed in your heart. And in your hand, you have the key to discovering that answer.

Meg studied the words while once again squeezing the small Bible that rested in her left hand. Opening it, she placed Nancy's note inside the pages and closed the book. But as the pages shut, the note went flying out. Picking it up, she reopened the book and reinserted the note. But once again when she closed it, the note fell to the floor.

Picking the note up for the third time, Meg reopened the Bible, and this time a passage that Nancy had underlined in red ink jumped out at her.

Don't just pretend to love others. Really love them. Hate what is wrong. Hold tightly to what is good. Love each other with genuine affection, and take delight in honoring each other. Never be lazy, but work hard and serve the Lord enthusiastically. Rejoice in our confident hope. Be patient in trouble, and keep on praying. When God's people are in need, be ready to help them. Always be eager to practice hospitality.

Bless those who persecute you. Don't curse them; pray that God will bless them. Be happy with those who are happy, and weep with those who weep. Live in harmony with each other. Don't be too proud to enjoy the company of ordinary people. And don't think you know it all!

Never pay back evil with more evil. Do things in such a way that everyone can see you are honorable. Do all that you can to live in peace with everyone.

Dear friends, never take revenge. Leave that to the righteous anger of God. For the Scriptures say,

"I will take revenge;
I will pay them back,"
says the LORD. Instead,
"If your enemies are hungry, feed them.
If they are thirsty, give them something to drink.
In doing this, you will heap
burning coals of shame on their heads."
Don't let evil conquer you, but conquer evil by doing good.

After reading the passage several times, Meg placed the note once again into the Bible, and this time it stayed in place. Setting the book down on the table to her right, Meg whispered, "You can't leave me alone, can you, Nancy? When you said that you left me a road map, you didn't say it would show me where I'd already been. And I don't like that. The question I've got now, the same one I had that night I came to see you and you had already gone, is where do I go from here?"

"Are you talking to me?" Katie asked as she popped into the room.

Meg shook her head. "No, just thinking about an old friend."

"Well, I'm going home now. Thanks for saving Jim."

"You take care," Meg gently answered as the young woman left the room. Now once more alone, Meg continued to silently speak to someone who had not been there for three months.

"Where do I go from here? Nancy, I know what you would say. You'd say that all I have to do to learn what I need to know is ask the One who made me and then search my own heart Well, this time, I'll listen. And this time, I will give it a try."

Walking out of the break room, down the hall, up a flight of stairs and around a corner brought her to the hospital's small chapel. There was no one there. Stepping in, she fell to her knees and began to pray. She did so unashamedly and out loud.

"Okay. Lord. It's just You and me now. I guess You've been waiting for this moment for a long time. I don't really know how to say this, but I'm sorry, for not only pushing You out of my life but for blaming You for all that has happened.

"It's pretty clear to me now that You didn't want Jim Thomas to get drunk and kill Steve. If Jim had been listening to You, well, that wouldn't have happened. What he did may have resulted from his choice, but it's obvious that his problem goes back beyond that night. Someone didn't care enough about him to reach out and love him. He didn't have a Steve, Nancy, or Heather, or anyone I guess. And if he did, he may have been just as stubborn about listening as I was.

"Lord, if You will just help him get well, I'll try to make up for what I've done. Of course having that boy listen to me, after all the things I put him through, will be a bigger miracle than You making him well. But if I can be used, I want to be used.

"Lord, I thought Jim Thomas was the enemy, but now I see that wasn't true. The enemy was what made him lose control ... the booze. There are many ways that I can make a difference through my witness on this subject. Help me to find a way.

"You know I haven't thanked You for anything in a long time. But now I want to. Thank You for a mother who told me about You, who has great faith in You, and who still loves me after all I've done. Thank you for my friends, especially Nancy, someone who loved me at my ugliest and whose kindness and understanding have done a great deal in helping me see a bit more clearly now.

"Finally, Lord, I don't know if she ever will be able to forgive me, but please give me the strength to humble myself to Heather. I walked out on her, took advantage of her nature, and then, when she looked to me for some kind of strength and guidance, I let her down.

"Without You I've done a real good job of messing my life up. I'm ready to admit that and I'm ready to not blame You for it.

"From this moment, I dedicate myself to being more of the person I need to be. Dear Jesus, I'm sorry, but work with me on this, please.

"Amen."

As Meg opened her eyes and raised her head, she saw a figure standing to her left. As she turned, her eyes met Heather's.

"I understand that you're a hero," Heather softly announced.

"No, I'm a jerk, who got lucky," Meg responded as she pulled her pregnant form from the pew. Pausing a moment, she continued, "Heather . . ."

"You don't have to say a thing," Heather responded. "I heard your prayer and I'm just glad to have you back. Whatever problems we had, they aren't important now. They happened when you weren't yourself."

As Meg rose, Heather opened her arms, and the two of them shared both tears of pain and thankfulness. After a long moment, Meg patted her friend on the back, wiped her eyes, and then stepping back, inquired, "What are you doing here?"

"I was worried about you," Heather replied. "Julie called me and told me what had happened. I thought you might need someone."

"I sure hope what I did was in time," Meg stated.

"It was."

"How do you know?" Meg demanded.

"I just know," Heather assured her. "I just know."

56

WHEN MEG OPENED THE DOOR, JIM THOMAS WAS WATCHING TELEVISION. As she came in, he quickly turned the set off. The look on his face told her he didn't know what to expect.

"How are you feeling?" Though her voice was calm, Meg's insides were shaking like the limbs of a willow tree fighting a gale force wind. She'd slept little but prayed a lot. Those prayers had centered on forgiveness and compassion. She'd prayed for complete healing for this young man. And she had prayed for her own strength in this moment.

"Fine." Jim's answer was short and accompanied by a worried nod.

Thomas, who was now a patient in room 211—Nancy's room—and it had been over sixteen hours since Meg had made the hardest decision of her life by deciding to save his life. Now after one night of observation, he would be going home, with no lasting effects from his experience.

As her big brown eyes stared warmly at him, the fear that he'd initially shown turned to confusion. He had to be asking himself where was the hard, cold demon who had confronted him just two days before.

"You had me a little scared," Meg continued after closing the gap between them. Then noticing the flowers and cards that decorated the entire room, she observed, "I'm glad you made it, and evidently I'm not the only one. I wonder if there are any cards and flowers left in Springfield?" She forced a laugh. When he didn't join her, she walked over to the window and looked outside.

This was going to be a lot harder than she imagined. He had no reason to trust her. Not now, not ever! She shouldn't even be in his room. She was the wrong nurse at the wrong time. As much as she wanted and needed forgiveness, it was simply too soon.

From behind her, he cleared his throat and finally spoke. "I don't understand why you did it."

She had to say what she had come in here to say, but it was hard and humbling. There simply couldn't be anything more difficult than admitting you were wrong unless it was that you were also ugly, mean, and evil. And she'd been all these things. So a simple "I'm sorry" was not enough. Where did she begin?

While letting the words sink in, Meg turned away from the window, strolled across the room, pulled a chair up close to the bed, and sat down. Crossing her legs, she placed her hands in her lap, just below her baby bump, and began.

"I don't know if you mean why I spent the last few months hounding you, maybe tormenting is a better word, or why I tried to save your life last night. But both of those questions deserve to be answered, and that's really why I'm here. For your sake and mine I need to try to make you understand not only what I became but what I'm trying hard to be at this moment."

"Jim," Meg's eyes met his and locked. His face still showed confusion, but at least it seemed some of the apprehension that had been etched there a few minutes ago was now gone. She smiled as she continued, "I don't know if you can ever forgive me, in fact, I don't expect you can, but I am sorry for everything I did. Something got into me, no, that's not true, the Spirit of God left me, or at least I decided I wasn't going to listen to that spirit any more, and I became an almost demonic instrument of hate. I mean . . ."

Meg paused and glanced over to the mirror. This was so hard. She was having to admit that hate had consumed her. That was an ugly picture. But she also had to be honest, he needed to know it all and she had to get it off her chest, for fear, that if she didn't, it could creep back into her life again.

"I'd be lying," she softly admitted as she turned back to face him, "if I didn't tell you that a big part of me wanted you to die when Katie brought you in. I had gotten so far from what I once was, what I should have been, that I wanted to walk away and do nothing for you. But there was a still, small voice, a pretty powerful voice, too, one that just wouldn't let me do that. It wasn't the nurse in me. It was that tiny bit of faith that was left in me."

Meg stopped for a moment. What she had said may have been enough, but for herself she needed to go further, to explain even more.

"I think that the Christian in me would have been dead, too, except for the very positive, loving influence of a young lady I met just a few months ago. As a matter of fact, I met her in this very room. Her name was Nancy, and in some very subtle ways, she kept after me to look inside myself. You know, I thought I had been able to ignore everything that she had said, but I guess that I didn't. She told me that it wasn't God striking out at me when Steve died. It was a shortcoming in us as human beings. If everyone would just try to be what God wanted, if we would just pay attention to His word and wishes, then things like this wouldn't happen."

Meg got up and walked over to the table where Nancy's iPod used to be. As she touched that spot, she was taken back to a time when music filled this room. If that same music were here now, it would sure help. She spun slowly around to face the patient.

"Jim, Nancy actually believed God was as sad as I was about Steve's death. She told me then, and now I believe it, that God cried with me. But she also said that God wasn't mad at you, and I couldn't buy that at that time. I thought He should have been. But Nancy said He wanted you to ask Him for help, to reach out to Him. And He was sad when you took a different road. Without Nancy, I'm not sure that I would have ever realized that. Her witness probably saved your life last night. It's folks like her who positively touch other people's lives. Then there are folks like me, who have done just the opposite. I affected you in ways that make me ashamed to the bone."

He was listening to every word she was saying, but was she getting through to him? Smiling again, she continued, this time intent on keeping her eyes right on his.

"Nancy was one of the first people I ever met, who never—not once—demanded that I think like or be like her. She was strong enough to know her own faith and not judge me for my lack of faith. I guess if I've ever known a real wise Christian, it was her."

"She sounds very special," Thomas said. "She sounds like someone I should meet."

Now hesitating, tears welling up in her eyes, Meg whispered, "I wish you could, but she died a few months ago. She had cancer." Meg stopped. She knew what she needed to say, but even after trying to put the words together all day, she still didn't know how to say it.

"Jim, I was very wrong. What I did to you was unforgivable. I have no right to ever expect you to forgive me, but I want to say that I am very sorry." Her words had come out in a halting manner and a chill ran down her neck as she waited for the response. It took an agonizingly long time for the young man to speak.

"Mrs. Richards," his voice was a little shaky, "I should be apologizing to you. I am the one who . . ."

"You were driving," Meg interrupted, "but the alcohol is why it happened. If it hadn't been for that, then there would have been no accident. It was the alcohol, not you. You can't change that past part of your life, but you can still put your life together. You can use what has happened to help others from letting it happen to them."

"Still," the boy began, but Meg once again cut him off before he could continue.

"Jim, I have a feeling that the alcohol and the partying were an attempt to replace something that you were missing in your life. It's just a guess, but I have a feeling that you were look-ing for something even on that night, and you probably still haven't found it. Heaven knows, I haven't helped you any."

"Mrs. Richards," Thomas's voice was now strong and sure, "if I'm missing something, then a lot of my friends are, too."

"I know. And all day long I've been looking for a way to do something to help you find it. I'm still not sure what I can do, but until I discover how, I've got something I want to share with you. Something that Nancy shared with me."

Reaching into her purse, Meg pulled out a new Bible. "Jim, I'm sure that you probably have got a bunch of these at home. Most of them probably have an inch or two of dust on them, but tonight I just thought this one might help you find an answer or two; at least to realize just how wrong I have been, and why now, I'm different.

"You see, I rediscovered an important part of me in this book. And I hope that you might find something, too."

After she handed Jim the black, leather bound book, she started to get up and leave. But before she could walk away, he made a request. "What did you read?"

Pulling the Bible from his hands, she leafed through the pages until she came to Romans 12:9-21. Using her index finger, she pointed to the verses.

"From here to here."

Taking the book back from her, he glanced back into the woman's eyes, and then marked the place with the Bible's ribbon, closed it, and set it beside him on the bed. She waited for him to say something, but his lips remained tightly drawn.

"Take care of yourself," Meg answered and left the room.

She sighed as she walked down the hall. Did she make an impact? Shaking her head, she figured that she would never know. But at least the hard words had been said. He may not have been humbled, but she had been. And admitting her mistakes had lifted the final heavy load off her shoulders.

She walked up to the nurses' station and looked over at Heather. Opening her arms, she hugged her friend.

"What was that for?" Heather asked.

"I'm back," she whispered. "The old Meg is back. Thank God she came back before I ruined any more lives."

57

Even after saving Jim Thomas's life, even after discovering Nancy's gift, the road back to where she had been was not an easy one. Meg had hurt too many people and made too many deep impressions to have everyone instantly trust and accept her. Yet the change took place, likely because the foundation had always been there. She wasn't as much discovering a new person as embracing the woman she'd always been—the one Steve had fallen in love with so many years ago. And she liked that Meg a lot.

Almost two months of hard work and kind actions had rebuilt most of the bridges Meg had burned during her campaign for vengeance. Some, like the hospital administrator, were still keeping a close eye on her—waiting for her to slip up. But the nurses trusted her again. In fact, they had thrown her a baby shower. And at that shower Nancy's husband, Joe, had shown up with a gift his late wife had ordered before she'd died. It was nothing big, nothing really special, just a tiny pink outfit. Yet Meg wondered why Nancy thought that she was going to have a girl. After all, she'd not even found out the baby's sex yet. She hadn't wanted to know.

As Steve had said time and time again, the apartment was too small to raise a kid in, so Meg had moved to an older, but well-maintained, two-bedroom frame home just a few blocks from her mother's. In the extra bedroom, Meg, her mother, and Heather spent a whole weekend decorating a nursery in Steve's favorite colors—red and blue.

Yet faith can only do so much. With each passing day that drew her nearer the birth of her child, her loneliness hovered over her like a cloud. Sometimes that cloud was dark and ominous. It brought with it pain, but no longer a cry for vengeance. Yet even though her need for Steve's love was still strong, her need for retribution was gone. While she didn't accept her loss as God's will, she was at peace with what happened.

Being alone was not something that she enjoyed, but it was no longer a time when she felt deserted. She had faith to support her. It wasn't the same kind of faith as her mother's, Meg was still a fighter and a questioner much more than an accepter, but it was a faith that fit her own personality. It was faith that once again worked for her.

At first, she had been unable to visit Steve's grave. Now she stopped by at least twice a week with fresh flowers. Once she cleaned up the grass and weeds around the new headstone, she sat down and informed him of the baby's latest kicks and the other events in her life. That one-way conversation brought tears to the eyes of observers, but it somehow made Meg feel like Steve was still a part of her life. She didn't want to give them up either.

Each night, before going to bed, Meg began a new tradition. She read the Bible Nancy left her. And every morning, just before she left for work, she'd reread the passage she knew that Nancy had meant for her to find.

Work was no longer an escape as it had been in the first weeks and months after Steve's death. She looked forward to each new day as an avenue for meeting new people and touching lives. With her quick smile and warm eyes, she was once more the nurse everyone requested. Except for missing Steve, her life couldn't have been more perfect. And it was that one empty place that pushed her on to do something meaningful, something positive and rewarding, something that she felt was a proper way for her to dedicate herself to Steve's memory.

Rather than bury the pain of Steve's death, Meg now talked about it. A local representative of Mothers Against Drunk Driving had by chance heard her speak in her Sunday school class in early August. That woman got Meg involved in MADD. She embraced this service with zeal and enthusiasm. She didn't hesitate to share her story with church and school groups, as well as legislative bodies, civic and social clubs. Each time she spoke, she felt as if she might just be saving someone else from going through what she had. Now, just days from her due date, she was looking forward to one of the most important speaking engagements of her life.

"Meg," Heather asked as they finished up another day of work, "are you sure you should go tonight? I mean, that child is due any day now."

"I've got to, Heather," Meg explained as she completed the count and prepared to check out. "There are going to be over five hundred high school kids there. And if just one of them take's note of what I say, then I'll have done something that might save a life."

"High school kids?" Heather replied ironically. "When I was in high school I blew off anything that anyone over twenty had to say. How are you going to make them hear you? Sweetheart, this is not going to be a picnic."

"I know and I'm scared," Meg answered. "Still, I've got to try. It's important to me. After all, drunk driving is the number one cause of death in people of that age. If I don't talk, then they'll get to watch a video or have a science teacher speak to them. And you know that the kids won't get much out of that."

Heather gave in. She wasn't going to get Meg to go home and rest, but she could add a stipulation. "Okay, I'll let you go, if you'll let me drive you and stay with you. I mean you might need a nurse!"

Smiling, Meg nodded. "Pick me up at six-thirty."

58

A FEW HOURS LATER, AS MEG LOOKED OUT AT THE PACKED AUDITORIUM she was glad that Heather had decided to come along. These kids, brought together simply as an extra credit assignment for school, did not appear to be a receptive audience. They were there only because they had to be. It was a grade, no more, and most of them were not going to give Meg either their attention or respect. It would be the toughest group she had ever addressed, but it was the one that probably needed to hear her words the most.

When the school superintendent introduced her, she couldn't help but note only a few of the kids seemed to be listening and even fewer responded with applause. The school principal had warned her she'd be speaking to the party animals, as it seemed the good kids didn't need the extra credit. So it was as if her captive audience was really made up of zoo animals and she was the raw meat. Most were talking and texting and some were even tossing a ball around. The supervisors had given up even trying to make them behave. Looking back at Heather for some support, she waddled her nine-months pregnant body out to the middle of the stage, deciding the best way to try to win the group over was by being honest.

Clearing her throat, she began, "You came here tonight to fulfill an assignment. I came here tonight to reveal to you something I think is very important. Something that I feel is a matter of life and death. Yet, what I'm going to say you have heard a hundred times and so you probably are wishing that I would just hand out a few brochures and let you go home. It's too important for me to do that and I only hope that you'll give me at least a few minutes of your time."

Even as she spoke, Meg could still hear the students—many of them talking to one another, some simply shuffling in their seats, and many being outright rowdy, but few, if any, were hearing her words. Silently, she uttered a short plea to God for some help. But as she went on it became more and more obvious this was going to be a wasted cause. The louder she spoke, the louder the noise made by those in the audience. Ten minutes into her speech, she glanced back toward Heather as if to say, I'm not doing a bit of good. I might as well give up.

Suddenly she heard someone in the back shout, "Shut up!" Even if they were rude enough to talk and text and not pay any attention to what she said, she still was shocked that anyone could have such gall to yell. Then she heard it again. This time the voice was even louder.

"Just shut up!"

As the voice echoed through the gym, her heart sank. Now she was sure she might as well give up and go home. Looking down at the podium, tears began to well up in her eyes. Her past was coming back to haunt her.

"Shut up," the voice shouted for the third time and suddenly the entire audience quit talking and turned to look at a figure quickly making his way down the aisle from the back of the room to the stage. Because of the spotlight directed at her, as well as the darkened gymnasium, Meg couldn't tell much about the young man, except that he was very agitated and in a big hurry to get to her. As he got closer, she was pretty sure she knew who he was. Too stunned to be scared and too confused to continue speaking, just like the others, she waited for the young man to do what it was he was going to do and that was humiliate her.

He climbed the six steps to the platform two at a time. Then, as his feet hit the stage and as his face was illuminated by the spotlight, Meg confirmed what she believed when she heard his shout. It was Jim Thomas.

She was sure he was here to make a fool out of here. He was going to expose what she was to the whole world. He was probably going to blame Steve and he'd make her look like a vengeful, stone-cold monster. She wanted to run, but there wasn't any place to go. So she was stuck in one spot, in front of a silent and gasping audience just as stunned as she was by what was happening.

Jim covered the fifteen feet to the platform in four more steps and suddenly he was standing beside her. Looking down, he demanded she move to the side. Meg responded by walking across the platform and toward the exit, almost as if running for cover, but as he began to speak, she stopped.

"You know me. I'm Jim Thomas. I'm the guy who was voted most likely to succeed last semester. I was the captain of the football, baseball, and basketball teams. Some of you considered me Mr. Cool. But I've changed a lot since I graduated and I think all of you need to hear about it."

The crowd was now completely silent. All eyes were on the young man and no one made a move to stop him from speaking. He had everyone's complete attention.

"Listen, because these are the facts," he continued. Then, pointing a finger at himself, he said in a strong voice, "I killed this woman's husband. I loaded myself up with some booze and killed him with my car. You know what, I was less drunk that night than I'd been at least a dozen times before. I used to get so wasted I didn't even remember driving home. But I remember that night in detail. So I was a lot less drunk than most of you are every Friday night. But I guess how drunk I was or wasn't didn't matter much to Mrs. Richards's husband. I was gone enough to kill him."

The boy's words were now rushing out at rapid-fire rate and he knew what he had to say.

"This is no joke. Since the time this meeting has started three people in this country have been killed by drunk drivers. I don't know how many more have been injured. But, to put it into perspective, if each of us—and you look around, there are a lot of us here tonight—starting at this very moment took the place of a victim, it is amazing how fast we would fall. By midnight, the whole first two rows would be dead. By tomorrow night, all of you sitting in the first nine rows would be lying in a morgue somewhere. By next week at this time, all of us, everyone in this room would be dead. Kind of frightening, isn't it?"

Meg took a few steps away from the exit back toward the stage. She didn't want the young man to go through this alone. She was going to join him. As she made her way back to the platform, he continued.

"You know, I killed someone. Do you know how hard that is to say? Well, it was real easy to do. Nobody here can afford not to listen to what this lady has to say. If it wasn't for me, she wouldn't know anything about this. Each night I pray that I will wake up from the nightmare that I created. But I can't change that now. It's too late! But you can. Don't let yourself make someone else as well-informed on widowhood and alcohol statistics as Mrs. Richards. Listen to her now."

Thomas looked back toward Meg. It was time for her to talk, his eyes said. They would listen. Meg took the few steps back to the podium. As she did, he started to leave, but she caught his hand.

"Please, stand here beside me," she asked. Then she turned toward the now quiet crowd. "It took a lot of courage for Jim to come up here and talk to you and it shows just how important he thinks this subject is." Glancing to her left, Meg said, "Thank you, Jim." Then, she continued.

"What Jim has to live with none of us can imagine nor would we want to. You see, as he said, he can't go back to fix the mistake he made. But, if you haven't made that mistake, you can change it before it happens.

"If a whole high school class were killed by drunk drivers, then something would be done. But the kind of abuse and death we are trying to tell you about doesn't happen that way. It happens one person at a time and usually the story is buried on the back page. We never see the ruined lives. Never feel the pain of the survivors.

"Kids, I'm not asking you to plead guilty for what you have done in the past. What I'm asking is for you to find something to replace the drinking and the driving. For me it is faith and a belief in God. I don't need to search for my highs anywhere else or by using anything else. I think that this would work for you, too. But whatever it is you choose, you need to find something to take the place of booze. You strive so hard every day to make adults think you are grown up. Well, booze controls you and your actions. The sign of real maturity is for you to be in total control."

The crowd was stone silent. They were taking in every word Meg said.

"Right now, if things don't change, in your lifetime, one in four of you will be seriously injured or killed by someone who is drinking and driving. Don't become a statistic and don't be the one responsible for continuing this sad trend. Stop your drinking and driving, tell your friends to stop, too. Not for my sake or my husband's or Jim Thomas's, but for yours.

"Thank you, and good night."

Meg turned and walked to the side of the stage with Thomas following. When they were safely in the wings, Meg looked up expecting to see a boy's face, but a man looked back.

"Why?" she asked.

"They needed to hear what you had to say," he answered. "I only wish I'd heard it a few years ago."

"But you put yourself on the line," she argued. "You knocked yourself. You didn't have to do that."

"No," he grimly replied, "I told it the way it was. None of them should have to experience what you or I have. I wanted them to feel a little bit of both yours and my pain, and maybe, just maybe, it will give some of the ones who need to hear it the worst something to think about before it's too late."

"Would it have helped you," Meg asked, "if someone like me had spoken to you back then?"

"I don't know if what happened tonight would have made a lasting impact, but what you showed me in my hospital room after I tried to kill myself would have made an impact no matter when it happened.

"You see, my parents gave me everything that I could've ever wanted, except for their time and their love. They bought me cars and gave me money, but they never took the time to give me limits or even care enough about me to respond in the right way to my big mistakes. I guess when I tried to cash in my life I was crying out to them and they still haven't heard me. You temporarily saved my life with your CPR, but it was the genuine caring that I felt when you came into my room the next day that give me a reason to live."

He paused a moment, ran his hand through his hair, and shook his head.

"You know, even when you were calling me and leaving those posters all over everywhere, making my life a living hell, I could understand why you were doing it. Now I know that you weren't right, but you loved your husband so much that you were willing to do anything and give everything to do something for him. That was real love, the kind I'd never known. It may have been misdirected, but it was real. If I'd been killed by someone like me, no one would have cared enough to give a second thought to punishing my killer."

"Jim," Meg said quietly, "what I displayed wasn't love, it was pure, selfish hate. Real love would have reached out to you and seen your needs. I missed those. I'm not sure that I knew what real unselfish love was until I had almost killed you."

"Mrs. Richards," Thomas smiled, his hand touching hers. "You didn't make me try to kill myself. I was looking for something, and if my parents or my friends had helped I might have had the strength to make it through what you did to me. Being hated is not that big a deal, but not being loved is. Now, thanks to you, I know that at least God loves me. That'll do for now."

Nodding in approval, Meg turned and walked toward Heather. Thomas hesitated for a moment before walking off in the opposite direction. Suddenly stopping, Meg whirled around and hollered at her one-time enemy.

"Do you really think we made an impact tonight?"

He nodded.

"Would you like to work together—you and me?" she asked. "I think that by showing both sides of this story honestly we could wake some people up. Besides, I believe what God has been able to do in bringing us together is something people need to see, too. So do you want to give it a try?"

Smiling, Jim responded, "I'd like that a lot."

"Okay, then," Meg replied enthusiastically, "I'll call you soon. And I won't hang up this time."

The boy waved and walked across the stage toward the steps that led to the floor. But before he got completely out of earshot, Meg's voice caught his attention one more time.

"Jim," she shouted. "God does love you, and I do, too. Don't ever doubt that or forget it."

Thomas didn't respond with any more than a small wave but she knew her words had struck home. He would be all right from now on.

"Well," a smiling Heather noted as the two of them left the school and got into the car, "I'm proud of you, Meg. You're something very special. I'm glad that I came along, even if you didn't need a nurse."

"Thanks, Heather," Meg answered, "but you are needed."

"What do you mean?"

"I've been experiencing labor pains for at least half an hour, and if you don't hurry and get to the hospital, you may get to deliver this child yourself. So let's get moving!"

59

For the next few hours, as her labor progressed at a normal rate, Meg thought mostly about Steve and how much he had looked forward to this moment. Even though this brought a degree of pain, it no longer created feelings of hate. She was fine now, lonely but fine. She could now remember and not want to die. She could think of good times with a smile. She was healing.

Meg glanced over at Heather, who was almost asleep in a far chair. The combination of getting up early for work and now having to stay with Meg all night had taken its toll.

"Heather," Meg whispered.

"Huh?" came the startled reply.

"You fogging out on me?"

"No," Heather answered, rubbing her face, "I just had something in my eye, and I thought that if I closed it for a moment it might find its way out."

"Sure!"

"No, I'm serious."

"Hi, you two lucky, off-duty nurses." Jan's greeting was typical of her cheery "it's time for a laugh" manner. After checking Meg's vitals and the baby's heart rate, she announced, "I have some good news and some bad news. Which do you want to hear first?"

"My baby," Meg gasped, fearing the worst, "it's all right?"

"Beating away at 140," Jan answered.

"Then what?" Heather asked.

"Which do you want first?" the on-duty nurse asked again.

"The bad!" both Heather and Meg yelled back.

"Okay, Dr. Colvin has taken ill. Nothing serious, but he had to go home."

"So what's the other part?" Meg demanded.

"Because old Otis can't be here, we've decided you'll have to go home and have the baby another time!"

"Sure, Greer," Meg shrugged, "now that you've made your weak attempt at humor, tell us what is really going on."

"Didn't you like my joke?" Jan seemed genuinely disappointed. "All right, here is the real story. Otis is sick and he's calling in a sub. The sub is Dr. Drew Meyer. He just joined the staff, and if you haven't seen him . . . well, suffice it to say, he is a hunk. One look at him, Meg, and you won't need any anesthesia."

Meg was very disappointed Dr. Colvin couldn't be the one to deliver her baby. He'd delivered her, and she had such faith in him. After a moment of contemplating the change, she looked back at Jan and asked, "Tell me about this new guy."

"Well," the nurse began, "he's about six-foot-two, has these dreamy blue eyes, and . . ."

"Not that," Meg cut her off. "I don't care what he looks like. Where did he come from?"

"Oh, that." Jan sounded very disappointed. "He's from Arkansas. I think he went to Rice Med. I know that he worked in some highly experimental programs for a few years. Dr. Colvin was as pleased as punch that we got him. The only reason he ended up here, rather than a big-city hospital, was that he had an uncle or someone who lived in Springfield who needed some kind of help. Evidently, the old man didn't have any kids, and Drew was the only one willing to step up to the plate. When you see him, you won't put me down for talking about his looks. I mean, this guy is a real . . ." Evidently noting Meg's bored expression, she cut her observation short and continued with the professional run down.

"Don't worry about it, you're in good hands." Jan couldn't resist adding, "Oh, what I wouldn't give to be in his hands!"

"Don't you have somewhere you need to be?" Heather asked.

"No," Jan answered. "Meg is my only patient right now."

"Why don't you go find another one?" Heather suggested.

"Okay," Jan acted hurt, even though she wasn't, "I can take a hint. I'll go check the streets. Maybe they're filled with pregnant ladies in labor tonight! Later, girls!" With a wave, she was gone.

"Can you believe her?" Heather asked.

"Sure," Meg responded. "She acts just like you."

The two women grinned at each other and waited as the time slowly passed and the contractions grew closer and closer together. Eventually Meg became interested in a late-night talk show, and Heather once again drifted off. Then a male voice brought both of them back into the present.

"I understand that one of you is having a baby. Now which one is it?"

"Jan was right!" Heather said.

"By Jan, I assume that you're talking about Nurse Greer. Now what was she so right about?" the doctor asked.

Realizing what she had said, Heather attempted to cover up her embarrassment by explaining herself. "Well, what I mean is that Jan said you were a good doctor."

Sensing her explanation had backed her even deeper into a corner, she tried again. "What she said was that you would be here just when I needed you." Satisfied that she had extracted herself from the hole she had put herself in, Heather smiled.

"Why do you need me?" the doctor asked Heather.

"No," Heather stammered, "I didn't mean me. I meant *we*. When we needed you."

The doctor cut her off and offered his hand. "My name is Dr. Meyer, but you can call me Drew. Now, if you can remember, I'd like to know your name?"

"A-a-a Heather," the nurse answered while gazing into his eyes. "Heather Rodgers. I'm a nurse."

"Congratulations. You know your name and your occupation. We'll go for the birth date tomorrow." Smiling at Meg, he understatedly asked, "I take it you're having the baby?"

"What was your first clue?" Meg groaned.

"Oh, I really had an unfair advantage," the doctor answered, a gleam now evident in his eye. "I saw a picture of a pregnant woman is a medical book once, it must have been about five years ago, and you look a whole lot like that. You did pose for that picture, didn't you?"

"No!" Meg smiled. "Five years ago I was much thinner."

"Anyway," the doctor continued, "you can call me Drew, and your name is?"

Meg, taking the same tact, responded, "I have a feeling that since you've already looked at my chart you know my name. But just in case you don't know what a chart is, it's Meg."

"The charts at this hospital are called Meg?" he asked, almost seriously.

"No," Meg smiled. "I am! And having Jan doing stand up comedy is enough for one hospital."

"Well, then, I will cut the jokes and take a look at you, Meg."

After a few moments of examination, complete with a great deal of the expected poking and prodding, Drew smiled and offhandedly remarked, "You're right! You're going to have a baby. As a matter of fact, pretty soon! So I'll get some folks, and we'll take you to the delivery room."

"Oh, my," Heather sighed after the doctor left. "Jan was right. He is a hunk."

"Heather," Meg inquired, "were you working on your breathing exercises while he was in here?"

Blushing, Heather turned her back to Meg and pretended to search for something in her purse. A minute later, Jan reentered the room, took one look at Heather, shrugged her shoulders, and stated, "I don't have to ask what you thought of the good doctor, it's written all over your face." Turning toward Meg, she then added, "Do you suppose we can bring her down to earth long enough to get her to help me get you across the hall?"

Jan's request resulted in immediate action and within moments, Meg found herself in the delivery room. The contractions were now very close together and much more intense. She watched as a team of nurses, including Meg's old friend Molli, hooked up monitors to measure all her vital signs. She smiled when they finally started the fetal heart monitor. As the machine echoed at a steady rate, Jan announced to everyone, "Told you all that it was going to be a girl. Look at that, a pulse rate right at 145. You got any girls' names picked out, Meg?"

Meg just shook her head and then added her own insight. "Sorry, Jan, it is going to be a boy."

She knew she was just minutes away from holding her child, and everything was proceeding just as it should be. Steve would have been so proud of her. She was doing this without anything for the pain. Looking up at Heather, she observed, "You know, Steve always said I was such a wimp when it came to pain. But look at me, I'm doing great. No problems at all."

No sooner had she spoken than she suddenly felt like someone had jabbed a pitchfork into her side. She screamed twice and then groaned, "What was that?"

"That was pain, wimp," Heather answered. "Now, breathe."

"Coming down nicely," the doctor said as he reentered the room and checked Meg's progress. "Did you say something a while ago, young lady? I thought I heard you way down the hall."

Meg shook her head, knowing her scream had probably awakened the whole wing. After Dr. Meyer smiled at his patient, he looked toward Molli and said, "Okay, let's disconnect the external monitor and introduce the internal one."

Meg immediately missed the clip-clapping of the baby's heartbeat when the nurse pulled the external monitor. The steady sound helped take her mind off the pain. Still, she knew it wouldn't be more than a few seconds before the internal one was introduced and the steady beat would return.

After a few moments, she heard Dr. Meyer's voice, muffled by his mask. "Why don't you go ahead and put the external back in place."

If Meg hadn't been a nurse, she might have been worried. But there was no urgency in the doctor's voice, and she knew that occasionally an internal just can't be positioned properly. Molli placed the external back into its previous position. But there was no sound. Meg looked up and urged the nurse on, "C'mon, Molli, get it right. The baby's moved a little. Just find him. Surely after as many times as you've done this, you can get it in the right place. You had it a while ago. Just find it again."

As the seconds ticked by, Molli struggled to once again position the monitor and find the baby's heartbeat. Shrugging her shoulders at the doctor, she continued to search. It had now been almost a minute and then she got something.

"Lub-dub . . . lub-dub . . . lub-dub."

The machine and the heart sounded much different just a few moments before. Something wasn't right. That heartbeat was too slow. Meg counted then she looked up at Heather and saw the worry on her face.

"Doctor, we're at less than thirty," Molli calmly but urgently stated. "We appear to be . . ." She didn't finish her statement. She didn't need to.

Dr. Meyer already knew what she was going to say, and he was frantically moving his hand around in the birth canal. "Nurse, get me some Betadine," he ordered.

Looking around the room, Jan quickly replied, "I don't see any, doctor."

"There is some PhisoHex over there," Meg jumped in, the nurse in her taking over and attempting to control her fear as a mother facing the prospect of losing her baby.

"Okay, that'll do. Hand it here!" the doctor answered as he reached to grab it. Refusing to wait until someone told her something, Meg asked, "Is it the cord?"

"Yeah, Meg, it is." Suddenly the doctor sounded like an old friend, not someone she had just met. His manner, his eyes, and his relaxed control told her that she was in good hands. She had faith in this man.

Looking back at him, she nodded and calmly said, "We had better go for it, hadn't we? After all, it's our only real option. C'mon, get the knife out! I don't care if it kills me, cut me! Save my baby! I don't want to hear the 'dark music' again."

"What?" the doctor asked.

"Nothing," Meg sadly replied.

60

"Okay folks, let's get ready for a stat," Dr. Meyer barked.

Jan flew out of the room barking out orders. "You, scrub for a C-section on the double. Molli, get me an anesthesia and a permit. Get Dr. Jones here and make it snappy. Come on, folks, a life is in danger. Move it! Move it!"

Barbara Hankins had just arrived in the waiting room when all of the activity broke loose. Grabbing Jan as she ran by, she asked "What's going on?"

"It's under control," Jan answered. Then seeing Heather coming out into the hall, she hollered, "Heather, tell Meg's mother what's going down!"

"Ms. Hankins," Heather's anxious greeting belied her obvious fear. "There's not that much to worry about." Then she looked back toward the delivery room and added, "They know what they're doing in there."

"What's the problem? Is it my daughter?"

Shaking her head, Heather took a deep breath to calm herself down and then explained, "It seems that the umbilical cord is wound in such a way that combined with the pressure caused by Meg's pelvic bone it is acting kind of like a tourniquet. It's cutting off the baby's blood supply."

After taking a moment to comprehend what she'd been told, Mrs. Hankins grabbed Heather's arm and demanded, "What's going on? What are they doing? Is the baby going to die? Meg can't take another tragedy in her life. It would kill her. I think it would kill me, too."

"Don't worry," Heather's show of confidence was immediately reassuring to the woman. "They're going to have to do a C-section and we all know that's pretty common. Jan is just putting the team together right now."

"Where's Dr. Colvin? Is he with her?" Barbara looked past Heather hoping to see inside the room, but the door was shut.

"No, he's sick," Heather explained. "But Dr. Meyer is there, and he's very good. I mean, this is his specialty."

The nurse didn't really know if her last statement was correct, but she knew that the words would help keep Barbara calm. Leading the woman by the arm, Heather suggested, "Let's go over here and sit down. After all, in a few moments you're going to be a grandmother. We need to talk about this."

61

IN THE ROOM, THE MONITOR WAS STILL REGISTERING A VERY SLOW HEART rate. Dr. Meyer did the best he could to relieve the pressure on the baby's neck, but time was not on his side. Meg knew that he had two, maybe three, minutes left and then, even if the baby survived, there would probably be brain damage.

Hearing a voice, he glanced up. "Did you say something?" he asked Meg.

Sweat was pouring down Meg's face. Her hospital gown was drenched.

"I was praying," Meg answered.

Nodding, the doctor asked, "You want to pray together?"

"That would be nice," Meg moaned, as another series of sharp pains hit her.

"Okay," Dr. Meyer answered. "Seeing as how you're so involved in making those breathing exercises work, I'll start.

"Lord, each child is special, and we all know that. But I can see that this child has a very special mother, a mother who can teach him more with a gentle look than most people can with a lifetime of words. Please, give us the ability and the faith to use what we've learned to give this child life. We now entrust our abilities and training to Your hands. Amen."

"Amen," Meg breathed.

Molli hurried back into the room. "Everything's set. Everyone will be here in a matter of seconds." Then, stopping to look at the monitor, she cried out, "Doctor. The baby's heartbeat has increased to fifty!"

The door burst opened and four more figures rushed in. "Jones here, Dr. Meyer. Sorry we haven't had a chance to meet until now."

"No problem," Meyers told the newest member of his team. "Will you take over for me, doctor, while I scrub."

"Can you sign this?" Jan asked Meg. Despite the pain, Meg reached out and scribbled her name on the release form. Taking the form and laying it aside, Jan took a cloth and wiped Meg's face. "We're going to make it, kid, don't worry."

Meanwhile, Molli was scrubbing Meg down and prepping her for the delivery. All was proceeding as it had to.

Dr. Meyer rushed back into the room, now ready to go in. "Where's the anesthesia?" he demanded.

"I ordered it!" Jan shot back.

Moving up to where Meg could see him face-to-face, the doctor leaned over and softly informed her, "If I don't get something for you in the next thirty seconds, I'm going to have to use a local. It'll still probably hurt really bad."

"Don't worry about it," Meg replied. "Don't lose my baby. You go for it! Do it now!"

"She's here," Molli cried.

Standing over her head, anesthetist Jenny Cheek began to frantically rattle off all the standard questions. "Are you allergic to anything? What is your height and weight? When did you last eat?"

"We've got to have it," the doctor urgently pleaded.

"I know, I know," Jenny said. "It's just taking a while to work on her. She's too pumped up. Give me just a little more time."

"We don't have more time," Dr. Meyer answered, his voice still calm but now showing the urgency of the moment.

"I think it's beginning to take effect," Jenny assured him.

Meg grew dizzy, but she could still focus enough to see the doctor raise his hand, a scalpel in it, and plunge it toward her stomach. Then, just before the blade touched her, the lights went out and she drifted off to an empty, black void.

62

"Oh, my stomach, my stomach." Meg moaned.

"Hey, how are you doing?" The man's voice sounded as if it were twenty feet away. Meg wondered why in the world he was talking to someone else rather than her. After all, she was the one who was hurt so badly.

"My baby, my baby?" Meg mumbled. Her eyes were now open but unable to focus, yet she was beginning to remember what she had been through.

"My baby, my baby?" she pleaded.

"Seven pounds, ten ounces." The man's voice now sounded much closer. "She's a girl."

"Oh, thank God," Meg sighed and almost drifted back into the black void she had just left.

A few minutes later, she came out of it again. This time her mind was clear and she recognized the hospital's newest doctor standing over her. He was smiling. Judging from the fact that he didn't look like he'd shaved recently, she must have been out of it for a while.

"I'll tell you what," the doctor said, grinning broadly. "When we put you under, we really put you under."

"What time is it?" Meg asked.

"About nine," Meyer answered and then added, "at night!"

The presence of the doctor scared Meg a little. They usually hung around and waited for patients to come out from under anesthesia only when they had bad news. A chill ran down her spine as she realized that her baby might not be perfectly healthy. Scared to know the truth but afraid to wait, Meg blurted out, "Is she okay?"

"Well, considering what she put us through to get here, she's probably in better shape than anyone who was in that room this morning."

He paused to make sure Meg was following all he was saying. "We've got her in the special care unit as a precaution and also because Nurse Greer didn't want to let her out of her sight, but her Apgar was five over eight. So, you can see that she'll be fine. As a matter of fact, I'm sure that she feels a whole lot better than you do.

"You know," the doctor rambled on, "I was reading the paper after we got you out of trouble and realized that your baby was born at the exact moment of sunrise. I was wondering what the odds were of that?"

"I don't care, just so he's healthy," Meg answered.

"Watch yourself, nurse," he warned. "The baby is a girl."

"Oh, yeah," Meg sighed. "I was so sure that it was going to be a boy. I was going to name it Steven after his father. I guess I'll have to come up with something else now."

"Meg, I heard about your husband." Dr. Meyer's tone was now soft and sincere. "Jan—I mean, Nurse Greer—told me. I'm very sorry."

"Well, I've kind of worked through it," Meg explained. "That is, if you ever work through something like that."

"I'm not sure that you ever do."

His words and the manner in which he said them made Meg believe that he had been through something similar.

Carefully choosing her own words, she said, "I'm guessing that you lost someone once."

Getting up from his chair, the doctor stuck his hands in his coat pocket and walked to the window. Opening the blind and looking outside, he grimly stated, "My wife and our child . . ."

Waiting a moment, he turned back toward Meg. "Lisa and I had been married for only three years, and Missy wasn't planned. I guess the best and worst things in life aren't. She was a year old. I was in my last year of med school and the two of them were on the way home from her mother's one day. They hit a wet spot in the road." He paused a moment to compose himself, then continued. "They didn't even live long enough to get to the hospital. It was nobody's fault. I still wish that there were something or someone I could blame. But there isn't. It just happened.

"You know," his blue eyes were fixed on Meg's brown ones, "For six years I was so mad, I couldn't even pray. This morning when we were fighting for your baby's life, you broke through all of that anger. I didn't want to have someone else lose a wife or a child and so I turned back to God. I prayed for the first time in six years. I did it because I didn't want your husband to have to go through what I went through. Later, I found out about the accident. Kind of ironic, I was praying for someone who had already died. You were the one who showed me a thing or two in there today!"

Neither of them spoke for a few moments. Finally, Meg broke the silence.

"Sometimes when we hurt, we forget that others hurt, too. It sounds like you buried yourself in your work. Well, I buried myself in my hate and I almost killed someone with that hate. I certainly hurt a lot of folks. You, at least, devoted your life to helping people. Yet, at a moment when a life hung in the balance, I broke down the wall I had constructed between myself and God. Who knows, maybe now, you have, too."

"I wouldn't go that far," he said quietly. "I think that deep down inside, I'm still bitter and angry. But maybe I'm ready to start working through it. Maybe I tore a brick out of the wall anyway."

"If I can help . . ." Meg smiled.

"Don't worry. I've got a great deal of my energy invested in you. I'll check in on you—and often. Now, I'm going home and getting some sleep. You take advantage of this opportunity to rest, too. You may not have another one for a long while!" With that warning, he walked through the door and disappeared.

Grabbing the pager on the side of the bed, she called the nurse's station. "Nurse?"

"Yes?" Meg immediately recognized Jan's voice.

"When can I see my baby?"

"I've scheduled a visit right after her college graduation," Jan explained. "She's mine 'til then." Waiting a moment, she continued. "How about an hour or so? Less, if you're good. But I guarantee you, she's still going to like me better!"

Meg pushed the button and called back, "Hey, Greer!"

"Yeah," the nurse finally answered.

"You're still not funny." Meg then dropped the intercom back on the bed. As she moved in an attempt to find a more comfortable position, she felt the stabbing of pain caused by the C-section. "I didn't realize that it would hurt this much," she moaned.

Just when she finally got comfortable, she detected the sounds of footsteps—the squishy kind that only nurses' shoes made, and seconds later, Molli and Jan robustly knocked her door wide open.

Meg grinned as Jan said, "It's about time that you were awake. You've been lazy for too long!"

"We've got some questions for you," Molli added.

The two nurses pulled chairs up to the side of Meg's bed, and Molli, taking the top off of her pen, readied herself to record the answers.

"This morning," Jan began, "you fogged out on us before we had a chance to ask a very important question. This case cannot be closed without the answer." Glancing across the bed she asked, "Nurse Cassle, are you getting all of this?"

"Oh, yes, inspector," Molli answered.

"Oh, don't make me laugh," Meg begged. "It hurts too much."

Taking no pity, Jan continued. "Nurse Cassle, I told you she was a wimp, didn't I? Next, she'll be begging off and asking for pain meds. Anyway, where was I? Oh, yes. So, before you find some other reason to wimp out and go to sleep for another ten hours, we thought we'd better get this down on paper. Otherwise, the way you make decisions and answer questions, your child might end up suffering from some kind of long-lasting trauma."

"Are you ready for a visitor?" Meg heard the door open again, and this time it was Heather asking the question. As Meg looked up, Heather continued. "I think she's ready for you."

Heather held a tiny, wrapped bundle in her arms. It seemed to take her a lifetime just to walk the five steps from the door to the new mother's bed. Meg automatically reached out for her child. She was ready for a mother's most magical moment.

"Not yet," Molli said. "Let's get you sitting up first."

Grabbing the control, Jan warned, "Meg, this is going to pull on those stitches. So be ready for some pain."

Meg didn't feel a thing as the bed rolled upward. Oblivious to the pain that must have been there, Meg once again held her hands out and this time, Heather carefully handed the slightly squirming form to her. After peaking at the round face, the red nose, the hairless head, and the blue eyes, tears began to flow, not only from Meg's eyes but from the three other nurses, too.

"My baby, she's perfect," Meg cooed, gently touching the little girl's face. "Thank you, Lord," she silently breathed, kissing the child on the forehead.

"Meg," Jan interjected, "we need a name."

"A name," Meg thought. She'd been so convinced it would be a boy she had never considered a girl's name. As she stared at the tiny beautiful face, a small hand curled around her own finger. Meg marveled at the child's innocent beauty and slowly shook her head.

"Tell you what, girls," she sighed. "If I had known just how bright this day would be, I might have not struggled for so long in the darkness."

"Meg," it was Molli's voice this time. "We need a name. She can't go through life being called Female Richards."

Suddenly remembering the time of her daughter's birth as well as a friend who had brought another kind of light, Meg smiled and whispered, "Her name is Dawn. Yes, that's it. This is Nancy Dawn Richards!"

Discussion Questions

1. Would you have advised Meg to view or not to view her husband's body? What do you think you would have done in her shoes?

2. Why did Steve's death cause Meg to walk away from her faith?

3. If Steve had died in a different way do you believe that Meg would have responded differently?

4. Why do you feel Meg didn't want to keep her baby? If you had been her friend what would you have said to make her change her mind?

5. Nancy knew she was dying. Do you think it would be easier or harder for a person in her position to embrace faith and feel the Lord's hand? Why?

6. District Attorney Web Jones put his own ambitions ahead of his responsibilities. Do you think most people in his position would have done the same thing?

7. Do you believe that our court system favors those with money and influence? Why or why not?

8. Do you think the punishment Jim Thomas received from the courts was the right one? If you were the judge, what penalty would you have assessed and why?

9. Meg sought her own kind of justice. What would you have advised her to do if you were her friend?

10. Meg's mother tried to connect with her daughter but just couldn't do it. Why do you suppose this was the case? Whose fault was it?

11. Meg's prayers were answered. She had Jim Thomas right where she wanted him. Why do you believe she didn't

walk away and claim victory? What drove her to save him?

12. Who was the wisest person in Meg's life and why?

13. Jim came to help Meg when she was in trouble at the meeting. What drove the young man to challenge the audience to listen?

14. Meg named her baby Dawn. Discuss the symbolism of this choice as it relates to Meg's life.

Want to learn more about author
Ace Collins and check out other great fiction
from Abingdon Press?

Sign up for our fiction newsletter at
www.AbingdonPress.com/Fiction
to read interviews with your favorite authors, find tips
for starting a reading group, and stay posted on what
new titles are on the horizon. It's a place to connect
with other fiction readers or post a
comment about this book.

Be sure to visit Ace online!

www.acecollins.com

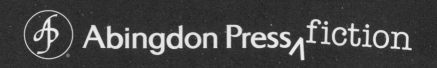